The Lyons Den

The Lyons Den

Kendra Norman-Bellamy

www.urbanchristianonline.net

Urban Books, LLC
78 East Industry Court
Deer Park, NY 11729

ISBN 13: 978-1-60162-815-2
ISBN 10: 1-60162-815-3

First Mass Market Printing January 2012
First Trade Paperback Printing April 2009
Printed in the United States of America

10 9 8 7 6 5 4 3 2 1

*This is a work of fiction. Any references or similarities to
actual events, real people, living, or dead, or to real locales
are intended to give the novel a sense of reality. Any simi-
larity in other names, characters, places, and incidents is
entirely coincidental.*

Distributed by Kensington Publishing Corp.
Submit Wholesale Orders to:
Kensington Publishing Corp.
C/O Penguin Group (USA) Inc.
Attention: Order Processing
405 Murray Hill Parkway
East Rutherford, NJ 07073-2316
Phone: 1-800-526-0275
Fax: 1-800-227-9604

Dedication

And the guard stood, every man with his weapons in his hand, round about the king, from the right corner of the temple to the left corner of the temple, along by the altar and the temple. (2 Kings 11:11)

Dedicated to the members of the **Security Staff of Total Grace Christian Center** (Decatur, GA). Your jobs, not only as police officers, but also as church security, are ones that should be celebrated and revered. In a society where the deterioration of morals leaves no one safe from harm's way, your assignments, that involve guarding the men and women of God, are appreciated more than you know.

As you protect them, may God's hands continue to protect you.

Acknowledgments

In everything give thanks, for this is the will of God concerning you. (1 Thessalonians 5:18)

Every blessing that I've ever received in life has come from the **Lord**, including my gift for writing. For without Him, I am nothing. I thank Him for keeping the ideas coming, and for allowing what I write to be a source of encouragement, enlightenment and entertainment to others.

I thank my husband, **Jonathan**, and my daughters, **Brittney and Crystal**, for their quiet, but mammoth support; and my parents, **Bishop H.H. & Mrs. Francine Norman**, for perpetually reminding me to stay true to myself and true to my faith.

I'm thankful for my guardian angel, **Jimmy** (1968-1995) for the motivation and the memories; and the entire **Holmes Family** for continuing to love and embrace me as a part of you.

Much appreciation goes to my siblings, **Crystal, Harold, Cynthia and Kimberly,** for their unfailing love; and my cousin, **Terrance**, for fulfilling the multi-faceted roles necessary to help orchestrate my career. Eternal gratefulness also goes to my godparents, **Aunt Joyce and Uncle Irvin**, for the seeds they've sown in my life.

A special thank-you to my attorney and agent, **Carlton**, for looking out for my best interests and my publicist, **Rhonda**, for introducing me to book clubs, bookstores and book readers across the globe.

I thank "my girls," **Heather, Gloria and Deborah**, for personifying the true meaning of friendship from childhood through adulthood; and for my sister in Christ, **Lisa** (Papered Wonders) for making me look good on paper through the production of my marketing material.

A big shout-out to **Anointed Authors on Tour** members—Vivi, Tia, Michelle, Norma, Shewanda and Vanessa—for being a bond of sisterhood unlike any other; and to **Victoria, Timmothy, Travis, Jacquelin, Keith, Hank, Eric, Patricia,** and all of the members of **The Writer's Hut** for the enormous roles they have played in my life and my career.

My appreciation for **Bishop Johnathan and Dr. Toni Alvarado (Total Grace Christian Center)** is immeasurable. They are such awesome role models of what marriage, ministry and mentors should look like.

Clive, Emily and Gerald . . . well, I just couldn't pass up this chance to mention the navigation systems that help keep the ministry of **Cruisin' For Christ** afloat.

I thank my **Urban Christian** family for embracing me as a person and as a writer; and I thank all of the **book clubs and other readers** who have chosen to read my books and have allowed my stories to take them on literary journeys time and time again.

Finally, to those who know me well know that, when I write, I prefer music over any other sound. And as always, I end my acknowledgments by saluting all those talents whose music and lyrics helped to get me through my current project. So, I thank **Melvin Williams, Fred Hammond, Brian McKnight, Five Men on a Stool, The Clark Sisters and India Arie** for providing the positive and powerful music and lyrics that helped me create *The Lyons Den*.

Prologue

Am I being punked? The whole thing had started out being funny. A strange hang-up call here, an anonymous letter there—each ridiculous installment from the unknown perpetrator had served as a source of entertainment for Lieutenant Stuart Lyons . . . until now.

Stuart stood in his front yard fully dressed for work and with not an amused bone in his body. All of the beautiful flowers he'd spent hours planting in his yard had been yanked from the roots and were strewn across his front lawn. So much for him receiving Shelton Heights' "Best Landscape Award" for the second consecutive year. That was bad enough, but it wasn't the worst of the story. It was his cruiser that had him staring in anger-driven disbelief, as it sat lopsided in the driveway with both right tires slashed. On the side of Stuart's squad car, written in shoddy big bold capital letters that appeared to have been inscribed with a broad-tip paint brush, were the same words that had been signed to every hoax that had been played on him for the past several weeks: "DR. A. H. SATAN."

"Who did that to your car, Daddy?"

Looking over his shoulder, Stuart saw his inquisitive son, Tyler, standing in the open doorway of their split-level home, peering through his new corrective lenses and still wearing his backpack. Shelled in grey bricks, theirs was one of the few houses in the neighborhood that wasn't ranch style.

Thirteen-year-old Tyler was the one who'd discovered Stuart's vandalized car while on his way to join his schoolmates at the bus stop located at the mouth of the Shelton Heights subdivision. When Tyler ran back into the house and alerted his father of his findings, Stuart did the first thing that came natural for him. He ordered his son back into the house, drew his loaded weapon, and walked outside his front door, carefully surveying his surroundings every step of the way. When Stuart was certain that there was no current danger, he called for backup and waited.

"I don't know who did it, son. Just stay in the house." Stuart's voice was lifeless.

"But I'm gonna miss the bus."

"I said, stay in the house. And close the door." A firmer tone took over, and the brief debate came to an immediate end with Tyler's obedience.

Sirens in the distance grew louder, signaling that help was only moments away. Still dressed in his official police gear, Stuart walked the full circumference of his squad car. Other than the writing on the side and the slashed tires, there was no visible destruction.

"Morning, Lieutenant. You okay? Any damage other than your cruiser? Did you spot any suspicious people hanging around?" The thread of questions came from Sergeant Allen Bowden, an officer who was Stuart's subordinate, but one who he considered his friend.

Stuart shook his head, his anger gradually being replaced by the desire to single-handedly solve the mystery. "Whoever did this was probably long gone before it was discovered. See?" He rubbed his index finger across the wording. "The paint is already dry. This and the tires are the only damage." As he spoke, Stuart watched other officers walk around his house, closely inspecting it for hidden clues.

"You know, this Dr. Satan character has taken it too far now. This isn't funny anymore," Allen pointed out. "This nut doesn't even have respect for the law. You might want to think about getting yourself some protection, Stu."

Generally, when they were on the clock, Stuart and Allen referred to each other by their official titles. But with none of the other officers in listening range, there was no real need for formalities.

Stuart tapped the holster on his hip that housed his weapon. "I've got all the protection I need."

"I'm serious, Stu."

"So am I," Stuart assured him. "But the more I study this fool's M.O., the more I believe this is just some snot-nosed kid that needs a good butt-whipping."

"What is it about his method of operation that makes you think he's a juvenile?"

"Are you kidding me? Look at this." Stuart pointed at the penmanship that defaced his car. "This mess had to be written by some kid; you with me? It's sloppy and immature, just like the signature on the letters has been."

For as far back as his teen years, forty-two-year-old Stuart Aaron Lyons had owned what his friends referred to as a "you-with-me" habit that frequently found its way into his sentences. This was especially true when he became impassioned or excited about any topic of conversation.

Allen nodded as if he understood, and Stuart continued.

"Probably some flunky with nothing better to do, so he gets his kicks from writing anonymous letters and damaging property."

"Got any troublemakers out here?" Allen looked around the quiet subdivision as he asked, like the front doors of houses were going to swing open and boys wearing saggy jeans and excessive bling-bling were going to step out with their hands raised, confessing, "I am, sir. I'm a troublemaker."

"I don't know any personally, but what neighborhood doesn't have its share of idiots?" Stuart replied. The emotions brewing inside of him continued.

"I suppose you could be right. It just seems like this guy—whoever he is—is going way out of his way to make you a target. Why would he single you out to badger with threatening letters? And now this? What's the motive?"

Without an immediate answer to offer, Stuart quietly watched another official car whip into an available space at the end of his driveway. The door opened, and Irving Over street, Deputy Chief of the Criminal Investigation

Division, stepped from the vehicle. Two of the other attending officers walked across the lawn to meet the chief, and Stuart could hear them talking in low volumes, filling him in on the sketchy details.

The mounting number of law enforcement vehicles and flashing lights had caught the attention of some of the neighbors, who now stood on their porches or watched the drama from their front lawns. The commotion had interrupted whatever they had been doing. Some were dressed for work; others still in their night clothes. Stuart studied every one of them, searching for any indication that they'd been involved. He saw nothing.

"Somebody around here had to have seen or heard something," Overstreet said to the two officers. "Ask around and see what you can find out."

"Yes, sir," one of them said before both dispersed to neighboring yards.

Deputy Chief Overstreet flashed a sympathetic smile toward Stuart, and the men exchanged pleasantries before Irving removed his glasses and then his hat. He used his fingers to gather hairs that had strayed from his toupee, carefully pushed them back into the rest of the hairpiece, and then stepped closer to the car to get a better look at the markings.

Stuart shot a glance in Allen's direction and saw the same hilarity in his comrade's eyes that he knew showed in his own. He made a mental note to bring up the comical sighting at a later date, so they could laugh freely. Chief Overstreet was second in command only to the Chief of Police and it would not be a wise move on either man's part to express amusement in his presence.

"You got yourself a live one here, Lieutenant," Over street surmised, replacing his hat and spectacles. "They tell me this isn't the first time you've heard from this fella. Is that true?"

Stuart wondered who'd divulged the little-known information, but didn't ask. "Yes, it's true. It's been going on for about three months now. This is the first time he's touched any of my property, though. I didn't even know he knew where I lived. Every other contact I've had from him has been mail that I get at work every few days. I received a few hang-up calls at the precinct that were a little suspicious, too. But this is the first time the kid did anything like this."

"Kid?" Irving Overstreet's eyebrows rose. "You think you know who's responsible for this?"

"Possibly. My gut feeling tells me that it's a juvenile, and the more I think about it, the more certain I am. You know, I was the first officer on the scene at Columbia High School a couple of months ago when they had that big fight. We arrested a few guys that day, and they weren't pleased about it. One of those boys was more outspoken and defiant than the others, and he did threaten that we hadn't seen the last of him. I'm not saying he's the one who's doing this, but high school kids aren't like they were a few years ago; you with me? These days, they don't forget stuff easily, and if they have violent tendencies, like these guys did, they're used to getting revenge."

Deputy Chief Overstreet twisted his lips and appeared to be biting the inside of his mouth. Then he gave his head a slow, thoughtful nod. "You could be right. We'll pull the kid's record and have him checked out. You let us take care of it, Lyons. I know you're a little ticked off about this, who wouldn't be? But leave this to the people who are paid specifically to handle investigations, okay?"

"Will do, Chief."

"Good deal. We're going to have the car dusted for fingerprints, and I want you to be sure to turn in any letters that you've gotten too. We may be able to wrap this up pretty easily. Kids can be pretty naïve. Let's hope that this one wasn't smart enough to ensure that he didn't leave behind any evidence. I'll see you at the station, Lieutenant. You too, Sergeant."

With a wave of his hand, Deputy Chief Overstreet turned, exchanged a few words with a newly arrived detective, and then strolled toward his car. A brief silence iced over them before Allen Bowden's voice dissolved it.

"You wanna catch a ride in with me? I think it's pretty clear that this baby won't be going anywhere today," he concluded, pointing at the crippled vehicle that was now being photographed by a detective.

Stuart turned to look toward his front door and then back at Allen. "Tyler has missed the bus, so we'll have to drop him off at school first."

"No problem."

"I kinda want to wait until my yard is clear first though," Stuart said, his eyes scanning the half dozen men still working the scene.

Allen followed him to his house, and they both sat on the steps that led to the porch. "So you really think one of the high school kids did this?"

Stuart looked out into his community. Most of the nosey neighbors had dispersed, having offered no help to the inquiring police officers. "Who knows? That's just an early assumption, but I wouldn't be surprised."

A skeptical grunt escaped Allen's throat, capturing Stuart's full attention.

"What does that mean? You don't agree?"

"Like you said, who knows?" Allen said. "I was just wondering; that's all."

"About what?"

"Well, you *do* live in Shelton Heights." Allen raised one eyebrow like that was supposed to give more clarity to his statement.

Stuart shrugged his shoulders and looked even more clueless than before. "And?"

"Don't play dumb, man. You know the mythology that's attached to this neighborhood."

Stuart folded his arms and then snickered and shook his head simultaneously. "I can't even believe you shaped your mouth to say that."

"I'm just saying."

"And I'm just saying too," Stuart debated. "What's the root word of mythology? Myth, right? What's a myth? A fable. A fairy tale. A lie, basically."

"Strange stuff happens out here all the time, man," Allen pointed out. "You can't deny that."

"I know you're not going to bring up what happened to my pastor two years ago, or what happened to Pete Jericho last year with the whole Iraq incident. All of that stuff sounded bizarre at the time that it was happening, but in the end, there was a practical explanation for both."

Allen nodded slowly. "That's true for those two events, yes. But we don't even have to think back that far to cite some *unexplainable* happenings out here."

Stuart rolled his eyes to the heavens, knowing exactly what direction Allen was headed to validate his point.

"You know I'm telling the truth, Stu. What about last December when that bear broke down that old couple's front door in the middle of the night and charged through their living room, tearing up everything in its path?"

"We see bears in these parts all the time, Allen."

"Not in thirty-three-degree temperature, we don't. Bears hibernate in the winter. They aren't breaking into folks' houses."

"They do when a city is constantly demolishing all of its woodland to build dwelling places to house its overpopulation. The wild-life doesn't have anywhere to hibernate any-more, so what they're doing is fighting for what's rightfully theirs."

"Are we taking away the outer space too?" Allen mocked. "Just a few months ago, on New Year's Day when that meteorite fell out of nowhere and killed that brother two or three streets over who was outside taking down his Christmas decorations—was that because our city is demolishing the outer space to build houses for our ever-growing population of Martians?"

Though the man's tragic death was a sad occurrence, Stuart couldn't help but laugh at the combination of Allen's choice of words and his facial expression. "Okay," Stuart conceded, "you make a good point with that one."

"Man, over the years you have to admit that, per capita, the Shelton Heights subdivision has had more than its share of peculiar events. Some of them are explainable, yes; but some of them continue to be unsolved mysteries. This is a sinister sector of Atlanta, plain and simple. I mean, I don't consider myself to be superstitious or nothing, but let's face it, Stu: the identity of Dr. A.H. Satan may very well be as simple as some vengeful kid that you booked after a schoolyard brawl. But you can't totally rule out the possibility that it could also be that the ghost of that warlock, Old Man Shelton Heights, just went and got himself a pen name—and he's decided to make you the lead character in his next bestseller."

Chapter One

Stuart awakened early Saturday morning, just as he'd done for the past five days. The knowledge that someone had come onto his property while he was asleep, and managed to do such extensive damage to his car without stirring him, made him a bit paranoid. Amateurish letters to the station were one thing, but disrespecting his property was too close for comfort; and it made him feel more uneasy than he had admitted to anyone.

Standing at his bedroom window, Stuart peeped through a small opening in his security blinds that the fingers of his left hand provided. In his right hand, he held a model 4586 Smith & Wesson .45-caliber semi-automatic pistol. It was just after five o'clock in the morning, and the sun was still laying low. In his mind, Stuart suggested that his harasser did the same. He'd been given a replacement vehicle, and there had been no signs of a follow-up appearance by his wannabe stalker, but if the decision for a repeat performance hit the faceless, nameless man, so would a bullet.

Regardless of Sergeant Bowden's remarks about the late Mr. Shelton Heights and the namesake upscale community that was built with his money just days before the self-proclaimed sorcerer was found dead on the grounds thereof, Stuart refused to consider his plight had anything to do with "the legend" surrounding the neighborhood. Though it was believed that the heart attack suffered by eighty-eight-year-old Shelton Heights was arbitrary, the autopsy was inconclusive, leaving many to wonder if an armed robber had frightened the old man to death. Mr. Heights was believed to be the most well-to-do citizen of Atlanta, Georgia; but when his body was found, he was carrying no money and no wallet. The truth behind his death died with the warlock, but over the years, it seemed that his spirit still lurked, and chose to haunt those who had taken advantage of the affordable housing in a neighborhood whose domiciles he never intended to sell at such a deflated cost.

Ever since inception, the Shelton Heights subdivision had been riddled with folklore. Because of it, dwellers moved out as quickly as they moved in. Most of the people who purchased homes there did so just to resell them to new transplants into Atlanta who'd not yet heard the myth, hoping to make a sizeable profit. As fabulous as the houses in the neighborhood were, superstitions made them difficult to sell. Therefore, structures that could easily vend for $300,000 in other areas of the city had to be sold for half as much in Shelton Heights. It was a bargain for those who dared to dispel the myths; but the better part of those who at one time took on the challenge would eventually move out because of uncanny, ambiguous occurrences.

Stepping away from his lookout spot, Stuart sat on the side of his bed, debating whether or not he should try and get a little more sleep. As with most Saturdays, he was off from work, and generally, he took advantage of the opportunity to sleep in late. But this week's mishap would not allot him a smidgen of peace, and Stuart was sure that lying back down would only accumulate wasted time that he could use to do something constructive, or at least, enjoyable.

Still in his pajamas, and with nothing but socks on his feet, Stuart retrieved a silver key from his nightstand drawer and stepped from his room as quietly as he could. His four-bedroom home was a spacious one, and he wasn't overly concerned that he'd awaken his son who slept in one of the rooms upstairs. But for the past eighteen months, he had also shared a home with his sister, Kenyatta, and she was a shallow sleeper. She'd been that way ever since a bitter divorce forced her to move from Jacksonville, Florida, to Atlanta, Georgia.

Like Stuart, Kenyatta rarely worked on Saturdays, and Tyler often spent much of the weekend horseback riding with his friends in Greene Pastures, a champion horse breeding farm owned by Stuart's friend, Hunter Greene, who was also the father of one of Tyler's best school buddies.

Passing his sister's room door and rounding the corner at the end of the hall, Stuart used the single key to unlock the door that led to his favorite room in the house: the den. That space was kept locked because it was his personal sanctuary: a place of work—a place of worship. The place where he felt his prayers were most heard. Stuart never could quite single out one thing that made it his preferred room, but he had concluded that much of it was due to the solitude that he often found there, especially on his days away from the chaos that frequently surrounded his line of work.

Fully furnished in neutral colors right down to the eggshell couch, oatmeal walls and deep tan coffee tables, the den had such a welcoming feel that Stuart could almost sense it hug him when he entered. A stocked entertainment console was nestled against one wall beside a five-tier glass-encased bookshelf, and in a corner nearest his door was a sturdy maplewood desk that housed his flat-screen Gateway computer. The den served as not only a place of privacy, but also a place of worship. It was here where Stuart found a level of closeness to God that seemed to escape him in other areas of his home.

The way Stuart figured it, he had at least two hours before Kenyatta would awaken and possibly three before Tyler would begin begging for a ride to Greene Pastures. His eyes burning from the lack of sleep, Stuart powered up his computer and waited for his home screen to appear. Among other things, he was what his sister called a "big kid" who collected the latest tech gadgets. Stuart carried a cell phone on each hip (one for business and one for personal use), had the latest iPod, digital camera, and computer software programs available on the market. Had he not turned to law enforcement as a career choice, no doubt, he would have become an electronic engineer.

Glancing at his watch, Stuart noted that the time was five forty. It was still early, but he hoped his favorite online friend had reason to awaken prematurely today, too. For the past four months, he'd been chatting frequently with Candice Powell, a woman who he had yet to meet. Stuart had been apprehensive about registering with the popular online Christian matchmaking site, but after watching televised advertisements about its success rate, he made the decision to give it a try. After connecting with three women, none of whom held his interest for more than two weeks, Stuart was ready to call it quits. It was then that Candice contacted him by way of a note left in the email box associated with his online profile.

Hi, Stuart. I'm a thirty-something-year-old math teacher in New York City. I reviewed your profile and noted that we had quite a bit in common. Despite what this note may lead you to believe, I'm not an aggressive woman. In fact, I've never initiated communication with anyone on this site before, but I admit that I was immediately drawn to your profile. If you would like to chat sometime, please feel free to leave a note.

Be blessed,
Candice

Stuart almost didn't reply. After all, the three women before her sounded like they had good sense too. Talisa, Anita, and Marilyn were a gynecologist, librarian and associate pastor, respectively. By their third correspondence, Talisa had sent him a highly inappropriate photo of herself wherein she gave the gynecological breakdown of each part of the full-color image. By week two of Stuart's contact with Anita, she had warned him not to mess over her because the mistake of doing so had cost her last boyfriend a "knife-carved tattoo that he didn't have to pay for." And the day before Stuart ended his affiliation with the great Evangelist Marilyn Lassinger, she had sent him an email that prophetically detailed how the Lord was commanding him to marry her in exactly three hundred days so they could work together in ministry, and so he could become the "Boaz" she'd been praying for in her times of "laying before the Lord." Stuart had been on secular dating sites that were less stressful.

Before typing in his note, Stuart pulled his reading glasses from his desk drawer and placed them on his face. He rarely used them, even when reading, but his tired eyes needed the support today.

Hi, Candice. I woke up early this morning and couldn't go back to sleep, so I thought I'd check and see if you were up too. It's Saturday, and since you don't have to work, I imagine that you're sleeping in, but I thought I'd give it a try anyway. If you happen to be there, hit me back.

Peace,
Stuart

At an even height of six-foot-tall and with a skin tone that he'd once heard a woman refer to as "a minute before midnight," Stuart epitomized tall, dark and handsome to the letter. He belonged to one of the fastest growing, most esteemed churches in the state of Georgia and, arguably, he held one of the most revered jobs in the country.

"Why do you need to find a woman on the Internet?" His sister, Kenyatta, had asked this question many times.

In fact, Stuart had asked himself the same question, wondering why it had been so difficult for him to find true love. Most of his closest friends were either married or in exclusive relationships with women who seemed to be in it for the long haul. Hunter and Jade Greene had been married for two years and were so much in love that, even to other lovers, it was almost sickening. A year ago, trouble had rocked Pete and Jan Jericho's thirteen-year marriage, but ever since Pete returned from Iraq and had retired from the Marines, they'd been inseparable. Even Jerome Tides, Jade's brother, and self-proclaimed bachelor for life, had his choice of women.

Ironically, Jerome, a former bad boy who served ten years in prison for a part he played in an armed robbery, was Stuart's best friend of them all. The two of them were often teased about their friendship. A law officer forming a brotherhood with a man who still had thirteen years of probation to serve just didn't happen every day. But despite his past, Jerome had two women currently vying for his attention; one was Stuart's own sister, and the other was Ingrid Battles.

Ingrid was Jade's best friend from Virginia who accepted the offer to be Jade's executive assistant in her booming private psychology firm, and had moved to Atlanta a few months ago to fulfill her duties. Kwame, who was Stuart's friend by way of Hunter, was single, but he was unattached by choice. Kwame wasn't ready to settle down, and he only dated women who felt the same.

For Stuart, twelve years of bachelorhood was more than enough. He wasn't just looking for a woman—he was in search of a wife. The single father had once been married and, for the most part, enjoyed it. His marriage to Natasha "Tasha" Lyons, who had since chosen to go back to her maiden name of Dennis, had lasted for nine years. But the strong love that was needed to sustain their relationship fizzled somewhere between years seven and eight. As with most dissolved marriages, the split was bitter at first, but it had long since become amicable.

Upon the initial separation, Tyler lived with Tasha, and spent weekends with Stuart. Shortly after the child's fourth birthday, Tasha, a registered nurse by profession, connected with Nurse Finders, a company who placed transitory health-care workers in facilities across the nation, whenever the need arose. The opportunity was too great for her to pass up. Her connection with them opened the door for Tasha to substantially increase her income while doing one of her favorite things: traveling.

Because of the demand, Tasha's assignments kept her away for stretches of six, eight, and sometimes, twelve weeks at a time while she temporarily filled positions in hospitals as far away as Seattle, Washington, and Boston, Massachusetts. Stuart was the more stable parent, and together, they agreed that he would take on physical custody of Tyler. The job came with no regrets from Stuart. His son meant more to him than life itself. And Tyler's bond with his mother remained strong through lengthy weekly telephone chats.

Since the divorce, Stuart had been no stranger to dating, but serious love interests had been few. Women found him attractive, and indeed, he enjoyed their admiration and companionship. But there always seemed to be a long-term personal agenda hidden behind their short-term perfect personalities. And his lack of finding Ms. Right couldn't be blamed on a sparse harvest. New Hope Church had a bumper crop of available women. Finding a saved woman wasn't a problem. Finding a genuine one was.

The idea of the traditional family appealed to Stuart, and he desired to give marriage another try, but having been there and having done that before, he needed to be sure that his next wife was sent from God. After all, it was no longer just about him. He had a son to consider, and loving Tyler wouldn't be an option for her. He hoped that she—whoever *she* was—would require the same of him for her children, if she had any.

At Stuart's age, he figured that whatever woman he ultimately partnered with would have at least one child. He had to be realistic in his thinking. Stuart knew that he'd never date a woman too much younger than he, and there was a good chance that a sister in his age bracket would have been married before, or at least have a child that was the result of a previous relationship. And, besides, he couldn't expect something of her that he couldn't give in return. Whoever married him would become an instant mother, so he was prepared to become an instant father as well. Oddly enough, the woman who was currently holding his interest was thirty-six, had never been married, and had no dependents.

Candice: *Hey, you! Good to hear from you.*

Stuart had been so occupied with his own thoughts that it startled him when the note from Candice popped up on his instant messenger screen. He liked it better when they chatted this way. There was less waiting time than with emails. Instant messenger was the next best thing to talking on the phone, which was something else that he and Candice hadn't yet done. A follow-up message appeared, and Stuart immersed himself in her words.

Candice: *Yes, I'm up, believe it or not. I just logged on the computer to print out an answer sheet and saw your note. I have a ton of papers to grade, and I have to prepare a test for my students to take on Monday. Since I have a full day at church tomorrow, I thought I'd rise early today and get this stuff knocked out so that I can have the latter part of the day to relax. What got you up so early on an off day?*

Stuart hadn't shared with Candice any of what had been going on with him and his harasser. He'd come close to mentioning it to her in a previous chat session, but he chose not to for reasons he hadn't yet admitted. Stuart was captivated by Candice, but didn't know why. It wasn't based on her physical makeup. He'd never met her in person, and frankly, from what he could tell by the personal information on her written profile, Candice didn't really have the bodily manifestation of a woman most men would be attracted to. True enough, her head-shot depicted the face of an attractive woman with a magnetic smile. But her biographical sketch told what one never would have guessed from her photo. Detailed information included the descriptive words, "vertically challenged" and "more to love" and Stuart knew what those phrases meant. It was just a politically correct way of saying, "I'm short and fat," traits not often revealed on a dating site.

Her honesty was refreshing, and Stuart was drawn to the woman living on the other side of his computer screen. Candice shared his passion for cultivating children, his appreciation of the arts, his enjoyment of the outdoors, and most importantly, his love for Christ. Nothing about her seemed bogus or pretentious, and the ample dimensions of her heart overshadowed any qualms he might have about the length of her stature and the breadth of her body.

Stuart: *I've been dealing with a possible stalker and until we find out who he is or what his agenda is, I probably won't sleep too well.*

Stuart typed the words without giving it a second thought; but he paused before clicking on the button that would deliver the message to Candice. Once the message was sent, Stuart sat back in his chair and held his breath in anticipation of her retort. For a few moments, there was no response, and all he could hear was his own heartbeat.

Candice: *When you say "stalker," are you referring to a fan, as in someone who is overly infatuated with you? Or do you mean an enemy, someone who is out to do you harm?*

It was the question that Stuart dreaded, but if a relationship was possible between the two of them, she might as well know all the facts now.

Stuart: *From the looks of things, it's someone who has it in for me. It started a couple of months ago with me getting letters and phone calls, but Monday morning, the tires on my car were slashed.*

Stuart imagined that, on the other side of the screen, Candice's eyes were bulging.

Candice: *Letters? Phone calls? Slashed tires? This sounds serious, Stuart. Why am I just hearing about it? We've been chatting for more than a couple of months. Why didn't you tell me before now?*

He could see the hysteria in her words. Stuart closed his eyes and then reopened them again.

Stuart: *Because I was afraid of this.*

Candice: *Afraid of what?*

All the while that Stuart typed his response, he wondered if he was doing the right thing by baring his soul, but not once did the momentum of his fingers break as they typed on his keyboard.

Stuart: *I was afraid that you would freak out on me and then conclude that you didn't want to be involved with a man who is possibly being hunted by a psychopath.*

For a long while after he sent his reply, no words came back to him. Stuart counted the seconds and wondered how painful the punishment for his honesty would be.

Candice: *So is that what we are? Involved?*

Only when Stuart saw Candice's words appear on the screen did he remember to breathe. His chest felt tight, like he hadn't exhaled since sitting back in his chair after sending her the initial message about the violation of his property. Stuart stared at her question for a short time and then slowly placed his fingers back on the keyboard.

Stuart: *I don't know. Are we?*

Candice: *Don't ask me. You're the one who said it. I teach math, not English, so I'm not into a lot of word interpretation or the dissecting of sentences.*

A grin parted Stuart's lips and then stretched them across his face, displaying white teeth that seemed whiter all because of his skin's hue. In all the months they'd been chatting, he'd never felt as though they were flirting with each other. This morning, he did. Maybe it was time to move to a new stage in their undefined relationship.

Stuart: *Why don't we talk more about it and see?* He hoped she'd agree.

Candice: *Talk? You mean over the phone?*

He nodded his head as if she could see him.

Stuart: *For starters, yes; but I do have some vacation days coming to me. With your permission, I'd like to come to New York and meet you. Maybe we could have dinner?*

He ended the last statement with a question mark, hoping that doing so would prevent Candice from feeling pressured.

Candice: *Let's chat about it some more later. Meanwhile, I'd better get back to grad-*

ing these papers, or my evening won't be as free as I planned.

Hers wasn't quite the response that Stuart was hoping for, but he found Candice's hesitation to be refreshing. It was good to know that she didn't jump at the first opportunity to meet him. He would bet his last dime that the other three before her would have.

Stuart: *Okay. But can I at least have your number so I can call you sometime?*

Hearing her voice would be a nice consolation prize.

Candice: *I'll tell you what. You give me your number and let me give you a call.*

Stuart laughed out loud, and his heart fluttered. Four months had passed since their atypical introduction, and he felt like his site membership was finally paying off. As he typed in his cell phone number, Stuart found himself praying that she'd use it soon. He sent his good-bye message and yawned as he prepared to shut down his system.

Candice: *Stuart?*

The one-word call from her appeared just before Stuart clicked the icon that would have disconnected his Internet. Seeing it perked up his tired body like a jolt of caffeine.

Stuart: *Yes?*

Candice: *Promise me you'll be careful, okay? I try not to worry about you, but I do. I'll be praying for you that our all-seeing God will send His ministering angels to protect you and your son from any evils that seek to do you harm.*

Stuart was unprepared for the joy that raced through his body. Moisture glossed his eyes, and fine bumps decorated the full length of his arms. Taking a moment to collect himself, he placed his fingers on the keyboard for his final response.

Stuart: *Thanks, Candice. You can't imagine how much it means to me to have your concern and your prayers. I'll be careful. I promise.*

Chapter Two

"Come on in, Stu. You look tired, man. What you been up to?" Hunter Greene stepped aside so that Stuart could enter his massive five-bedroom, three-bath home.

"I'm all right." Stuart looked around. No matter how many times he visited this show-place of a dwelling place, it enthralled him. With its high ceilings, shiny hardwood floors and expensive artwork, the house was so immaculate that it looked virtually unlived in. "Just woke up too early, that's all."

"Woke up early? Man, you'd better take advantage of these Saturdays that you have off." He looked beyond the open door and then back at Stuart. "Where's Tyler?"

"He saw Malik, Kyla and the others and headed straight to the pasture." Stuart released a brief chuckle. "Bet you didn't know, when you started breeding horses, that what you were actually doing was preparing a weekend day camp for Malik's friends."

Hunter laughed with him. "Naw, man, it's cool. The kids get to have fun, and the horses get the exercise that they need all at the same time." He sat on the sofa opposite Stuart and sobered. "Any word on the cat that slashed your tires the other day?"

Shaking his head, Stuart replied, "Not really. They've pretty much ruled out the high school kid who I first suspected. Turns out that his mom sent him to live with his father in Jersey after he got locked up for that fight. His old man has a tight rein on him, and that boy hardly has the freedom to leave the house, let alone leave the state, which is what he would have had to do in order to mark up my car. I still don't necessarily see him as innocent, though."

"How come?" Hunter asked as he got up from the couch and walked into the kitchen.

Stuart raised his voice to be certain that Hunter could hear his reply. "He could easily have had some of his boys do it. I mean, he was a part of a school gang, and if he's really ticked about being shipped off to his dad's, he could have conspired with some of the other kids who are still here, telling them to seek revenge on his behalf, you with me? It wouldn't be at all farfetched for him to be indirectly involved in this whole mess."

"I see your point." Hunter reappeared from the kitchen, handed Stuart a glass of cola and then returned to his seat to polish off the glass of ice cold milk he'd been drinking when Stuart arrived. "If the police have ruled out this kid you suspect, then they must have someone else in mind. Do they?"

"No. At least, not anyone that they've mentioned to me."

A knock on the door invaded their private time.

"You expecting a yard full of kids today?" Stuart asked in the middle of a yawn.

"No, but that doesn't mean I won't end up with a full yard." Hunter laughed. "That's probably your boy, Jerome. He said he was coming over today. We were thinking of going out back for a little game of one-on-one. But with you here—"

Stuart threw a carefree wave of his hand in Hunter's direction. "Don't let me stop you. I'll keep score. As tired as I am, that's about all I can contribute."

Hunter opened the door, and when Stuart saw two men standing there, he knew that tired or not, he had inaudibly been drafted into the pending game. Both Jerome Tides and Peter Jericho walked into the house, noisily exchanging greetings with Hunter before approaching the living room, where Stuart continued to relax.

"What's up, gentlemen?" Stuart said, standing and embracing each man before returning to his place on the sofa.

"Man, get up," Jerome ordered, motioning with his hands for added effect. "We 'bout to go out back and shoot some hoops. Pete thought he was gonna be a third wheel, but with you here, we can have a fair game of two on two."

"Can you guys sit down for a minute first?" Stuart asked with deep lines in his forehead. "Geez, man, have some manners. You don't just come to another man's house and take advantage of his amenities without first exchanging some dialogue."

Hunter laughed as he sat. "That's Stu's way of saying he's tired and he wants to get some rest before getting the beat-down on the court."

"Whatever," Stuart said, knowing full well it was the truth.

"You do look tired, man," Peter observed. "You worked late last night?"

Stuart sat forward in his seat and pondered whether he should open up to the men he trusted most. They all knew about Monday's occurrence, but they didn't know everything that had happened since.

"What's up, Stu?" Jerome said, nudging his friend's leg. "Looks like you got something on your mind."

Rubbing his hand across his shaven head, Stuart said, "I do, I guess."

"Let's hear it," Peter urged when Stuart hesitated.

"I'm tired because I don't sleep well lately. I haven't mentioned this to my sister or to Tyler because I don't want to upset either of them and have them tossing and turning too. But ever since this Dr. Satan fool came up in my yard and jacked up my car, I don't sleep soundly anymore. Every little noise wakes me up, and even when I don't hear any noises, I'm up before the sun."

"Have you gotten any more letters or anything?" Hunter wanted to know.

Shaking his head from side to side, Stuart gave his silent answer. "But just the knowledge that he's still out there and he knows where I live is messing with my head."

Jerome released a dry laugh. "Well, maybe you ought to tell Kenyatta about it. I don't think she'd be afraid. If anything the crook would be scared of her."

The thought of his gun-toting, smack-talking sister made Stuart laugh too. "I don't know, man. I mean, she puts up a believable front, but behind that tough exterior, I don't think she has the courage to shoot anybody. If she did, she probably would have killed that ex-husband of hers."

"You still think that kid you arrested is behind this?" Peter asked as Hunter returned from another trip to the kitchen brandishing two more glasses of soda for his most recent guests.

"I don't know." Stuart didn't feel like going through the entire story again. "There's a good chance that he didn't do it, but the whole thing just seems too childish for it to be the work of an adult."

"Well, you know my bride is a psychologist," Hunter began.

Jerome released a heavy sigh. "Dang, man. You and my sister have been married for two years. You can stop calling her your bride anytime you get ready, okay? Her name is Jade. Say it with me, man, *Jade*." Jerome's quip was met with laughter from Stuart and Peter.

"Shut up, stupid," Hunter said, picking up a decorative pillow and tossing it in Jerome's direction. He then turned to Stuart and continued. "My *bride* had an interesting theory that I thought was worth mentioning."

"Everybody's got a theory," Stuart said, thinking of Allen and his mention of the Shelton Heights myth.

"But this one might be worth the police looking into," Hunter maintained.

"Yeah? Well, let's hear it." Stuart drank the last of his cola and placed the empty glass on the coaster on the coffee table in front of him.

Wasting no time explaining himself, Hunter probed, "Kenyatta's ex. What kind of man is he?"

"What are you saying? You think Joe could have done this?" Stuart looked him straight in the eyes in anticipation of Hunter's reply.

"Why not? Isn't he a violent man? Didn't you say that he was abusive to your sister?" Hunter gestured his hands like it was a no-brainer.

Stuart thoughtfully twisted the silver ring he sometimes wore on the middle finger of his right hand. He'd never given Joseph King a second thought. Could he be behind all the mayhem? "Joe was verbally and emotionally abusive," he revealed, still mulling over the question in his mind. "Kenyatta said that he threatened to do stuff to her all the time, but he never actually hit her; not even when his drunken mind was telling him that she was cheating on him.

"He did a lot of crazy stuff, like he'd follow her around, spying on her, and he embarrassed her a few times by showing up drunk at church or on her job, causing a scene." Stuart recalled other incidents that he'd been told about. "When he got really angry, he'd go into rages and throw and kick stuff, like a kid having a tantrum, but he never hit her. Kenyatta's decision to finally leave for good was made when Joe got mad once and took a carving knife and started stabbing her side of the bed."

"Sounds pretty violent to me," Peter pointed out.

"I don't know." Stuart still had his doubts. "Joe was more stupid than anything else. I think he was half-scared of Kenyatta, to tell the truth."

"Who wouldn't be?" Jerome mumbled.

"But you just said that he was jealous and would follow her around," Hunter recapped. "Does he know that Kenyatta's here in Atlanta?"

Shrugging his shoulders, Stuart said, "I don't know. I don't think Kenyatta's heard from him since she had her cell number changed last year, a couple of months after moving here. She didn't tell him where she was going. As a matter of fact, she didn't even tell him that she was leaving. She packed up and left one day while he was at work. Kenyatta could have gone anywhere. I'm not her only sibling. My parents had four kids, and all of us live in different areas of the country."

"But he knows where each of you live, right?" Jerome asked.

"He knows what states we live in, yes—he probably even knows what cities we live in. But he doesn't know *where* we live, you with me? He and Kenyatta weren't married that long, and none of us liked him from the start, so it's not like we ever invited him to our houses for dinner or anything. And of the four of us, why would he automatically assume she's with me?"

"By the process of elimination," Peter reasoned. "Between then and now, he's had plenty of time to scout out your other siblings and conclude that Kenyatta's not with any of them. You were probably just next on the list, Stu. He could have been watching your house for a while and now knows that she's with you."

"But I told you, he doesn't know where I live."

"If he really wanted to know where you lived, he could find it," Hunter said, fingering his goatee. "I think we're on to something here. Jade counsels women all the time who are afraid of their jealous men. They know what those men are capable of doing even if they haven't done it yet. If Joe has found out that Kenyatta took refuge with you, he might see you as the other man and is out to get you."

Stuart sat up straight. "The other man? Joe knows I'm Kenyatta's brother. Even if he does know she's living with me, he knows I ain't no other man."

"In his twisted mind you might be," Hunter said. "Not the other man as in Kenyatta's lover, but the other man as in the man she chose over him. In the end, you *are* a man and you did take her in. So Joe sees you as the reason she divorced him. Brother or no brother, she left him and came to you."

Jerome laughed. "Man, my baby sister's got you sounding just like her. Jade kills me with that psychology mess. She was trying to break it down to me as to why I acted out the way I did as a kid and ended up in prison as an adult. I listened to all that mumbo jumbo that she dished out, and I guess it made some sense. But I already know the main reason I did what I did. I was full of the devil. That was my problem, and if Joe is the one hunting Stu down, that's his problem too. I mean, look at the signature that he leaves behind. Dr. A.H. Satan. It don't get no clearer than that, dude."

"I still don't get why he'd come after me," Stuart added. "If Joe wants to come after Kenyatta's man, he'll come after Jerome."

"Look out, now," Peter said with a hearty laugh.

Jerome grinned in Stuart's direction and then shook his head in denial. "Man, I can't fool with your sister. She's cute and all, and she got them *real* nice childbearing hips; but I ain't going back to prison, and that's just where I'll end up if I hook up with her. Being around deadly weapons is in direct violation of my parole; and guns, for Kenyatta, are like American Express cards. She don't leave home without one."

"I told you before," Stuart said, "that if anybody is able to deliver her from that pistol-packing demon, it's you. If you told her that if she did away with that revolver, you'd make her your girl, we'd never see Kenyatta with a gun again."

"You say that like you really believe it," Jerome commented.

"Man, I do."

"Hold up, now," Hunter said, raising his hand to stop the conversation. "My bride's not here, so I have to represent, 'cause if she were here, Jade would put in a word for her best friend. Kenyatta's name isn't the only one in the hat where Jerome is concerned, you know."

"Oh, man. Here we go," Peter said, falling back on the sofa cushions.

"I'm not trying to force Ingrid on you, brother-in-law," Hunter told Jerome, "but you know she's sweet on you, and I think you're attracted to her too."

Stuart jumped in with a matter-of-fact tone. "The man spent ten years in prison where he didn't see nothing but other men. *Ten* years. He ain't been free but two years, so yeah, he's attracted. If you put on a skirt, a wig and some make-up, he'll probably be attracted to you too."

"Man, I'll bust you upside your big ol' bald head," Jerome threatened over the laughter that filled the room. "I ain't knocking either one of them. Both Kenyatta and Ingrid are fine women, and I like them both for different reasons. But I ain't about to settle down with either one of them. Not yet, anyway. Like Mother said, God will show me if either of them is the one for me."

"I love me some Mrs. Tides," Peter said with a reflective smile. "I'd bet my money on her advice. Her wise counsel was instrumental in convincing Jan to give our marriage another chance. If she hadn't talked to my wife that Sunday at church, Jan never would have flown to California to meet me when I came back from Iraq."

Hunter sighed and rolled his eyes. "If I have to hear that doggone story one more time . . ."

"What?" Peter challenged. "We always got to listen to you talk about your *bride*. Why can't I talk about Jan once in a while?"

"Hold up." Stuart used both his hands to give the time-out signal. "I thought we were supposed to be talking about me and the identity of my stalker. How did we get on the subject of women?"

"It always comes back to women, my man," Jerome said. "You gotta know that by now."

"Speaking of women," Peter said. "Why is everybody trying to push both Kenyatta and Ingrid off on Jerome? Stuart's a free man. Why can't Ingrid be turned on to how great a catch Stuart is? That would make Jerome's decision a lot easier."

"There's a thought," Hunter said with raised eyebrows.

"Hey! How y'all just gonna come and try to take a lady from a brotha?" Jerome protested. He turned and looked at Peter, scowling. "How you know I want to make my decision easy? Did you hear any complaints from me?"

"Aw, man, you just like having two women pawing at you," Peter said.

"And what man wouldn't?" Jerome replied with a wide grin.

"I can make all of your decisions easy," Stuart announced. "I'm not interested in Ingrid, so that's the end of that."

"What's wrong with Ingrid?" Hunter asked. "She's pretty, she's employed, she's saved . . . and I think she's saved for real this time, because Jade said she hasn't heard her cuss not once since she went to the altar to rededicate her life to God a couple of months ago."

"Well, if you had brought her to my attention a couple of months ago, maybe I would be interested," Stuart said over the laughter. "It's too late now, so let's move on."

The room quieted for the first time in a while, and Jerome, Hunter and Peter looked at Stuart with quizzical eyes.

Jerome was the first to speak. "Stu, you done met somebody and didn't tell me?" When Stuart failed to immediately reply, Jerome added, "How you gonna leave your boy in the dark like that?"

"You're dating, man?" Hunter grilled. "Who is she? Do we know her?"

Stuart rubbed his temples as though the inquisition was giving him a pounding headache, but in reality, he was glad for the opportunity to finally talk about Candice.

Peter hit him on the arm and said, "Man, you might as well tell us, 'cause we're not letting it go until you do."

Looking at the men, Stuart could hold back his smile no longer. "Okay, but keep this under wraps for now, okay?" The men nodded in agreement. "I'm not dating, exactly, and to tell the truth, I haven't really *met* someone either, not in the true sense of the word. But I have become very fascinated with a woman named Candice. You don't know her, so don't even try to figure out who she is. She lives in New York, and I've been communicating with her through a Christian online dating site."

"Kenyatta told me that you had joined one of those sites," Jerome revealed, "but she didn't tell me you'd made a connection with anyone special."

"That's because she doesn't know," Stuart said. "The only person that I've even mentioned Candice to is Tyler, and he wasn't interested in the conversation enough for me to be concerned that he'd tell any of you guys. I kind of wanted to keep it on the low-low until I knew it was something that could turn into something."

"So, are you saying this is serious?" Hunter asked.

"Too early to tell," Stuart admitted. "But I think it's headed in that direction. All we've done is chat online. We connected for the first time about four months ago, and for the past eight weeks or so, I've made her my exclusive online friend. When we chatted this morning, I took it a step further," he added with a smile.

"I gave her my number, and she's supposed to call me soon. It'll be our first time talking live."

"Sounds like you're happy, at least," Peter said. "That's good, Stu."

"I don't know. I tried online dating once a few years ago," Hunter revealed. "Worst mistake of my life. I met a corporate girl in Savannah, Georgia, named Melva, who managed a string of restaurants and described herself as resembling Vivica Fox. After a few weeks of chatting online and on the phone, I decided to check her out a little more. I called her house, and her roommate was all too excited to tell me where I could find her the next day. So, I traveled to Savannah the next morning, and I arrived at the restaurant around two, wearing a baseball cap and sunglasses so she wouldn't recognize me if she saw me, right?" Hunter laughed and continued. "When I asked the first worker I saw to point Melva out to me . . . oooooooweeee!" He squeezed his eyes shut as if trying to block out the remembrance of it all. "When she looked at me and said, 'I'm Melva. How can I help you?' I told her I had the wrong person, turned around, and hauled my tail right out of there and never looked back."

"I gather she didn't look like Vivica Fox," Stuart said with a laugh.

"Shoot, naw!" Hunter said, shaking his head. "She looked like *Jamie* Foxx in a bad wig. You remember when *In Living Color* used to come on in the late eighties, early nineties? Remember Wanda, the ugly female character with the big butt and lipstick on her teeth that Jamie Foxx used to play? That's what she looked like."

Stuart, Peter and Jerome doubled over in laughter.

When he was finally able to speak, Stuart said, "Well, I don't think Candice lied about her appearance. If she were going to lie, I don't think she would have described herself the way she did. If she'd compared herself to some Hollywood star like Vivica, then I would probably be doubtful. I'm pretty confident that Candice is cool."

"Well, as long as she's the truth, I'm happy for you," Jerome said. "I hope it works out, man. Wish I could go with you to New York when you meet her for the first time, but it'll be a while before a brotha can travel outside of the state of Georgia."

"I know," Stuart said with a sympathetic sigh. "I wish you could come too. You miss out on so much with all your legal restraints. Being on parole is kind of like being in hell, huh?"

"Naw, man," Peter jumped in. "I've been in hell. Got to know it on a first-name basis, and its name is Iraq."

The room quieted, as if each man was trying to imagine himself in that tortuous place. Peter had spent seven days in the captivity of murderous Iraqi soldiers, wondering if he would live or die.

"Well, I guess it has lots of names, because I've been in hell too," Jerome insisted, breaking the elongated silence. "Its name is *prison*. When you've spent time behind the iron curtains of prison, believe me when I say that parole feels like a piece of heaven."

Jerome's testament was followed by another solemn silence. This time, it was interrupted by Hunter's voice.

"Well, I haven't been *in* hell, but I've looked it straight in the eyes. It may have many names, but it ain't got but one face. I may not know what it feels like, but it looks like Jamie Foxx wearing a bad wig with a big butt and lipstick on its teeth."

Stuart dropped his head in his hands, but couldn't hear his own laughter for the roaring sounds that came from the men surrounding him. "I'm gonna tell Reverend Tides to pray for you," Stuart said when he finally caught his breath. "He may not know it, but his son-in-law needs Jesus in a special way."

Hunter stood up from the sofa. "Yeah? Well, I'm not the one with a doctor whose initials are A.H. and whose last name is Satan following me around. You're the one who needs Jesus in a special way, man," he said. "Come on and let's play some ball. Maybe while we're out here, we'll come up with a plan to find out if this crazy tire-slasher is some kid from the high school or your ex-brother-in-law."

Chapter Three

Ever since she was a little girl, growing up in the town of Greenwood, South Carolina, Sunday had been Candice Powell's favorite day of the week. Back then, it was because every Sunday afternoon, her parents would load their six children into their early-model Ford van and drive eighteen miles to her paternal grandparents' house for dinner. Candice's maternal grandparents had died in a car accident before Candice was even born, so her only introduction to them was in photographs that her mom had on display in the home. But she knew her dad's parents, Clayton and Ora Lee Powell, well and she loved them dearly.

Grandpa Clayton was probably well-to-do by most people's definition, especially for a black man in the late nineteen-sixties and early seventies. Candice's grandparents lived in a large wood-framed house with what, to her childhood eyes, seemed like miles of land separating them from the nearest neighbor. Her grandfather had always supported his family with the work of his hands and the hands of the men he hired. He was a farmer who planted acres of tobacco each year. It was the only crop that he cultivated—everything else was livestock. In one fence, he bred pigs and cows, and in another, chickens. What he didn't sell to the markets, Ora Lee cooked for the family.

Candice's father had nine siblings, all of whom still lived in Greenwood at the time. Every Sunday afternoon, the home that Clayton and Ora Lee Powell lived in would be bursting at the seams with children and grandchildren. Candice had long ago moved from South Carolina, and so much about her life had changed since then. But one thing that still held true was that she still loved Sundays.

These days, her love for the first day of the week had different roots. Candice hadn't grown up in the church like many of the members of Redemption Tabernacle, the church where she worshipped each Sunday. Her family wasn't a spiritually grounded one by any means. Grandpa Clayton's god was his work. He gave his farming job all the glory for providing for his family, and those views were passed along to all of his offspring, including Candice's father. Abraham Powell had the name of one of the greatest men in the Bible, but that was about as close to the scripture as he ever came. Candice couldn't even recall ever seeing a Bible in their home. Abraham didn't believe in any living being that he couldn't physically see or touch, and he made sure that his family knew it. If Minnie Powell didn't share her husband's hardnosed beliefs, she never voiced it.

"Ain't no such thing as the Easter bunny, ain't no such thing as Santa Claus, ain't no such thing as the tooth fairy, ain't no so such thing as the devil, and ain't no such thing as God," Abraham often said, and always in that order.

Both Candice's parents were in their seventies now. They were in reasonably good health and still lived in Greenwood, South Carolina, occupying the big house that her father's parents' deaths had left vacant. Not much about her parents had changed over the years, including their atheistic beliefs. Candice had tried to share the message of Jesus Christ with them many times over the past three years since she'd given her heart to God, but all of her urging had fallen on deaf ears. Minnie basically ignored her middle daughter, and her father called her crazy, saying she had been brainwashed.

"Next thing you know, that cult you in gonna have you doing something that's gonna get you in trouble that you can't get out of," Abraham warned with a full mouth of food and pointing his fork in his daughter's direction as they all sat, eating dinner last Christmas. "You gonna end up dead like them folks that was following that Jones fella in the seventies, and that other crazy preacher out there in Waco, Texas. And if you don't end up dead, you gonna end up in trouble with the law. Just remember this day that I'm telling you this, Candice. I love you 'cause you my daughter. But if you get locked up for the sake of your religion, I don't want no parts of it. You hear me?"

Candice constantly prayed that her parents and siblings would find salvation before it was too late. The thought of people she loved so dearly being eternally lost was depressing, but Candice knew that surrendering to God would have to be their choice.

Taking one last look at herself in the mirror, Candice grabbed her purse and Bible and headed for the front door of her apartment. Ev-

ery year since she'd moved to this faster, more
progressive city, she'd vowed to buy a house of
her own. But every time she began the search
for one, she convinced herself that it would
be an unnecessary purchase. She was a single
woman with no children. She didn't even have
a pet that required added space, so it made no
sense to invest in a house. But Candice promised herself that by the time she was forty, if she
was still single, she'd purchase a condo. It was
a three-year plan that she hoped *not* to cash in
on.

   Since the age of twenty-three, when she made
a conscious decision to break her family's vicious cycle, Candice had put her career first.
That was when she became the first Powell to
seek a higher education. By the time she began
her freshman year at Lander University, many
of those with whom she'd completed high school
had already graduated college and were em-
barking on careers. The discouragement that
she got from her family caused her to struggle
in her first year at Lander, but Candice trans-
ferred to Anderson University in Anderson,
South Carolina, in her sophomore year and
began to refocus. She became her own greatest rival, daring herself to become what many
thought she couldn't.

All that was expected of the Powell children was the bare minimum. Each of her siblings had finished high school, but none of them reached any higher. Her dad reared all three of her brothers to be mechanics, a self-taught line of work Abraham had been in for most of his life. And Minnie groomed her daughters to be dutiful housewives and mothers. Both of Candice's sisters, one older and one younger than she, were married by age twenty, and by the time Candice graduated from Anderson University with a Bachelor of Science degree and her Secondary Teacher Certification, they had families of their own.

Candice had to fight for everything she'd ever achieved. She had little or no support to encourage her, nobody to share her victories with, and nobody's shoulder to lean on when she needed to cry. Sometimes she wondered if she'd made the right choice to be her own person and move away from her family.

"You gon' put me in my grave yet, Candice," her mother said during one of their recent telephone chats. "You'll be forty in a few years, and all you got to show for it is paper."

"Paper?" Candice asked as if she didn't already know.

"That's right—paper. All you got is a degree and money, and neither one of 'em ain't nothing but paper."

Candice wanted to laugh. Since when did teaching become a lucrative job? It was a career choice to follow only if you had a desire to educate children. The money that was earned from it was certainly nothing to write home about.

But Candice didn't even have the chance to defend that point before her mother spoke again.

"That's all that a whole lot of women who took the route you took got. I ain't saying that it's anything wrong with having a little money, I reckon we all need some every now and then. But what good is having money when you ain't got nobody to spend it on but you? Don't you even want to get married, Candice?" Minnie asked the question like her daughter's singleness was an incurable disease.

"I do, Mama. I just haven't met the right person yet."

"And you ain't gonna meet one either," Minnie scolded. "Candice, you should've stayed in Greenwood and found you a decent, hardworking man, like me and Abraham tried to tell you.

You know Ralph and Pearleen Johnson's boy always was sweet on you. He would have been glad to marry you. Them Johnson boys were always decent and hardworking. And they got that good hair too. You would have had some pretty babies."

When Candice heard her mother use backward phrases like "good hair," every homesick bone in her body was healed. And she couldn't even believe that Minnie would dangle the likes of Darrell Johnson in her face as if he were a worthy prize. Even if she had stayed in Greenwood, he wouldn't have had a chance.

"Mama, Darrell Johnson's breath smelled like he had little men in his mouth tossing around little doo-doo balls; and he had more rotten teeth than good ones before we even got out of high school. I can only imagine what his mouth looks like now. Plus, he always smelled like week-old urine. Rumor was that he was still wetting his bed at the age of seventeen. Why in the world would I want to marry something like that?"

"Teeth can be fixed, and urine ain't nothing that a little soap and water can't take care of," Minnie shot back to Candice's disgust. "That's why Abraham be so outdone with you, girl.

You got yourself a little education, and now you think you better than everybody else."

Candice's eyes had filled with tears at the accusation. The emotion was driven more by aggravation than hurt. "That's not true, Mama. I just know what I want, and Darrell Johnson is not it."

"Whether he was it or not, it's too late now. Raggedy teeth, stank breath and all, he got a wife and two young'uns that could have been yours if you had-a just been like your sisters. You worrying about the wrong thing. Your breath is clean, and your teeth are pretty, and what you got? Nobody, Candice. And now you out there in the big city with all them pretty boys who half-scared to get their hands dirty. And they got so many women to choose from that they ain't in no hurry to settle down. Living up there, you'll be fifty years old and still by yourself."

"I don't receive that, Mama. I'll get married when God says so. Just wait and see." Candice said that and then ended their conversation to escape the sting of any further tongue-lashing. There had been times in the past when Minnie had prophesied a future of lifelong singleness and Candice believed it. But this budding relationship with Stuart Lyons was headed in the right direction to make the prophecy false.

It had been a long time since Candice had felt about a man the way she felt about Stuart. She tried daily not to get her emotions too involved in the cyber relationship for fear that she'd end up with a broken heart. Again. Stuart's request for a telephone conversation had caught her off-guard. She should have seen it coming; after all, they'd been chatting for four whole months. But when he asked, she was caught unprepared. Candice desperately wanted to talk to Stuart, but she knew she had to proceed with caution. There were things about herself that she hadn't yet told the police lieutenant, and for now, she wanted to keep it that way.

Redemption Tabernacle was about a half-hour drive from Candice's apartment, but her deep thoughts seemed to usher her there in record time. She parked her burgundy Avalon in the half-empty lot of the storefront worship center and retrieved her belongings before getting out and taking the short walk to the entrance. The male usher who was on duty to attend the front door today, opened it to allow her inside.

"Good morning, Sister Powell," he greeted, handing her an envelope for her morning donation and then walking her up the aisle and directing her to the corner of the pew where she generally sat.

Redemption Tabernacle was among the smaller churches in the city. The ministry didn't have a weekly televised broadcast, the pastor's face couldn't be found on a single roadside billboard, and the congregation didn't include any of the city's many professional athletes, politicians or recording artists. On its roll, the church had roughly two hundred members, and the edifice was equipped to accommodate them; but on any given Sunday, Redemption Tabernacle was fortunate if a third of its members showed up. Despite that, the services were always lively and Candice never failed to go home feeling rejuvenated enough to take on the week ahead.

Soon after she got situated in her seat, the associate pastor, Cornell Pratt, took the stand and opened with prayer. Candice didn't miss the admiring glance that he threw her way en route to the podium, and she didn't miss the one that followed just before he reclaimed his pulpit chair. Aside from being Pastor Goode's right-hand man, Cornell also taught World His-

tory at the same school where Candice taught
math. He was handsome enough to give a second look, and many of the female students at
the high school adored him, but Candice could
find no real attraction. Perhaps his age had
something to do with it. Cornell had just turned
thirty on Valentine's Day, and he treated himself by asking out the woman he'd had a crush
on since they began working together.

Candice felt indebted to Cornell on some
level. He'd been the one to invite her to Redemption Tabernacle, and had it not been for
his persistence, hers would most likely still be
a lost soul, searching for something to fill a
void that only Jesus could satisfy. But gratefulness was all that Candice felt for Cornell. The
evening she spent at dinner with him, celebrating his birthday, was an enjoyable one. Their
conversation flowed, chatting about common
issues surrounding school and church. For
Candice, it was like sharing dinner with her
younger brother. However, Cornell felt a deeper
connection and had told her so on more than
one occasion.

Standing as the praise and worship leaders
took the floor, Candice clapped and swayed to

the music provided by the keyboard situated on one side of the church and the full set of drums in the opposite corner. They were the only musical instruments that the small organization had, but the musicians played skillfully and ushered in the Holy Spirit.

As the praise and worship service came to a close, Pastor Emily Goode took to the speaker's stand. Pastor Goode was a high-energy, hat-wearing, late-fifty-something-year-old preacher who always looked like she'd just stepped out of the pages of *Vogue*. She was at least fifty pounds heavier than a woman her height should be, but despite that, she looked ten years younger than her age. Her tawny-colored skin showed very few wrinkles, and not a glimmer of gray showed in her hair as it hung in ringlets that bounced past her shoulders. Pastor Goode rarely wore the same outfit more than twice a season, and today, it was a red-and-black skirt suit, the hemline decorated in diamond-like jewels. The heels of her matching two-tone sandals appeared to be at least three-inches high, and the straps seemed to hang on for dear life and beg for mercy as the preacher's plump feet hung over the edges.

Candice smiled at that thought while her hands flipped the pages of her Bible as directed, coming to a rest at Matthew, seventh chapter.

"God's opening up doors for many of us," Pastor Goode began, dabbing at beads of perspiration leftover from her holy dance during praise and worship. "The sad part about it is that God has done all the work, and all we got to do is put one foot in front of the other and walk on through; and some of us are too afraid to do it. Who knows what I'm talking about this afternoon?"

A chorus of responses validating the pastor's point filled the room. Candice sat in silence, pondering what was said and wondering if she were among the guilty.

"Follow along with me in the text today," Pastor Goode instructed. "Look at verse seven, and when you're ready to read along with me, say, amen."

"Amen." There were less than sixty people in the building, but the acoustics made it sound like far more. Those same voices echoed as they read along with the preacher.

Ask, and it shall be given you; seek, and ye shall find; knock, and it shall be opened unto you:

"But it doesn't stop there," Pastor Goode pointed out. "See that colon? That's not a period. The Lord had more to say to His people.

We miss out on our blessings when we stop God short of what His Word says. If you want to get the fullness of the blessing, you have to have a full knowledge of the scripture. Amen?"

"Amen," the congregation agreed.

"Let's read on."

"For every one that asketh receiveth; and he that seeketh findeth; and to him that knocketh it shall be opened." The congregants' voices bounced off the walls.

"See, when God says something and then goes back and stresses His point, that means He really wants to be sure you're getting what He's saying," Pastor Goode expounded. "Many times, we ask God for things, seek His face for the desires of our hearts and knock on heaven's door for answers; and when He grants us our prayers, we don't even trust Him enough to walk out on faith to get it."

As her pastor preached, Candice's mind drifted to Stuart. It was true that she had been praying for someone special to share her life with.

In the short span of years since she had come to know the Lord, Candice had asked for many things like a deeper relationship with her Savior and a heart to forgive those who'd all but emotionally crippled her. Then there were the more materialistic requests: a job that allowed her to nurture children, a home in a neighborhood where she could feel safe living alone, freedom from the debt that she accumulated during her college years, a reliable vehicle so she could stop riding public transit, etcetera. All of it, God had been gracious to provide.

In recent months, her most earnest prayer was to connect with someone who she could share a future with; someone who would be spiritually compatible; someone who wouldn't handle her heart as though it were nothing more than the wrapping that covered the gift that he really wanted to get to; someone unlike the man who had hurt her in the past.

When the benediction was given two hours after the opening prayer, Candice felt as though God had spoken to her. It was time to stop second-guessing herself . . . and Stuart. She'd still exercise caution and take it slowly, but after hearing today's message, she had come to the conclusion that she was ready to walk through the door that the Lord had opened for her. She just had to plan carefully so that . . .

"Hi, Candice. Good to see you today."

Startled, Candice's arms jerked, causing her purse to fall on the floor, scattering much of its contents onto the carpet.

"I'm sorry." Cornell immediately bent to collect the spill. "I didn't mean to sneak up on you like that."

Embarrassment flushed Candice's face as she lowered to help him. "I've got it, Minister Pratt." She always referred to him in his clerical capacity when at church.

"No, it's my fault, let me get it," he said, scooping up her cosmetic items in one hand and passing them to her. "I hope I got everything." Cornell searched the area around them as he spoke. Once he was certain he had, he turned his attention back to Candice. "Do you have any plans for this afternoon? I'd love to take you to dinner."

"Oh, um . . . thanks, but I can't. I have some work to do this afternoon."

"Oh?" Cornell looked disappointed. "Something to prepare for tomorrow's class?"

"Huh? Yeah," Candice said, making a mental note to do something classroom-related when she got home so she wouldn't be guilty of telling a lie in the church.

"You can't even spare a couple of hours?"

"No, I can't. I've put this off long enough. I need to go ahead and get it done."

Cornell was persistent. "Need any help? I mean, I know I'm not a math whiz or anything, but I'm pretty good with numbers when I want to be."

Candice offered a sensitive smile. She didn't quite understand Cornell's motivation. She was several years older than he and had, for the most part, rejected anything that even resembled an advance from him. Still, he seemed determined to foster some type of relationship with her that expanded beyond church and business. If she didn't think he'd misconstrue it, Candice would be willing to be a casual friend. She hadn't had a close friend in years, and the thought of having one trustworthy, platonic friend appealed to her. But Candice was smart enough to know that Cornell wasn't the person to fill that vacancy.

"What do you say?" Cornell pressed. His face was near pleading when he added, "I can stop by KFC or wherever you want and pick up dinner and bring it over. It'll be fun." He touched Candice's arms with his last word.

"Thanks, Cornell . . . Minister Pratt," Candice quickly corrected. "But I work better when I'm alone." This time she wasn't lying.

Cornell's smile showed no trace of defeat. "See you at work tomorrow?" He half-stated, half-asked, while waving and backing away all at the same time.

Nodding, Candice said, "Sure. See you at work."

Chapter Four

Thought maybe U had scared me off, didn't U, Stuart Lyons? Just b-cuz U hadn't heard from me in a week don't mean I'm gone. Maybe U didn't hear from me last week b-cuz I liked U last week. Or maybe I just had better things to do than haunt U. Now I'm back and I know where U live and I know U don't live alone. R U scared?

DR. A.H. SATAN

Stuart's hands trembled. Not from fear, but from seething anger that was nearing its boiling point. In the seven days that had passed since his car had been vandalized, Stuart had prayed that Dr. Satan would have had enough entertainment for one lifetime and would move on, leaving him alone. But now, not only was the deranged man threatening him, but also his sister and his son. And while Kenyatta might be able to protect herself, Stuart knew that Tyler couldn't.

"Until we can make an arrest, we may have to put you under protective custody, Lieutenant," said Donald Reinhart, Dekalb County Chief of Police, after looking over the letter again and then for the second time, passing it along to Chief Overstreet, who readily agreed.

"I think so too. This guy may be crazy, but he's not stupid. He's smart enough to type the letters or mask his true penmanship so sloppily that we can't identify him by his handwriting. And he uses gloves or some other form of protection so that we can't detect fingerprints on the paper or envelopes."

"Maybe he doesn't need gloves. Maybe he doesn't have fingerprints to hide."

All of the men gathered in the small conference room of the police station turned their attention toward Sergeant Allen Bowden. He had mumbled the words as though talking to himself, but Stuart couldn't believe he'd said them at all.

"What's that, Sergeant?" Chief Reinhart said.

Surely he won't repeat himself, Stuart thought. Allen would never be that stupid.

"I said, maybe he doesn't need gloves. Maybe he doesn't have fingerprints to hide."

Stuart looked at Allen like he had lost his mind. It was with much the same expression that all of the other officers looked at him.

"Okay, just hear me out," Allen said, holding up a hand to stop words from the others that had not yet even been spoken.

Stuart shook his head, knowing what the man was going to say. "You all know the whole story behind the Shelton Heights subdivision, right?"

With reserved caution, each man nodded.

"Well, what if this is another one of those weird things that only happens to people who live in Shelton Heights?"

"Are you *serious*, Sergeant?" Chief Overstreet said the words with an overtone of skepticism and a telling scowl.

"Yes, sir." Allen's voice was unwavering. "We, the members of the Dekalb County police force, know better than anyone how unexplainable some of the things that go on in that neighborhood are. I'm not telling you to believe in ghosts. Heck, I'm not even sure I believe in them; not on the broad scale anyway. But I'm kind of inclined to believe that old man, Shelton Heights, is not resting in peace. People have gone missing or turned up dead in the strangest ways in that community. Has anybody other than me even considered the fact that it could be the ghost of Shelton Heights that's spooking Stuart?"

"Do you want to be placed on medical leave or something?" Stuart blurted, standing in indignation. "Is that why you keep bringing up this nonsense?"

"Calm down, Lyons," Chief Reinhart said, motioning with his hands for Stuart to return to his seat.

"There's a fool on the loose who is threatening my family," Stuart said, still standing and still fuming. "How am I supposed to calm down? I got a nut who's got it in for me for no apparent reason, and a friend whose best explanation is that a ghost . . . a *ghost*, Chief . . . he actually thinks a ghost is the offender. That's just like saying that there is nothing that can be done about this."

"That's not the case," Chief Reinhart assured. "We will catch this perpetrator."

"Not if Sergeant Bowden can help it, we won't," Stuart stressed. "If he can get the rest of you to start believing his ghost theory, you'll stop looking. I mean, what's the use in looking? You can't see a ghost and you sure can't arrest one."

"I didn't mean that we should give up, I was just saying." Allen's voice was quiet, and he seemed embarrassed by the outburst he'd caused.

"I was just saying, too," Stuart sputtered.

"Calm down, Lyons," the Chief of Police reiterated. "We won't get anything done if we lose our cool here. Reading between the lines, it does appear that this guy is making an indirect threat to your boy, but it's not going to happen. If we have to put your house under twenty-four-hour surveillance, it won't happen."

Stuart slowly sank back into the chair behind him and rubbed his hands over the top of his head. Aside from a mustache and his eyebrows, his face was as clean-shaven as his dome, but right now, he wished he had enough hair somewhere to pull as hard as he could. Never in his life had he been so frustrated or felt so helpless. The week had started out on a positive note. Candice had called Sunday night, and they spoke for two solid hours, making plans for their first meeting. She sounded as beautiful as her spirit, though her voice lacked the northern accent that Stuart had imagined a New Yorker would have.

She was far more receptive to the idea of coming to Atlanta for a brief visit than she was of him flying to New York to see her. Stuart was elated when she said she'd come in on Friday night and agreed to them spending much of the day together on Saturday. But he was a bit disappointed when Candice rejected his idea that she remain in Atlanta until Sunday evening, allowing them time to attend worship service together at New Hope Church and share dinner afterward.

Citing that she needed to return home as quickly as possible so she could prepare herself for work on Monday, Candice sounded regretful that she couldn't stay longer. Stuart liked that. And in hindsight, he even appreciated the fact that she rejected his offer to pay for her flight and her two-night hotel stay. He really did want to contribute something to the trip, especially since it was more his idea than hers; but Candice insisted on paying her own way. Stuart figured that she didn't want to feel obligated to him in any way, and he completely understood.

"I cannot believe that a woman is finally leading my brother by the nostrils," Kenyatta said over dinner on Sunday night when Stuart finally informed her.

"Nobody has Stuart Lyons by the nostrils," he replied.

"Oh, you're hooked all right." His sister laughed. "I can't wait to meet her."

Her laugh quickly turned to a sour grimace when Stuart told her that she wouldn't get that opportunity.

"How you gonna bring some woman around that you're interested in and not let me and Tyler meet her?"

"I didn't say that Tyler wouldn't meet her; I said you wouldn't. Tyler will be with me when I pick her up from the airport, but he'll be here with you when Candice and I go out."

"Why can't I come along when you pick her up from the airport?"

"Because, Kenyatta." Stuart's voice was unyielding. "It's way too soon to be introducing her to family. I don't want her to feel uncomfortable."

"And who is Tyler, if he ain't family?" Kenyatta pressed, pointing the prongs of her fork at Stuart. "Besides, if this girl is somebody you're interested in, she needs to pass the Kenyatta test. She can't just roll up in here and hook up with my brother without my approval."

"See?" Stuart's voice was accusing. "That's why you're not meeting her. You're always trying to intimidate somebody, and I won't let you do that to Candice. Besides, I don't recall you getting my approval before you hooked up with crazy Joe."

That had been enough to temporarily shut down Kenyatta, and the remembrance of it was enough to snap Stuart back to the present. He looked at both Chief Overstreet and Chief Reinhart.

"I have somebody that I want you guys to check out."

Both men looked at Stuart, but it was Allen who spoke up first.

"You have a realistic possibility in mind who you think might be doing this?"

Serving him a glare that teetered on the edge of menacing, Stuart said, "Well, it might not be as realistic of a possibility as a frickin' *ghost*, Sergeant Bowden; but yeah, I think this person might qualify as a possibility."

Allen's posture sank.

"Who is it, Lieutenant?" Chief Overstreet asked, motioning for one of the accompanying detectives to step closer with his pad and pencil in hand.

"My sister lives with me," Stuart began, after taking a breath to calm his renewed anger. "She's been my housemate for a little over a year now, ever since she broke away from her abusive husband."

The mention of an abusive husband clearly got Chief Reinhart's attention. "Is he a violent person?"

Stuart shrugged. It wasn't the first time he'd been asked that question. "I guess it's all in the manner of how you define violent. He was very controlling of her—at least, he tried to be, anyway. If you know my sister, you know that, at times, controlling her is about as doable as controlling a rabid bulldog, but her ex gave it the old college try. He never hit her, but he constantly threatened to, and was even known to threaten her with a deadly weapon. It would be safe to say he had violent tendencies."

"And he knows that your sister resides with you?" Chief Overstreet asked.

"He didn't in the beginning, but I'm thinking he's found out and he's not too happy about it. Joe and I have never gotten along, so I think he'd be pretty angry if he found out she was with me."

Chief Reinhart nodded. "Well, he certainly has motive, and it sounds like he's capable of scheming up such a plan."

"I agree," Chief Overstreet said. "You say his name is Joe?"

"Joseph," Stuart said. "Joseph King. He lives in Jacksonville, Florida. I can give you his last known address."

"Good, good," Chief Overstreet said, removing his hat, revealing a toupee that, today, had been placed too far to the left. "This makes sense," he said, thinking aloud and then replacing his hat. "If this guy lives in Jacksonville, it would explain why his pranks are always spaced and possibly why it took so long for him to break the cycle of letter-writing and actually mar your property. If he were local, it would stand to reason that he would probably make some kind of physical threat on a more consistent basis. But because any actual contact would require that he physically be in Atlanta, he can only do that when it becomes convenient."

"That's good reasoning," Chief Reinhart said, patting Chief Overstreet on the back like the case was all but closed.

Stuart felt a building confidence too. He'd waved it off when his friends consistently brought up Joe's name during their talk last week. But the more he thought of it, the surer he became that Joseph King was the one they were looking for.

"Stop by my office, Lyons," Chief Overstreet ordered. "I want to get more information from you, including Joe's physical address and his place of employment. Before taking him into custody for questioning, I need to check out a few things." The chief turned away, and his deputies followed, with Chief Reinhart bringing up the rear.

Stuart began following them too, but stopped at the sound of his name being called. He turned to see Allen standing in the same spot he'd occupied for the duration of the discussion, his hat in his hands.

"Yes?"

"Can we talk a minute?" Allen asked.

Stuart exhaled and then took a few steps in Allen's direction. "What do you want, Sergeant? And let me make it clear up front that I don't have the time or the patience for any more talk about ghosts. Not today."

Taking his cue from Stuart, Allen addressed his superior in his official capacity too. "I'm sorry, Lieutenant. I just wanted to make sure all the bases were covered."

"So you thought you'd throw it out there that I'm just doomed?"

Allen shook his head using short, quick motions. "That's not at all what I was trying to do. I was just . . . well, if there is even the slightest chance that there could be some truth behind this whole Shelton Heights thing, wouldn't you want to know? I mean, wouldn't you want to know the fullness of what you're up against?"

"You know what? I'm losing respect for myself just because I'm standing here listening to you." Stuart turned to leave but was stopped again by Allen's voice.

"Lieutenant Lyons, all I'm saying is the only way to find out why this crazy stuff is happening is to check out everything, even the unlikely."

"I don't have anything against checking out the unlikely, Sergeant. It's the unfeasible that I don't want to waste time on. You with me? The whole legend of Shelton Heights is about as real as *The Legend of Sleepy Hollow*. I believe Old Man Shelton Heights's spirit is lurking around Atlanta about as much as I believe the Headless Horseman—who, if you recall, was supposed to be the ghost of some soldier who got his block blown off by a cannonball—is riding around during the night looking for his head."

The room was quiet momentarily, and then Allen spoke again. "You could be right; this whole Shelton Heights myth may have nothing to do with what's happening with you. As a matter of fact, I hope you *are* right. But what if you're not?"

Stuart placed his hands on his hips and shook his head. "You just won't give up, will you? You would just rather believe there's no hope for me, wouldn't you?"

"No, Lieutenant. Even if the myth is true, it doesn't mean your fate is sealed. Crazy things have happened to other people in that subdivision that didn't end in their demise. It's almost like Old Man Heights just gets a kick out of haunting the folks who live in his community, and after he's had his fill, he moves on. I've been studying the pattern out there, and he's never hit the same family twice."

Stuart stood silent for a moment, looking into the serious eyes of his friend. "I keep forgetting that you were raised by your grandparents and they believed in this kind of stuff." Stuart ran his hand over the top of his head and then placed his hat there. "You know what, Bowden? I give up, okay? You go right ahead and keep researching your Shelton Heights mystery. But please don't bring it up at another meeting with Chief Reinhart and Chief Overstreet, you with me? It's bad enough that I think you're losing it. If everybody starts thinking the same, you're liable to be relieved of your duties."

"Deal," Allen agreed. He smiled like a kid who had just been given permission to play in the mud.

Stuart turned back toward the door and resumed his exit. "I don't know which one of us is crazier, you, for seriously considering a dead man's spirit as a possible suspect, or me, for permitting you to do it."

Chapter Five

Women of Hope, a ministry within New Hope Church that was founded just for those sisters who had been spiritually, mentally, or physically wounded, had grown by leaps and bounds since its inception two years ago. The founder of it, Dr. Jade Tides-Greene—daughter of Reverend B.T. Tides and wife of Hunter Greene—never knew that it would become one of the most active ministries within her father's church; and certainly not in such a short time. Attendance at the weekly meetings had increased so much that they'd had to move it out of the forty-person-capacity classroom in which it began and into a room more than twice that size.

Now, even women who had no history of neglect or abuse came just to take part in the worship and fellowship. Women of Hope had, in essence, expanded into a ministry for women in all walks of life who just felt the need for encouragement and a deeper trust in God.

As he did every Thursday, tonight, Hunter escorted his wife into the room and helped her set up her belongings in preparation for the evening's gathering. Jade watched both him and their son as they reorganized the chairs so they would be just the way she liked them for her chat session. Turning back around to face the oversized dry-erase board on the front wall, Jade smiled to herself while she wrote down pointers for those who would be joining her shortly.

"You need us to do anything else, babe?" Hunter's voice was close behind her.

Jade turned again, and Hunter was close enough for her to reach out and touch. And she wanted to, too. That man seemed to get more irresistible every day. Broad-shouldered and tall, with caramel-colored skin and brown eyes that seemed to tease her every time he looked at her.

Like the overwhelming majority of brothers between the ages of twenty and fifty who attended New Hope, Hunter sported a clean-shaven head. His mustache and goatee were always neatly trimmed, just the way Jade liked them.

Boy, if we weren't at church, I'd show you what else I needed you to do. Jade almost laughed at her thought. But as inappropriate as it may have been, she knew that being in the church wasn't the thing keeping her from wrapping her arms around her husband's neck and tasting the lips she had just feasted on before they left home.

"Where did you put the papers, Daddy?"

That was the only thing stopping Jade from giving Hunter a sample of her brewing passion. Malik was in the room with them.

Finding them, Malik added, "You want me to pass these out, Ma?"

Ma. He'd been calling Jade that ever since the day she married his father. Still, she relished the sound of it. "Yes, sweetie," Jade said, breaking her stare with Hunter and connecting eyes with her son. "If you'd place one in every chair, that would be very helpful. Thanks."

Hunter's chuckle brought her attention back on him. He knew her well, and Jade was fully aware that he hadn't failed to notice her earlier smoldering look.

"Would you like me to help him lay those out, or is there something or some*one* else that you'd like me to lay out on those seats?"

"Hunter!" Jade said in a harsh whisper. She cut her eyes toward Malik and then turned them back to her husband. "We're in the Lord's house."

"Not in the sanctuary," he replied, adding a boyish shrug.

"It's all a part of the church, so it's still the Lord's house."

"True," Hunter said with a nod, stepping closer and putting one arm around Jade's waist. "But I believe that somewhere in the *Lord's* Word, it tells us that marriage is honorable in all, and the bed is undefiled."

His increased closeness made the temperature in the room seem ten degrees higher. Jade was in a serious battle with her flesh when she said, "The *bed*, Hunter, not the chairs at the church."

"Well, if we turn them the right way, we could—"

"Hunter!" Jade could feel the color rushing from her face, and her neck felt like someone had just lit a match to it. She used her hand to remove his arm from her waist. "Now, behave yourself and go help Malik."

Hunter laughed as he backed away. "If I didn't have this appointment this afternoon,

I'd stay here and rush you through this class so we could get home and undefile our bed."

"What's that mean?" Malik asked, causing Hunter to laugh even harder.

Not knowing what to say in response, Jade looked toward her husband in a mixture of terror and panic.

Hunter came to her rescue. "It means good, son."

"Good?" The thirteen-year-old looked to be deep in thought as he pondered the word. "So you want to go home and make your bed good?"

"Yeah. Yeah, that's exactly what I want to do." Hunter released a short chuckle that received a silent reprimand from Jade.

Apparently satisfied with the answer, Malik resumed his task, and Hunter winked toward his wife before going to assist. They had just placed paperwork in the final chair when the door to the classroom opened and members of Women of Hope began filing in.

"Good evening, ladies," Jade greeted. "Just grab a seat, and we'll get started shortly. Don't mind my men. They'll be out of here in a minute."

"Hey, girl," Kenyatta said, approaching Jade and delivering a warm hug.

"Good to see you," Jade said. "I thought you said you weren't going to make it tonight."

A look of concern flashed across Kenyatta's flawlessly made-up face. She was as pretty as her brother was handsome, but the complexion of her skin wasn't nearly as dark as Stuart's. "I know, but I had to end up skipping the after-hours staff meeting on my job because I got called to the police station to answer some questions."

Jade's eyes grew large, and she lowered her voice to keep their conversation private. "The police station?" She knew Kenyatta's reputation for carrying a gun and immediately wondered if that had been the reason for her summons. "Is everything okay? You're not in any trouble, are you?"

Patting Jade on the back for reassurance, Kenyatta replied, "No, but it looks like my ex has found out where I am, and he's acting the straight fool about it."

Although Jade had never met Joseph King in person, Kenyatta had shared her story of abuse with the members of Women of Hope when she first joined the group. She had never admitted being afraid of the man, but Jade knew that to some degree, Kenyatta did fear him. "Is this something that you want to vent about in tonight's meeting?" Jade asked. "I'll be sure to give you the time you need."

Kenyatta shook her head, refusing the offer. "I do want to talk about it, but not with the whole group. You think the girls and I can grab a bite to eat after the meeting, maybe?"

"The girls" consisted of Jade, Kenyatta and Jan. And simply because Kenyatta knew she wouldn't have a choice, Ingrid was also included.

"We'll see what the others have planned for later, and if they're all free, I'm sure they would love to lend you their ears. But definitely I'll be available to you."

"Thanks, Jade."

When the door opened again, Jade looked toward it and saw her brother standing in the open doorway. She bit her lip when she noticed he stepped aside and allowed Ingrid to walk in ahead of him. Had they come together? The thought filtered through Jade's mind as she tried to think of something to say that would keep Kenyatta from noticing the pair, but she couldn't create a quick-enough diversion.

For a moment, Kenyatta stood silent with her hands on her hips, looking as though Ingrid had no right to speak to Jerome, let alone smile at him. Kenyatta immediately made a step toward the door, and Jade grabbed her by the arm.

"Kenyatta King, let me tell you something." Jade made her voice as firm as she could. "If you want to turn my brother completely off, you just go over there and create a scene." She was sure that was enough to make Kenyatta change her decision. But just in case it wasn't, Jade added, "And let's not forget that we are in church. This is not the time or the place for you to go all . . . *Kenyatta* on us."

Jade didn't know if Kenyatta backed down because of what she'd said or because Ingrid had now found a seat while Jerome headed toward Hunter. Whichever was the case, Jade was grateful enough to breathe a sigh of relief. "Go grab a seat before you're one of the ones who have to settle for a seat in the rear," she told Kenyatta while pointing in the direction of another group of women coming through the door. "You know how much you hate sitting in the back of the class."

Kenyatta complied, returning a smile and a wave from Jerome in the process. Jade whispered a soft prayer of thanks.

Even when they were in school, Jerome served as a lure for the opposite sex. Back then, he was also a magnet for trouble. Ten years in prison and a commitment to God had changed the latter, but not the former.

"We're gonna get out of your way, sweetheart," Hunter said as he, Jerome and Malik approached. "It's about time for you to get started."

Jade embraced him. "Thanks, baby."

"Stu told me to tell you that you can leave the room in whatever shape it's in when you're done, sis," Jerome reported. "He said that he'd be sure that the janitorial crew puts all the chairs back in place and do any clean up that is necessary."

"Is Stuart riding with you all?"

"Yeah," Hunter said. "I'm gonna drop Malik off at Kwame's," he said, referring to his best friend and second-in-command at *Atlanta Weekly Chronicles*. "He won't be going to the prison with us today, so he agreed to watch the kids. He'll have Tyler and Kyla too. Once we drop Malik off, we'll pick up everybody else."

"Will all of you be able to fit in the Range Rover?" Jade counted the men in her mind.

"Well, since Jackson is out on the road," Hunter said, referring to Jade's oldest brother, "it'll just be me, Jerome, Stuart, Pete and your dad in the Range Rover. Any other brothers from the prison ministry that will be coming will be in a second vehicle.

"Okay," Jade said. "Be careful. I'll see you at home later tonight."

Hunter winked. "I'll be needing you to wait up for me."

Smiling, Jade replied, "And I'll be needing to wait up."

Jerome made a gagging noise and said, "And I'll be needing a barf bag."

When the door closed behind the brethren's departure, Jade turned to her full classroom of hope-seeking sisters and smiled. "Are we ready to begin?" It was her standard opening line.

"Amen!" The answer was nearly lost in a chorus of accompanying loud cheers and thunderous handclaps—the standard reply.

"Let us all stand and grab the hand of the sister beside you as a display of unity and support as we go to the Lord in prayer." Jade stepped out in the floor with the others and stood in the open space left for her between Jan and Ingrid.

When each of the sixty or so women had a hand linked in hers, Jade bowed her head and prayed. "Heavenly Father, we thank You for every home that is represented through those who have gathered here this evening. There are troubled women here tonight who came to seek your will, your guidance and protection. Father, assure them that they have come to the right place for you promised to be our present help in the time of trouble. I ask that you touch every heart and mind in this circle. Allow your presence to saturate this room, to fill every nook and every corner, leaving no space for the devil. With You as our weapon of warfare, we rebuke the evils of Satan that seek to harm us. Send him and all of his devious angels back to the pits of hell in Your Son, Jesus, name."

Jade paused for a long while, and during that space of time, all that could be heard were expressions of worship coming from the women around her. Some spoke words identifiable to the common ear, and others spoke in unknown tongues as the Spirit of God moved upon them. When the sounds of worship began to abate, Jade continued.

"Cover our families under your blood, Lord. You told us to pray for those that trespass against us; so even if they are named among our enemies, we ask that you bless our husbands. Some of us have been mistreated at their hands, but we pray for them that you do what you have to do to bring them to the foot

of the cross. We curse the hands of the enemy
that will try to continue to use our husbands to
our detriment. There is a spirit of fear in the
room, but we ask for deliverance from trepi-
dation, knowing that you are the Almighty
God and with you, nothing by any means shall
harm us. Give us peace, Lord. We speak peace.
And in all things we give you glory and honor
because You are most worthy. Amen.

"Amen," the women said under one strong
voice.

When Jade looked out into the room, her
eyes immediately locked on Kenyatta, who
was dabbing at the corners of her eyes. While
tears were commonplace in their weekly sessions, in all the time Kenyatta had been a part
of Women of Hope, Jade could never recall a
moment when she had seen her shed a tear.
Seeing it was proof that the thought of Joseph
King deviously scheming to harm her, whether
directly or indirectly, was more troubling and
frightening for Kenyatta than she was willing
to admit.

Chapter Six

Phillips State Prison was an institution where Jerome Tides had wasted ten years of his life. An entire decade of holidays, birthdays, family reunions, vacations, weddings and graduations had been missed all because he chose to reject the teachings of his parents and embrace a life of sin and crime. Although Jerome had been blessed to be released at his first parole eligibility hearing, and had promised his father that he would join him in New Hope's prison ministry, putting that pledge into action had been beyond difficult. From age twenty-six to thirty-six, Jerome had been forced to sleep on thin mattresses, relieve himself in public urinals, and live in daily fear of losing his manhood and/or his life. Once he was free, it just seemed stupid to voluntarily walk back into the facility for any reason—even to spread the Gospel of Jesus Christ.

"Son, you have to do this," Reverend Tides had told him that first month as Jerome sat on the side of his bed in the home he shared with Kwame at the time. His father had come to pick him up for what was to be his first active prison ministry assignment, and Jerome was falling apart at the thought of it.

"I can't, Dad," he'd said. Jerome's eyes were pleading and he was unashamed of the tears that painted streaks on his face. At four years short of forty, he was rocking back and forth, hugging himself with crossed arms, lamenting like a mother who had lost her child. "I know what I promised you, and I thought I could do it, but I can't."

"Never mind what you promised me, Jerome," his father had explained. "You made a vow to God that you'd do this and He is the one who you are reneging on if you don't follow through. A miracle from heaven delivered you from physical and spiritual bondage, son; and there are hundreds of men at that prison who are still locked up and lost. They need to see your testimony, Jerome. Don't rob them of the chance to know that there is a God who is able to deliver them too."

"I'm sorry, Dad. I can't do it. I'm so sorry."

Reverend Tides had embraced him that day and allowed Jerome to cry on his shoulder. He didn't say that he understood, but Jerome felt that he did. Before leaving, his father prayed with him, asking God to give his son the strength for the mission that had been divinely placed upon his shoulders. And God heard.

Three nights later, while Jerome slept, he dreamed of walking into prisons and using his bare hands to pull away bars that confined the inmates, allowing them to walk out into freedom. It was then that he knew, without doubt, that he had to conquer the phobias paralyzing the ministry within him. And the next month when the prison ministry gathered, Jerome was ready for the challenge.

But even now, nearly two full years later, he trembled a bit when the barbed wire fence came into view as Hunter maneuvered his truck onto the penal complex property. He found a parking spot that had an empty space beside it, so that they and the second vehicle of men that trailed them could park side by side.

The conversation in Hunter's truck—mostly talk about Stuart's still unidentified stalker—had been flowing freely en route to the prison; but the closer they'd gotten, the less Jerome spoke. By the time the waving flags that marked the distant spot of the prison location could be seen, Jerome had become completely silent. His reaction was typical, so none of the other men questioned him.

As they did each second Thursday evening when the Bible-bearing brethren arrived, Phillips State Prison's employees warmly greeted Reverend Tides and the men of New Hope Church. They and their belongings were taken through the normal process of passing through metal detectors, and then assigned officials escorted them to the room where they would meet with the incarcerated men. Coming to the prayer and Bible Study sessions was voluntary, and when Reverend Tides started the ministry eighteen months ago, there would be more men from New Hope present than inmates. Now, almost every month, they could look forward to ministering to at least fifty brothers of all ethnic backgrounds, willing to hear the messages of hope. One man's presence, in particular, made Jerome's own discomfort worth dealing with.

"What up, church boy?"

It was a nickname that used to infuriate Jerome during his prison years, but one that he now accepted as the compliment that it was.

Jerome stopped his mission of passing out New Testament Bibles to the incoming men and walked toward the owner of the voice that had said the words. Pressing his fist against the one that Rocky offered, Jerome answered, "What it do, brotha? Good to see you. Always good to see you." And he meant every word of it.

Rocky had been Jerome's cellmate for the last few months of his imprisonment, but Jerome had never viewed him as a friend until the final days. He didn't know the man's last name then, and he didn't know it now. Rocky had been known as one of the toughest men behind the iron curtains of Phillips State Prison. He was six-foot-five, and at the time when Jerome was released, he weighed in at 250 pounds. Jerome didn't ask, but looking at him now, he guessed that Rocky had put on at least another fifteen pounds of solid muscle in the past year. He was a massive human being, and although he'd made some noticeable changes for the better in the three months since Jerome had convinced him to start attending the meetings, still, nobody bothered Rocky. Whether he *would* kill a man with his bare hands or not, everyone knew that he *could*.

Rocky had turned forty on New Year's Day, and every birthday since his nineteenth had been spent in confinement. It would be almost another four years before he would even become eligible for parole. Like Jerome, Rocky had been with the wrong people, at the wrong place, at the wrong time. But unlike Jerome, Rocky was determined to be the mastermind behind the drug-related armed robbery he was involved in. And whereas the man who was shot during Jerome's crime survived, the one who starred in Rocky's story didn't.

The bullet that killed the eighteen-year-old victim proved not to have come from Rocky's gun, but in exchange for lighter sentences, all of his co-conspirators and so-called friends identified him as the ring leader who had arranged the heist. Rocky had refuted the accusation, fingering another man, but his arguments went unheard. The man who was convicted of the murder got life without the possibility of parole. Rocky got twenty-five years to life. And even with the changes that he'd made, Jerome often wondered if Rocky would seek out the men who betrayed him once he was released—*if* he was released. Jerome would bet anything that with each passing year, those tattling men worried over that possibility too.

Rocky gave Jerome what was, no doubt, what he defined as a light punch to the arm. "You looking good, nig . . . I mean, dude."

Jerome laughed through the throbbing pain and then handed to Peter Jericho the remaining Bibles that he held in his hand so that he could finish the job that Jerome started. During his frequent visits to see Rocky, Jerome had been trying to convince him to rid his dialogue of the *N* word, and accomplishing the feat had been an uphill battle for the imprisoned thug. But he was making noteworthy progress.

"You're looking good too, Rocky," Jerome replied. "Frighteningly *huge*, but good. Still hitting the weights every day, I see."

Rocky's laugh was a satisfied one. He flexed his arms with pride, displaying muscles that would make some professional body builders envious. "Gotta keep everybody in check so they don't get confused about who's the man around here," he remarked. "You know what I mean?"

Nodding, Jerome said, "I hear ya."

"Brother Rocky, it's a blessing to see you again. How are you today?"

Jerome stepped aside as his father approached with an outstretched hand. Reverend Tides had learned many of the men's names in the time that they'd been making their monthly visits.

"Thanks, Rev," Rocky said. "Some days I'm good, some days I ain't. Today has been a pretty good one."

"Well, thank God for today," Reverend Tides said.

Rocky said nothing in response. Just sported a sort of crooked grin and gave his shoulders a slight shrug.

Jerome noticed that around his father, Rocky took on a meek demeanor that was otherwise hidden.

"I think the men are ready, Reverend Tides," Stuart said, joining the threesome.

At his words, Rocky walked away, navigating around the room briefly before deciding which chair he wanted, and then motioning for the inmate who occupied it to move elsewhere.

Jerome shook his head at the sight of it. Some things never changed.

Reverend Tides sat in a chair in the center of the floor, making him the focal point of everyone in the room. The brothers from New Hope sat in chairs that were positioned farther back. In all, there were twelve men who had been handpicked by the pastor to serve in the prison ministry. All of those chosen were now saved and filled with the Holy Spirit, but at one time they had either been locked up or had a history of dealing closely with other men who had been incarcerated. Reverend Tides needed those in this ministry to be men who could relate to those to whom they'd be ministering.

With the absence of Jackson and Kwame, only ten were present today. All of them sat, with the exception of Stuart, who took seriously his position as lead security for Reverend Tides. He stationed himself not five feet from his pastor.

Phillips State Prison made sure that the room was secured well. There were alert armed guards standing alongside the walls and near the single exit door, but Stuart still posted himself near Reverend Tides, as though he thought the others were too far away to offer adequate protection should something go awry. The employees of the prison were familiar with Stuart and his position with the Dekalb County force. His act of overprotection went without debate.

Reverend Tides always began their meetings with prayer, and this evening was no different. Jerome lowered his head, but his eyes remained open and he scanned the room while his father prayed. Although Reverend Tides had asked that everyone bow their heads, a few of the inmates didn't feel the need to comply. They were quiet and respectful during the brief prayer, but their heads remained upright and their eyes open.

When Reverend Tides began speaking, his voice was unruffled and almost tranquil, a stark contrast from the authoritative tone used when he preached from the pulpit on Sunday mornings. Jerome appreciated his father's versatility and self-control. Because of it, he could speak to any sect of people without bringing embarrassment on his calling or his congregation.

"Just before we dismissed from our meeting last month," Reverend Tides was saying, "I asked each of you to write down one thing that you wanted the Lord to do in your life. Some of you dropped your written desires in the box that was provided, and others of you didn't. Doing so was your choice, so if you didn't participate, there is no harm done. But for those who did, I believe the Lord honors your compliance." The pastor paused and seemed to make eye contact with each man and then continued. "I sealed those requests in a large envelope and I have had that envelope under the prayer mat that I kneel on each day during my times with the Lord. As I promised, I didn't read any of them, but God has all-seeing eyes. He knows what you wrote."

At that moment, Rocky's uncharacteristic squirming caught Jerome's attention, who couldn't help but wonder what his former cellmate had written on his paper. One of the things Rocky had shared with Jerome during their cell-sharing days was the hatred he had for his father—the man who had not only mistreated all of his own children, but also repeatedly abused Rocky's mother. Rocky told Jerome that he not only wished his father would die, but wished he could be the one to kill him. It was a deep-seated hatred unlike any Jerome had ever known.

Now, as he looked at Rocky's bulky figure fight for a more comfortable position, Jerome wondered if, on the paper that had been made a part of Reverend Tide's morning meditation, Rocky had asked God to grant his father a cruel death. The pastor's words pushed Jerome's grim thoughts aside.

"As I was praying over your requests a few days ago, the Lord brought to my heart Mat-

thew 6:33, and I want to share that passage
with you. Matthew is the first book in your New
Testament Bibles." Reverend Tides turned the
pages of his own full-sized Bible as he spoke,
and the men followed suit.

"It's a simple but profound passage of scripture, that in laymen's terms, plainly tells us
that our number one concern should be to do
those things that are pleasing to God, and when
we look to do those things that are righteous or
good in the eyesight of our Lord and Savior,
He will give us our hearts' desires. The truth of
the matter is that until we seek to please God,
we really don't know what to do with the good
that our Creator gives us. That's why we find
ourselves choosing the wrong friends, making bad decisions and going down the wrong
paths," Reverend Tides explained. "In our
sinful natures, we don't know how to handle
certain situations. Many times, we don't even
know how to handle God's blessings."

Jerome looked at his father's profile as he
spoke, and for the first time, he saw an older
image of himself. Since childhood, he'd been
identified as the son who looked most like B.T.
Tides. Jerome never saw it. Probably because
he didn't want to. But now he recognized the
likeness clearly, and to be frank, Jerome didn't

quite know how to process it. The resemblance was more than physical. Even as Reverend Tides spoke, expounding on the Word of God, oddly, Jerome felt as though the words were coming from his own lips. Unconsciously, he touched his mouth, making sure that the voice he was hearing wasn't his own.

"How many of you have gifts?" Reverend Tides was asking. "I'm talking about talents, something that you're good at and you know you're good at it?"

Several of the men's hands crept into the air.

Reverend Tides took a moment to take in the sight and then said, "Now, how many of you are willing to admit that you've misused those talents? And because of it, the same interests and abilities that should have been used to help you become doctors, lawyers, mechanics, educators, counselors, policemen, scientists, construction workers, even preachers—are the same abilities that landed you here."

The hands went up even slower this time, but for many of the men, the silent confession was finally made.

Jerome found himself balling his hand into a fist, fighting the urge to raise it in the air with the others. He remembered his own childhood, teen and younger adult years. The same hands that, as a child, he'd used to spoil private property with graffiti were now used to help write articles for one of the most successful black-owned newspapers in the country. The same hands that were once used to hotwire and steal cars were now used to repair them for those who didn't have "real mechanic" money to pay. The same hands that were once used to distribute drugs to strung-out addicts had just been used a short while ago to pass out Bibles to inmates.

"That's what the Word is getting at today," Reverend Tides said, invading Jerome's thoughts once more. "All of those desires that you wrote on your papers last month; those are the 'all these other things' that the scripture makes reference to. God doesn't need to add all these wonderful benefits to our lives before we first come to the place where we have surrendered our hearts to Him. Because when we put Him first, we will know how to properly use the gifts He gives. We will use them to His glory and not to fulfill our own lusts or to our own detriment."

Reverend Tides kept talking, and the men continued to listen. Thirty minutes passed as though it were fifteen, and it was time to open the floor for discussion. Rarely were questions posed by the inmates on a voluntary basis. The after-study dialogue was most often generated when Reverend Tides would ask the men questions, prompting them to answer and sometimes debate. The same protocol was followed on this evening.

Twenty minutes later, Reverend Tides was giving the closing prayer. It had been another productive evening for the prison ministry.

"Well, I guess it's back to the cozy mansion for me." Rocky made the facetious remark as he approached the place where Jerome and Stuart stood together talking.

"It's just temporary, man," Jerome said, pressing his smaller fist against Rocky's larger one once more.

"Yeah," was Rocky's only response, and even it was said through a breathy sigh.

It saddened Jerome to hear the defeat in his friend's voice. A thousand clichés like, "Stay positive" and "Keep your chin up" flowed through his mind, but Jerome had been there. He knew how hopeless life felt when one was forced to live it behind bars. It was barely living at all; and he wouldn't dare insult Rocky by tossing out words that would be meaningless to him.

"I'll be out here to see you next week." Jerome hoped that would bring at least a morsel of cheer. When he was in prison, knowing he could look forward to a visit with someone who cared was always an encouragement.

Rocky grinned and rendered a slight upward jerk of his head, indicating that it had done the same for him. "A'ight. I'ma hold you to that."

"Well, well," another inmate said as he drew near them, interrupting Jerome's reply. His face wasn't familiar. He was a newbie among the men at the gathering.

Rocky's earlier smile dissolved in an instant, and he focused an ominous glare at the man who dared to talk without first getting his permission. "You don't see me talkin'? Fool, I'll bust you in the face."

The man retreated a little and cast his eyes toward the floor like a youngster who knew he'd have to pay for his misbehavior once the "company" was gone.

Stuart looked at Jerome, as though searching for confirmation that Rocky's rule over the others was normal behavior. Without uttering a word, Jerome told him that it was.

"I'm gon' bounce," Rocky said, finally bringing his eyes back to Jerome's and returning his tone to normal.

"That's a good idea," Jerome said. Then looking up into Rocky's eyes, he added, "And remember what we talked about a couple of weeks ago. Stay out of trouble, my friend. Can I count on you to do that?"

"Long as they let me." Rocky sported a partial grin and then backed away, giving their uninvited guest one last look of warning in the process.

"How are you, brother?" Jerome said, turning to the man and extending a hand. It was always encouraging to see someone new in the midst. "Hope you enjoyed the fellowship."

The man, relatively short in stature, appeared to be in his thirties and wore a hairstyle that resembled that of Snoop Dog. He looked up at Jerome, paused, and then accepted his offered handshake, but didn't respond.

When Stuart extended his arm, the man looked at Stuart's hand and sneered. "You don't even know who I am, do you?"

Resting his rejected hand by his side, Stuart asked, "Should I?"

The man uttered a single swear word, a dry snicker, and then added, "Probably not. Y'all crooked cops arrest so many innocent people 'til y'all don't remember one from the next."

"Are you saying that I arrested you?"

"Eleven years, three months, and sixteen days ago." There was no uncertainty in the man's voice.

Stuart was at least six inches taller than his accuser, but that didn't seem to intimidate the man.

Jerome made eye-contact with one of the armed guards that stood near Reverend Tides, conveying a silent message to him that his services might be needed more elsewhere.

"That's a long time," Stuart pointed out. "Are you sure it was me?"

"Oh, I'm sure. Ain't that many men in the world as black as you. I won't never forget that face, playa. You the reason my son ended up being raised by some man that he didn't even like. Oh, I ain't never gonna forget you, punk. You can bank on that one."

"Is everything okay?" The approaching guard's hand was on his holster as he asked.

"I think this gentleman needs to go back to his cell." If Stuart felt at all at risk by the man's threat, there was no sign of it in his eyes or his voice. He returned the man's stare without flinching.

"Come on, Blake. Let's go," the guard ordered, placing his hand on the man's forearm in the process.

"Why I gotta go? I ain't did nothing wrong." The man, who just moments ago, had been on the verge of being hostile now acted more like a whiny teenager whose misbehavior was being rewarded with a trip to the principal's office.

"You just threatened a law officer," Stuart said. "You don't think anything is wrong with that?"

The man's lips curled downward as if he was going to cry. No tears came from the man's eyes, but he maintained the look of regret when he lowered his sights to the floor and muttered, "Sorry."

Jerome narrowed his eyes, hardly believing the scene before him. This man had to have spent some time in the psych ward. Jerome shook his head from side to side and then looked at Stuart to see if he would respond to the man's warped apology.

The guard was the one to speak, and his words validated Jerome's earlier thought. "There's at least one in every prison," he said with a half-grin. "He's harmless. Whatever he said he didn't mean it, Lieutenant. I'll take him back to his cell."

"Yeah, I didn't mean it," the man moaned. Then bringing his eyes up for the first time in a while, he set his lips in a pout and then mumbled, "The devil . . . he the one made me do it."

As the guard pulled the man away, Jerome heard the crack of his own neck as he snapped his face toward Stuart. "Did you hear that? Huh, Stu? Did you hear what that man just said?"

Stuart didn't answer with his lips, but the expression of his eyes was deafening.

Chapter Seven

Ingrid Battles chewed a lukewarm french fry much longer than necessary as she sat sharing a table with two women she genuinely liked, and one that she simply tolerated. If the feeling wasn't mutual, Ingrid might have a reason to feel bad. But it was, and that was no secret to anybody. For the first thirty minutes, while they ate appetizers, drank beverages and waited for their main courses, Kenyatta had basically talked in code about her situation. Ingrid struggled not to laugh at the thought that the woman she'd long ago coined a pretentious drama queen considered her too naïve to decipher what was really going on.

Finally, getting fed up with the charade, Jade said, "Kenyatta, we are all women over thirty, and we've all had issues with a man in our lives at one time or another. The only way the three of us are going to be able to give you some constructive feedback is for you to tell us what's going on."

"I really wasn't looking for feedback from all *three* of you." Kenyatta's words were calculated, and accompanied by a twist of her mouth and a slight roll of her neck.

Ingrid bit the inside of her bottom lip, forcing herself not to speak. *Jesus, Jesus, Jesus . . .*

Reverend Tides had preached a recent sermon, saying that the more a person called on the name of Jesus in the time of trouble, the less likely they'd be to sin. Ingrid felt a sin coming on that would likely get her thrown out of the doors of Ruby Tuesday and straight into the fiery pits of hell.

Jesus, Jesus, Jesus . . .

"Well, there are *three* of us here, and neither I nor Ingrid are going anywhere before we eat our food, so you might as well come on with it." Jan spouted the response with just as much attitude as Kenyatta had given hers.

Ingrid appreciated Jan's attempt to act as though she thought Kenyatta's snide comment could have been directed at either of them, but she wasn't fooled in the least bit. Rotating the name of Jesus in her head was taking effect, though. Ingrid could feel her rising blood begin to recede. Not only that, but Jan's comeback must have been enough to make Kenyatta feel outnumbered, because by the time their meals arrived, she'd opened up. It was like pouring Heinz Ketchup from a newly unsealed bottle, but her words eventually began to flow.

And for the past hour, for the first time since meeting Kenyatta three months ago, Ingrid felt sorry for her.

"Do you really think that Joe is capable of harming Stuart or Tyler?" Jade asked in a hushed tone as she leaned across the table.

"If you had asked me that a week ago, I would have said no," Kenyatta answered. "I mean, Joe's no saint by any definition, and he's done and said some crazy stuff in the past, but I've never defined him as a wacko, and that's exactly what he is if he's doing all this."

The age-old adage, *It takes one to know one,* dashed through Ingrid's mind while she sipped from her half-full glass of lemonade. Indeed, Joe sounded like a man on the brink of insanity, but as far as Ingrid was concerned, he and Kenyatta were two peas in a pod. She'd wager her last dollar that the Dooney & Bourke handbag nestled between Kenyatta and the divider that separated their booth from the next one housed a loaded revolver. With Kenyatta, twenty-four hours a day, there could be a murder waiting to happen; and if that wasn't a good definition of a wacko, Ingrid didn't know what was.

"When was the last time you spoke to your husband, Kenyatta?" Jan asked.

"*Ex*-husband," Kenyatta corrected. "I haven't spoken to that man since the day I left. There has been absolutely no communication between the two of us."

"He didn't try to call you on your cell or anything? I mean, I'm sure you eventually changed the number, but didn't he make an attempt to call prior to you changing it?"

"Jan, I didn't just change my cell number, I changed my cell phone and my cell carrier," Kenyatta stressed. "And I had probably done that before he realized that I was really gone. I'd left that man so many times that it wasn't even funny; but I'd never be gone for more than forty-eight hours before coming back. It was all a game to Joe. He knew I'd eventually come home. Shoot, he probably even knew which hotel I'd retreat to. I was trying to make him realize how difficult his life would be without me, but he couldn't have cared less. Every time I'd come back home, he'd have this smug I-knew-you'd-come-back look on his face. Not once in all of the temporary break-ups that we had did he ever call me. Not once."

"But it's been a year, Kenyatta," Jade pointed out. "You think he thought you were at the hotel all this time? I don't think so. He would have had to have known before now that you weren't coming home. That's the part that doesn't make sense. Why wait until now to start reacting to your leaving?"

"Exactly," Jan said. "The divorce has been final for how many months now? He signed the papers. He knows you're gone for real."

Kenyatta shrugged and then cast a brief look at Ingrid, like she wasn't sure if what she had to say next should be said in front of "the help."

Child, please! Those were the callous words that ran through Ingrid's mind and she hoped that they would somehow convey loud and clear through her own eyes that rolled toward the ceiling. Ingrid didn't know if Kenyatta got her message or not, but after a short silence, she continued speaking.

"When I went to the police station yesterday for questioning, the police said that they believe Joe's been looking for me for a while and only recently figured out that I've been living with my brother. Stu apparently started getting the letters a number of weeks ago, but he didn't take them seriously. It wasn't until his car got damaged that he stopped seeing it as a laughing matter. He said that one of the guys at the station says we've been singled out by . . ." Kenyatta paused, took a quick glance around their surroundings, and then whispered, "Shelton Heights."

"Oh, please, not that again," Jade said. And in apparent agreement, Jan flung her hands up in the air and fell dramatically back against the seat, wretched.

"Why y'all acting like that? Both of you got caught up in the effects of the curse," Kenyatta accused. "What makes you think the same couldn't be happening to me?"

Ingrid had heard about the whole Shelton Heights myth back when Jade and her family were grieving over what they thought was the death of Reverend Tides. But since she moved to Atlanta, she'd not heard much more about it.

When the table quieted, Ingrid wanted to press Kenyatta to keep talking, but if she wanted to hear more about Shelton Heights, Ingrid knew she'd have to get it from one of the others. Deciding on her best friend, she turned to her left and looked at Jade. "I thought all that was laid to rest after Reverend Tides was found alive."

"No, it wasn't." Kenyatta's voice was almost accusing. "Plenty of strange stuff has happened since Reverend Tides."

Jan laughed. "The legend surrounding that old man will never be permanently pushed aside. When Pete was captured as a POW in Iraq, who do you think was blamed for it?"

"Shelton Heights?" Ingrid was glad to finally be an active part of the conversation.

"Exactly. They even had me believing it." Jan grimaced as she continued. "And the main one who was trying to tear my marriage apart was also the main one drilling the legend in my head."

Jade nodded. "Yeah, your cousin Rachel was a hot mess."

"Don't even call that skank's name in my presence," Jan said, the lines in her forehead deepening. "Just the sound of it makes me want to hurl."

"Well, tell us how you *really* feel," Ingrid said with a laugh that ran around the table, but fizzled when it reached Kenyatta.

"I thought this was about *my* problem," Kenyatta said, pointing to herself, showing off perfectly salon-manicured nails. "See, I knew that having *three* other people here would throw things off track. Can we try to focus, please?"

Jesus, Jesus, Jesus, Jesus, Jesus. Ingrid drank from her straw again.

"Look, Kenyatta," Jade said. "The point we're trying to make is that there is no Shelton Heights curse. The one lesson that we all should have learned from my dad's sudden disappearance and Pete and Jan's unexplained break-up is that there is always a valid reason behind the oddities that happen in Shelton Heights."

"And the explanation for Stuart's situation is probably rooted in your ex-husband," Jan added. "From what you've told us, it seems pretty obvious. I mean, look at the facts. You left Joe and he's not pleased about it. He thought he had you trained and under the control of his rule. You broke away and found refuge with Stuart. Now he's after the one who you ran to so that he can get to you. He probably figures that if he can scare you enough or cause enough trouble for your family, you'll go back to him, in spite of the divorce."

"That's good reasoning, Jan," Jade said in an approving tone.

"Well, I do what I can," was Jan's reply.

"Are the police going to make an arrest?" Jade asked.

As Kenyatta chewed on a strip of fried chicken, it was difficult to decipher if the mumble she replied was a yes or a no.

After swallowing down several gulps of water, she added, "Last I heard, the police were going to find out if Joe was at work on the day that the damage was done to Stu's car. If he wasn't, that's all the evidence they'll need in order to obtain a warrant for his arrest and bring him in for questioning."

The table quieted once more, and Ingrid was sure that she saw tears accumulating in Kenyatta's eyes. Jade must have seen them too.

"Are you prepared for the what ifs?" Jade asked, once again leaning in closer. "If Joe is picked up for questioning and then charged with committing these acts, are you prepared to have to face him again?"

"Face him again?" Kenyatta's eyes shot up to meet Jade's. "Why would I have to face him? He hasn't done anything to me. Stu is the one who will have to face him, not me."

Ingrid sucked more of her beverage to swallow down words that her mouth wanted to express. Was Kenyatta born this stupid, or did a private tutor get hired somewhere along the way? The words resonated in Ingrid's head so loudly that they caused a ringing in her ears.

"Kenyatta, if this goes to court, you do know that you'll have to testify for the prosecution, don't you?" Jade's voice was so much more comforting than the one screaming in Ingrid's head.

"Sweetheart, you would be a key witness," Jade continued. "Nobody knows better than you the details of Joe's erratic and controlling behavior. They would need your testimony of his abusive tendencies to prove that he's capable of this kind of thing."

When Ingrid saw Kenyatta dab at the corners of her eyes, smudging her once-perfect eyeliner, her heart softened. Ingrid had dated her share of losers, but she couldn't imagine ever dating an abusive man, let alone marrying one. And the thought that he could also be so imbalanced that he'd be terrorizing her family was just too much to consider.

"I just don't understand it," Kenyatta said in a voice barely above a whisper. "He couldn't love me, or else he would have treated me right when he had me."

"Some people don't know what love is, Kenyatta," Jade said, reaching across the table and touching her hand. "For some of them, it's more about the head than the heart. They confuse love with possessiveness and control, and when they feel like that misplaced power is being taken to them, love has been stripped too. And they react accordingly."

"Do you think he could be jealous?" Kenyatta asked. "I mean, could it be that he had to see me happy elsewhere for it to really kick in with him that I no longer love him?"

"That's very possible," Jade said, nodding her head in the process. "Hunter and I were talking about this not long ago. Although Stuart is your biological brother and not another man in the sense that most of us think of it, Joe may very well see him as such. To him, Stuart is the man who is keeping the two of you apart; therefore, Stuart is the man who robbed him of the one he loves—however twisted that love may be. In essence, Stuart is the man who stripped control away from him. So, what does he do? He goes after Stuart."

Kenyatta scowled. "Who's talking about Stuart? I'm saying, do you think Joe has heard about me and Jerome and has decided that he doesn't want another man to have me."

Although she, too, thought Kenyatta's words were ludicrous, Ingrid couldn't believe it when she heard Jade break into a laugh that boomed around the restaurant. She thought that as a professional, the trained psychologist would have a better capacity to maintain control—even in the most ridiculous of situations.

A pain shot through Ingrid's side as she looked to the left and noted that the laughter wasn't coming from Jade. Diverting her watery eyes to the seat across from her, she perceived that it wasn't coming from Jan either. Only then did Ingrid come to the full realization that the pain in her side was a direct result of her own outburst of emotions.

"Ingrid!" Jan scolded, kicking her beneath the table.

In response, as she fought to catch her breath, Ingrid managed a feeble, "Sorry," and then she wiped the water from her eyes and picked up her glass to drown the residual laughter that bounced in her belly.

"Not half as sorry as you 'bout to be," Kenyatta huffed, grabbing her purse.

"Don't you dare!" Jade warned in a raised voice, drawing attention to their corner booth.

Ingrid's heart pounded in her chest, but she shooed away the fear that threatened to show

on her face. She stared across the table at Kenyatta, who looked like she would wish death
on Ingrid if she had a genie in a bottle with
only one unfulfilled wish left.

"She didn't mean it, Kenyatta, it's okay," Jade
said, her voice now gentle, resembling that
of a negotiator trying to persuade a would-be
jumper from the edge of a bridge.

As Ingrid saw her best friend using her trained
abilities to calm Kenyatta, her fear turned to anger. *Why is everybody always trying to cater
to this nut's psychosis?* she wondered.

Ingrid had moved to Atlanta after years of
living in Virginia, but had spent most of her
formative years in Illinois. Working as an executive secretary in the city of Virginia Beach,
she had been schooled on poise and profes-
sionalism, but in the streets of Chicago's south
side, she'd learned how to fight. Ingrid knew
that the lessons of Virginia Beach were best,
but when it came to the battle that was churn-
ing on the inside of her, Chicago was threatening to win.

Jesus, Jesus, Jesus, Jesus . . .

"Let me out, Jan. I'm leaving," Kenyatta said
suddenly, pulling her hand away from Jade's
grasp. "I don't have time for this mess."

"You don't have to leave," Jan coaxed. "It's over now, Kenyatta."

Jade must have read Ingrid's thoughts and realized that Kenyatta's leaving was for the best. "Let her out, Jan," she said, still sounding like the psychologist she was. "I'll get with you later to finish this if you want to talk more, Kenyatta. You have my number."

"Long as you come *alone*." Kenyatta glared at Ingrid and tossed a ten-dollar bill on the table.

The three remaining women watched Kenyatta's wide hips sway as she headed for the door, pushing it open with far more force than necessary.

When it closed behind her, Ingrid breathed a sigh of relief and smiled to herself. Reverend Tides was right. The name of Jesus was powerful indeed; and the mere fact that she'd gotten through the ordeal with not even as much as a desire to string together a garland of curse words and use them as a noose to wrap around Kenyatta's neck was all the confirmation Ingrid needed to be certain that God had really given her a spiritual makeover.

"Well, I guess that's that," Jade said, reaching into Kenyatta's abandoned plate and transferring her untouched chicken strips to her own.

Jan looked at Ingrid and shook her head. "I can't believe you did that."

Ingrid sipped more lemonade, and when her throat was amply irrigated, she offered the only defense she could think of. "I said sorry."

Chapter Eight

"Daddy, the light's green." Wincing, Stuart eased his foot on the gas pedal and replied, "Yeah. I . . . I know it's green, son. You should always wait a couple of seconds before proceeding because you never know if the person coming from the other direction is gonna try to beat their light. If they do, and you start driving as soon as the light turns green for you, then that could result in an accident. You with me?"

"Yes, sir." Tyler played along, but he knew his father had just been too preoccupied with thoughts of meeting his new computer friend to notice the traffic light change.

"You remember what I told you, Tyler," Stuart said. "You mind your manners when we meet Ms. Candice, okay?"

"Yes, sir." Tyler didn't understand what all the fuss was about. His father was acting as though this woman was going to be the first one he'd ever gone out with. He had watched Stuart leave the house on several occasions to pick up a date for the evening, but Tyler had never seen him this nervous. "Daddy?"

"Yeah, son?"

"How long is Ms. Candice gonna be in town?"

"Just until Sunday morning."

"So, is she coming to church with us?"

"She can't. She has to be on a flight that leaves early Sunday morning."

Tyler made an attempt to quickly calculate the short visit. He was never that great in math. "So, she's just flying in tonight, and she's gonna have to turn around and leave right back out in twenty-four hours?"

"She'll be here a little longer than twenty-four hours, but yeah, it'll be a short visit."

Tyler could hear regret in his father's voice.

"She has to get back to New York to prepare for work," Stuart explained, "so, right now, you and I are going to pick her up from the airport and take her to get something to eat, if she's up to it. Then, we'll take her to her hotel. Tomorrow, I'll pick her up from the hotel, and she and I will spend some time together. You'll be at home with Kenyatta while Candice and I hang out. You good with that?"

To be perfectly honest, he wasn't. There were few people on earth that Tyler loved more than his Aunt Kenyatta, but he certainly didn't want to spend the day with her. Especially not a Saturday. As a social worker, Kenyatta worked on Saturdays only on those rare times when she was on call. Many a Saturday, Tyler had known his aunt to spend several hours shopping, only to come home with one bag to show for her excursion.

Once, about six months ago, he'd been forced to accompany her when she went to the beauty salon to have her hair styled. And while she sat in rollers under a dryer, a woman who spoke broken English sat beside Kenyatta and gave her a manicure and pedicure. That was the day that Tyler thanked God that he was born male. And after six hours of sitting in the salon, he made up his mind then and there, that the only way he'd ever get a girlfriend or a wife was if her hair, hands and feet were naturally pretty. Mrs. Tyler Lyons would have no need for a salon of any kind.

It was on weekends like this one that he wished his mom wasn't off somewhere filling a job assignment. Tasha liked to shop too, but when he was with her, she mostly just shopped for him, going to toy stores and electronic outlets where he could buy the latest video game. When he spent time with her a couple of months ago, she took him to Sports Authority and got him a licensed Dwayne Wade basketball jersey. Those were the type of shopping sprees that Tyler didn't mind.

"Can I go ride the horses in Greene Pastures instead of staying home tomorrow?" Tyler just had to find a way to avoid his babysitting aunt.

"I don't know about that, man," Stuart said. "Rain is in the forecast, and you know Hunter doesn't let you guys ride the horses when it rains."

"Well, can I just go and hang out with Malik at their house? We don't have to ride the horses."

"I'll have to check and see what Hunter has scheduled for his family," his father replied. "You can't just assume that it will be okay for you to spend the day at their house." Stuart turned and looked at him briefly before focusing back on the road ahead. "Why are you trying to avoid Kenyatta?"

"I'm not," Tyler insisted. *Avoid* sounded like too strong of a word. "It's just that I don't want to follow her around from store to store while she shops and stuff. That's boring, Daddy, and she don't *never* get tired. I'd rather do just about anything else than that."

"You got some money?"

Tyler stole a glance toward his father and hesitated. He didn't particularly like the introduction to whatever Stuart was going to say. Tyler was tempted to lie, but his father gave him an allowance every week, and he knew Stuart's question was really just a rhetorical one. "Yes, sir."

"Okay, then how about you offer to take your friends out to the movies tomorrow? I know there's something playing that you want to see; there always is. You could treat Malik, Kyla, K.P., and maybe even the Lowman boys to a matinee."

"*All* of them?" Tyler frowned and shook his head. "That's a lot of money, Daddy. Why can't they pay their own way?"

"Because the person whose idea it is should pay," Stuart reasoned.

"Okay. Then why can't *you* pay? It was your idea, not mine."

The thought that invaded Tyler's mind had rolled off his tongue before he could stop it. For a moment, the boy thought the silence that blanketed his father's Land Rover was the prelude to a painful swat—a just reward for his snide remark.

"How about this," Stuart said. "How about I drop the question mark from behind my original questions and turn them into statements."

Tyler swallowed hard at the stern and unyielding tone of his father's voice. He knew his best bet was to sit still and listen; and that was just what he did.

"You are going to offer to take your friends to the movies tomorrow. So, check your bank, Mr. Stingy. You'll make the offer to all five of them, and don't let me find out that you left anybody out or made them feel like you didn't really want to do it. You with me? You'll *insist* on treating all five of them to a movie, and when I turn to look at you, if I so much as see any outward sign that you don't want to do this, you'll also treat them to lunch."

Tyler could feel the heat of his dad's eyes as Stuart glanced at him not once, but three times. Tyler didn't flinch. Given a choice, he would have taken the swat, but his father was no dummy. Stuart knew that hitting Tyler in his pockets would be far more painful that hitting him across the arm or leg.

Tyler stared straight ahead, trying not to even blink for fear that Stuart would read it as a reaction that meant he didn't want to follow through with the order given.

The movie would set Tyler back enough. He didn't need six lunches added to the tab, especially with friends who had the appetites that his possessed. The punishment hurt, but looking on the bright side, Tyler decided that he'd rather spend those hours with his friends than following his aunt all over town while she got girlied up for the week—even if the deal would cost him a healthy sum.

Other than the music that streamed from the jazz CD that had been playing during their route to Hartsfield-Jackson International Airport, the last few miles of the trip were quiet. Friday's rush-hour traffic made the voyage take longer than usual, and Tyler saw Stuart glance at his watch more than a few times.

"What time does her plane land?" Tyler asked as they pulled onto the airport's property. Stuart had told him once before, but he thought that talking would lessen the anxiety that was mounting on his father's face. Before Stuart could answer the question, the cell phone that hung on his left hip rang. That was Stuart's personal phone.

Looking at the caller ID, he paused. "Private?" Stuart said it like he wasn't even sure he wanted to take the call. When he finally answered, he greeted the caller with a simple, "Stuart Lyons."

Tyler watched his father's expression. When Stuart broke into a smile, he knew right away that the woman from the computer was on the other end.

"Hey, Ms. Lady." His tone changed entirely, as if rain from heaven had fallen on the earlier dry greeting. "Have you gotten off the plane yet?" There was a momentary pause and then he said, "Already? Wow, that was quick. Well, I'm glad you landed safely, but I wish you had stayed inside until I got there. I didn't want you waiting outside."

After another lapse of time, during which all Tyler could hear was indecipherable chatter on the other end of the line, his dad said, "Okay, well, I'm turning in now, and since you're already outside, I'm heading toward the pick-up area outside of the Delta baggage claim exit doors instead of going in the parking garage. You did fly Delta, right?"

Stuart listened and nodded like Candice could see his reaction.

"Okay, I'm within view," Stuart said into the phone. "There are a lot of folks standing out this evening. How will I know which is you?"

Tyler stared out the side window and scanned the faces of many of the people who waited for transportation. Among the women, he wondered which was Candice. His eyes connected with a woman, standing near one of the courtesy benches, wearing denim jeans and a red top. She caught his attention because she was holding a cell phone to her ear and watching the passing cars intently. "I think that's her, Daddy," he said, pointing.

Stuart shook his head. "I don't think so, Tyler." Then into the phone he said, "Candice, wave or something. I'm in a white Land Rover. Do you see me?"

The woman on the cell phone turned, scanned the line of vehicles, and then waved, validating Tyler's presumption. "See?" he said with knowing pride. "I told you that was her."

Stuart ended the call and navigated his truck to the curb.

Tyler noted the confused look stamped on his dad's face just before Stuart opened his door to get out.

"Get in the back, Tyler. Let Ms. Candice have the front seat."

"Okay, Daddy." Tyler was glad to do it. Getting out gave him the opportunity to have an excuse to overhear whatever his nervous father would say to this woman once he walked around to assist her with her garment and overnight bags. Tyler took his time getting out, all the while, watching Stuart.

"Candice?" Stuart said her name like he wasn't sure.

"Hi, Stuart." Candice seemed nervous too, but her smile was pretty. "Good to finally meet you."

"Same here." Stuart ignored Candice's outstretched hand and bent to hug her. While there, he placed a quick kiss on her cheek. Then he took one bag from her shoulder and the other from her hand and then turned to Tyler. "This is my son, Tyler. Tyler, come over and say hello to Ms. Candice."

Suddenly feeling a bit shy and flushed, Tyler grinned, pushed his glasses up on his nose, and took the steps that closed the distance between them. "Hi, Ms. Candice."

"Hi, Tyler." If her smile came with a price tag, it would break the bank.

Tyler was counting on a hug like his father had gotten, but the pretty lady offered her his hand, and he just wasn't bold enough to initiate an embrace as his dad had done. The blowing of a horn caught all of their attention.

"I guess we'd better move and let some of these other cars get in here to pick up folks," Stuart said, motioning for Tyler to get in the vehicle and then holding open the front passenger door for Candice.

When Tyler climbed in, he slid to the far end of the seat so that he sat behind his father with a good view of Candice's profile. Seeing her, he better understood his dad's nervous tension on the ride over.

Stuart had told him that his "computer friend" was attractive, but he had downplayed her beauty by far. Tyler thought she was one of the prettiest women he'd seen in quite some time. She didn't fit the description of a model or anything. After all, all the models that appeared on television were much taller and thinner. Candice was relatively short. Tyler guessed that she was just a little taller than his five-two stature. But then again, her shoes had heels, so without them, they may have stood eye to eye. Height aside, her face was pretty enough to be placed on any magazine cover.

"How was your flight?" Stuart steered onto the interstate.

"Huh? Oh, it was good." She seemed preoccupied with her own thoughts.

"Did it feel long? Are you tired?"

Candice looked at Stuart and smiled. "No, it didn't feel long at all. Seems like I was here in no time, actually."

"That's good," he replied.

Tyler couldn't see his father's face, but he could tell that Stuart was smiling.

"Are you hungry? Would you like to get something to eat?" Stuart offered, his tone hopeful.

"No . . . no, thanks," Candice replied. "I ate a full meal before leaving home."

Tyler was hoping she'd said yes, too. He could sure use a burger.

Stuart laughed. "How many hours ago was that? You can't still be full from what you ate before leaving home."

"Well, airlines still serve refreshments, too," Candice said. "Plus, I had snacks in my bag, so I'm good."

"You sure?"

Stuart gave her a chance to change her mind, and Tyler had the feeling that his dad was praying that she did.

"I'm sure," Candice said, dashing both their hopes. "Thanks, though. I think I just need to get some rest. I left school early today and didn't get any rest between then and getting here."

"Okay." Stuart sounded like he understood. "What hotel did you book?"

"Wingate Inn."

"Wingate Inn? I didn't realize Stone Mountain had a Win-gate Inn."

"It's in Atlanta," she said, pulling out a sheet of paper in the process. "Thirty-six hundred Piedmont Road."

"In Buckhead? You booked a room in Buckhead?"

Candice looked at Stuart. "Is Buckhead a bad area?"

"No, not at all," Stuart said. "Buckhead is nice. It's just so far away, that's all."

"Is it an inconvenience for you?"

She looked at Stuart with concern, and Tyler braced his back against the seat, hoping his dad gave the answer she was searching for.

"No, it's not inconvenient." Stuart was smiling again.

"Rush-hour traffic might make it about a forty-minute drive from here, but that'll give us a little time to talk."

Tyler was still staring at Candice's profile when she turned and looked at him. The fact that she'd caught him looking made him sit back farther in the seat, hoping the setting sun would hide his embarrassment.

"What grade are you in, Tyler?"

"Thirteenth."

"Thirteenth!" Stuart exclaimed. The truck weaved a bit in the road as he tried to spot Tyler through the rearview mirror.

"I mean, eighth," he quickly corrected. "I'm thirteen years old." If he didn't think he'd die doing it, Tyler would have opened the door and bailed out onto the highway. Candice had to think he was half-retarded, but she didn't act like she did.

"Thirteen, huh?" she said, sporting the pretty smile that was the cause of Tyler's blunder. "I'll bet you're excited to be a teenager."

"Yes, ma'am." It wasn't particularly true. He didn't really feel any differently than he did at twelve, but agreeing with Candice just seemed like the right thing to do.

"What's your favorite subject?"

Tyler cleared his throat, then answered, "English."

"Really?" She smiled again. "I'm a teacher. Did your dad tell you?"

"No, ma'am."

"Oh." Candice turned back around and sat quietly.

Tyler got the feeling that she thought she'd said too much. Stuart must have felt the same.

"It's okay," he said in a lowered voice that he probably thought Tyler couldn't hear. Then raising it to a more audible level, Stuart added, "Ms. Candice teaches high school math. Maybe she can tell you what you have to look forward to next year."

Tyler guessed that his father said that because he'd been having trouble with the subject earlier in the school year.

His math teacher, Mrs. Kirkland, was a stoic-faced woman with half-framed glasses that sat on the end of her nose. And with her rotund upper body that was held up by a set of the skinniest legs he'd ever seen, Mrs. Kirkland's shape reminded Tyler of an overstuffed bullfrog. If she looked like Candice, he'd be an "A" student.

Most of the chatter for the duration of the ride into Buck head flowed between Stuart and Candice. The more they talked, the more they seemed at ease with each other. Tyler tried not to smile about that, but he smiled in spite of himself. Every now and then, one of them would say something to give him permission to participate.

As Stuart guided his truck into an open parking space at Wingate Inn, flashes of lightning began to streak across the sky.

"Looks like rain is on the way," Candice observed. "Not the best weekend to come into town, I guess."

"I beg to differ," Stuart said, flashing a mannish grin before climbing from the vehicle and taking quick steps to walk around and let his new lady friend out. "You stay here, Tyler. I'm going to make sure Ms. Candice gets checked in okay, and I'll be right back. Keep the doors locked."

Tyler settled back in his seat and watched out of the window as his father and Candice walked side by side toward the hotel's entrance.

The front parking lot was well-lit, and Tyler watched their every move. While they stood at the check-in counter of the hotel, his eyes never left them. The glass doors kept their words muted from Tyler's ears, but the body language was earsplitting to his eyes.

Stuart must have said something hilarious, because Candice's pretty smile suddenly broke into a full-sized laugh that ended with a gentle touch to Stuart's arm.

For some unexplainable reason, Tyler laughed too. There was something about this lady that he liked, and apparently, that was something he and his father had in common.

Chapter Nine

Last night, Candice had tossed and turned. Unsettled nerves assailed her stomach like enemies doing battle. It was the first Friday night in weeks that she didn't spend at least an hour on the computer chatting with Sergeant Stuart Lyons. Candice couldn't believe she'd forgotten to bring her laptop along for the ride. But meeting him face to face had been a wonderful substitute for their normal online fellowship. The ride to the hotel had been quicker than she wished, but it was enough time to validate her cyber attraction to the respected lawman.

"You know he's going to have questions," Candice said to the reflection that stared back at her in the mirror over the bathroom basin. "I just hope your answers are good enough."

Candice had seen the interrogation in Stuart's eyes last night when he and his son met her on the curb at the airport. The look of uncertainty that he gave her upon their introduction didn't surprise her. She knew he'd be a bit bewildered, and for good reason. *Totally truthful* didn't exactly describe her online profile, and Candice was fully aware that Tyler's presence was the only reason Stuart hadn't confronted her on the inconsistencies last night. As she looked at her side profile, she hoped that Sergeant Lyons was pleased, in spite of her dishonesty.

Stepping from the bathroom and into the spacious bedroom, Candice felt the coolness of the polished hardwood floors against her bare feet. She sat on the side of the bed and smoothed on a generous portion of scented lotion before slipping her feet into pink peephole sandals that gave the world a teasing glimpse of her perfectly manicured toes. The shoes would only give her five-feet-three-inch body a two-and-a-half-inch boost, but she had a full day ahead and needed to be comfortable.

When her cell phone rang, Candice did a double-take toward the digital clock that sat on the nightstand. Stuart had told her he would call when he was within ten minutes of the hotel. The plan was for him to pick her up at noon, but it was just five minutes past eleven, and Candice hadn't put on her dress or her makeup.

Immediately, her already troubled nerves began dancing to the beat of a song whose tempo
was twice as upbeat. Candice placed her left
hand over her stomach and took in a deep breath
before pulling her phone from her purse. When
she saw the number on the ID screen, she was
relieved.

"Hello?"

"Candice, where you at?" It was her mother.
"I called your house and left a message last
night, and you ain't never called me back. And
I've been calling you since eight o'clock this
morning. I finally decided that I'd try your cell.
Where you at?" she repeated.

Her mother never called her at such an early
hour. Candice's nerves switched gears. "Hey,
Mama. I'm not at home, so I never got your calls
or your messages. I'm . . . I'm out and about
right now, getting ready for a date. What's
the matter?" She didn't see the need to reveal
where she was. It would only raise questions
she wasn't ready to answer.

"A date? Hush yo' mouth!"

The fact that her mother didn't sound frantic
eased Candice's earlier fears that something
awful had happened to prompt her constant
calling; but she wasn't too sure how she felt
about her mother's reaction to her announce-

ment. Minnie Powell sounded as if she thought her daughter's dating was a miracle comparable to that of Moses parting the Red Sea.

"You got a man, Candice?" Minnie said, still sounding doubtful. "Or are you just making this up cause you think I'm gonna start in on you 'bout not having one?"

"I didn't say I had a man, Mama." Candice rolled her eyes to the ceiling and wished her mom could see her doing it. "I said I had a date."

"So, what you sayin'?" Minnie's voice had dropped to a terrified whisper. "It's a woman? You gon' kill your mama, girl. Please don't tell me you goin' the other way now. I know the odds are against you in the big city, but stick with what you know, baby."

"Mama!" Candice couldn't believe her ears and could barely think of what to say next. She exhaled so heavily that a grunting sound escaped her lungs. "Mama, I have a date with a man, okay. It's only our first date, so I can't very well call him *my* man. That's all I'm saying." Candice released another labored breath and decided she wanted nothing more than to change the subject. "What's wrong, Mama?

Why have you been trying to call me? Is everything okay?"

"Umph. Might not be much good in me telling you this now, seeing that you got a date and all."

Candice frowned. "What does my having a date have to do with anything?"

After a slight pause, Minnie continued, and caution set the standard for her pace. "Well . . . things between Darrell Johnson and his wife wasn't as good as I thought it was."

At the introductory sentence, Candice fell backward on the mattress, keeping the phone at her ear. She couldn't believe her mother was still holding on to hope that was not only unattainable, but nearing two decades old.

"Me and your daddy ran into Darrell's mama at the grocery store last night, and she said that gal packed up her stuff and the children and moved out. Said something 'bout her being nothing but a gold digger."

"A gold digger?" Candice laughed out loud and made a visual picture of the man her mother had tried to hook her up with years ago. "Mama, Darrell doesn't have any gold. Not unless he went and put some in his mouth to replace those rotten teeth."

There was no amusement in Minnie's reply. "I done told you 'bout that, girl. Darrell's a good man, and I promise you, that gal gon' be sorry she left him. She thinks the grass is greener on the other side, but she'll be hard pressed to find a man that will treat her as good as a Johnson boy. She so busy looking at what other folks got and wanting it for herself that she can't see that what she had was good."

"Well, I'm sorry for what happened to Darrell's marriage, Mama, I really am. But his breakup doesn't have any bearing on me."

"Pearleen said he asked about you. She said she don't believe he ever got over you. Umph. That sure don't surprise me none."

"Once again, Mama, I'm not interested. Maybe the current Mrs. Darrell Johnson will come to her senses and see all the good in her husband that you see. I hope it works out for them, but I'm not interested."

Candice's dry response brought silence from the other end, and she could tell that her mother was trying to think of what to say next. Meanwhile, Candice looked at the clock and knew that her time was running out. She needed to get started if she were going to be ready when Stuart arrived.

"What this boy look like that you going out with today?"

"He's very handsome, Mama."

"Is he tall and high yella with wavy hair like Darrell?"

Candice took a breath. If her cell phone battery died right now, it would be a blessing straight from God. "No, Mama, as a matter of fact, he's not. He's tall, yes, but he's very dark, and as for hair, he has none."

"You goin' out with some bald-headed black boy?"

Candice had taken all she could for one day. "Yes, I am, Mama. He's very much bald, and very much black. Not only that, but he'll very much be here in just a few minutes, and I still haven't finished getting dressed. I have to go now, okay?"

"All right, but call me later and tell me how it went."

"Okay, Mama," Candice agreed, having no intention of following through.

Placing her cell back into her purse, she raced to the bathroom to start the finishing touches. Keeping with natural tones, she brushed her caramel skin with powder and then brushed on bronze eye shadow before lining her eyes, using a dark brown pencil.

Once her lips were glossed with raisin-colored lipstick, Candice combed her shoulder-length hair that had been flat-ironed earlier, and added a swooping bang that tucked behind her left ear. With that done, she scampered back to the room to put on her outfit.

The statement Candice was trying to make was one of simple elegance. She wanted her outfit to say, *I'm casual, but I'm still sexy.* Two days ago, she had gone shopping specifically for today's rendezvous with Stuart. She had purchased two outfits; one for the first half of the date, and another to slip into before dinner. They would be spending several hours together, plenty of time to get to know all that either of them would need to know in order to make an informed decision of whether or not they could, or would even want to, take their relationship to the next level.

The day's agenda was set. They would share lunch, eating at On The Border Restaurant, which, in comfortable shoes, was within walking distance from the hotel where Candice was staying.

Mexican was her favorite cuisine, and she knew that Stuart had that in mind when he planned the day. After lunch, the two of them would spend some time at nearby Lenox Square.

Stuart said they weren't going necessarily for the purpose of shopping, but he thought it would be a good place to walk off the food they'd eaten while taking in the sites of one of Atlanta's premiere shopping centers.

Candice was looking forward to it. Shopping might not be the order of the day, but there was no way she would walk through the mall and not purchase something.

AMC Buckhead was the nearest cinema, and it was there they would go and take in a movie of choice. Candice had never been a real theatre buff, probably because she didn't date much. Her choice was always to wait until the movie was released on DVD, and then watch it in the comfort of her own home. She wasn't even up to date on the latest blockbuster films being released. The choice of films would be left to Stuart's discretion.

After the movie, Stuart promised to take her on an extended tour of the city. They'd canvass the Buckhead District and then the downtown area before heading to Stone Mountain. She had heard a lot about Greene Pastures, where Stuart said he'd take her to see the champion horses that his friend bred.

Perhaps the event of the day she was most looking forward to was dinner. During their

online chats, Stuart had raved about The Pecan, a black-owned fine-dining restaurant in
College Park, Georgia. He said that he had
made their reservation the next morning after she'd accepted his invitation to visit him.
That's how popular the eatery was. If reservations weren't made in advance, the chances of
getting a seat in the establishment were slim
to none.

Candice had barely had the chance to slip
on the silk-blend cream-white slacks complemented by a soft pink mock two-piece blouse
before the phone on the nightstand rang.
There must have been something that the
front desk personnel needed to tell her. Was
Stuart already waiting downstairs?

"Hello?"

"Good morning."

Stuart's voice took her by surprise. The sound
of his suave tone sent a chill up her spine.

"Are you almost ready?"

Candice calmed herself. "Good morning.
Yes, I'm almost ready. Are you downstairs?"
The clock said that it was eleven fifty-four. If
Stuart was downstairs already, he was six min-
utes early.

"Not quite. I told you I'd call ahead, remember? I'm not far away, though. I'll be there in less than ten minutes."

"Okay." The fluttering in Candice's stomach had returned. "When you called me on the hotel phone instead of my cell, I was thrown off."

Stuart chuckled. "Well, I would have called you on your cell, but you've never given me the number."

For a split second, Candice's voice was lodged in her throat. She'd forgotten that she had deliberately not given Stuart her personal contact information. Now, she'd stupidly opened the door for him to expect to receive it; but Candice still wasn't ready to allow him that privilege. She couldn't do it just yet.

With her mind racing at the same pace of her heart, she blurted, "Okay, well, I just have to grab my change of clothing, and I'll meet you in the lobby."

"Uh, um . . . okay." Stuart didn't sound like his usual confident self.

Candice closed her eyes, knowing he was baffled by her blatant avoidance of his insinuation. "See you in a few," she said, hopeful that she sounded far more carefree than she felt.

With no time to punish herself for the last moments of the conversation, Candice opened the closet door and retrieved the outfit she'd wear later. The knee-length, spaghetti-strap cocktail dress was the perfect shade of royal blue, the color that Stuart had revealed as his favorite. She had shopped for three hours and gone to at least ten stores before she found a dress worthy of this evening's dinner date. Candice placed the dress back into the garment bag she'd removed it from last night and zipped the closure. She'd need to bring it along with her, since she and Stuart had made plans to change clothing at the home of Hunter and Jade Greene. From her overnight bag, Candice pulled out a pair of silver dress sandals. The four-inch heels would lengthen her legs a bit more tonight.

Within minutes, she had given herself one last look-over and was headed to the elevator on her floor. When Candice stepped out and took the short walk to the hotel lobby, she saw Stuart headed toward the entrance. His timing was perfect; and so was he, dressed in white linen slacks and a blue short-sleeved shirt made of the same material. The shirt showed off the toned muscles in his arms, and the combined gentle colors were a ravishing contrast against his skin.

"Hey, beautiful," he said, apparently just as impressed with Candice as she was with him.

"Thank you." Candice accepted his second kiss to her cheek in as many days. "You look quite good yourself."

"I knew how enchanting you would be, so I did my best to measure up." He winked, took the garment bag from her arm and then added, "Ready?"

"Yes, I'm ready."

Chapter Ten

Stuart stole another look at Candice as he steered his truck into the near-full parking lot of On The Border Restaurant. She looked beautiful and nervous as she fidgeted with the strap of her purse that lay across her lap. Something about her uneasiness appealed to him. Perhaps it was because he was nervous too, and knowing he wasn't alone served as a source of comfort.

"Are you going to be able to find anything on the menu here that you want to eat?" Candice asked, grabbing back Stuart's attention as she stepped from the vehicle with his assistance.

Stuart nodded. "Why would you think otherwise? Because if memory serves me correctly, you said that you liked seafood, soul food and Chinese, in that order."

Impressed with the fact that she'd taken such detailed notes during that one-time conversation, Stuart grinned. "I like Mexican, too. It's not in the top three on my list, but I like it."

The adornment of On The Border was festive and very true to the culture of its cuisine. The walls displayed sombreros, colorful maracas, and even a few photos of bull fighters and scenes of Mexican sunrises. Stuart noted that Candice barely even looked at the decoration, and what she did notice didn't seem to impress her in the least. He supposed that this didn't compare to the Mexican restaurants in New York City.

"How many?" the hostess asked when she approached.

It was a redundant question that always irked Stuart just a bit. Every time a greeter asked it, he was always tempted to respond with, "How many of us do you see?" No doubt, the question was one they were trained to ask, in case more party members were on the way; but that didn't diminish his annoyance.

"Two," Stuart answered. "And if we can have a booth, we'd appreciate it."

"Sure, sir. Follow me."

While they trailed the courteous woman, Stuart found himself repressing a laugh. Her wide rear end immediately made him think of the woman that Hunter had talked about as they prepared to play basketball in his backyard several days ago.

"Will this be good?" She stopped at a booth situated in the restaurant's corner.

"This is perfect. Thank you." Stuart gave Candice a chance to sit before he slid on the seat across from her. "So, what do you think of our fair city so far?" he asked, jumping right in.

Candice diverted her eyes, choosing not to look at him directly. "What's there not to like?"

"Nothing like southern hospitality, right?"

"You act like I've never been to the South," she replied, looking at him briefly before focusing her eyes on the menu.

Stuart was intrigued. "Have you?"

"Sure I have. I was born in the South, Stuart. I never told you that?"

That explains the reason she lacks a northern accent. "What part of the South?"

"South Carolina."

Taking the menu from her hands so he could get her undivided attention, Stuart said, "No, you never told me that. But let's focus on the things you *did* tell me instead."

Candice tucked stray hairs that had fallen from her bangs back behind her ears before she responded. "What do you mean?"

"I mean, I took your online profile to be fact, and it really wasn't. What's up with that?" When she looked at him, Stuart knew right away that, although his question seemed to make her uncomfortable, it wasn't one she hadn't expected.

"What do you mean?" she repeated.

"Is your real name Candice Powell?"

She looked at him in disbelief. "Of course it is."

"Can I call you Candy?"

"No." Her reply left no room for doubt. She softened her sharp answer by calmly adding, "I'd rather you didn't."

A moment of silence passed before Stuart asked, "Are you really a school teacher?"

"Yes, I am, Stuart, and you can stop the needless interrogation now. I know what you're getting at."

"I figured you did." Stuart looked directly at her, although Candice chose to keep her gaze on the woodwork of the table.

"You're referring to the way I described myself in my profile."

Stuart sat back in his seat and nodded. "I know my eyes aren't as young as they used to be, but you're a far cry from short and overweight."

"To be fair, I *am* relatively short, and I never said I was overweight either," Candice defended.

Stuart wasn't about to let her off that easily. "I believe the exact words you used were 'vertically challenged' and 'more to love,' so while you didn't say it directly, I think your page alluded to it, don't you?"

Their waiter approached at that moment, and Stuart imagined that Candice was relieved that he brought with him two glasses of cold water. She immediately began to sip from hers, probably to wet the dehydrated throat that the heat of his questions had created.

"Are you ready to order?" the server asked, placing a tray of complimentary chips and salsa on the table between them.

"Give us a few minutes," Stuart said.

When the waiter walked away, Stuart placed Candice's menu back on the table in front of her and rethought his decision to pounce on her with such aggressiveness. She may not have been completely upfront with him, but the last thing he wanted was to run her away. It would be nice to know why she'd misrepresented herself, but knowing the answers wasn't worth the risk. Deciding to leave it alone, Stuart opened his menu and scanned his choices.

"Are you disappointed?" Candice's question brought his eyes back to her. She was looking at him now too.

"Excuse me?"

"Do you feel let down because the physical person you imagined me to be isn't the person I am?"

Stuart closed his menu and reached across the table for Candice's hand. She vacillated, but gently placed hers in his and stared at their connection as his fingers locked her hand in place. He said nothing until her eyes came back to meet his again.

"No man in his right mind would be disappointed with the physical you, Candice. You're absolutely beautiful, and you're a smart, classy, Christian woman. But that's what makes this so confusing. If you have all of this to offer, why would you try and make believe you're something that you're not?"

Stuart watched the slow rise and fall of Candice's chest. Then she said, "It wasn't always that way. A co-worker of mine got me turned on to the whole idea of finding a mate online. At first, I was dead set against the notion of it, but then I thought I'd give it a try. This one is the third site that I've been a member of. The first two were Christian sites as well, but I don't know what to make of the so-called Christian men that I'd get messages from. I know men are physical creatures, but I just kind of expected a little bit more tact and respect from those who call themselves men of God."

Still not quite understanding, Stuart dug for more. "So, you wanted to make yourself what you considered to be less appealing so that men would back off?"

Candice shrugged, almost as if she didn't quite understand why she'd done what she'd done. "I think I wanted to be sure that the next man who showed interest in me wasn't quite so shallow. I wanted his attraction to me to be deeper than the physical."

"And so it is," Stuart said.

"Is it?" Candice challenged.

"What do you mean?"

"I mean, is your attraction to me deeper than the physical, or is your preference short and full-figured? You just sat here and called me to the carpet on misrepresenting myself, and although you said you weren't disappointed, you were apparently disillusioned enough to bring it up. Maybe you connected with me because the physical persona that I fudged to weed out the shallow just happened to be the physical traits that you look for in a woman."

Stuart was falling in love at warp speed. Candice was everything that appealed to him. Even her challenges were fascinating. Without realizing it, he tightened his hold on her hand. "There seems to be a lot that neither of us knows about one another." His speech was interrupted by another visit from their server.

"Are you ready to order now, or would you like some more time?"

"Oh," Stuart said, releasing Candice's hand and once again grabbing his menu. "I apologize; it's my fault."

"No problem," the young man replied. "If you'd like a few more minutes—"

"You know what? I'll just have a chicken quesadilla with rice," Candice said.

Stuart looked at her and snickered. He could tell she wanted to get rid of the server just as much as he did. "I'll have the same," he said. "And give me extra chicken and extra cheese."

"I'll get those orders placed for you right away." The waiter took their menus and disappeared.

"So, what is this that I don't know about you?" Candice asked, picking up where they'd left off.

"I'm unlike most men in the sense that I can't say that I have a physical preference, where a woman is concerned."

"Really?" Her eyes narrowed, and her head cocked as though she didn't believe him.

"Really," Stuart reiterated. "Don't get me wrong, a woman would need to have an attractive face to get my attention, but as far as height, weight, and skin complexion . . . I don't have a preference, really. I mean, I wouldn't want to date a midget, but you're proof that short is cute. And while I'm definitely not into Amazon women, as long as I don't have to look up at her, a tall woman is fine too." Stuart sipped from his glass and shrugged. "Granted, I have never dated outside my race, but I've been known to go out with women who were fair-skinned to the point of being freckle-faced, and I've also dated much darker women." He chuckled and added, "They've never been quite as dark as I am, but then again, God didn't give this hue to everybody. This is kingdom-ordered chocolate right here."

His last comment brought an approving smile from Candice. "I like your complexion."

"Thank you." Stuart found it hard to stop

smiling. "I had to grow into an appreciation for the dark man that I am. As a kid, I was teased a lot for being blacker than most Blacks. I had a complex for years. Now, I appreciate the man that God made me. I wouldn't trade my skin for any other skin in the world."

Candice brought her hands together in a soft applause. When she was done, she probed further. "So, have you ever dated an overweight woman?"

Stuart nodded. "Yep, and I've dated thin women."

"You've dated a lot, I see," Candice said, with what sounded like a twinge of jealousy.

"I have," Stuart admitted, enjoying the twinge. "Haven't done much lately, but I've done my share. The one thing that dating has taught me is that you can't judge a book by its cover."

"Meaning?"

"Judging a woman by her shell only would be very one-dimensional. I think it's all in how a woman carries herself. I've seen full-figured women who could outshine a model-sized woman any day of the week. And I've seen petite women like you who could stop traffic even during rush hour."

"You're such a flatterer."

"It's true," Stuart said, not missing a beat.

The corners of Candice's lips curved upward. "So, if I had put my real physical traits on my profile, that wouldn't have caught your eye any quicker than the fabricated ones?"

"No. I have women of all sizes in my family, and my opinion could be biased, but I think they're all attractive. My sister—the one who lives with me—looks flawlessly pretty on most days." To Candice's amusement, Stuart quickly added, "But I wouldn't date her."

"Well, I should hope not. She *is* your sister."

"No. I wouldn't date her even if she weren't."

Candice placed her glass on the provided coaster and looked at him. Her expression brought deep lines to the space between her eyebrows. "Why not?"

Stuart chuckled, glad for a chance to explain himself. "Kenyatta is . . . how should I put this?" He wanted to be careful not to paint a negative picture of his sister to Candice, but at the same time, he wanted to be truthful. "Kenyatta can be very overbearing. That's a trait I don't care for in a woman."

Candice's interest was piqued now; Stuart could tell. "What else don't you care for in a woman?" she prodded.

"Women who are loud, meddlesome, love to gossip or who keep drama going all the time," he explained. "I can't deal with that."

"Is that what ended your first marriage?"

Candice had caught him off guard with that question. He hadn't expected to be discussing his previous marriage with her, at least, not on their first date. Stuart's prolonged silence prompted Candice to withdraw her question.

"I'm sorry. That's none of my business. I didn't mean to pry."

"No, it's okay," he said, taking a moment to collect his thoughts. Stuart made it a point never to talk badly about his former wife. He didn't know if that choice was made more out of respect for her or respect for their son. Whichever was the case, he wouldn't do it. "I've been divorced for a long time. Twelve years. Tyler wasn't quite a year old when Tasha and I split. We get along much better as Tyler's parents than we did as husband and wife. She respects me. I respect her. Sometimes I genuinely forget why we broke up; you with me? None of it really matters at this point anyway. We married young, and I think that as we grew up in the nine years that we were husband and wife, we also grew apart. At the end, we couldn't seem to see eye to eye on much of anything."

"But isn't it said that opposites attract?" Candice offered.

"That may be true in some instances, but not in ours. If we were saved at the time we were going through the rough patches, we may have been able to work it out, but we weren't. I mean, we went to church, but speaking for myself, I will readily admit that I wasn't in the spiritual place that I needed to be in at that time. If she's honest, she'd say the same for herself. She's an excellent mom to Tyler, though."

Wanting to get the spotlight off him for a while, Stuart took his turn to ask a question. "What about you? What attracts you to the opposite sex?"

Candice placed her elbows on the table and rested her chin on her crossed hands. "I know this is going to sound hypocritical after what I did with my online profile, but one of the things I look for in a man is honesty. My biggest issue in past relationships is getting a man to be genuine and honest. And faithful," she added.

"The worst relationship I ever had was prior to my getting saved and establishing a personal bond with the Lord. And when I look back on it, I guess that's something that should be expected. He was a sinner, thus, he did sinful things. I was a sinner, so I reacted as such. But so-called Christian men haven't been much better."

"I've run into the same problem with Christian women," Stuart said, his mind quickly thinking back to the females he'd met on the site prior to Candice.

The discussion at their table stopped and, for several moments, Stuart gazed across the table and looked into Candice's soul as she locked eyes with him. Not once did she turn away from him, and what Stuart saw in her eyes made his heart pound harder with every pump of blood.

"So," she whispered, her voice carrying a noticeable quiver, "with both of us realizing the risks and knowing that people are not always what they portray themselves to be, how do we know if we can trust each other?"

"I guess we don't," Stuart said, reaching across the table again, in search of her hand. "But if you're willing to take a chance on me, I'm willing to do the same with you."

Chapter Eleven

Everything had gone so well that Stuart found himself waiting for the axe to fall. There was no way that this girl could be as perfect as she seemed. Not perfect by the dictionary's definition, but perfect for him. The more Stuart searched for the hidden flaw—the one thing that should make him take a step back and exercise caution—the more Stuart appreciated everything about Candice Powell. He had to in order to be headed in the direction in which he drove his truck now.

When Stuart had called ahead, the answering machine had picked up, signifying that Kenyatta wasn't at home. Since Tyler was out with his friends, Stuart supposed that Kenyatta would spend even more time shopping than she would have, had the boy been with her.

Initially, Stuart had no intention of bringing Candice to his house. Hunter and Jade had

given him an open invitation to bring her to
their house to change clothes. It would give
them a chance to meet her and allow her to
see Greene Pastures, as a part of her tour of
Atlanta. But deciding that he wanted to keep
Candice all to himself today, Stuart made an
impromptu change of plans and broke a car-
dinal rule in the meantime. After all, this was
only their first date, and he made it a point to
never bring a woman to his home on the first
date. But this wouldn't be the only rule he'd
break tonight.

Aside from talking to Candice about his severed marriage—another thing he'd never done
this early in a relationship—Stuart had also
held her hand during lunch, as they walked
through the mall, at the movies, as they walked
barefoot on the lawn of Stone Mountain Park,
and now, as they walked together toward his
front door. The light rainfall gave Stuart an
additional reason to stand close to Candice as
they shared an umbrella. Candice seemed a bit
nervous as he opened the door and motioned
for her to walk in ahead of him. Her garment
bag was placed over his unoccupied arm, and
he laid it across the living room couch as he
closed the door behind him.

"You have a very nice place," Candice re-marked, looking around the living room but not moving from the place where she stood.

Stuart's smile said that he appreciated her praise—and the way her slacks kissed her curves. "I know we're headed out, but would you like something to drink?"

"No, no thank you. I think I'll be fine until dinner."

"You're not too disappointed about not vis-iting Greene Pastures, are you?" Stuart didn't want Candice to be dissatisfied about any of her time with him.

"Not at all," she answered. "The rain would have put a damper on things anyway, I sup-pose."

He was just about to offer her a seat when Candice began walking toward his entertain-ment center, where photos lined one of the shelves. She studied each picture as if trying to store images into her memory bank for later recall.

"Is this you as a child?" she asked, turning to look at him while pointing at a small-framed photo.

Stuart knew which picture she was refer-ring to, but he used the moment as an added opportunity to walk closer, just so he could be standing near her again. "Yeah, that's me." He picked up the photo. "I think I was about Tyler's age when I took this one."

"I really didn't see a lot of resemblance between the two of you when I met him last night," Candice admitted, "but looking at you at his age, I can see the likeness."

"Yeah, he took his complexion and most of his facial features from his mother," Stuart said as he returned the photo to its rightful place. "But he has a lot of my ways. He's definitely his daddy's son."

"You sound like a proud papa."

Stuart looked at Candice and saw her looking up at him with admiring eyes. She had an infectious smile, and returning it didn't even seem to be optional. "I am. Tyler is . . . well, I don't know. I guess you can say that he's my heart. My son means the world to me, and as long as God gives me breath in my body, Tyler will never want for anything that he needs."

"That's refreshing to hear," Candice praised. "As a teacher, I see kids—especially boys—that really need that love and positive reinforcement from their dads. Too many fathers aren't involved enough in their children's lives; particularly when they are no longer in a committed relationship with the child's mother.

It's always nice to see a parent—a father—care deeply for his child."

Stuart didn't readily know how to respond. He didn't really want to respond; not with words, anyway. What he craved was to take Candice in his arms and kiss her. It was another thing he never did on first dates, but she'd already made him break three other rules. One more wouldn't hurt.

"What time is our dinner reservation?" Candice backed away as she asked the question, and Stuart wondered if she could feel the heat building on the inside of him, seeping through his pores.

"Seven," he answered. "We've got a few minutes." Stuart walked over to the sofa and retrieved her garment bag.

"Come here. I have something I want to show you."

He had taken several steps down the hallway before she began following at a distance. Not looking behind him, but knowing that Candice was following, Stuart unlocked the door of his den, walked into the space and then stepped aside so that Candice could see his prized room.

For an extended period, she stood in the doorway, not fully entering the area, but looking around and taking in the fullness of it. "Wow. This is nice, Stuart. It's almost like a home within your home."

That was exactly what the room was to him, and Stuart couldn't have said it better. "I know." He reached for her. "Come on in. I want to show you all of it."

Candice pointed at the different areas of the den as she spoke. "It's like an office, a living room, and a kitchen, all in one." She giggled slightly when she noted the personal sized refrigerator in a far corner.

"And the couch lets out into a bed, so if push comes to shove, it can be a bedroom too." Stuart hoped his words didn't sound like he was insinuating anything. He glanced toward Candice, and she didn't appear to think so.

"Look at all the books," she observed, walking to the bookshelf that lined the wall adjacent to the sofa and retrieving a large hardcover book simply titled *Mandela*. A large black-and-white photo of the famed leader graced the book's front cover.

Stuart beamed, seeing that his favorite room had impressed Candice. "I wish I had time to read them all, but with my schedule, I have to fit it in where I can get it in." Nudging Candice's arm, he brought her attention back to his workspace. "This is the computer I'm always sitting in front of when we chat online."

As though it were a cherished piece of Smithsonian memorabilia, Candice took deliberate steps as she approached the station, and then cradling *Mandela* in one arm, she used a single finger of the opposing hand to graze the full length of the desk and then rounded it so that she stood in front of the blackened computer screen. Stuart watched a look of appreciation cross her face and he imagined that she was thinking to herself: So, this is the machine that brought us together.

"You wear glasses?" She picked up the frames and studied them closely. "I should have guessed it, since Tyler wears them."

Stuart smiled. "I don't wear them nearly as much as Tyler. That boy would trip over his own feet without his glasses. I only need them when I'm at the computer or sometimes if I'm reading fine print."

Candice handed the eyeglasses to him. "Put them on. Let me see what you look like in them."

Had the request been made by anyone else, Stuart would have likely refused. Although they were fashionable, he didn't care much for wearing the spectacles. But he couldn't say no

to Candice, and he watched her smile stretch
when he placed them on his face and looked
at her.

"Very handsome," she said. "They really become you."

On the inside, Stuart felt himself blush, but
it was a reaction that his dark skin kept secret.
"Thank you." After such a fine compliment, he
didn't want to take them off, but he did.

"This is really nice, Stuart." Candice turned
her body with the grace of a dancer and walked
across the floor until she reached the flat-
screen television that occupied floor space directly across from the couch. A coffee table, so
polished that she could see her reflection, separated the couch from the television. Candice
admired it for a moment and then took the liberty of sitting on the couch, rubbing the supple
leather covering with one hand. She slipped
her feet from her sandals and entangled her
toes in the plush hairs of the spacious throw-
rug that covered the floor surrounding her.

Enjoying the scene before him, Stuart said
nothing. He watched intently, licking his lips
and regretting that he'd have to soon end this
phase of the evening in order to make it to The
Pecan in time for their dinner reservations.
A part of him wanted to cancel the previous

plans and just spend the rest of the evening here with Candice. But with the unbecoming path that his mind was threatening to travel, and the added ambiance of light rainfall on the outside, Stuart knew that staying in wouldn't be best.

"Do you spend a lot of time in here?" Candice asked, breaking his smoldering thoughts.

Stuart used his bare hand to wipe away beads of sweat from the top of his head. Sweat that he didn't even know had begun forming. "Uh, yeah, I do," he said. "I come in here every morning before I go to work."

Taking cautious steps, he approached Candice, pausing to unload her garment bag on the arm of the couch farthest from her. Then he removed the television remote from the space closest to her and sat. Following her lead, Stuart removed his loafers and then propped his bare feet on the coffee table in front of them. In one smooth motion, he slipped his arm around her and allowed it to rest against the sofa pillows behind her. Candice didn't move away.

"To read?" she inquired as she readjusted her body so that her bare feet were now on the sofa and her back was nestled on the space that marked the dividing line of Stuart's shoulder and chest.

Stuart melted a little and heard a slight whimper that wishful thinking told him had come from Candice's throat and not his. "To pray," was his soft answer. Pray was something he needed to do right now as he closed his eyes and digested the fragrance of her hair.

"Oh, yeah?" She nestled closer. "So this is like the secret prayer closet where you come to worship?"

Stuart chuckled as much as a melted man could. "I suppose you could say that. But instead of calling it a secret closet, I prefer to call it The Lyons Den." He wished he hadn't even said it when the words caused her to pull away.

Candice looked at him with bright eyes and tilted her head to the side in a thoughtful pose. "The Lyons Den. I like that."

Stuart wanted to tell her that he liked it when she was resting against him. "Yeah," he opted to say. "In the Bible, Daniel prayed in a lion's den, so I thought I'd use my den as the place where I'd go to seek God."

"My pastor always says that there's nothing like a praying man."

Stuart offered a quiet nod and secretly held on to the hope that Candice would eventually return to her snuggling position.

"You have a great eye for interior decorating," she observed

"I try," Stuart said. It was hard to be modest when he'd been repeatedly told so. "I think I have a better eye for landscaping, though. You can't tell it right now, because I don't have flowers planted out front anymore." He grimaced a little, thinking of the culprit who destroyed his lawn scenery. "I'll plant again for next spring. Maybe you can come back so you can see it."

Candice's face displayed a shy grin. "Are you inviting?"

"I'm insisting," Stuart replied, hoping his gazing wasn't making her uncomfortable. Apparently, it wasn't. Answering his ongoing inward plea, Candice turned and nestled against him again, allowing *Mandela* to rest against her thighs. Stuart imagined that he could easily fall asleep with her in his arms like this. He closed his eyes and wished he could.

"You said you pray in this room. What do you pray about?" She asked like she really wanted to know.

"Everything." A deliberate whiff fed him another dose of the scent of her hair. "Lately, I've been praying quite a bit about this still unidentified person whose been harassing me."

It was a subject that the two of them had managed to avoid up until now.

"How's that going?"

"There's a lead, but not enough evidence yet to make an arrest."

To Stuart's chagrin, she moved away, turning to face him once more.

"There's a lead?" Candice looked surprised. "Who?"

Stuart fanned his hand as if it were no big deal. With the prime suspect being his own former brother-in-law, it wasn't a topic he wanted to delve in too deeply. "Just a guy who's never really been that fond of me."

Stuart wanted to get away from this subject matter altogether and back to whatever topic would bring Candice back to her previous position. But the clock on the wall told him that he'd had all the mental ecstasy he'd get for now. Reluctantly, he stood and pointed toward her garment bag. "Why don't you use this area to get dressed, and I'll change in my bedroom. We're cutting it close with our reservations and need to get going. There's a restroom behind those closed doors on the right, and there are wash cloths and towels, if you need them. If you need anything else, just holla."

"Thanks. I'll only be a minute," Candice promised.

Stuart doubted it. From his mother to his sisters to his ex-wife, he had never known it to take "a minute" for a woman to get ready to go anywhere. "I'll wait for you in the living room." Stuart closed the door as he exited.

Once in his own bedroom, he peeled off the clothes he'd been wearing all day and removed the plastic dry cleaning covering from the outfit that would replace it. The single-breasted black suit was one of Stuart's favorites that he always paired with shirts that complemented his skin tone. This evening, it would be a royal blue button-down number from Joseph A. Banks which he'd wear with no tie. He didn't want to be overdressed.

Ducking into the bathroom, Stuart did what he was certain that Candice was doing as well. He took his bath cloth and did a quick wash-up, to be sure he was fresh in the places that mattered the most. Time was working against them now, and as Stuart returned to his bedroom and began to get dressed, he only hoped that Candice wouldn't take too long. He had barely made his reappearance in the living room when the cell phone on his right hip rang. It was business, but Stuart hoped it wasn't business that needed his physical involvement.

"Stuart Lyons."

"Lieutenant, it's Sergeant Bowden."

Allen's formality told Stuart that he was at the precinct. "Hey, Allen. What's up?"

"Just calling to let you know that we got him, Lieutenant."

"Got who?" Stuart needed to hear words that verified his gut feeling.

"Joseph King," Allen confirmed. "He was picked up about an hour ago when he went in to work the night shift at the plant where he's employed."

"You're kidding me."

"No, sir. We got him. After it was established that he'd missed work on the Monday that your car was vandalized, we moved in. That, coupled with your sister's statements, should be enough to put him away. If you ask me, he doesn't have a leg to stand on." The satisfaction could be heard in Allen's voice when he added, "You can breathe easier now."

And Stuart did. It was disturbing to know that the damage had been done by someone who had once been a member of his family, but the relief of knowing he would no longer have to deal with the fear of leaving his son home alone or finding his property tampered with outweighed any disappointment he had in Joe. There was no love lost. After all, there had been very little there to begin with.

"That's great news, Allen," Stuart said. "I've gotta run, though. I have an appointment that I'm already running late for. Call me tomorrow afternoon and fill me in on the details."

"Will do, Lieutenant."

"What's great news?"

Stuart turned at the sound of Candice's voice and what he saw made him momentarily forget about the report he'd just received. With the speed of pouring molasses, Stuart's eyes scanned Candice's figure from head to toe, and then back to her head again. She looked striking in the royal blue dress.

"You're staring," she said, fidgeting under the glare of his eyes.

"You're stunning," Stuart replied.

"Thank you." Candice offered a soft smile and then added, "We're matching." She pointed at Stuart's shirt and then at her dress.

Stuart bit the inside of his mouth, punishing himself for the unrighteous thoughts racing through his head. "Did I tell you this was my favorite color?"

"Yes."

"So . . . one could say that you're wearing this dress for me?"

Candice fingered her hair like a nervous teenager and then replied, "One could say."

The hush that hovered in the living room was so thick that it nearly changed the lighting of the space. Stuart closed his eyes and inwardly prayed that God would supply him with the strength to follow the commands of the scripture. It was clear that he was going to need power beyond his own.

"Are you ready to go?" Candice asked, snapping him from his trance. "You've raved about this restaurant, and I'd hate to miss the experience."

Stuart extended his hand toward her so that she would join him and so he could take her garment bag from her arm. "Yeah, we'd better get going. These are our last few hours together. Let's not waste any time."

Candice gave him her bag and then linked her arm in his. "Agreed."

The rain had subsided as the two of them stepped out onto the front steps and headed for the awaiting Land Rover.

Stuart released a chuckle and said, "We've talked about everything. What on earth will we find to talk about over dinner?"

"How about your good news?" Candice suggested.

"Good news?"

"Yeah. The good news that the caller just gave you."

Stuart's thoughts had traveled so far away from the chat with Allen that it took a moment for him to rewind and refresh his memory. "Oh," he said as he held the passenger door open for her to enter. "That was the police station. They picked up a suspect in the stalking."

Candice froze and looked at him with eyes that told the full story of her surprise. "What? They caught someone? But how? I mean, when?"

Chapter Twelve

If water is a viable comparison to the Holy Spirit, then Sunday morning's service was equivalent to a dam break. As obvious as the presence of God was on a weekly basis at New Hope, this Sunday, His move in the midst was unusual. The anointing ran rampant, touching almost everyone in the building.

Jerome had never seen anything like it before. The praise dancers had long ago abandoned the grace of their normal flowing movements. Many of the ushers, who were trained to attend to the needs of the congregation, needed attending to themselves. People who typically showed emotion by occasionally closing their eyes and lifting their hands were dancing in the aisles or running around the church like the horses in Greene Pastures had done on yesterday. Jerome spent time there on Saturday, despite the threat of rain, playing with his nephew and his school friends as though he was the same age as they.

Then there were the men of New Hope, some of whom never showed much emotion at all. Today, they were walking the circumference of the floor. Some, like his brotherin-law, Hunter, were kneeling with their faces resting against the altar that surrounded the pulpit. Jerome himself was so overcome that he didn't know how to react. His knees buckled, his shoulders shook, and his eyes overflowed. Jerome had never felt the presence of God like this before. It felt overwhelming, even frightening; almost too much for him to handle. With legs that wobbled under the weight of his quivering body, Jerome, with blurred vision, navigated his way through the emotional crowd, making his way to the exit doors. He had to get out and away. "Are you okay, Brother Jerome?" The concern on the dutiful usher's face was telling. She served regularly at the entrance and exit doors, but Jerome didn't know her name. Pulling several sheets of fresh Kleenex tissue from a nearby box, the woman pressed them into his hands. "Are you okay?" she repeated.

Jerome tried to answer, but like a mute, no words would form. With trembling hands, he wiped away the flood of tears from his eyes and then looked helplessly in the middle-aged woman's face again, trying for a second time to respond to her still unanswered question. But his only reply was the appearance of more tears to replace the ones he'd just dried. Jerome imagined that this woman must have thought he was crazy, but her expression indicated otherwise.

Substantially shorter than he, she reached up and cupped his face in her hands. Jerome was no longer sure of the blur in front of him. The usher seemed to transform into someone no longer familiar. Maybe it was the overhead lights reflecting through his watery vision, but whatever the cause, her salt-and-pepper hair now shimmered like a mix of precious silver and sparkling coal, and the outline of her image began to glow.

"That's all right, Brother Jerome, you praise Him," she said, smiling all the while. "Let the Lord work on you, honey, you hear me? You ain't been through all that you been through just to sit in these here pews and watch your daddy preach. You just like David, that shepherd boy in the Bible who, compared to his brothers, didn't look like much-anothin'. Even his daddy didn't know his worth. When the man of God came looking for a king to crown, David's daddy lined up all his young'uns, except David. 'Cause although he loved that boy just like he did the others, he didn't have no inkling of the call that God had on David.

"Everybody always expected your brother, Jackson, to be a preacher 'cause he always looked and acted like one. Your sister could have turned out to be a preacher, and it wouldn't have surprised a soul. But you . . . bless God, you was the dirty little shepherd boy and didn't nobody expect nothing from you."

The woman paused long enough to purse her lips, close her eyes, and give her head a slow snake-like roll to the east and then a matching one to the west—like the Spirit of God was moving through her neck, riding on a slow rollercoaster. When she opened her eyes, she continued in a voice more authoritative than before.

"Jackson Tides is a preacher, and he's a good one. Can't nobody even come close to questioning his anointing. But make no mistake, son. You been called, too. From the day you were formed in your mama's belly, you were called and chosen by God. That's why the devil tried so hard to destroy you. 'Cause that old muskrat knew what you had in you all along. And just like the Lord did with David, He's about to call you up out of the sheep pen, clean you up, and do a new thing in your life."

She tightened her hold on Jerome's face, pressing his cheeks until his lips puckered out and he could taste the salt of his own tears. Her final words, a paraphrase of 1 Corinthians 2:9, were deliberate and perceptive. "Eyes have not seen, ears haven't heard, nor has it even been conceived in the hearts of man, what God is preparing you for."

In truth, Jerome was never sure if those were the actual last words the lady had spoken or not. But they were the last ones he heard. Following them, he felt a powerfully forceful, yet painless, current run through his body with the strength of a bolt of lightning. Jerome felt himself being lifted from the floor and the next thing he knew, he came to, feeling the weight of his father's body sprawled on top of him.

Reverend Tides repositioned himself, kneeling beside the spot where Jerome still lay flat on his back. Pressing his hands against Jerome's forehead as he often did when praying for a person, Reverend Tides repeated the words, "It is well," over and over again.

Searching the faces of those who stood, looking down at him, Jerome saw looks of joyful-
ness replace despair and concern. The faces
of medical personnel mingled with those of
his family and fellow church members. During early moments of disorientation, Jerome
reasoned that he must be in the hospital; then
he came to realize that the nurses standing over
him were New Hope's own on-staff profession-
als. The music that played in the background,
combined with the sounds of worship in the
atmosphere, was confirmation that they were
still in the sanctuary.

What happened?

Jerome felt confused and at peace, all at
the same time. He was clueless as to what
had transpired and how long he'd been un-
conscious to the goings-on around him. But
although there were no memories of his time
away, the intermission had brought him tran-
quility he'd never known.

Obviously satisfied that his son was okay
now, Reverend Tides stood to his feet with
the help of Stuart, his self-appointed personal
security guard. Peter Jericho and Kwame Williams served as human cranes, each position-
ing himself on either side of Jerome and lifting
him to a standing position.

As the crowd of onlookers and prayer warriors dispersed, they did so rejoicing, as though Jerome had been a paraplegic and was standing on his own for the first time.

"You good, man?" Kwame asked, inspecting Jerome closely.

Jerome nodded yes, but disorientation lingered in his eyes.

Peter looked as though he wanted to say something too, but he was literally pushed aside by First Lady Mildred Tides, who proceeded to throw her arms around Jerome's waist, locking him in a grip so tight that he thought she'd snap his spine.

Jerome had no idea his mother was so strong. When she loosened him, she looked up in Jerome's face and then grabbed his cheeks in much the same manner the usher did earlier. Only, instead of talking to him, Mildred pulled Jerome's face down to hers and planted a firm kiss on his nose. She used to do that when he and his siblings were children and had fallen during horseplay, hurting themselves.

Jerome blinked hard at the recollection of the endearing gesture. Mildred said nothing, but her high-glossed lips were stretched into a wide grin when she turned away, and in essence, danced all the way back to the front of the church, where other praisers were still at work.

"You all right, bruh?" Stuart asked, his hand firmly planted on Jerome's shoulder.

Jerome wondered why everyone was acting as though they'd never seen the Spirit move on him before today. "Yeah. Yeah, I'm fine." He had barely gotten the words out of his mouth before Stuart abandoned him to guard Reverend Tides, who had begun his own trek down the aisle, headed back to the pulpit.

Convinced their friend needed no further special attention, both Kwame and Peter patted Jerome on the back and walked away.

Still feeling a bit bewildered by it all, Jerome turned and made his way back toward the same exit door where he'd been stopped on the first attempt. He was no longer being bombarded by the Holy Spirit, but he still felt the need for fresher air. Jerome halfway expected not to see the usher at the post, fully prepared to accept the possibility that an angel had interrupted him earlier. But as Jerome paused and looked to his right before pushing open the door, the woman tossed him a knowing smile, raised her eyebrows into a high arch, and nodded her head as if to say, "God's gonna use you, boy. Just you wait and see!"

The air was much cooler in the vestibule. All the praising on the inside of the sanctuary had brought on a mild heat wave. Jerome reached up to wipe away what he thought was sweat from his face, but when he looked at the oily substance his hand collected, he knew that it wasn't perspiration. The familiar smell of the olive oil suddenly slapped him across the nose, and he was glad that he hadn't unwittingly wiped his hands against the fabric of his pants.

Making long and quick strides, Jerome walked into the bathroom, taking care not to touch anything en route. Once there, he stood in front of one of the sinks and laughed at his own gleaming reflection in the mirror.

"No wonder Mother's lips were so shiny after she kissed me," he said aloud.

Laughing again, Jerome immediately turned on the hot water and began pumping soap from the dispenser. There was enough anointed oil slathered on his face to fry a chicken. He looked like a well-polished chocolate drop. It took three washings, but Jerome finally could feel the natural surface of his skin. A few drops of the greasy substance had fallen on his shirt, but the black cotton fabric hid most of what he couldn't scrub away.

When he was done, Jerome stood for a long while, just staring at the image that stared back at him. There was a time in his life when he would have fought the usher's prophecy with all of his might. But nothing she'd said rang strange to his ears.

Ever since last week's visit to Phillips State Prison, Jerome had been feeling that there was more that God wanted him to do. Though preaching God's Word had never been on his list of things to do before he died, Jerome knew that trying to escape the inevitable would be a waste of his time. Everything the lady told him was confirmation of what God had been presenting to him by way of thoughts and dreams. And, among the many things that ten years in prison had taught him, the consequences of running from God were right up there at the top.

Just the thought of standing behind a pulpit, preaching to people who had been active members of the church longer than he, who had been reading the Bible longer than he, and who had been saved longer than he, was more than intimidating; it was downright frightening. Jerome didn't even begin to know how he would follow in the gargantuan footsteps of his dad, but there was no question that ministry was where God was calling him.

Blowing out a lung full of air, he rolled his eyes up toward the ceiling and said, "Okay, Lord. But on the real, you're gonna have to send a brotha some help, 'cause you know this ain't something your boy can do by himself."

Jerome imagined that his mother would scold him for using such lax language when talking to God, but even as children, they'd been taught that they could talk to the Father above using the same civil language that they used when talking to mortal man. Both Reverend and Mother Tides had taught their children that they didn't have to use sanctified words when praying. The last thing Jerome expected to be was the subject of another prison-to-the-pulpit story, but if that was what God wanted him to do, he was willing.

"As long as you send help, we've got a deal," he reminded God through a whisper as he pressed against the men's room door to exit.

"Jerome."

Jerome's heart leapt in his chest. The voice that called him was a familiar one, but he didn't expect to hear it coming from the dark corner adjacent to the door of the men's room. Jerome caught his breath, and then with an embarrassed chuckle, he said, "Ingrid. Woman, you scared me half to death. Don't ever creep up on a brotha like that."

"Well, you scared me half to death too, so now we're even."

There was a smile in Ingrid's voice as she spoke, but when she stepped from the shadows, Jerome could see she'd been crying. At first, he thought something was wrong, but then he remembered the moving of the Spirit on the inside. Ingrid had probably just been caught up along with everyone else.

Jerome relaxed his back against the wall and quickly noted Ingrid's attire. Today, she looked like a window-front mannequin in the champagne-colored skirt suit, which was tailored just right to flatter her already flattering figure. "I scared you half to death?"

"Yes, you did," she said, walking closer and placing her hands on her hips for emphasis.

Jerome's mind raced to try and figure out what she was talking about. Thanks to Kwame's ill-timed need to have spark plugs replaced on his car, Jerome had arrived at church a little later than normal this morning, but that was no reason for Ingrid to be concerned. He'd noticed that she hadn't called him once last week. That was odd, since he normally heard from her at least three times weekly, most times, more. The frequency of her calls was only upstaged by that of Kenyatta. Rarely ever did a day go by that Kenyatta didn't call.

"Are you mad at me or something?" Jerome asked, finding himself bracing in expectation of her answer. "Is that why you haven't called me? Because you're mad?"

Ingrid looked away and then back at Jerome. "I'm surprised you even noticed."

"Noticed what?"

"That I hadn't called."

Jerome laughed, feeling more at ease that Ingrid didn't seem upset. "How can I not notice? You go from calling every two or three days to not calling at all and I'm not gonna notice?"

"Well, you never said anything."

"I would have, had you called."

"You couldn't have picked up the phone and called me?" There was a definite challenge in Ingrid's tone.

Jerome shrugged his shoulders. "I guess I could have."

"I thought I'd give you a chance to miss me," Ingrid said, her eyes darting downward. "I thought if you missed me, maybe you would call me, for a change."

Jerome felt the strong need to apologize, but fought it off successfully. He had, in fact, missed his time of talking with Ingrid this past week, but he wasn't about to tell her that. After all, he wasn't obligated to call her, and he didn't want Ingrid to get the notion that he was. He'd never called her before. Why should he start now?

The lingering silence between them was growing stale.

"How did we get on this subject anyway?" Ingrid rescued them both.

Crossing his arms in front of him, Jerome refreshed her memory. "You said I scared you, and I was trying to figure out what I'd done to make you say that. I thought maybe you were gonna say that you'd been trying to call me, but couldn't get through or something."

The noise on the inside of the church had somewhat calmed, causing the echoing of Jerome's voice in the foyer to be more pronounced. Ingrid must have noticed it too, because she motioned for him to follow her, and then began walking toward the glass doors that led to the outside.

Jerome watched the heavy doors close behind his exit and then turned to face the scene in front of him. The overcast sky was evidence

that there was a good chance that today's
weather would be a repeat of yesterday's.

He took his time descending the steps to
join Ingrid, who had made a leaning post out
of one of the gigantic steel light poles that
lined the walkway leading to the church. Jerome noted how striking she looked, standing
there watching his approach. It would have
made for a captivating postcard image.

As was the case with Kenyatta, Jerome was
drawn to Ingrid immediately upon meeting
her. He'd met and grown fond of Kenyatta
first, but that didn't lessen the attraction he
felt for Ingrid when his sister introduced the
two of them when he had accompanied Jade
to the airport to pick up Ingrid that Wednesday evening. The two women—Kenyatta and
Ingrid—were so different that Jerome couldn't
make sense of why he found them both appealing.

By most people's definition, Kenyatta would
be considered the prettier of the two. On Kenyatta's worst day, her pricey and proficiently
applied cosmetics made her face look like it
belonged on a centerfold beauty ad. At her
best, she could give any runway model fash-
ioning the latest trends for full-figured women
a run for her money. Most days, Kenyatta wore

her hair in an up do, molded to such perfection that it nearly looked like it was painted on her head. Jerome often wondered how she slept without disturbing it. She could be a bit boisterous and a tad domineering at times, but Kenyatta's good traits outweighed her bad.

As for Ingrid, insignificant, but mildly noticeable adult acne scarring prevented her from sharing the unblemished skin of her rival. Very little make-up got the pleasure of kissing the sensitive skin of her coffee-colored face, and naturally thick eyelashes that many women would pay for made her every blink seem like a tease. She kept her nails well-groomed, but they didn't have perfectly matched, salon-applied French tips like Kenyatta's. Ingrid's short, layered, auburn-streaked hair was always neatly styled, but she'd once told Jerome that she went to the salon only to freshen her cut and her color. Everything in between, she did herself, including her own relaxers.

Though Kenyatta, hands down, made a more commanding physical statement, Jerome was drawn to Ingrid's heart. When he looked at her, he saw the female version of himself. Unlike Kenyatta, Ingrid hadn't been brought up in the church. The streets had served as Ingrid's guardian for much of her formative years. They

had done the same for Jerome, due to his deter-
mination to rebel. He and Ingrid had both suffered some setbacks in life that had delayed, but
not denied, their taking their place with God.

In the three or four months that Ingrid Battles had been in Atlanta, Jerome had seen her
grow spiritually. In the past several weeks, that
maturity had been obvious. Even Jade had
been skeptical of Ingrid's sincerity when she
first proclaimed her salvation two months ago.
After all, it wasn't the first time she'd done so.
Jade said Ingrid had gotten saved many times
when they lived in Virginia. Every time their
church had a revival, Ingrid claimed salvation; and each time, it was like having a case of
twenty-four-hour pneumonia. A few days, and
she'd be back to "normal," chasing every man
who wasn't attached to a woman or a respira-
tor, and cussing out everybody who even looked
like they wanted to reprimand her for doing it.
This time, though, when she stood at the altar
of New Hope Church, a genuine change had
been made, and that was what lured Jerome
the most.

"Awesome service, huh?" Ingrid's question
snapped Jerome from his idle staring.

He turned and looked at the massive structure behind him and nodded in agreement. "Awesome ain't even the word," Jerome said. He could feel the hairs on his arm stand at attention at the total recall. "But, man, I don't know if I could take the Spirit moving like that every Sunday."

"I know."

Ingrid's voice trembled during her two-word answer, and hearing it brought Jerome's sights back to her. He watched her use slender fingers to dab at tears that had begun mounting themselves in the corners of her eyes. It had been that kind of service, Jerome thought. His remembrance brought chills. Hers brought tears. Men and women were just different like that.

"I don't know what I would have done if they hadn't brought you back."

The words were as faint as a whisper in the wind, but Jerome heard her. He stepped closer, deep lines gathering between his brows. "Brought me back where?"

Ingrid looked up at him as though she thought the question was rhetorical. "I was so scared. I think, for a minute, everybody was, even your dad."

"What are you talking about, Ingrid?" Jerome's heart pounded at the insinuation.

"I'm talking about what happened in there." Her voice was laced with irritation, like she thought he knew more than he was revealing.

Jerome took two more steps, which had him standing within reach of Ingrid. He watched large tears gather in her eyes, dangle at the end of her rich lashes, and then melt quickly down her cheeks. Placing one of his hands on both of her arms, Jerome tried again, not knowing if he really wanted to know the answer. "What happened in there, Ingrid? Tell me."

"You mean, you don't know?"

"Not if it's something that scared you, I don't," he said. "I mean, I remember being swept up by the Holy Spirit, but that's pretty much it. When I came out if it, Daddy was laying on top of me, and some of everybody was standing around me. I heard Daddy praying, and saw Mother crying, but that's it."

In one surge, Ingrid lunged into Jerome's chest and wept without restraint, puzzling him even more. What had happened? And why was Ingrid making such a big deal out of it?

He wrapped his arms around her, trying to provide the comfort she needed. The brisk spring breeze caused some of her hairs to wander into his face and tickle his nose. For a long while, they stood huddled together, Ingrid crying and Jerome asking God why. Ingrid had yet to address his questions, and God wasn't giving any immediate answers either.

As soon as she calmed and the opportunity presented itself, Jerome thought he'd give it one last try. He used his thumbs to wipe away the moisture on Ingrid's face that his shirt hadn't already absorbed.

"What happened, Ingrid?"

With her voice apparently held prisoner in a closed throat, Jerome was left with the task of reading her lips. Doing so wasn't difficult. There were only two words mouthed toward him in silence.

"You died."

Chapter Thirteen

Monday's wet roads, a direct result of a weekend of scattered showers, made rush-hour traffic almost unbearable. A drive that would normally take less than thirty minutes took well over an hour. Still, as Candice walked into her apartment and placed her carry-all on the living room sofa, she heard music. When she realized that the tune was the sound of humming coming from her own throat, she rested her back against the inside of her front door and beamed.

It had been ages since she felt like this . . . maybe never. Years ago, her father had warned her of making her heart accessible too quickly and too often. As a child, Abraham Powell's middle daughter was already showing signs of being a target for heartbreak, falling in love with every other star that hit the stage or the big screen. Between the ages of twelve and eighteen, Candice had fallen head over heels with pop idol Prince, actors Richard Gere and Denzel Washington, athletes Muhammad Ali and Julius "Dr. J" Erving, and all of the men who made up the gospel group, The Williams Brothers. By age twenty-one, romance novels had become an addiction. Candice was a hopeless romantic, strongly believing in the concepts of happily ever after and love at first sight.

Abraham Powell cautioned that any woman who believed in love at first sight was doing nothing more than asking for trouble. He reminded her of that forewarning years later with a very audible, "I told you so" that sounded all too cheerful to Candice's ears. She wanted to refute her father's victorious claim, but at the time, she was the living proof that validated his words. For three weeks, Candice had been lamenting a break-up that nearly robbed her of everything good.

Seven years had passed since then, but Candice still remembered every detail of the ordeal. Ephraim Polk, the man she was sure she'd spend the rest of her life with, had done the inconceivable. She'd had no doubt that the popular disc jockey was her soul mate. All signs pointed to it.

Ephraim was a true gentleman. He opened her car door, draped his jacket around her shoulders when she felt a chill, stood whenever she needed to leave the dinner table, and insisted on picking up the tab whenever they ate out—even if it was just a meal from McDonald's drive-thru. Ephraim shared her appreciation for good music, good movies and good friends. But all of that not withstanding, he made what Candice thought was her dream come true turn out to be her worst nightmare.

On the first anniversary of their "exclusive" relationship, Ephraim surprised Candice with a beautiful bouquet of roses that he had a high-end florist hand-deliver to her front door. Candice was astonished and elated—until she read the attached card.

Hey, Candy. (To this date, she hated that nickname because of him). *I know this is a cowardly way to do this, but I just need you to know that this relationship isn't working for me anymore. You're a beautiful and sweet girl and I know you'll be snatched up by somebody before you can even miss me. You're going to make some dude happy—it just won't be me. I know it may take a minute for you to forgive me for ending things like this, but when that day comes, I hope we can look back on this and laugh. I'm sorry it didn't work out.*

                              Ephraim

"Look back on this and laugh?" Candice recalled, repeating those words through vision blurred by anger and pain.

It had been no laughing matter. She balled up the card and threw it in the garbage can. Moments later, she'd retrieved it, read it again, and then tossed it back in with the other household compost. Another minute or two passed, and she pulled it out for the second time, hands trembling, reading words that, to her mind, made no sense. They'd just spent an intimate evening together two nights before. There were candles, wine, music, satin sheets—the whole nine yards. How had they gone from that to this in less than forty-eight hours? His dreadfully ugly words were in no way beautified by the red roses that accompanied them.

On the days when the sorrow was too much to bear, the shoulder of her pregnant best friend, Oneeka Stout, served as a sponge for Candice's never-ending flow. And on days when anger was the more prevalent emotion, Oneeka's ears also served as a trash compactor where Candice could empty every foul and vulgar name she could think of to call Ephraim.

Six months later, all of Candice's unreturned phone calls, ignored emails, obsessive knocks at Ephraim's front door, and mind-tormenting questions were finally answered. Ephraim welcomed his first child into the world, and three months after that, he got married. His bride was none other than Oneeka Stout, who would have been Candice's choice for maid of honor, had she been the one wearing the veil. All of the devastations, and the people who inflicted them, nearly made her lose her sanity—literally.

For many nights following the exposure of the long-time secret affair, Candice sat up late at night, thinking of ways to create a proper burial for the two Judases. She mulled over ideas of ways that she might be able to ignite a fire to their cozy little love nest while they slept. Visions of them crawling on hands and knees, trying to feel their way to safety while thick, black smoke choked the life out of them served as sunshine for Candice's otherwise cloudy days. Thoughts of firemen pulling their charred remains from the fire-gutted house

tickled Candice. It was a shame that an innocent baby would have to die too, but Candice
justified her twisted thinking by noting that
the baby would probably be better off dead
than be raised by liars and backstabbers like
his parents.

Despite Ephraim's written prediction, no
man had snatched up Candice—not before she
had a chance to miss him and not even long after she'd gotten past the hatred and hurt. Until
Stuart, Candice hadn't allowed another man
to get close enough to her to successfully woo
her. Ephraim's brutal deception caused Candice to second-guess every man. And because
of Oneeka, she had never become close friends
with another female. Distrust was the lingering
scar she carried from the seven-year-old ordeal.

Stuart was quickly taking her down a road
she once doubted she'd ever travel again. For
the first time since Ephraim, she felt like she
was ready to move forward with a part of her
life that, until now, had all but terrorized her.
Stuart seemed to be genuinely trustworthy.

But then again, so did Ephraim.

"Stop it, stop it, stop it!" Candice whispered
fiercely as she pressed her fingertips against
her temples. She was sick and tired of allowing

the deeds of Ephraim and his now *ex*-wife to control her life.

For months following "the incident," their blatant deceit had rendered her sleepless, tortured, and borderline suicidal. She spent countless nights lying awake, with her body coiled into a fetal position, and countless days lying in the same position on a leather couch that belonged to a professional who charged her $150 per hour to listen to her profess her pain. Over time, the open wound closed, but years later, Candice still carried the scars of betrayal. It wasn't until she gave her life to Christ that she was able to find solace. Even now, sometimes she struggled.

Candice remembered the day she found out that Ephraim had gone and done the same thing to Oneeka that he'd done to her. Their marriage was only three years old when the successful insurance agent reconnected with his cheating ways. Or maybe, it had just taken that long for him to get caught. All Candice knew for certain was that three years into Oneeka's marriage to Ephraim, it was discovered that he was having an affair with one of his wife's co-workers. Word on the street was that Oneeka had spent a year trying to convince him to stay with her and their two children, but it didn't work. He filed for divorce and, a year later, tied the knot with his newest "other woman."

"Stuart wouldn't do anything like that. He's a man of God, and that alone makes all the difference in the world." No one else was in Candice's living room with her, so her words were solely meant to reassure herself.

Still standing with her back against the front door, Candice's right hand fluttered to her chest. It was then she was reminded of the extra reason Stuart had given her to trust him. Unbuttoning her top three buttons and reaching inside her blouse, she pulled out a key that dangled at the end of the chain she wore around her neck. With her thumb and index finger, she stroked the surface of the key and reminisced.

They were standing outside the entranceway to the airport, where they'd been holding a disagreement for at least fifteen minutes. Candice had asked Stuart to drop her off at curbside check-in, but he'd insisted on parking the vehicle in the parking deck and walking her inside.

"I don't want you to walk inside with me," *Candice told him when they reached the airport's entranceway.*

"But I want to."

Candice took a deep breath. "I know you do and I appreciate it, Stuart. Really, I do. But I'm asking you to honor my wishes. I need you to just leave me here and let me do the rest of this by myself."

Stuart rubbed his hand across his smooth scalp in frustration. "Why?"

"Because you said your church starts service at eleven thirty. As head of security, you have to be there an hour early, right? It's already eight thirty, and it could easily take you an hour to drive back to Stone Mountain. I don't want to make you late for your duties."

Stuart looked down at his clothing. He was dressed in an olive green Brooks Brothers suit with Stacy Adams shoes to match. "It's not like I have to go home and get dressed or anything. Kenyatta and Tyler will be going to church together in Kenyatta's car, so I'm just gonna drive to New Hope straight from here." He took a quick look at his watch. "I've got plenty of time."

"Stuart—"

"What? You got another excuse?" he challenged. "I'm beginning to think you're just trying to get rid of me."

"No." He was getting upset, and that was the last thing Candice wanted. Their weekend had been too enchanting to end on a sour note. "No, Stuart, that's not it at all."

"Then, what is it?"

Candice took a moment to catch her breath . . . and to think. She had to think of something. "What would be the purpose, Stuart?"

"To be sure that you get in and find your way to the security lines without a problem," he answered.

"I won't have a problem. It's not like I don't know how to make my way through an airport."

"This is Hartsfield-Jackson—the busiest airport in the world, Candice, bar none. You may think LaGuardia is as crazy as it gets, but this one can be much worse. I know you've had to find your way through a busy airport before, but not this one."

Candice giggled, more out of nervousness than humor. "I flew into this one, remember? I found my way just fine."

Stuart missed a beat. "Finding your way in is a whole different ballgame than finding your way out."

"Stuart—"

"Okay," he blurted, flinging his arms in the air and then allowing them to fall by his sides. "You wanna know the real reason I want to walk you all the way to the security checkpoint? I want to do it because it'll give me more time with you. I want to spend more time with you, okay? Is that too much to ask?"

Candice's heart fluttered again just thinking about that moment. The confession was forced, but the sincerity of it was evident, and Stuart's vulnerability was endearing. *She'd stepped closer to him and stroked the sleeve of his suit jacket. The simple contact from her hand brought softness to his eyes as they stared down into hers.*

"Don't you see? That's the same reason that I need you to leave me now," she told him in a tone that was as gentle as her touch. "Your walking me in isn't going to make this any easier, Stuart. The longer you're with me, the harder it's going to be for me to leave you behind. It'll be simpler for me to separate from you right now than it will be for me to walk away, waving good-bye, fifteen or twenty minutes from now."

Candice could feel Stuart's rapid heartbeat drumming against her cheek when he pulled her in for a loving embrace. With his jacket open, his aroma—a mix of cologne and just plain maleness—seeped through the fibers of his shirt and into her nostrils, weakening every muscle in her body. For those fleeting yet significant moments, Candice felt as though God was giving her a taste of what heaven must be like.

When Stuart finally released her and took a step backward, Candice had to find her legs and steady herself. He didn't seem to notice her struggle.

"Okay," he conceded. Stuart lifted her chin so that her eyes met his again. "I don't like this, but we'll do it your way. This time."

Candice dropped her eyes to the pavement between them, hoping to hide her insurmountable relief. "Thank you."

Shoving both his hands in the pockets of his slacks, Stuart looked away for a second and then turned back to her. "So, when am I going to see you again?"

"I don't know," Candice answered with a shift of her feet. "We don't exactly live down the street from one another."

"I know," he agreed. "But I'd definitely like to pursue this. I hope you feel the same way."

Like they were being pulled by the force of a magnet, Candice's eyes were drawn back to

Stuart's. A nod accompanied her words. "I'd like that too."

Stuart smiled his approval and then said, "Until then, I have something for you."

Candice watched in anticipation as he reached inside his suit jacket and pulled out a white gift box. It looked like the kind of box that would be used to house earrings. Having not bought him anything, Candice suddenly felt self-conscious and thoughtless.

"It's nothing extravagant," Stuart said when she stared at the case, not reaching to accept it, "but it's very meaningful. Here, take it."

Candice hoped he couldn't see the slight trembling of her hands as she received his token. When she opened the box, she didn't exactly know what she was looking at, but she felt oddly overwhelmed.

As Stuart removed the object from its casing, he explained. "While most men who'd had the honor and pleasure of spending such an awesome day with such an amazing woman would have probably presented you with a bracelet or maybe a nice pair of earrings, I wanted to give you this."

He grabbed Candice's unoccupied hand and opened it, placing his presentation in her *palm and then manually closing her fingers around it. "This is the key to my den," he explained. "Remember, I told you that, of all the rooms in my house, my den was my favorite. It's the heart of my home. So, in essence, I've just given you the key to my heart. Handle it with care, okay?"*

At his words, Candice tightened her grip on the silver key and brought her closed fist to her chest. A tear escaped from both her eyes, but Stuart's thumbs stopped them before they could run the distance of her cheeks. Then, in a move even more unexpected, he brought his lips to hers and caressed them with a brief, gentle kiss before stepping away.

Candice swallowed, unable to move, unable to find any words to say.

"Next time, it's my turn," he said, licking his lips as though searching for lingering residue of what he'd sampled. "I'll look at my calendar and make plans to fly up to New York to see you. I'll do that real soon. I promise."

Candice swallowed again. This time twice.

"Good-bye, Candice Powell. See you online."

"Bye, Stuart," she whispered.

Candice enjoyed the view as he backed away from her and then turned to make the lonely trip back to the parking deck where he'd left his vehicle. Stuart looked back only

*once, to wave, before he rounded the corner
that would put him out of sight.*

The blaring sounds of Candice's telephone
brought her back to the reality that she was no
longer standing outside the entrance doors of
Hartsfield-Jackson. But the tears tickling her
jaw line were very real. She wiped them away
with her hands and reached for the phone,
thinking it would most likely be the familiar
voice of one of her parents calling for a report
on her weekend date.

"Hello?"

"Candice. How are you?"

It was a familiar voice all right, but not one
that belonged to either of her parents. Candice
sighed and used the arm of her couch as a
chair. "I'm fine, Cornell. How are you?"

"I'm blessed, praise the Lord," the minister
said. "I just wanted to call and check on you.
I saw you today at school, but I didn't get a
chance to speak to you. I wanted to tell you
that I missed you at church yesterday. It's not
like you to miss Sunday morning service, so I
was wondering if you were feeling well over
the weekend."

"I appreciate your concern, Cornell, but I'm
doing fine. I just had some other matters to

take care of yesterday, so I couldn't make it to church."

"Oh?" he pried. "Did you have to go out of town?"

"No," Candice said before she could stop herself. "No," she repeated, "I didn't go out of town. I just had some local business to attend to."

"I see," Cornell, said. He stalled, like he was waiting for her to explain further.

"Listen, Cornell; thanks for calling, but I've just walked in the house, and I need to get some things done. I'll be in service this coming Sunday."

"No chance I can see you before then?"

Candice bit her lip. Cornell Pratt was such a nice man and no doubt, many women would be flattered by his persistent advances. Candice wished he would find one who was. "Aside from passing one another in the school halls, I doubt it, Cornell. My classes are testing this week, and so are yours. Both of us have a ton of work to do."

"True," he replied, not sounding a bit discouraged. "I'll see you throughout the week, I'm sure."

After hearing Cornell hang up, Candice's shoulders slumped through a heavy exhale.

Her mind instantly went back to Stuart as she placed the phone on its cradle. His closing words were haunting her.

"I'll look at my calendar and make plans to fly up to New York to see you."

She'd been lucky enough to talk him out of paying for her flight ticket to Atlanta and to convince him not to walk her through the airport to the security checkpoint. But Candice knew that she'd need a whole lot more than luck to talk him out of flying to New York. But, somehow, she knew she had to think of something.

Chapter Fourteen

Twenty minutes had passed since their meals had been served, and most of the lively chatter at the table had been replaced by the popping sounds of crab legs being snapped by hungry men. Crabby D's, where the brothers had gathered to enjoy a casual meal, was a split-level seafood eatery that had recently relocated to the corner of Miller Road and Snapfinger Woods Drive in nearby Decatur. The empty tables around them on the upper floor proved that Crabby D's hadn't yet become the most popular seafood restaurant in the area. It was only a matter of time though. It had some of the best snow crab legs that money could buy.

"So, what's new with you guys?" Hunter asked. "Kwame, aren't you closing on your house soon?"

Nodding, Kwame said, "Yep. I'll be closing on the new house in just a few weeks. Maybe as soon as June first. Reverend Tides has already agreed to lay hands on it before I move in."

"Well, strap on your seatbelt, and secure your dreadlocks real good," Jerome teased, "'cause when Dad prays over a house, he *prays* over a house. When I moved into my apartment, he slung so much blessed oil that it was days before I could get that olive oil smell out of my crib."

The men laughed heartily.

"I'm being honored in a few weeks. Did I tell you?" Peter announced while using his napkin to wipe away globs of butter that had built up on his hands during the feast. "Me, Jan, and Kyla, are going to fly out to D.C. for a special recognition during a Memorial Day celebration there."

"That's great, Pete," Jerome said amidst congratulatory words from the others. A grin preceded his next words. "Is your mother-in-law going with you?"

"Nope. Ms. Leona thinks it's a sin to fly, so she won't be coming along." Pete laughed and concluded with, "Thank God for her righteous ignorance, 'cause I didn't want her there anyway."

"So, this is going to be like a mini reunion for you and the guys, huh?" Hunter said. "Are both the others gonna be there? Even the sick one?"

"Yeah." It was evident that Peter was looking forward to it. "The sick one—Louis Malloy—he's still undergoing treatment for post traumatic stress, but I hear he's much better now. And I talked to Flex today," he added, referring to a fellow marine he had bonded with and brought to Christ during the seven days they'd been prisoners of war in Iraq. "You know he's been floating on air since getting his family back in the church. His wife and son will be there too. It'll be our first time seeing each other since shortly after we were all rescued. And this will be the first time that our families will meet."

Jerome dipped his crab meat in the butter sauce. "Didn't I hear you say once before that Flex was thinking of reenlisting even though he was free to get out after the Iraq incident?"

Peter chuckled. "Yep, and he did. That Flex is a brave one. He's in the Marine Forces Reserve now."

Kwame shook his head slowly. "Braver than me, that's for darn sure. I'm not the least bit ashamed to say I wouldn't have been that brave."

Jerome answered with a grunt. "Man, that ain't brave, that's just crazy. Ain't that much bravery in the world."

Peter shook his head. "Nah, Flex isn't crazy. Flex is a marine."

"Well, you know they say marines are crazy," Jerome muttered.

"*They* don't know what they're talking about." Peter's tone was defensive. "Marines are trained to either survive or fight to the death. Marines are taught to defend at all costs. They're taught to be fearless and courageous. Flex was taught how to deal with the likes of terrorists."

"So were you," Hunter pointed out, "but you got out. Are you saying that you aren't brave?"

Peter shook his head. "Our situations were different. My family had fallen apart, and while I was on death row in that Iraqi prison, I thought I'd die without ever having a chance to put it back together again. Flex's home life was good. He hadn't screwed things up with his wife and kid. Had he been killed, at least he would have died having peace with God *and* his family. That wouldn't have been my testimony. And I promised God that if He allowed me to live and make it back to Jan and Kyla, they would become my primary focus. I miss active military life but I couldn't make good on that promise as long as I had to answer to Uncle Sam. I had to put things in perspective and decide what was most important to me."

"I heard that," Hunter said. "The right woman will make you put everything on the line, won't she?"

"Reminiscing about the time you almost lost your livelihood trying to impress my baby sister, are you?" Jerome mocked, lifting his glass to his lips for a sip.

"Shut up and wipe that sliver of meat off your cheek, crab face," Hunter said.

"Crab face?" Stuart burst into laughter. "You couldn't think of a more mature name to call him than that?"

"And speaking of women," Hunter said, looking directly at Stuart. "It's been three days since your lady friend left town. When are you planning to give us an update?"

"Yeah, Stu," Jerome chided. "Maybe now that somebody else is asking other than me, you'll give a better response than, 'We'll talk about it later.'"

Stuart looked at his best friend and narrowed his eyes. "You were always asking at the wrong time, Jerome. Every time you called to ask, it was just after a time when I'd gotten an earful from Kenyatta about her need to know everything about Candice."

"So, why are you being so secretive about Miss Candy?" Jerome teased.

"I'm not being secretive." Stuart cracked his last crab leg. "And don't call her Candy. She made it clear that she didn't like that nickname."

"So, are you gonna tell us or not?" It was Kwame's turn to probe.

Stuart smiled. He had wanted to talk about the events of last Saturday for days. Until now, the perfect time and place never lined up. But now, at the table he shared with his most trusted confidants in the near empty restaurant, seemed ideal. After a shrug that he tried to make appear as nonchalant as possible, Stuart said, "What do you want to know?"

"What was she like, man?" Hunter said. "I mean, our sons are good friends, so I won't pretend that Tyler didn't already tell Malik that this girl was pretty hot."

"Oh, he said that, did he?" Stuart interrupted.

"Those words exactly," Hunter reported. "So, I know she was easy on the eyes. But how was her personality? I mean, you met this sister on the Internet, man. You had to be holding your breath in preparation for just about anything."

With hands that had just been sanitized by a Wet Ones, Stuart reached into his pocket and pulled out his wallet. From it, he slid the photo of Candice that he'd printed off her webpage on the dating site. His quality color printer almost made the copy look as good as an original. Finding a clean spot in the middle of the table, Stuart gently placed the picture there for public viewing.

Peter whistled.

"Not bad," Kwame remarked. "Not bad at all."

Jerome peered closer. "If her bottom half is as tight as her top half, you've got yourself a winner, Stu."

Hunter picked up the picture and admired it further before handing it back to Stuart. "It's clear that you weren't disappointed with what you saw, but did it ever occur to you that you could have been?"

"Well, yeah, I'll admit that I was a little nervous at first. I wasn't worried about what she'd look like, exactly. I mean, in spite of your Jamie Foxx in a wig incident, I was pretty certain that the photo on Candice's site was her."

"And it was, obviously," Kwame said.

"Yeah, it was. She's even prettier in person." Stuart grinned and then put the photo away. "She fooled me a little bit on the rest of the description, though. I was expecting a short, heavyset girl, and she ended up being a little bit taller and a whole lot thinner than I pictured."

"And that's a bad thing?" Peter asked.

"No, not bad, just different than her online description. I was very pleased with who she was. Not just outside, but on the inside too. Candice is a very nice lady. She's smart, beautiful—"

"Saved?"

Jerome looked at Hunter and laughed. "Man, you sound like my daddy. That's exactly what he would have said."

"Well, that's important," Hunter insisted.

"I agree," Stuart added. "Yes, she's saved, and she has an awesome testimony, really. She grew up in a family that never prayed, never read the Bible, never went to church—nothing. But even with roots like that, she managed to find Christ."

"That's wonderful, man," Hunter said. "I'm getting good vibes on this one."

Hunter's words made Stuart smile. "So did I."

"So, where'd you go? What did you do?" Peter said. "Give us details."

All too happy to accommodate, Stuart said, "Well, as you know, she met Tyler first. They didn't talk too much on the ride from the airport, but they seemed to click right away. She complimented me on raising him well, and I can't tell you how many times Tyler told me that he liked Candice."

"This was Friday, right?" Kwame seemed to want to rush Stuart along.

"Tyler and Candice met on Friday, yeah," Stuart said. "It was late, and she was tired, so we just took her to her hotel and called it a night. Saturday, it was just me and her. We went to breakfast, lunch and dinner, saw a movie, went shopping, drove around the city looking at some historical sites, spent some time at my place—"

"Spent some time at your place?" the quartet echoed in unison.

"Yeah, what's wrong with that?" Stuart challenged, looking at each of them one at a time. "We had some time to kill after the movie, and we had been wearing the same clothes since breakfast. We needed to freshen up and change clothes for dinner."

"You both were supposed to come to my place for that," Hunter reminded him.

Stuart readjusted his seating position and said, "We weren't *supposed* to do it. You just extended the invitation. I appreciate that, but I decided to take her to my house instead."

"So, y'all changed clothes in the same house?" Jerome's normal tenor voice had reached a high alto.

"Oh, grow up," Stuart said, waving his hand in Jerome's direction. "Just 'cause *you* can't change clothes in the same house with a woman without acting like an idiot doesn't mean I can't. And remind me to never let my sister spend a whole day with you."

"So you changed clothes and went to the movies?" Hunter said.

"Yeah, but let's back it up a little," Stuart said. He continued feeding his brothers the details of how he'd given Candice a personal tour of the house, conveniently leaving out the tender moment they shared on the couch.

"Wait, wait, wait." Jerome's eyes grew wide as he held up one hand to stop Stuart in the middle of his recall. "Let me get this straight.

You took this girl into The Lyons Den? This must be serious."

Stuart had told Jerome things about The Lyons Den that the other men weren't privy to. He shot a glare of warning at Jerome and then continued. "Like I said, I took her through the whole house. Kenyatta wasn't home, so I figured the time was right. I could do it without her following us around, asking Candice all kinds of crazy questions."

"Well, she sounds like a nice lady," Peter said. "You think you'll see her again?"

"Definitely," Stuart said without a second thought. "I'm already looking into taking a long weekend and flying out that way."

"So, give it to us straight," Hunter said, leaning forward on his elbows. "Do you think this could be long-term? I mean, seriously, man. We're all too old to be playing games, here. Like Trix, the boyfriend-girlfriend thing is for kids. When a mature man reaches our age bracket, he's generally looking to meet a woman he sees as someone he can settle down with. Is Candice that kind of woman?"

Stuart thought over Hunter's words and then began a slow nod of his head. "Yes. Yes, she is."

Peter tapped his fingers on the table in front of him, apparently a move to call attention to himself. When he had the floor, he asked, "After only spending one Saturday with her, you think you know her well enough to draw that conclusion?"

"Obviously, since he took her in the den," Jerome mumbled.

"What's the big deal about her seeing his den?" Kwame asked.

Stuart jumped in. "Nothing."

Not seeming to get the silent message that his best friend wasn't particular about having to explain the topic, Jerome said, "It ain't just a den, man, it's *The Lyons Den*."

"And?" Kwame motioned for a deeper explanation.

"Wait," Hunter said, holding up one hand. "We are talking about an actual den, right? I mean, The Lyons Den isn't a code name for . . . *something else* of yours that you showed this girl, is it?"

A moment of silence passed before Stuart grasped the full meaning of Hunter's words. When it registered, he nearly choked on the water he'd been sipping from his straw. When he was able to regroup, Stuart's brows furrowed.

"Are you crazy? I can't even believe you asked that."

"Well, Jerome's acting all stupid," Hunter said. "I just thought there was something he knew that we didn't."

Peter agreed. "I know, right?"

Jerome gave Peter a matter-of-fact look. "Have you ever seen Stu's den?"

"Actually, no, I haven't. But, all things considered, I'm the new kid on the block. I've only been in Atlanta for a little over a year, and I've only been to Stuart's house three or four times, and on no occasion did I make it past his living room."

Jerome shot his eyes between Hunter to Kwame. "The two of you have known him for a while. Have either of you seen his den?"

The men exchanged glances before answering with a quiet synchronized shaking of their heads from side to side.

"But then again, we aren't his self-proclaimed best friend," Hunter reasoned. "It would make sense that you might have been in parts of his house that we haven't."

Jerome placed both his elbows on the table, on either side of his empty plate, and leaned in closer to Hunter. "Now, ask me if I've ever seen it?"

Hunter grimaced. "Why? You want to rub it in our faces that you've seen Stuart's den and we haven't? It ain't like we're gonna be jealous."

"Ask me," Jerome urged. "Just ask me."

Hunter sighed, but obeyed anyway. "Have you seen Stuart's den, Jerome?"

"As a matter of fact, no."

Stuart felt all eyes turn toward him. He took several swallows of water, knowing that he only had a few seconds to irrigate his throat in preparation to answer the next question.

"What's the big deal about the den, Stu?" Hunter inquired.

One last glare was aimed toward Jerome before Stuart answered. "There is no big deal. Crab face here is making way more out of it than it is."

"Hey!" Jerome warned, simultaneously wiping his face for more signs of residue.

Stuart continued. "It's just a room in the house that serves several special purposes for me."

"Like what?" Peter asked.

"I go there to unwind sometimes after a particularly stressful day at work," Stuart began. "My den is where I go to get away from Kenyatta on those days when she starts to wear on my nerves. I go there to get away from Tyler too. They both know that when I'm in the den, it means I'm off limits. I also often go there to pray," Stuart added. "For some reason I feel closer to God when I pray in my den. You with me? I feel like my prayers get through to heaven quicker and they get answered a little faster when I send them up from my den."

"That's pretty deep, bruh," Kwame stated.

"So, you actually really believe that nobody goes in that area when you're not at home?" Peter asked.

Jerome released a short laugh. "Kenyatta claims she's never been in there, but as nosey as your sister is, I find that hard to believe. I think she just won't admit it to me 'cause she thinks I'll slip up and tell you."

"No, she's never been in it." Stuart spoke with confidence. "She's seen it from the doorway a time or two when she just happened to be nearby when I opened the door, but she's never been in there. I keep it locked, and she doesn't have a key."

"So, that's why Jerome says this Candice must be special," Hunter reasoned. "You haven't allowed family or friends in there, but you've allowed Candice."

"See what I mean?" Jerome stated. "Nobody has a key to this space but him, and the first person he lets in is Candice.

Before stating his next revelation, Stuart sat back in his chair and briefly rubbed his full stomach. "Actually, Tyler has a spare key that can be used for emergency purposes only. He's been inside the den a few times, but never without my permission. Other than him, Candice is the only one who's had the privilege of a full tour of The Lyons Den."

"The Lyons Den," Hunter repeated. "I like that. It's almost as cool as the name I gave my horse breeding business."

"Yeah," Kwame said, grinning. "I always get a kick out of saying, 'in Greene Pastures' when people ask me where I go to ride horses."

"And what about my stint in Iraq?" Peter offered with a smile of his own. "You know, Flex and Colonel Goodman, my commanding officer, named it Battle of Jericho."

"Hey, Kwame," Jerome called. "We need to do something so that we can get named after some great moment in biblical history."

"Yeah," Kwame agreed, tapping his chin thought-fully.

Hunter repositioned himself in his seat. "Well, since both of you have served time in the big house and so did Paul and Silas, that might be a biblical reference you can relate to."

"Ha, ha, ha," Kwame mimicked, "why don't y'all call up TV One and see if they're interested in casting the three of you in an African-American version of *The Three Stooges*?"

"Man, we're your friends," Stuart said, wiping his eyes with a napkin. "We're not laughing at you, we're laughing *with* you."

"You see either one of us laughing?" Kwame pointed to himself and then to Jerome.

"And speaking of friends," Jerome said over the residual snickering, "just when was one of my *friends* gonna tell me that I died last Sunday?"

The laughter ceased, and the rest of the world seemed to follow its lead.

Jerome sat back, looked at each one of the men, and then folded his arms across his chest. "Seems to me that a better biblical reference for me would be the story of Lazarus. What do you guys think?"

Chapter Fifteen

"You had to do what?" Stuart looked at Chiefs Overstreet and Reinhart as though both men had lost their minds. For Stuart, the past few days since Saturday had been some of the happiest in recent years, and the past few nights since that time had been some of the most restful. Now, with six words, Chief Reinhart was threatening to erase all of the good from the past six days.

"We had to let him go." Chief Reinhart repeated the words as though Stuart's question wasn't rhetorical and he really hadn't heard him the first time.

"When did—? How could—? Why would—?" Stuart babbled. "I thought we had the evidence we needed to charge him."

"No, Lyons," Deputy Chief Overstreet said. "We had enough to justify our need to pick him up and hold him for questioning. But that was just circumstantial evidence. We hoped it would lead us to concrete evidence to indict him, but that didn't happen. His alibi panned out, and we couldn't continue to hold him just because we still had our personal doubts. He was released on his own accord this morning."

"So you admit it," Stuart said, pulling up on his belt and tucking his starched shirt deeper in his pants. "You do believe Joe is the one that's been doing all this."

"He's not been personally doing it," Chief Reinhart said. "But there's still a possibility that he could have had it done. Truth is, it doesn't matter what we believe. We need proof."

"But when you guys picked him up, Sergeant Bowden said that Joe had missed work on the same Monday that the crime was carried out. He was a prime suspect. Why couldn't he have done it?"

Before answering, Chief Reinhart sipped from a steaming cup of coffee, taking special care not to burn his tongue. "Like Chief Overstreet said, our prime suspect, as you call him, had an alibi to justify his whereabouts. We checked it out, and it's legit. The guy definitely has a chip on his shoulder. He confessed to not being your biggest fan and even admitted to being ticked off that his ex-wife walked out on him. But there's no crime in either of those things. You know the law, Lieutenant Lyons. If we're going to hold him, we need substantiated proof that he had something to do with the constant threats and the defacing of official government property. We don't have that, so we had to let him go."

"What about the fact that I didn't receive one letter or a single threat of any kind from the infamous Dr. A.H. Satan while Joe was in custody?" Stuart was grasping at straws. He knew what the response was going to be before he even posed the question.

"Mr. King was held for five days, Lieutenant," Chief Overstreet said, placing his own coffee mug on the table in the precinct conference room where they talked. "Even before we picked up him up, there had been times that you'd gone for a five-day stretch, and sometimes longer, without being hounded. Based on that alone, the fact that five days passed without a threat during the time the suspect was in custody could easily be coincidental. It wouldn't stand up in any court of law and you know it."

Stuart pounded the side of his fist against the wall nearest him. "So, what you're telling me is that we're back at square one."

"Basically," Chief Reinhart said. "But whoever this guy is, he isn't going to get away."

"What do you mean, whoever this guy is, Chief? It's Joseph King. I know it, you know it, and Joe knows it."

"I'm as sure as you are that he has something to do with this," Chief Reinhart said, clearly stating his suspicions for the first time. "But until we get the proof we need, he's free to go back to Jacksonville, Florida and resume life."

"So, he can resume his life, but I can't resume mine." Stuart's annoyance resonated in his words.

"He's not going to get away with it, Lieutenant," Chief Overstreet promised. "We're going to be watching him closely, especially for the next few weeks. We've got friends on the force in Jacksonville who'll do it for us. If he so much as throws a chewing gum wrapper out of his car window on a freeway, we'll have him pulled over and ordered to pay the stiffest fine the law allows. If he can't pay it, he'll serve time. Anything we can do to keep him confined until we can get the proof we need, we'll do it."

Chief Reinhart nodded in agreement. "He's smart, but he's not that smart. No matter how carefully he has planned out his revenge against you, there has to be some holes in the strategy. If there's an accomplice here in Atlanta acting on his behalf, he'll slip up soon enough. And when he does, he won't take the fall by himself. They rarely do. I don't care how much hush money Mr. King has paid him or what kind of vow of secrecy he's taken. By the time we finish with him, he'll be singing like Andrea Bocelli."

Andrea Bocelli? In Stuart's neighborhood, that slot in a sentence was always filled with artists whose first names were the only ones needed—like Usher, Luther or Patty.

"I'm sorry we couldn't give you better news on a Friday morning so that your week could end on a high note," Chief Overstreet said, adding a pat on Stuart's shoulder for emphasis.

"Yeah, me too." Stuart stared at the white wall in front of him.

"If you want some police protection, or if you want us to set up surveillance at your home, just let us know," Chief Reinhart added as both men began walking toward the door.

Stuart hoped to God that it didn't come to that. "Thanks, Chief." He turned to face both of them. "I appreciate everything that's being done."

The room door opened behind Chief Overstreet's pull. "Mark my words, Lyons. We'll get him." He uttered a vulgarity to describe the culprit, and then added, "Nobody messes with one of our own and gets away with it for too long."

The men left the door open when they made their exits, and for a short while Stuart stared into the adjacent hallway, looking at nothing in particular. Thoughts crammed his brain as he pulled out a chair from the conference room table and sat. Stuart needed to get to his desk and catch up on some paperwork, but right now, he was too preoccupied to focus.

Who could be doing this? The question echoed through his head. It simply had to be Joe. There was no one else to suspect. Chief Overstreet and Chief Reinhart were right. Joe may not be the one carrying out the deeds, but his hands were dirty. No doubt about it.

A tap at the door broke Stuart's train of thought.

"Got a minute, Lieutenant?" Allen asked.

Stuart sat back in his chair. "Yeah. Come on in."

When Sergeant Bowden walked inside the room, he closed the door behind him. Stuart eyed him as he rounded the table and then plopped heavily in the chair directly across from him. Anguish could be seen on Allen's face before he spoke; and when he began talking, the same distress could be heard in his voice.

"I'm sorry, Stu. I was sure that the key would be thrown away once we picked him up. I was shocked to hear that, that creep got released."

"Yeah," Stuart said, rubbing his face with his hands. The reaction was more out of frustration than anything else. "Chief said he was released this morning."

Allen slapped the table top with his palm and swore. "I just don't get it," he barked. "This guy is guilty. I know he is."

"Yeah, well, a guilty man with no evidence is a guilty man roaming the streets." Stuart tried to sound calm, like he really believed the law book was playing fair, but on the inside, he was fuming. The longer he stayed on the force, the more he understood why policemen sometimes planted evidence on people just to be able to make a legal arrest. When blatantly guilty people got away with crimes, sometimes the unlawful setups didn't seem so bad. If it resulted in getting a bad guy off the streets, what was the harm? "We couldn't hold him without evidence," he concluded despite his thoughts.

"I know," Allen said. "This sucks."

Seconds passed with only silence talking. The scraping sounds of Allen's chair against the floor snapped the quietness.

"I'm about to go out on patrol. You want to ride along? It'll give you the opportunity to get some fresh air. I know with the news you got, this precinct is smothering you."

It really was, but Stuart had work of his own to do. He couldn't let the pressure get the best of him. "Thanks, Allen, but I need to stick close to my desk today. I'll be all right."

Allen nodded quietly and started for the door. He stopped in mid-stride and turned to look at Stuart.

Stuart didn't return his gaze, but he could feel Allen's eyes on him.

"Listen, Stu. I have a friend who is in real estate—"

"Don't start with that nonsense, Allen." Stuart wasn't in the mood to talk about Shelton Heights, the man, nor Shelton Heights, the community.

"I'm just saying—"

"That'll be all, Sergeant Bowden." Stuart's use of Allen's title was intentional. He knew if he pulled rank, it would put an immediate stop

to the conversation that Allen was determined
to have.

"Yes, sir."

It worked.

As Allen finished his trek to the door and then
opened it, Stuart's voice stopped him again.

"Sergeant?"

Allen turned to face him again. "Yes?"

"Do me a favor, will you?"

"Sure, Lieutenant. What is it?"

"While you're out on patrol, swing by the
school and canvas that area for me."

Allen tilted his head to the side. "Redan
Middle School?"

"Yeah," Stuart said. He stood, walked to the
door, closed it shut and then turned toward
Allen. "Joe was just released a few hours ago,
and he may or may not have left the area yet.
I can take care of myself, but I just need to be
sure he's not lurking around my son."

"Right," Allen said with a nod. "I know what
he looks like. If I see him anywhere even near
the school grounds, I'll call you right away."

"No." Stuart locked eyes Allen. "Shoot to kill
first. Then call me."

Allen straightened his neck as though he
was a serviceman coming to complete atten-

tion. Then he eased his hand to his holster and stroked it before nodding silently and allowing his arm to again rest by his side. "I gotcha covered, Lieutenant."

"And I've got you covered," Stuart promised, knowing that Allen needed no further explanation.

"I'll find an inconspicuous area near there to park my car, and I'll survey that area for about an hour or so while I'm out. Before coming back here, I'll also drive by your house, just to be sure."

"'Preciate it," Stuart said.

"No problem, Lieutenant. I'll check back with you later."

With Allen gone, Stuart was alone again. He felt a sharp pang in his side and wondered if the fingers of God had just pinched him—a punishment for the direct order he'd given his subordinate, and the indirect promise he'd made to make sure Allen wouldn't be disciplined for carrying it out. The pain, though momentary, was nearly unbearable, and he had to ease back to his chair to find relief. Stuart massaged the right side of his body and then propped his elbows on the table and buried his face in his hands. He wanted to pray and ask God for forgiveness for his act of anger, but

Stuart knew that his heart wouldn't have been in the apology. At the moment, nothing would satisfy him more than to receive a call from Allen saying he'd seen Joe prowling near the school grounds and had blown his head off.

When Stuart's cell phone rang, he bounced from his chair, his heart pounding. It was too soon. There hadn't been enough time for Allen to have even driven out of the police station parking lot yet, let alone enough time for him to have driven to the school. The realization that it was his personal cell ringing and not the one he used for business purposes helped to steady Stuart's hand as he pulled the phone out of his pocket. The caller ID showed the number as private. It had to be Candice.

"Stuart Lyons."

"Well, good morning, Mr. Lyons."

Her voice sounded like music to his ears.

"It is now." Stuart felt the tension of the morning drain from his body, being replaced by a new and far more pleasant kind of stimulation.

"Why'd you say it like that? Did your day get off to a bad start or something?"

Stuart needed to get to work, but he needed to talk to Candice, too. "You could say that," he confessed. "They released Joe this morning."

"Who?"

"Joseph King. My former brother-in-law."

Candice's gasp could be heard through the telephone. "Not the guy who was stalking you?"

"Yeah. That's the one."

"They've released him already? But, why?"

Stuart sank back down into the chair. "Not enough evidence to hold him."

"You're kidding."

"I wish I was." Stuart closed his eyes and used his thumb and middle finger to rub them. "They thought for sure we'd be able to nail him, but other than him missing work the same day my cruiser was vandalized, they had nothing. Makes me want to take the law into my own hands and take care of that idiot myself."

"You can't do that, Stuart. I mean, I know you're upset about this, and so am I, but if they couldn't get the evidence they needed, maybe there's a reason for that."

"What are you saying?"

"I'm saying maybe they couldn't find the evidence because there is none. Maybe this guy is innocent after all."

Stuart's laugh was short and dry. "Innocent? Not hardly. Joe's a jerk."

"He might be a jerk, but that doesn't make him a stalker," Candice said. "You don't know for certain that he did this, and if he's been investigated and the police haven't found anything, then maybe that means—"

"That don't mean *jack*," Stuart cut in. His voice was sharper than he intended for it to be, but then again, he didn't expect Candice to take Joe's side. "Guilty people fall through the cracks all the time in this business, Candice. There are too many arrows pointing to Joe. He's guilty; we just weren't able to pin him down."

Her voice remained calm in spite of Stuart's. "I'm not saying he's not guilty. But until you can prove it—"

"What?" Stuart challenged, cutting her off for the second time. "What are you saying? Until he does something that clearly shows him as the guilty party, I should leave him alone? Is that what you're saying?" Stuart didn't give her a chance to respond before he spoke again. "What do you suggest I allow him to do, Candice? Hurt my kid? Am I supposed to stand around and wait for him to take out his anger for me on Tyler and then while my son is laid up in the hospital or being buried six feet under, I can then find satisfaction in the fact that *now* we can put him in jail for good? Is that what you're saying?"

The line was dead silent for several moments, and Stuart was starting to believe that Candice had hung up on him during his rant. He was just about to call out her name when she responded.

"This is clearly not a good time," she said. Her voice was a whisper compared to the elevation of Stuart's during his tirade. "I'm gonna go. My next class will be starting shortly."

"Yeah," Stuart said. "You do that."

When he heard the disconnection on the other end, Stuart continued to hold the cell phone to his ear. Closing his eyes, he felt the throbbing of his temples that was rhythmically synchronized with the hammering of his heart. He couldn't believe he'd just taken out his frustrations on the woman he loved.

Love. There it was. It was the first time he'd fully admitted to himself that he loved Candice. Stuart pulled the phone from his ear and immediately pressed the button to find his address book. Then he remembered. He didn't have Candice's phone number. He couldn't call her back to apologize. Not now. Not ever. If at some point, she didn't call him, he'd just ruined the best thing that had happened to him in a long time. And after his little telephone tantrum, Stuart couldn't blame her one bit if she didn't call.

Standing, Stuart forcefully kicked his chair under that table. If he could have, he would have kicked himself in the rear instead. Through clinched teeth, he said, "What an absolutely *marvelous* morning this had turned out to be!"

Chapter Sixteen

"Our pizza's here," Ingrid announced as she walked into Jade's office, carrying the large flat box, filling the room with the smell of pepperoni, ham and cheese. She had just locked the front door and put up the "Out To Lunch" sign to give them the hour of privacy they'd need.

"Great." Jade immediately began clearing her desk to make room for the fresh baked delivery.

Ingrid laughed when Jade sped through a grace that was barely comprehensible and then opened the top of the box to indulge. "Jade, girl, I remember a time when you wouldn't touch pizza," she said as she reached for a slice of her own. "Moving to Georgia sure did change you. When we were in Virginia, you acted like eating one slice of pizza was a sin that came with an automatic ten-pound punishment."

Jade laughed. "A moment on the lips, a life-time on the hips."

"Yep," Ingrid said through her chewing. "That's what you used to say. But this is the fourth time in the last three weeks that we've eaten pizza for lunch. I guess everything changes once you get a good man, huh? You fight to keep your figure to catch their attention, and then once you've got them, you can ease up on the deprivation."

Jade pulled her food away from her lips and looked at Ingrid. "What are you saying? Are you saying I've gotten fat since I've been married?"

Ingrid huffed. "Oh, yeah, Jade, you're just a common beach whale now." She rolled her eyes and continued. "Girl, you know you haven't gained any weight since you've been married. Not yet, anyway. A few more dates with Big Daddy, a.k.a. Papa John's, and both of us are gonna blow up. And I haven't gotten my man yet, so I can't be trying to keep up with you."

Jade placed her portion of uneaten pizza on the napkin in front of her. "Can I tell you a secret with your promise to keep it to yourself for now?"

"Girl, yeah," Ingrid said, her native New York accent heavily lacing her words. She felt a ripple of worry at Jade's sudden change of expression. "You know you can tell me anything, girl, and you know it stays right here. What is it? Did Kenyatta say something bad about me? She's planning to shoot me, isn't she?"

Jade laughed and picked up a napkin to wipe her hands. "How many times do I have to tell you that Kenyatta is all talk? I can't believe you actually think she's capable of shooting somebody."

"And you don't?" Ingrid watched Jade's face as she reassessed the question. "Uh-huh," Ingrid mumbled. "You know just as well as I do that, that girl is a murder in the making."

"No, she's not," Jade defended. "She's a bit much at times, I agree. But underneath that no-nonsense exterior, I think she's all heart."

"All heart? Well, she ought to get an Oscar, a Tony *and* a Golden Globe for the way she so successfully hides her soft side." Ingrid's words were saturated with sarcasm.

Jade said, "Kenyatta's just one of those girls who doesn't take a lot of flack, that's all. She's a lot like you when you think about it. That's probably why the two of you don't get along so well. You're too much alike."

"In what way?" Ingrid said, clearly offended by the comparison. "Other than the fact that we both apparently have the same taste in men, I don't see a lick of likeness between us."

"Speaking of which," Jade said, grinning. "How's the battle of the broads coming along?"

"There is no battle of the broads," Ingrid said. "Not anymore, anyway. I gave up."

"You what?"

She saw the look of shock on Jade's face. "I gave up. Remember that talk you and I had a couple of weeks ago where you reminded me that, according to God's Word, a man was supposed to find a wife and not the other way around?"

"I remember." Jade picked up her pizza and began eating again, but never took her eyes off of Ingrid.

"Well, I did some thinking and some praying and decided that I was done chasing your brother. I haven't called him in almost two weeks now."

"Wow," Jade said. "I don't even know what to say. That's quite a change. Good for you, Ingrid."

Shaking her head from side to side, Ingrid's doubt was clear. "I don't know if it's good or not. I was hoping that you already knew about this, but I see you didn't."

"How would I have known?" Jade managed to say through a mouth full of food. "You didn't tell me until now."

"Yeah, but if Jerome had missed me enough, I'm sure he would have mentioned to you by now that he hadn't heard from me." Ingrid didn't even try to hide her disappointment. "I really like Jerome, Jade. I like everything about him, from the way he looks, to the way he acts, to the way he talks, to the way he dresses, to the way—"

"Everything," Jade said. "I get it."

"No, you don't, Jade." Ingrid migrated away from the desk and settled on the leather couch that sat in the middle of the office. Her lying down on it was almost involuntary. It just seemed like the right thing to do. "All of that is just the physical stuff," she added. "Shallow stuff, really, when you think about it." Ingrid closed her eyes to block out the overhead lights that were usually turned off during an actual session. "My attraction to him runs a lot deeper than that."

"How so?" Jade asked. The muffled sounds of her words let Ingrid know that she was still eating.

"I like his testimony, you know what I mean?"

"Where God has brought him from," Jade offered.

"Yeah. But not only where God has brought him from, but where I know God is going to take him."

"Daddy is always saying that Jerome has a special calling on his life. And after last Sunday, Mother has been saying the same."

Ingrid sat up straight and faced Jade. "Girl, if he hadn't come back to us Sunday, I would have died along with him."

"He scared all of us, Ingrid," Jade said after turning up her cup of water for a brief drink.

"But I wasn't just scared, I was terrified." Unexpected warm tears raced quietly down Ingrid's face at the remembrance of it all. "When Reverend Tides was stretched out on top of Jerome, praying, and all the ministerial staff and then the medical staff was called for assistance, I thought I was gonna breathe my last breath. The thick crowd prevented me from being able to see Jerome, but I heard people saying he was dead." Ingrid's voice cracked, and she used her hand to whisk away the tears that had pooled at her chin. "When I heard that, my chest started tightening up, and I felt the air being squeezed out of my lungs. If Jerome had died, Reverend Tides would have had to preach back-to-back funerals."

Ingrid pulled Kleenex from the box that always sat on the table beside the sofa and dabbed at her face. She hadn't intended to say all of that, and she certainly didn't expect to cry, but her emotions had a mind of their own. Ingrid saw Jade approaching her and felt the movement of the couch when she sat beside her.

"Ingrid, I'm going to ask you something, and I want you to be completely honest with me."

"Okay. What?" She wadded the tissue in her hand and looked at Jade.

"Are you in love with my brother?"

Ingrid's eyes blinked in rapid succession. "Why would you ask me that?"

"Well, for starters, you're a mess. Look at you over here weeping over a hypothetical situation. Jerome is fine. Like I said, we all had a scare, but God restored him and he's fine now. And secondly, there is only one man in my life who I would say if he died I'd want to die too, and that's Hunter. My husband. The man who shares my heart, my life, and my bed. The man I'm in love with. Not only are you and Jerome not married, but you're not intimately involved. Yet, you're ready to keel over if anything happens to him. Dying is not something a girl would want to do for just any man, Ingrid. Now, I'll ask you again. Are you in love with my brother?"

Ingrid's sights dropped to her clasped hands. "I've never felt for another man what I feel for him. And if wanting to die just by reason of his death means that I'm in love with him, then I guess I am."

"Whoa," Jade said after taking a moment, perhaps to digest Ingrid's words. "Girl, I'm so sorry that I've not taken your feelings for my brother seriously before now. I thought you were just attracted to him. I mean, he's a handsome eligible bachelor, and I just thought you were . . . well, I don't know what I thought, actually. I guess I just figured it was a lot simpler than it really is. Like it was with Demetrius Miller back in Virginia."

"Demetrius Miller?" Ingrid's face contorted. She couldn't believe her friend could even think to compare Jerome to the therapist whose office was adjacent to Jade's. Besides, Demetrius was too busy trying to get his hooks into Jade to even notice she existed.

"Yeah," Jade said, shrugging. "You used to fawn over him all the time."

"I just thought he was fine, cute, and looked sensational in a suit. I wasn't interested in a relationship with him. He was a pompous pain in the butt."

"That's what I used to tell you, but you acted like you couldn't see it."

"I was just momentarily blinded by all the fineness," Ingrid said. "He was just eye-candy. Candy that had coconut in the middle, and I hate coconut. So, basically, underneath the milk chocolate, he was just a bunch of yucky, flaky stuff."

Jade laughed at Ingrid's analogy. "But that's just it. I didn't think you were genuinely interested in a relationship with Jerome either. Not a serious one, anyway. To tell the honest truth, I thought that half of the reason you showed interest in him at all was to aggravate Kenyatta."

"Oh, please." Ingrid was surprised that as long as she and Jade had been friends, Jade didn't know her any better than that. "There's no way I'd let Kenyatta control my life like that." Her eyes dropped again, and so did her voice. "But I saw the way she kept smirking at me during last night's Women of Hope meeting."

"I didn't notice anything," Jade said. "I really wish the two of you got along better. I hate that I have two women in my life who I consider to be good friends of mine, but the two of them don't care for each other. Every time the girls get together, I feel like I have to walk on eggs with you two for fear that one will think I'm unfairly siding with the other. Do you know how uncomfortable that is?"

Ingrid stood from the couch and took a few steps toward the window. "Well, you can just make it easier on yourself and do what your brother did."

"What did my brother do?"

"He chose Kenyatta."

Ingrid felt the gap between them closing as Jade took quick steps to join her at the window.

"I'm not *choosing* anyone, Ingrid. I'm both your friend and Kenyatta's, but if I could only be a friend to one of you and was forced to make that kind of a choice, you know very well that you and I have been through too much for me to just walk away."

Smiling, Ingrid turned to face Jade. She could see that her friend meant every word of what she'd just said. "Thanks. It's good to know that I won't have to lose both of you."

"And who says Jerome has chosen Kenyatta?" Jade inquired. "It's true that he hasn't mentioned to me that you haven't called him over the past couple of weeks, but he's also not mentioned anything about Kenyatta."

"Yeah, but you know as well as I do that Kenyatta hasn't stopped calling him, and I'm sure the two of them have been out together too. What that means is that now his time isn't divided between us. Now, she has his full attention, and he probably thinks that because I haven't called, it means I don't care." Ingrid released a laden lung full of air. "I hope I did the right thing. I know I don't get it right all the time, Jade. I'm new at this thing . . . this Christian walk, I mean. I really want to live like God wants me to live, and I went home and read and reread that scripture myself after you pointed it out. And if God meant it to denote that it's the man's duty to find a wife and not a woman's to try and find herself a man, then I want to be obedient to Him."

Jade placed her hand on Ingrid's arm. "That's a great way to think, Ingrid. If every new Christian made it a priority to follow God's Word, they'd find themselves blessed beyond measure. When you obey God unconditionally, even when it means doing something that you don't necessarily want to do, He blesses you in ways you can't even imagine."

"Blessed beyond measure." Ingrid repeated the words softly, trying hard to hold on to them and will them into her life. "So, that means if following God's plan for my life makes me miss out on Jerome, then there must be someone out there who is even better for me, right?"

"Amen."

Ingrid tried to smile, but the corners of her mouth wouldn't cooperate. Instead, her lips pursed, and through her nostrils, escaped a gust of forced breath. "You're right. Forget Jerome." Those two words left a bad taste on her pallet, but she stood strong. "It's time for Ingrid Battles to focus on fulfilling whatever assignments God has for her."

"You go, girl." A jovial beam seemed to overtake Jade's face. "And your first assignment is to say you'll agree to be godmother to my baby."

Like a progressive slideshow, Ingrid's eyes went from the size of dimes to nickels to quarters. Her bottom lip dropped, and her hands moved slowly toward Jade's belly. "Oh, my God," she gasped, barely able to form the words. "You're—? You're—? Jade, are you—?"

Jade answered Ingrid's incomplete question with a nod to accompany the grin that had seemed to become a permanent fixture on her face. "That's the secret I was getting ready to tell you at the start of this conversation."

"Does Hunter—?"

"Not yet," Jade said.

"So, I'm the first to know?"

"Yes. I haven't even told Daddy and Mother yet."

"Oh, my goodness, Jade. How long have you known? How far along are you? What's your due date?"

"Too many questions," Jade said through giggles that seemed to trip over each other as they escaped her throat. "I just found out this morning. That's why I told you I'd be in at ten instead of nine. I had a nine o'clock appointment. I'm seven weeks late and I'd never been late before, so I knew I probably was expecting. But I wanted to find out for certain before mentioning it to Hunter. According to Dr. Doreen Connolly, I'm actually ten weeks pregnant. My due date is the week before Thanksgiving. Did I answer all your questions?"

Ingrid reached out and embraced Jade. "He's going to be so happy, girl. Wow. I can't believe you're pregnant!"

"You think so?" There was a hint of concern in Jade's eyes. "You really think Hunter will be happy?"

"Of course. Why wouldn't he be? That man loves you to death."

"I know he does. But I'm just a little bit nervous, I guess. This wasn't planned, and I was the one responsible to take precautions. I missed a couple of pills a few weeks ago, but didn't think that would be enough to override all the times that I took them on schedule. Hunter and I never talked about starting a family this soon. We've only been married a year and a half."

Ingrid flipped her wrist and smacked her lips. "Girl, please. He's going to be ecstatic. I guarantee it."

"I hope so." Jade placed her hands over her still-flat stomach. Her smile returned.

"You're having a baby, Jade."

"I know."

"Can you believe it?"

"No. Can you?"

"No, I can't." Ingrid danced a little jig. "My little girl is pregnant!"

Chapter Seventeen

The drive to Phillips State Prison was un-usually quiet. It was Friday night and, as promised, Jerome was on his way to visit Rocky. His former cellmate didn't get many visitors. Rocky's mother only came to check on him once a month; and her visits were only that frequent when she could sneak and do so without Rocky's father's knowledge.

The years he'd spent behind bars had toned down Rocky in some aspects, but the hatred he had for his abusive and neglectful father had only festered over time. And from what Jerome had been told, the feeling was mutual.

Jerome looked to his right. "You okay?"

Stuart hadn't said much since they'd pulled out of his driveway in Shelton Heights more than half an hour ago. It wasn't customary for his best friend to accompany him on his re-current visits to see Rocky, but tonight, for his own reasons, Jerome had asked him to come along and Stuart had reluctantly agreed.

"Yeah, man. I just had a rough day at work, that's all." Stuart head rested against the window as if he were trying to catch a nap. But his eyes were wide open, seeming to stare at nothing in particular.

"That's real jacked up about Joe," Jerome said, hoping to dethrone the reigning silence. "Maybe the release is temporary. If they find something soon, they'll pick him back up."

Having spent a decade of his life behind bars, it was hard for Jerome to wish prison life on anyone; even those he wasn't particularly fond of. But if Joseph King was really the one making Stuart's life miserable, he needed to pay his debt to society, just like every other criminal.

"They *are* still watching him, right?" Jerome asked when Stuart gave no voluntary feedback.

"Yeah," was Stuart's half-hearted reply.

Jerome glanced at him again. "So, why are you looking so glum? You look like you've lost your best friend."

"I have."

This time Jerome's glance was longer, but he brought his eyes back to the road in time to steady the car in its lane. "What's that supposed to mean? I thought I was your best friend. I ain't gone nowhere."

Stuart straightened his posture, and Jerome saw white teeth appear from behind his lips. It was faint, but it was the first smile he'd seen from him since they began their ride. But even that feeble display of emotions disappeared almost as quickly as it appeared.

Stuart inhaled and exhaled, adding a grunt that seemed to underscore whatever he was feeling on the inside.

"Yeah, you're still my boy," he told Jerome. "But Candice has her place right up there at the top, too. At least, she did."

The car swerved again. "What do you mean? Just two days ago, we were talking about how she was the only person you allowed in the den. Now, you sound like y'all done called it quits or something. What's up with that?"

Stuart leaned back against the headrest and stared straight ahead.

"Well?" Jerome urged. "Are you gonna tell me or not?"

"I think I messed things up."

"How? And don't make me beg you for every little detail. We'll be at Phillips in a little while, and I want you to lay it all out on the line before we get there."

Jerome didn't know exactly what he expected to hear, but what he heard wasn't it. He sat in silence while Stuart verbally and mentally relived the telephone conversation he'd had with Candice earlier that day. Jerome wanted to offer some kind of reassurance that everything would be fine, but when he found out that Stuart didn't even have the option of calling her and smoothing things over, the future of the still-new relationship looked bleak even in Jerome's eyes.

"How do you not have her phone number?"

"I just never got it from her. She never offered to give it to me, and I didn't want to press. I dangled the idea in front of her a few times, but she didn't take the bait. I figured she'd give it to me if she wanted me to have it."

Jerome shook his head. "Man, I don't believe you. There's no way in the world that would have happened to me."

"Women are a little more cautious these days, Jerome. Candice and I met online. We'd talked a few times, but this was our first time meeting. When you really think about it, I suppose I can't blame her. We chatted online for months before she even felt comfortable enough to call me. I understood that. Women can't be too careful. Smart ones don't just hand out their numbers to guys just because they ask for it."

Jerome smirked. "Yeah? Your sister's smart. But she gave me her number the first time I asked."

"That's different."

"How's it different?"

Stuart pointed at him with a finger that was as stiff as his voice. "Don't get cocky, 'cause you ain't all that. If Kenyatta didn't trust me, she never would have given you her number. You're her brother's best friend. So, even though she may not have known you so well, she knows I would have warned her if you were trouble."

There's nothing like a good friend to set you straight, Stuart thought.

"So, what are you gonna do now? Can't you go to SuperPages.com and look her up online?"

"I tried that when I got home from work today. Can you believe there's not one Candice Powell listed? There were several C. Powells scattered all over the state in the Bronx, Albany, Amityville, Brooklyn . . . you name it. I must have dialed thirty or thirty-five numbers. I called every number on the Web site, but none was Candice. Not my Candice, anyway. Her number is apparently unlisted. If I had an address, I'd just buy a ticket and fly out there, but I wouldn't know where to go once I landed."

"You don't know her phone number, you don't know her address, but you let her in The Lyons Den. I don't get it." Jerome navigated his car in the visitors' parking lot of Phillips State Prison.

"Showing her my den and allowing her to peruse my personal space had nothing to do with knowing her number or address. Besides, this whole mess is my fault. I'm the one who created it. Not Candice. She was trying to get me to see this Joe thing from all angles, and it just wasn't what I wanted to hear at the time. You with me?"

"Yeah, man, I'm with you on that," Jerome said. He shut off the engine, but didn't reach for his door handle. It was clear that Stuart needed to vent, and he decided it was best to let him get it all out before going inside.

"I took my frustrations out on her, and it wasn't fair," Stuart said. "I can't help but think that she was left to believe that she'd only been allowed to see one side of me when she was here last weekend. The way I chopped her head off on the phone, I'll bet you anything that she's now thinking that I'm capable of being callous or even violent if she doesn't agree with me on everything. This is one hundred percent my fault, but there's nothing I can do to set the record straight if she doesn't call me."

Jerome stared straight ahead at the barbed wire-bordered campus where he wasted so much of his life. This place held lifelong memories for him. Some good. Some bad. It was here that he'd fought to keep his life. It was here that he'd fought to keep his manhood. But it was also here that he found Christ. That one day in his tenure at Phillips made the other nine years and three hundred sixty-four days worth it.

"It felt right, man," Jerome heard Stuart say.

"What?"

"I said, it felt right, to let Candice in my den, I mean."

"Oh." Jerome nodded his head. "Having regrets now?"

"No," Stuart answered. "It felt right then, and it feels right now. You don't know nothing about that right now, but one day when you meet the right girl, you'll know what it feels like. And if you stupidly allow her to slip through your fingers due to your own stubbornness, then you'll also know what I'm going through. It's not a good feeling, let me tell you."

Jerome leaned his head back on the headrest. While this moment wasn't ideal, it was the perfect segue to address the real reason why he wanted Stuart to accompany him today. "I think I already know that feeling."

"You already know what feeling?"

"The feeling of letting my dumb pride and stubbornness allow what could be the right girl to slip through my fingers."

The car was silent for several moments, and Jerome could see Stuart staring in his direction from the front passenger seat.

"Well, seeing that you and Kenyatta were just out together a couple of nights ago, I suppose it's safe to assume that you're not talking about her."

Turning to glance at him and then returning his eyes to the scene provided by the windshield in front of him, Jerome replied, "No." The blank expression Stuart offered wasn't exactly a look that gave Jerome permission to delve deeper, but he chose to anyway. "I haven't heard from her in two weeks."

"Ingrid?" Stuart guessed.

"Yeah." Jerome tossed another fleeting look toward his friend, wishing he could decipher what was going through his mind. "Are you mad?"

Stuart faced the compound in front of them and gave his head a slow shake from side to side. "Like I said, when it's right, you know it's right."

"I didn't really know it was right until she stopped calling. Until then, I guess I just took it for granted that she'd always be there. I don't know if she'll talk to me or not now, but not having her in my life made me realize that I want her in my life."

Stuart grunted. "Well, at least you know how to get in touch with her."

"Yeah," Jerome replied.

"So, why haven't you called her? Why has it been two weeks since you've spoken to her?"

Jerome ran his hands over his naturally wavy fade. "It hasn't been two weeks since I talked to her, it's just been two weeks since we've spoken by phone. I talked to her at church last Sunday. She was the one who told me that I stopped breathing, remember?"

"And you haven't spoken to her since then?"

"No."

"Why not?"

Jerome squirmed in his seat. It felt a bit uncomfortable talking to Stuart about the woman who had essentially beat out his sister in the mêlée for Jerome's affections. "To tell the truth," he admitted, "I'm . . . well, scared, I guess."

"Scared of what? Being in love?"

Jerome's body jerked forward. "I ain't said all that, now. A brotha ain't said nothing about being in love."

"Whatever." Stuart didn't even try to mask the fact that he didn't believe him. "So, what is it that you're afraid of?"

"Man, I ain't never had to go after no girl, you know what I'm saying? My whole life— since I was a kid growing up in Perry Homes— the only thing I've had to do is fight them off if I wasn't interested. I've never had to work for no woman's attention before. I don't even know if I know how to. I just figured I'd wait it out and she'd eventually call back. Didn't think it would take this long, though."

Stuart reached for the handle beside him and opened his door, apparently as a gesture to let Jerome know he had heard enough and was ready to get down to the business of why they'd come to Phillips State Prison in the first place. There was a certain austerity to Stuart's voice as he said, "Well, you're not a kid anymore, Jerome, and these aren't little girls you're dealing with here. These are grown women. Good, decent grown women, one of which is my sister. So, since you seem to have made your decision on which one of them you actually have some *real* feelings for, I suggest you stop playing kid games and be a man.

Now, it's up to you whether or not you pick up the phone and call Ingrid, but with Kenyatta, you ain't got a choice. You with me? You've got twenty-four hours, Jerome, *twenty-four* to call her and let her know what's up. Let her know where your heart is, so she doesn't waste any more of her time. Don't string my sister along, man. You with me?"

Jerome swallowed in unrestrained astonishment. He'd never heard Stuart take on that tone before. Not with him, anyway. "Yeah, man, I'm with you. You're right. I gotta set everything straight. Kenyatta deserves that. I'll call her."

Jerome was certain that Stuart didn't hear the last sentence. By the time he'd said it, his friend had already exited the car and closed the door behind him.

Chapter Eighteen

"You remember Stuart Lyons from the prison ministry gatherings?"

At Jerome's introduction, Stuart stepped forward and extended his hand toward Rocky. The friendly gesture was accepted, but not with any level of enthusiasm.

"Yeah, I remember him," Rocky said. "You're the badge, right?"

Stuart raised his eyebrows. *The badge?* "I've been called a lot of things, but that's a first."

"You wear one, don't you?" The chip on Rocky's shoulder today was almost visible to the natural eye.

"When I'm in uniform, yes," Stuart said, hoping what he did for a living wasn't the cause for Rocky's demeanor.

"I'm surprised you're here," Rocky commented with a half-smirk, looking at Stuart as though he was sizing him up. "Ain't you coming to see me the same thing as a man goin' back to the heap after he done thrown out the trash?"

Though Rocky towered over him by a few inches, Stuart held eye contact. "No, it's not the same thing," he replied.

Then for effect, Stuart looked around the visiting area and added, "But I don't see any trash in here anyway, do you?"

Rocky pulled out the chair nearest him and dropped his body weight onto the seat with a force that caused an attention-grabbing thud. "Yeah, yeah, yeah," he said, "'cause God don't make no junk, right?"

Stuart hadn't heard that one in a while, but as clichéd as it was, it still held true. He replied with a simple, "Right."

Jerome and Stuart joined Rocky at the table, and for a moment, neither of them spoke. During those quiet seconds, Stuart's eyes grazed the room. It was typical and drab, but the smell of a fresh coat of ivory paint still lingered. For security purposes, the space was well-lit. The only furniture provided were tables and chairs—all made of durable plastic—also for security purposes. Most of the tables were occupied by convicts and women who held the current position as their love interests.

As Stuart's eyes scanned, they froze when he saw the man he simply knew as Blake. He'd always remember the hateful face and vengeful eyes of the man who obliquely threatened him during the last prison ministry meeting. Blake shared a table with a young man that Stuart could only guess was his son. From a distance, it was difficult to recognize any telltale resemblance between the two, but the distance did nothing to fade the matching contempt in their stares. It wasn't hard to figure out the kinship.

Stuart's stomach churned. What he felt at the moment wasn't exactly fear, but something about the two men deeply disturbed him. He turned away and pretended that his attention was in greater demand at his own table.

Rocky appeared to be one of only a small fraction of men who were not being visited by females who barely looked legal. No doubt, these women had been convinced to wait it out so that their incarcerated boyfriends could make good on their vows to stay out of trouble, be better men, marry them, or whatever other lie they could convince their girlfriends to believe. In his line of business, Stuart had seen and heard it all. Subconsciously, he shook his head at the sight of it.

"So, how've you been?" Jerome posed, drawing Stuart back to the center of the room where they sat.

Rocky spread his massive arms out and in an elevated, condescending voice, said, "Man, look around you. It don't get no better than this. How many people you know who get to live in a house big enough to sleep over a thousand grown men? Man, my joint come wit' twenty-four-hour armed security, and there ain't been not one cat to ever try to break in on me to steal all my valuables." Rocky's laugh was bitter, and then cursing aloud, he repeated, "It don't get no better than this."

Not sure how to respond to the vinegary outburst, Stuart remained quiet. He glanced at one of the guards standing nearby whose hand had immediately become glued to his holster about midway through Rocky's outburst. Buford, Georgia, where Phillips State Prison was located, was an entirely different county than where Stuart served as a public servant, and he had no jurisdiction here. Still, the guard looked at him as if asking permission to handcuff the prisoner and take him back to his cage. A silent shake of Stuart's head brought the guard and his arms back to a relaxed state.

"Calm down and talk to me, man," Jerome said, leaning in closer to Rocky but not attempting to touch him. "Something's got you ticked off today. What is it?"

Stuart looked across the table at Rocky and was sure that he saw shadows of emotion in his eyes. In all the times the men of New Hope's prison ministry had gathered at Phillips, and in all the times Stuart had seen Rocky, this was the first time he'd noted even a trace of anguish on the man's face. Stuart was familiar with Rocky's witty side, and he'd seen him in his element of putting the fear of God in his fellow inmates. But this was the first time he'd been introduced to sadness in the man.

The roughness of the skin on Rocky's face could be heard when he rubbed his salt-and-pepper five o'clock shadow with his hand. "Nothing," he mumbled.

"Rocky—"

"I said, nothing." His demeanor was rigid.

"Come on, dude."

"Look, church boy—"

"No, *you* look."

During the exchange, Stuart felt as though he was watching a tennis match as his eyes floated back and forth from one man to the other. Though Rocky appeared to be somewhere around forty years old, the younger Jerome assumed the role of mentor, with no hesitation. His last words had come through an authoritative whisper that had Stuart looking back at the guard who was posted nearby. This time, though, the man's attention was elsewhere, and Jerome's order hadn't been loud enough to alert him.

"This is me you talkin' to, Rocky," Jerome continued. His tone wasn't nearly as commanding now. "Man, it wasn't that long ago that we shared the same *suite* inside this armored palace that can house over a thousand men. I know you, so don't even try to play me like that. Now, what's up with you?"

Rocky rolled his eyes and turned away.

"Look at me, Rocky." The larger man complied with surprisingly low reluctance, and Jerome continued. "Remember when I told you that God had made you my personal assignment? That He had orchestrated it so that we'd be placed in the same cell for those three or four short months—just long enough for us to connect right before He allowed me to be released? Remember when I said no matter how many of your peeps bounced on you, I was gonna be here whether you wanted me to or not? Do you remember me telling you all that?"

"Yeah. So what?"

"So, here I am, that's what. Talk to me, man. If something's messing with you on the inside, you can tell me about it."

When Rocky's eyes broke away from Jerome's and roamed toward Stuart, Stuart read the message loud and clear. He was the reason Rocky wasn't talking. Some level of confidence had been established between the two former cellmates, but all Rocky knew about Stuart was that he was a cop. And Stuart imagined that very few people ranked lower than cops on Rocky's totem pole.

"I'm gonna step out," Stuart offered as he prepared to stand. "I'll wait for you on the outside."

"No," Jerome said, stopping him midway between standing and sitting.

At a snail's pace, Stuart lowered himself back in his chair and looked at his friend with uncertainty. "You sure? I don't mind the wait."

"He's gotta learn that there are more people in the world than me that he can trust," Jerome said. He hastily held up his hand to stop Rocky's protest before he could even voice it.

"Listen, Rocky. Stuart's my boy, and whatever you say to him stays with him."

"Unless it's something incriminating." At first, Stuart thought the words were just said in his own mind, but when Rocky and Jerome both snapped their faces in his direction, Stuart knew he'd spoken out loud. "I'm sorry," he added, "but I'd rather just step out if it's incriminating, because I'm sworn to uphold the law."

"Typical cop," Rocky hissed.

Stuart stood up again to leave, but this time it was Rocky's words that stopped his motion.

"The badge can stay," he said to Jerome, opting not to look at Stuart. "It ain't like I'm about to confess to being a terrorist or nothing."

"It's up to you." Stuart kept his focus on Rocky. "If you want me to leave, I'll leave. Whatever it is that you're gonna say, if you don't want me to hear it, I'll go."

Rocky shrugged his shoulders and then nodded his head in the direction of Stuart's chair. "If you say he's cool, church boy, then there ain't no reason he can't stay."

"He's cool, Rocky. Really, he is," Jerome assured.

A quilt of quietness began weaving itself in the space surrounding them, but Rocky's voice put a halt to that, too.

"It ain't rocket science. I'm just tired of this place, man." His words were still directed at Jerome.

Stuart's eyes were glued on the tattoos that decorated Rocky's biceps, and he imagined how drunk or high any man would have to be in order to sit through such a long and painful process. But as drawn to the talented artwork as Stuart was, he listened to every word Rocky spoke.

"I was barely nineteen when I got locked up," he said. "It's been . . ." Rocky stopped and looked at his hands, pulling down one finger at a time while he counted silently. A moment later, he'd already given up. "It's been so long, I can't even keep up no more, man. I'm tired. I'm just tired." Rocky rubbed his forehead like the thought of it was giving him a headache.

There was a time when Stuart used to think that inmates that spent an extended amount of time behind bars eventually got used to the confinement, and to them, it became as comfortable and natural as home. But the stories Jerome had shared with him had convinced him otherwise. Rocky's visible torment was additional confirmation.

"Have you been keeping on the straight and narrow like we talked about during my last few nights here?" Jerome asked.

When Rocky answered, Stuart had to stifle a smile at the effort it took for the inmate to keep his dialogue clean. But it was a good feeling to know that Jerome and the other brothers of the prison ministry had had such a positive impact on the man's life.

"It ain't been all that hard to do," Rocky said in his indirect answer. "I done kicked enough . . . butt around here to seal my reputation. I don't have to fight no more. Bad news travels fast, so even the new nig . . . I mean, even the new men that get thrown in this joint know what's up. But being good don't mean . . . it don't mean crap in this joint, and you know it, man. I'm gonna have to spend the rest of my life here."

"Not necessarily, Rocky," Jerome interjected. "You're coming up on twenty-five years soon. Don't you get your first hearing then?"

Twenty-five? Stuart couldn't even fathom it.

"Don't even try it, church boy." Rocky scowled. "You and me both know that these fools ain't gonna let me out of here."

"No, I *don't* know that," Jerome insisted. "They let me out, didn't they? And when I had my doubts, you were the one who kept reassuring me that they'd hand me the key."

"But your boys didn't lie on you and finger you as the man who planned the whole takedown. Them . . ." Rocky seemed to search for an adjective that wouldn't be too offensive, and settled for saying, "Them no-good punks I was with got everybody believing I put that whole thing together, and there ain't no way these white folks gonna let me out of here when they think I'm the cause of killing one of their own."

There were fewer things in life that annoyed Stuart more than hearing a man of color blame white America for his sins. But as he looked across the table at Rocky, he believed him. Not that white people were the reason he was in jail, but that he wasn't the mastermind behind the crime that he'd been a part of committing. Rocky didn't order the victim's murder. Stuart was sure of it.

"When is your parole hearing?" Stuart asked.

Rocky glared at him with a mixture of distrust and hatred.

His voice was filled with cynicism when he spewed, "Why? You gonna put in a good word for me or something?"

Stuart said nothing, just returned Rocky's stare, until he won the silent war. Rocky was the first to turn away. And he was also the first to break the lingering hush.

"Three and a half years," he mumbled. Then Rocky turned his eyes back to Jerome. "That's too long to wait."

"What's three and a half years, when you compare it to the almost twenty-two that you've already served?" Jerome asked. "The worst is definitely behind you."

Rocky shook his head slowly. "I can't explain it, but it's different. Most of these twenty-two years, I ain't gave a . . . flip about nothing. I didn't care if I lived or died, so I sure didn't care if I stayed in prison or got out. But the last few months have been rough. Rougher than all the other time I spent locked up put together. I done missed twenty-one Mother's Days since I been in here, man. I ain't cared about none of them, mostly 'cause I ain't cared nothing about my mama. Not after what she stood by and let that piece of . . . my sorry daddy do to our family. But I was sitting in the library to-day, looking at one of the newspapers, and saw all the Mother's Day specials stores are having 'cause of Sunday. And I just started thinking 'bout how I ain't gave my mama nothing on Mother's Day since I was thirteen years old. I ain't told her I loved her since I was ten.

I ain't saying that I ain't still mad at her, but it hit me today that the reason Mama didn't stand up for us was 'cause she was too scared to stand up for herself, let alone anybody else. She still is. She was just as scared of that fool as we were. She still is. And the reason she ain't been coming to see me every week is 'cause she couldn't. She still can't. Not if she don't want to be turned into a punching bag. My mama—poor thing—is doing the best she can do. And I ain't being no help to her 'cause I'm locked up in this hole, feeling like killing my own daddy, instead of protecting my mama." Rocky balled his right hand into a fist and stopped the motion of his arm just before he would have slammed it against the table. "Lately, everything about being in this joint just reminds me of what I ain't got and what I ain't did."

That's God working on you, brother. Stuart wanted to clap his hands together in praise as the thought filtered through his head. He exchanged glances with Jerome and knew that they'd drawn the same conclusion. Neither of them voiced it, though.

Rocky stared down at the plastic-top table and continued. "I don't know why, but three and a half of years waiting on a parole hearing, knowing that they're most likely gonna tell me I need to serve out my whole life sentence, is just too long to wait. Lately, I been thinking crazy stuff."

He had Stuart's and Jerome's full attention again.

"Crazy stuff like what?" Jerome asked.

Rocky never looked up from the table. "You know."

"No, I don't know, Rocky. Tell me."

"Ending it all."

Stuart's only reaction was to close his eyes. He'd figured out what Rocky was going to say before he said it, but the words still struck Stuart's soul, prompting a quick, silent prayer.

"No, Rocky," Jerome's voice was pleading, but lowered, probably to guarantee their conversation remained private. "That's the enemy trying to get you to destroy yourself. To destroy your future," Jerome added.

When Rocky raised his eyes, Stuart saw liquid pooling around the bottom of them.

"What future?" A profane word escaped his lips, and Rocky made no attempt to apologize for it. His teeth were clenched together when he added, "Man, I ain't got no future."

"Yes—you—do." Stuart sounded out each word as though each stood alone. He was unable to stop his unsolicited participation. Rocky didn't acknowledge his sudden input, but Stuart continued anyway. "Don't you see, Rocky? This is a setup. If you didn't have a future, if God didn't have something waiting on the other side of these prison walls for you, the devil wouldn't be planting seeds of suicide in your mind."

"That's right," Jerome agreed, patting Stuart's back as though cheering him on to continue.

Stuart saw Rocky's jaws tighten, followed by the bobbing of his Adam's apple, and he knew it was an increased attempt to keep his pooling emotions from spilling over.

"Rocky," Stuart said, not minding that the man still hadn't looked in his direction, "you've been incarcerated for more than twenty-one years, man. You with me? Twenty-one years. That's a long time, and there's not an honest man anywhere who can't understand your frustration. Especially when you're serving it knowing that you're not guilty of what you've been charged."

It was the first time Rocky had looked at him in a while. In his eyes was an openness that Stuart hadn't seen before now. It was as though Stuart's words, signifying that he believed in Rocky's proclaimed innocence, meant something to the man.

"And watch this," Jerome said, using an introductory phrase that his father often used in the pulpit when he was preparing to bring home a point. "All these twenty-one and a half years you been in here and you ain't never thought about ending your life. Somebody else's maybe—but not your own. But as soon as you start coming to the prison ministry gatherings and listening to the Word that my dad's been sharing with you and the other guys, then Satan starts making you want to do something stupid. Something that once you realize how stupid it is, you can't take it back. You know why he's messing with your mind like this, Rocky?"

"Because *you* may not realize that God has a calling on your life," Stuart cut in.

"But you can bet your bottom dollar that the devil knows," Jerome finished. "He knows, and he wants to snuff the life out of you before you can fulfill it."

"Don't let him win, Rocky," Stuart said as he watched a thin, moist trail seep out of the corner of Rocky's eye and run down the crease that edged his nose. "Don't let him win."

Chapter Nineteen

It had been quite a Sunday at New Hope. Today, the members had the rare pleasure of listening to a message brought to them by the church's beloved first lady. Mildred Tides wasn't a licensed minister, and although Reverend Tides insisted that she had "the calling," Mother Tides never accepted the offer to be ordained.

"Too many pastors' wives wearing the title of co-pastor," she often said. "I believe that God calls just as many women to preach as He does men, but it just baffles me that just about every televangelist or mega-church pastor that you see and hear about has his wife as his co-pastor. Nowadays, it just seems like it's a fad or something."

With or without her official "preaching papers," Mildred handled her own on Mother's Day Sunday, citing 1 Kings, seventeenth chapter as her focus scripture.

"One of the benefits of loving God with all of our heart is that through our love, we cover our children under His protective power. I'll bet y'all didn't know that."

"Amen!" The crowd shouted the word as though they knew it, even if they didn't. "That's right, sisters." Then for clarification, Mother Tides eyed the deacon's corner and added, "I'm talking to the sisters right now." Then looking back out at the congregation, she said, "Women of God, our children can be saved from trouble and snatched from the hands of danger by way of our servitude to and love for our Lord and Savior. Do y'all hear what I'm saying?"

"Amen," they reiterated.

"The widow woman in this passage of scripture was never even given a name," Mother Tides pointed out, "but she teaches us a powerful lesson. It's not important that we know her name because it wasn't about her anyhow," Mildred said. "It's never about us, women of God, it's about Jesus!"

That brought another eruption of praise.

"This is the same woman who, some time earlier, was down to her last meal due to famine brought on by a drought that had covered the land. She was planning to prepare a last supper for herself and her son, and after eating it, they were going to die. But then the man of God came along, hungry and asking for food. Realizing that he was one of God's chosen ones, the woman prepared that last meal just like she'd planned, but instead of she and her son eating it, she gave it to the prophet, Elijah. And the Word of God tells us that because of her sacrifice, the Lord kept her barrels—her modern-day refrigerator—full every day, saving her and her son from certain death. Are y'all following me this morning?"

"We're following you, Mama. Preach the Word!"

Hunter chuckled as he took a long side-glance at his wife. Jade looked particularly ravishing today in the violet tapered Ann Klein skirt suit that he had given her early this morning as a Mother's Day gift. Hunter felt like patting himself on the back for making such a perfect selection.

Jade honored his request and wore her long, thick hair in its natural state. It was silky straight when she pressed it, which she often did for Sunday morning service. But when she washed her hair and allowed it to air dry as she did last night, Hunter always fought the urge to mingle his fingers in the resulting mass of large spiraling reddish-brown curls. There was something about the way she looked when she wore it that way that nudged at all of Hunter's senses. Today was no exception, and although he was enjoying his motherin-law's message, he looked forward to the benediction.

"Now, the scripture tells us, this woman was once again, in need," Mildred Tides taught, lassoing Hunter's thoughts back to more spiritual matters. "In verse seventeen, the Bible says that her son fell sick and died, leaving her not only a widow, as she had been before, but also childless. But how many of you know that there's nothing too hard for the Lord?"

Shouts of "Amen" came from every area of the sanctuary.

"He's not only a right-now God, He's a retroactive God," she sputtered. "He's not only able to stop something from happening, but even if it done already happened, the God we serve is a God who can go back and undo it."

"Say it, Mama, say it!" Jade's yell stood out amongst the other voices around them.

"Amen," Hunter agreed. He knew where Mother Tides was going with this sermon. He was among many who'd virtually seen a reenactment of it just days ago as Jerome lay lifeless in the center aisle.

"The Word of God tells us that this woman found the same prophet that she'd fed her last meal to and told him of her plight," Mildred said. "She entrusted the body of her dead son to the man of God, and Elijah took the boy, laid him on his own bed, and stretched his body on top of the boy's body. Just to show you that I'm not making this up, follow along with me as I read verse twenty-two." Mildred paused and then read aloud, "And the Lord heard the voice of Elijah; and the soul of the child came into him again, and what?"

"He revived." The congregation finished the text in unison.

"God breathed life back into that widow's son," Mildred said, her voice beginning to become unsteady. "God brought him back to life, sisters. Many of us want God to breathe life back into our finances, back into our relationships, back into our health, back into our careers, but we haven't loved God with all our hearts as this woman did. We haven't given Him our last as this widow did. We haven't given Him our children as this mother did."

Tears began to stream down Mother Tides's face. She turned to where Jerome stood, just a few feet down from Hunter. "Y'all see that boy right there?"

People were already beginning to jump up and down and shout praises to God in the places where they stood. They were there last Sunday, too, and they'd seen the miracle for themselves.

"Jerome came to me this morning and bought me a gift that was wrapped so pretty, I didn't even want to tear open the paper. But do you know what I told him? I told him that this year, he is my Mother's Day gift. I got three children, and I love them all; God knows I love them all."

Mildred's tears were flowing heavily now. Hunter batted back his own emotions as he watched a stream mow its way down Jade's cheeks. He retrieved a handkerchief from his pocket and pressed it into his wife's hand.

Mother Tides continued. "But my son was dead, y'all, and God brought him back to life. I think about all the sacrifices that me and Reverend Tides have made down through the years. I remember us barely having food to eat because we were trying to feed homeless people who we knew were only coming to our little storefront church for the free meal that would curb the hunger that drug use had left behind.

"I remember the time we lived in a little raggedy two-bedroom apartment and could barely make our subsidized rent because we had to be sure the rent on the church was paid. I remember nights of eating by candlelight, not because we were trying to be romantic, but because we used the little money we had to pay the light bill at that little place we called a church that was located on the bad end of Memorial Drive."

By now, people were running up the aisles and around the church, praising God while First Lady Tides stepped out of her shoes and walked the pulpit, squeezing a pink laced handkerchief in one hand and holding a cordless microphone in the other. Reverend Tides was walking behind her, cheering her on with enthusiastic words and waving a church fan at her, as though she needed cooling off.

"For days, months and even years, we struggled," Mother Tides cried. "Many a days, I wondered what good was coming of the trials and tribulations. Then God started adding souls to that little storefront mission, and that was good. Then He blessed us to lay the foundation for this church, and that was good. Then He made the way for me and Reverend Tides to move our family into a nicer home, and that was good. But when I thought about all the years of long days and sleepless nights we'd endured, it still didn't seem like enough."

"Preach, Mama!" Jade said.

"Then two years ago, I was put in the place of this woman in our scripture text. The devil tried to kill my husband. He had me thinking I was a widow woman, but bless the name of Jesus! God stepped in and snatched my husband from the clutch of the enemy and rescued him from certain death."

"Yes!" Jade screamed with uplifted hands.

"I thanked God with all I had in me," Mildred said. "But since then, there were still days when I didn't feel like the scales were balancing," she admitted. "After all God had done, sometimes it just didn't feel like He'd done enough. Every now and then, I would still think about all the heartaches and headaches we endured for the sake of the ministry and about all that we have given and gone without so that God's work could continue. And when I added it all up, it just didn't seem like a fair deal. But, Lord have mercy, y'all!" she heaved. "When I saw my baby boy lying dead on the floor, and when I saw the same man of God that I'd sacrificed everything for and with stretch his body across Jerome's and pray for his soul to return. And when God breathed life back into my son, I put an end to my pity party. I quit feeling like God owed me something. I told the Lord that if He don't do nothing else for Mother Mildred Tides, He done done enough! I said, He done done enough for me to praise Him all the days of my life!"

Through vision distorted by tears of joy, Hunter saw Jerome walk to the altar and crumple to the floor on his knees, his face pressed into the carpet. His whole body shook with obvious weeping. Jade edged by Hunter and the others on their row and ran to her brother. She dropped on the floor beside him, put her arm around his shoulder, and they cried together. Seconds later, Jackson had vacated his space in the pulpit and joined his younger brother and baby sister in worship.

"Happy Mother's Day to me, y'all," Mother Tides declared into the microphone. "Praise God to the highest! Happy Mother's Day to me!"

Atlanta Fish Market was a fine dining restaurant located on Pharr Road in the Buckhead District of metropolitan Atlanta, and Hunter decided it was the best place for him and Malik to take Jade in celebration of Mother's Day. No doubt, the restaurants in the Stone Mountain area would be crowded with after-church clientele, and as much as possible, he wanted to avoid the long wait and the noisy crowds. An outpouring of the Holy Spirit had caused today's service to go on longer than usual, and that had probably helped them avoid some of the multitude that had likely been at Atlanta Fish Market earlier.

The hostess seated Hunter and his family at one of the square varnished wooden tables with place settings for four. She removed the fourth setting and handed each of them a menu, letting them know that their waitress would be with them shortly.

"Why have you never brought me here before?" Jade asked as she looked around at the high ceiling and the large globe lights that hung from it.

"Got to keep a few surprises in my pocket that I can pull out when I need to," Hunter replied.

"Oh?" Jade challenged. "Is this the only surprise you have in your pocket for me today?"

Hunter's grin was brazen. "You want to check and see?"

"Aw, man," Malik whined, dropping his menu on the table. "Can I call Mr. Pete and ask him to come pick me up?"

Hunter burst into laughter, and Jade joined him. "Sorry, sport," he said. "I forgot you were here. We'll behave."

"Besides," Jade added, reaching across the table to nudge Malik, "today's Mother's Day, and I want to spend it with both of you. Besides, Pete took Jan and Kyla out to eat as well."

"Well, I can call Mr. Stuart," Malik offered. "Tyler said he and that lady he had started dating broke up. And he also said that Uncle Jerome picked Ms. Ingrid over his aunt, so I'm thinking that Tyler's whole family probably went straight home after church."

Hunter gave his son a look of warning. "You and Tyler talk way too much about stuff that's not your concern," he said. "Go wash your hands for dinner."

"But Mama has that hand sanitizer—"

Hunter laid down his menu and tilted his head. "I didn't ask you what your mama had. Now, go wash your hands."

Malik stood to obey the command given.

"Twice," Hunter added, knowing that saying so was all that was needed for Malik to get the message that he needed a few minutes alone to talk to Jade. When Malik was out of listening range, Hunter turned to Jade. "Did Jerome pick Ingrid?"

Jade nodded. "Apparently so. I didn't know about it until after service today, though. Ingrid said he called her yesterday and left a message for her to call him back. She didn't get the request until she got home late last night after going to the salon for her color treatment. When she called him back, he told her that he'd missed her and he wanted to get to know her better. Ingrid said he never once brought up Kenyatta's name, but made it clear that he wanted to make his relationship with her—meaning Ingrid—an exclusive one."

"Wow," Hunter said. "I wonder what brought that on."

"I don't know, but I saw Stuart and Jerome laughing together in the foyer after Stuart had accompanied Dad to his office. So, whatever happened didn't seem to affect their relationship. I do need to call Kenyatta, though. I didn't see her at church today."

Hunter thought for a moment and then said, "Neither did I, and she never misses Sunday worship."

"I imagine she's a bit upset about all this," Jade said.

"I always thought Ingrid was more into Jerome than Kenyatta."

"What do you mean?"

Hunter took a sip of his water. "I mean, I felt that her heart was more into it than Kenyatta's."

"Really?"

Hunter noted the surprise on Jade's face. "Why are you looking like that?"

"Because Ingrid and I had just had a talk on Friday during lunch and she told me that she was in love with Jerome. I felt so stupid because, as close as I am to her, I hadn't picked up on just how serious she was about him. Now I feel even more dimwitted, hearing you say that you saw it too."

Hunter smiled and then winked. "I think men pick up on these things a little bit more than women. A man knows when a woman loves him even if she doesn't think he knows."

"You think Jerome knew?"

"I'm sure he did. It's hard for a man not to feel a woman's love. If she doesn't express it with her mouth, he can see it in her eyes."

Jade's lips curled into a smile. "So did you know I loved you before I admitted it?"

"All day long," Hunter replied.

"And did you already love me, or did your love blossom later on?"

Hunter reached across the table and grabbed Jade's hand. "I think I loved you even before I knew I loved you." When Hunter kissed the tips of Jade's fingers, he caught a glimpse of Malik standing in the distance and laughed out loud.

Jade turned and saw him standing there too. She pulled her hand from Hunter and motioned for Malik to join them at the table. "He's so sweet," she whispered to Hunter. "He wanted to be sure he'd given us enough time."

When Malik reclaimed the seat beside his father, Hunter asked, "Did you wash your hands?"

"Five times," Malik said, holding them up for Hunter to see.

When the waitress came to take their orders, Hunter did a double take when Jade ordered an appetizer of a half pound of the Alaskan Red King Crab Legs and an entrée that consisted of a full pound and a half of the same. After the waitress had taken all of their orders and left the table, Hunter couldn't resist the chance to tease his wife.

"Hungry?" he asked as he turned his glass up to his mouth to drink.

Jade grinned. "Yes, why?"

"No reason," Hunter said. "I just hope you're able to fit into the other half of your Mother's Day gift this evening after you've eating all that."

Jade smiled like she already knew what the gift was. "Am I going to have it on long enough for it to even matter?"

"Okay, I'm gonna go and wash my hands again," Malik said, preparing to rise from his seat.

"No, Malik, honey. We're sorry," Jade said over Hunter's laughter. "You don't have to wash your hands. We'll behave. We promise. Don't we, Hunter?"

"Speak for yourself, baby."

"Hunter . . ."

"Okay," Hunter said, still chuckling. "But we need to eat fast."

"Am I gonna be like this when I get in my thirties?" Malik asked.

Hunter shook his head. "No, son. I wasn't like this when I got in my thirties, either. I didn't get like this 'til I got in love. It's not an age thing, believe me. When you find a woman that you love as much as I love your mother, all bets are off. You don't even get mad when she orders too much food, even though you already know that you'll end up with a doggie bag, taking home the leftovers."

Malik snickered.

"I don't need a doggie bag," Jade insisted. "I told you, I'm hungry."

"Hungry enough to eat two pounds of crab legs all by yourself?"

Jade leaned forward on her elbows. "Who says I'm going to eat them all by myself?"

Hunter looked at Malik and then back at Jade. "Baby, we ordered our own meals. We don't want the crab legs today. You're gonna have to eat all of them by yourself."

"No, I won't. Not technically, anyway."

Hunter narrowed his eyes, trying to decipher her coded words. "What's that supposed to mean?"

After a pause and an audible and visible exhale, Jade said, "It means I'm eating for two. I'm pregnant, Hunter."

Malik gasped and jolted forward in his seat.

For a short while, all Hunter could do was stare straight ahead into his wife's eyes. "You're pregnant?" he managed to whisper.

Jade nodded, and tears immediately welled in her eyes. "Tell me you're happy, sweetheart." Her voice was beseeching, like him saying so was a matter of life and death.

There were numerous emotions running through Hunter's body: shock, disbelief, fear, nervousness . . . but the most prevalent of them all was happiness.

"I am," he whispered, grabbing her hand once more and pressing the back of it against his cheek.

"Tell me the truth, Hunter. I know this wasn't planned—"

"Yes, it was, baby. Not by us, maybe, but there's no timing more perfect than God's. He planned it this way, and I'm happy. Believe me, sweetheart, I'm very happy."

Jade breathed a sigh of relief and then looked at Malik. "Are *you* happy?"

Hunter looked at him too. He couldn't remember the last time he'd seen his son grin so widely.

"Yes, ma'am," Malik managed to say. His answer made her smile even wider.

Hunter looked across the table at Jade and wondered if the pregnancy was the reason his wife had been looking particularly appetizing over the past few weeks. "Thank you, baby."

"For what?" Jade was blushing.

"For making me a daddy all over again and for helping me to give Malik the family he deserves."

Jade placed her hand on her stomach and said, "No, Hunter. Thank *you*." She looked at Malik and smiled. "Both of you."

The tender family moment was broken when Hunter's eyes navigated above Jade's shoulder and spotted a couple being escorted by the hostess. They weren't looking at him, but Hunter's sights locked on to them and wouldn't let go. It was the woman, especially, who grabbed his attention, and it only took him a second to figure out why she looked so familiar. His bottom lip fell, and he watched her and her date follow the hostess to a table near where his family sat.

"Hunter?" Jade said. She glanced at the pretty woman and then back at her husband.

Hunter turned his attention away from the woman, but his eyes had already seen all they needed to see.

"Hunter?" Jade repeated.

"Oh, my God." Hunter drowned his whisper with gulps of water. *What is she doing here? And who is the man she's with?*

Jade's mouth opened to comment, but the waitress who delivered their meals halted whatever Jade was going to say. For Hunter, the interruption served as a much-needed moment to regain some level of composure.

Chapter Twenty

"Can I see you for a moment, Lieutenant?" Stuart spun around and saw Chief Overstreet standing in an open doorway down the hall, holding a familiar blue binder in his hand. Only a few feet of space separated Stuart from Deputy Chief Irving Overstreet, but his feet felt like concrete blocks as he walked toward him. The chief stepped aside to allow Stuart entrance into the room, and then he closed the door behind them. Knowing what this meeting was going to be about, Stuart found a chair and sat. He wanted to scream, punch a hole in the wall, smash a window, shatter a coffee cup against the floor . . . anything to release the mounting frustration that permeated every fiber of his being.

"I hear you received another threat," the chief said. He held up the binder, as if Stuart needed a visual aid to jar his memory. His voice was calmer than normal, probably as a means of ensuring he didn't push Stuart over the edge. It was obvious he was already teetering.

Stuart leaned back in his chair and exhaled. His eyes were glued to the binder and the bold black letters that defaced it. If there were really such a thing as a person's blood heating to a boil, his was. Stuart clenched his teeth and said, "He's gone way too far this time. He's blatantly threatening my son."

Earlier on this Monday morning, before reporting to work, Stuart walked out of his front door to retrieve his copy of *The Atlanta Journal-Constitution* and he found his son's notebook lying on the front porch. When Tyler got home from school on Friday, he'd told Stuart that he'd misplaced it, claiming that it was on his desk when his class went to lunch, but when they returned, he couldn't find it anywhere. Because of it, Tyler had been forced to do make-up work as a punishment for the homework assignment he couldn't turn in on time.

"This man not only knows what school Tyler attends," Stuart told Chief Overstreet, "but the mere fact that he was able to confiscate my boy's notebook lets me know that he also knows Tyler's class schedule and where he sits in the classroom." The thought of it all made Stuart tremble with near uncontrollable fury. "If I find out who this mad man is, I'm not gonna wait 'til he hurts my son to take action. I'm gonna kill him, Chief."

"You can't do that, Lyons."

"Oh, but I can . . . and I will." Venom dripped from Stuart's words. "I don't care if it sends me to death row. I will shoot him execution-style at point-blank range, in the center of his forehead, if that's what it takes to protect my son."

"Lieutenant—"

"I mean it, Chief."

"I know you do, and that's the part that concerns me. Let us do our job, Lieutenant. We'll find him."

"You haven't been able to find him yet," Stuart accused.

"We will find him, Lieutenant," Chief Overstreet stressed. "Mark my words. We'll find him, and we'll find him before he can even come close to harming your son."

"He's already come close!" Stuart slammed his hands on the table. The sound echoed throughout the room and was followed by a brief hush.

Unruffled, the chief reiterated, "Let us do our job, Lyons."

Stuart struggled to settle himself. "I started to keep him out of school today, but I couldn't. He had tests to take."

"He'll be fine," Chief Overstreet guaranteed. "As a matter of fact, we have a patrol posted at the school to keep it under surveillance all day."

"I know," Stuart said. "Sergeant Bowden told me that he volunteered to be posted there. I appreciate what you're doing, Chief, but I can't keep living my life like this."

"I understand."

"No, you don't!" Stuart snapped again. "Everybody keeps telling me that they understand, but none of you do. You ain't even got a clue! I can barely sleep at night, realizing that at any time, some sick, twisted moron might light a match to my home. Now, on top of worrying at night, I've got to be wondering whether or not my son and maybe even my sister are safe during the daylight hours. This is messed up, Chief."

"I know, Lieutenant. Have you given any thought to sending the boy to live with his mother until all of this clears?"

Frown lines etched themselves on Stuart's face. "Tasha is traveling on extended business. She's somewhere in California or Chicago.

She'll probably be back in the next couple of weeks, and I was praying that all this was cleared up before that time."

"Does she know what's going on?"

Nodding, Stuart said, "Tyler told her about the patrol car, but I don't think she made too much of it. I'm gonna instruct him not to tell her about what happened today. I can't have Tasha thinking that living with me is hazardous to our son. We got a good thing going here, and I don't want to disturb it. I want Tyler with me, and I'll do whatever has to be done to make sure he's safe staying there."

Stuart stood from his chair and walked the length of the room, trying to regain the control that he could feel slipping away. "Doesn't it seem just a bit awkward to you that this happened just days after we released Joe? Is this not enough to pick him up again?"

Chief Overstreet scratched his head, bringing attention to the famed hairpiece that he never seemed to place correctly. "We still haven't given up on Joseph King, but even with this new act of revenge, we can't pick him up. We've had him watched closely ever since he returned to Florida; but so far, we have nothing. He hasn't even so much as parked in a handicap spot. He was in Jacksonville all weekend, and he's at work this morning. If he has something to do with your son's notebook being lifted from the school on Friday and being placed on your doorstep today, his dirty work is being done by a second party."

Stuart's exhale sounded more like an irritated growl. Following it, the room quieted, and all that could be heard was his shoes clicking against the recently buffed floor of the meeting room. He stopped in his tracks as a thought struck him, causing him to mumble the words, "Maybe Candice was right."

"Beg your pardon?"

Stuart shook his head, wondering if he should even bother to share it. But what if Candice *was* right? "I was just thinking," Stuart said out loud, "is there a possibility that my former brother-in-law has nothing to do with this after all?"

Chief Overstreet ran his hand through the unflattering wig on his head, shifting it to the right just enough to almost even it out. "Anything's possible, Lieutenant," he said. "Like I said, if he is involved, he has a cut man. Why do you ask?"

"Blake." Stuart blurted the name mindlessly.

"Beg your pardon?"

When Stuart smoothed his hands over his freshly shaven head, he felt traces of perspiration. "There's a man, an inmate at Phillips State Prison by the name of Blake."

Irving Overstreet quickly whipped out a notepad from his pocket. "Last name?"

Stuart thought for a moment. "I don't know."

"Black? White? Latino?"

"Black."

"What's your relationship to him? How are you connected?"

"Some years ago, I arrested him, and he was put away as a result of it. He's still serving time for that offense, and he's very bitter. Bitter to the point that all these years later, he immediately recognized me when he came to our church's prison ministry gathering. It's like my face was carved into his brain or something. I don't remember anything about the arrest, but he does, and he had no problem with voicing his disdain."

"He said something to you?" Chief Overstreet looked up at Stuart.

"Yeah. The guards there say he's mentally unstable, and from the looks of it, they're right. He almost seems to have multiple personalities, talking calmly one minute and chopping my head off the next. Reminds me of that character—Ernest T.—from *The Andy Griffith Show*."

Chief Overstreet nodded, indicating that he remembered the deranged, neurotic character too.

"He talked about losing the woman he loved and his son because of me," Stuart said. "From what I could gather, the woman he was involved with at the time of his arrest broke off their relationship after he was charged, and she eventually married another man. According to Blake, his son hated this other man, and both he and his son have held a grudge against me ever since, blaming me for their not being able to share a life."

"You think they could be collaborating on what's happening to you?"

Stuart returned to his seat, hoping that sitting would slow his racing blood. "He said something to me right before they led him back to his cell that day. He said, 'The devil made me do it.'"

Not readily making the connection, Irving replied, "What does that have to do with anything?"

"Look at the notebook in your hand, Chief. Look at the signature marking left behind on every deed this maniac does."

"Dr. A.H. Satan," the chief mumbled.

"Right," Stuart said. "Satan—the devil—they're one and the same."

"I think I'm definitely on to something here," Chief Overstreet said, as though he had uncovered the clue unassisted. "Is this the only time you've seen this Blake fella?"

"I went with a friend of mine to visit another inmate on this past Friday. I saw Blake in the visitation area, talking with a young man that I'm certain was his son. If looks could kill, I'd be a dead man right now. I'm not saying that they're involved in any way, but—"

"But they have major motive, and with his son on the loose, Blake certainly has means," Chief Overstreet said. "I'm certain Reinhart can get somebody over to Phillips State Prison who can question this Blake guy. And finding his son should be a piece of cake."

Stuart used both his hands to rub his face, wishing he could wipe away the misery. His life was being flushed like tainted water in a commode, and he seemed not to have control over any of it. Things had gradually gone from bad to worse. Stuart's stalker had gotten under his skin to the point of making him drive away the woman he loved, and now, this crazed man was getting far too close to Tyler for Stuart's comfort. He couldn't chance losing custody of his son. Something had to give . . . and fast.

"Are you going to be all right, Lieutenant?"

"Yeah, Chief. I'll be fine." Stuart put forth a valiant effort to voice a confidence he didn't feel.

"We're going to move on this new lead right away," Chief Overstreet promised. "Mentally unstable or not, if this man is behind this, he's gonna pay."

Stuart was going to thank the man, but the vibrating sensation of his left hip placed his response on pause. It was his personal cell, and he grabbed it anxiously, hoping that the caller ID would show the word PRIVATE. If so, there was a chance that Candice had finally decided to call. Stuart had sent her an email through the dating site early this morning before coming to work. It was the second one he'd sent—both times asking her to call. But disappointment ran through Stuart's veins when Hunter's number was displayed on the caller ID screen.

"I'll let you get that," Chief Overstreet said. "You know where to find me if you need me."

Stuart pressed the button to answer just as the conference room door closed behind the chief. "Hey, Hunter. What's up?"

"Calling to check on you, bruh. Jerome told me you got hit again today."

Stuart didn't feel like reliving it all over again, but he opened up anyway. "Yeah, and this time, Joe was at work, so he's looking less and less like the culprit."

"So, what do you do next?"

"Remember the guy at the prison that I told you all about on the ride home from our last ministry meeting at Phillips?"

"The loony tune?"

Stuart chuckled. "Yeah, that one. We're in the process of checking him out. I saw him when Jerome and I went to visit Rocky on Friday, and the look he gave me, coupled with what he said the first time he saw me, is enough reason to have him questioned. He's got plenty of cause to want to see me suffer."

"Hmmm," was all that Hunter said in reply.

"What?" Stuart asked. "You sound like you have your doubts."

"No, no," Hunter quickly responded. "I agree. He does have motive and definitely should be checked out. I was just thinking about something else."

"What's that?"

Hunter paused, like he was mulling over whether or not he should say what was on his mind. "I need you to be real open-minded about this, okay? Don't be so quick to write me off on what I'm about to say, but don't be too quick to jump to conclusions either."

"O—kay." Stuart dragged out the word.

"Where is Candice right now?"

The question took Stuart aback. "In New York. My guess is that she's at the school where she teaches. I don't know."

"So, you still haven't heard from her since the spat you all had last week?"

"No, I haven't." Stuart had an uneasy feeling in the pit of his stomach. "Sent her a couple of emails, but she hasn't responded. Why are you asking me about Candice?"

"I saw her yesterday, Stu."

Stuart's eyebrows squeezed together. "What? That's impossible."

"Malik and I treated Jade to Atlanta Fish Market for Mother's Day. We drove to Buckhead to eat there after church yesterday."

"What would she be doing there? What would she be doing in Atlanta at all?" Stuart shook the cobwebs from his head. "It was probably just another lady who favored her, Hunter. You've never seen Candice in person, so you could have easily been mistaken."

"I'm not mistaken, man. It was definitely her. She was with . . . well, she was with another man."

The words were like quick, painful jabs to Stuart's stomach. Before he could respond, Hunter spoke again.

"It could have been her brother or some other relative, for that matter, so don't jump to conclusions. They weren't hugging or acting like lovers or anything, but they came in the restaurant together and shared a booth. They sat near us, and the reason I'm sure it was her is because not only was she the spitting image of the photograph you showed us, but also because I heard the man say her name several times while I was straining to eavesdrop on their conversation. Jade heard it as well, and we heard your name slip in the conversation a few times, too."

Stuart swallowed and braced himself for the answer to the question he had yet to ask. "What were they saying about me?"

"Couldn't hear well enough to pick up the full discussion. We just caught small bits and pieces. But they definitely talked about Joe being released. We picked up on that much."

"Joe being released? Why would they be—" Stuart's eyes grew large. "Oh, God," he whispered. His face and palms were sweating. "You don't think . . . No. It couldn't be."

"Don't jump to any conclusions, Stu," Hunter repeated his earlier statement. "I just thought you should know. I knew you didn't mention her being in town again, and the whole thing just seemed a bit odd to me. You know, her being with this other guy and them having this private discussion about you. I just think it would be a good idea to check it out. I mean, you did meet this girl over the Internet. I know you trust her, and I know you're in . . . well, *very fond* of her, Stu, but maybe you need to check her out more thoroughly. You know what I mean?"

Chapter Twenty-one

"Jerome and I have our official first date to-morrow night." Ingrid's smile stretched from one ear to the other.

It was Tuesday evening, and as the two of them shared a rare weekday dinner at Ruby Tuesday, Jade looked at her best friend and saw a whole different girl than the one she was talking to just last week. There was no sign of the emotional wreck that moaned at the thought that Jerome had chosen another over her, and cried at the remembrance of the Sunday morning that he stopped breathing. That woman had been replaced by one who could barely contain herself. It had been a long time since Jade had seen Ingrid this happy. She hoped that what was about to transpire wouldn't change all that.

"Where is he taking you?" Jade asked, glancing in the direction of the entrance doors and trying to keep the conversation flowing.

Ingrid shrugged her left shoulder but failed in her attempt to look carefree. "He didn't say. I guess he wants it to be a surprise. It doesn't matter where we go, actually. We could sit outside on the porch and talk all night, for all I care. I'm just looking forward to spending some time together as a bona fide couple."

Jade giggled.

"I know I sound like a stupid teenager," Ingrid said, waving off Jade's response with a flip of her wrist, "but I don't care. For the first time, I feel like I'm about to enter a relationship that's going somewhere. Every guy I've ever dated, since I started dating at sixteen, has been shallow and self-serving. I've always been left feeling that they were in it for one thing and one thing only. But, stupidly, I'd never learn from one mistake to the next, and I'd be all too eager to jump into the next relationship, doing whatever I needed to do to hold on to *my man*." When she said the last two words, Ingrid made quotation mark gestures with her fingers. "Right now, I'm just as excited as I ever was with entering any of those so-called relationships, but this time everything feels different and, and, and . . . right. Am I making any sense?"

Jade nodded. "Yes, you are. It's a great feeling." When the door of the restaurant opened, Jade looked up. Then, leaning in close to Ingrid, she said, "Hold on to that feeling, okay?"

"Huh?"

"I should have known this was some kind of setup," Kenyatta snapped as soon as she and Jan reached the table where the other two women sat. "I'm going home. I don't have time for this mess."

"What's going on here, Jade?" Ingrid's deep brown skin paled.

"Wait," Jade said. She slid from the booth and stood beside Kenyatta. "Don't leave, Kenyatta. I know this was sneaky on our part, but—"

"Our?" Kenyatta glared at Jan.

"It was mostly Jade's idea," Jan quickly put in.

Jade rolled her eyes at Jan and then turned back to Kenyatta. "But you're here now, so you may as well join us. Besides, you rode here in Jan's car. She's not leaving, so neither can you."

"Is that the best you can do? Girl, there's a MARTA bus leaving from somewhere near here every fifteen minutes," Kenyatta retorted.

"You think I need to ride in Jan's car? I can find a way home. *Trust me.*"

Jade gently touched Kenyatta's arm, hoping to calm her. "Come on and have a seat. You're causing a scene."

Kenyatta's face twisted, and her neck began to roll. "Causing a scene? Oh, baby girl, you ain't seen nothing yet. I ain't even got started. How y'all gonna let her talk y'all into bringing me up here so she could try to rub this mess in my face?"

"I didn't have anything to do with this," Ingrid defended. "I didn't know you were coming here."

Growing embarrassment was causing Jade to steam. She hadn't counted on not being able to keep everybody under control, and the wandering eyes of nearby patrons told her that her neat little scheme wasn't working out quite as planned. "Ladies, ladies," she said in a voice just above a whisper. "Let's calm down, okay? Ingrid is right, Kenyatta. She's just as surprised to see you as you are to see her. This was my and Jan's doing."

"But mostly Jade's," Jan restated.

"I guess that marine mentality that Pete has—that *thing* that makes him willing to die for his fellow man—just hasn't rubbed off on you, huh?" Jade said to Jan while motioning for her to sit in the booth beside Ingrid. She then looked back at Kenyatta and said, "Just sit here beside me for a minute, okay? We need to talk and get some things in the open. Just us girlfriends."

Kenyatta's upper lip curled. "She ain't one of my friends. She's y'all's friend."

"I'll tell you what," Ingrid said. "She can stay, and I'll leave. I don't need to deal with her or her bad attitude."

"Who you calling somebody with a bad attitude?" Kenyatta asked, opening her purse and dipping her hand inside. "I got your bad attitude."

"Stop it!" Jade's voice was elevated as she grabbed the strap of Kenyatta's pocketbook and snatched it from her shoulder. The weight of the bag made her wonder just what was on the inside of it. Did she really have a gun in her purse? Jade didn't have time to give it a second thought. She tossed the expensive, heavy leather bag in the corner of the booth, sat beside it, and then looked up at Kenyatta, who was still standing. "Now, sit down!" she ordered in a harsh whisper. When Kenyatta continued to stand, Jade felt her heart pound under the daunting glare of the woman's eyes.

She swallowed, gritted her teeth, and kept her face set, and her voice stern. "I said, sit down!"

A wave of relief gushed through Jade's body when the padding of the space beside her sank under the weight of Kenyatta's full hips. All four women remained quiet for several moments, and Jade used that time to drink from her glass of tea, trying to wash down the discomfort brought on by the scene they'd caused.

The waitress approached their table with caution. "Is this everyone in your party? Are . . . are you all ready to order now?"

Still, no one spoke. Jade looked across the table at Jan, who returned her uncertain gaze.

"Can you bring us a couple of your sample platters?" Jade asked. "That and some water for the two who just joined us should be sufficient. Thank you."

"I'll get that order placed right away for you, ma'am." The girl carefully gathered all of the menus and left them alone.

"All of this over a man?" Jan blurted all of a sudden. "This is crazy."

"It certainly is," Jade agreed.

"Well, if that ain't the pot calling the kettle black," Kenyatta shot. She looked at Jade. "When you and Hunter started dating, you made him fire that lady who used to be his right hand at *Atlanta Weekly Chronicles* 'cause she used to be all up in his face."

"Not a word of that is true," Jade defended. "Hunter's a grown man now, and he was a grown man then. I never once suggested that he fire Diane. He made that decision on his own because of her persistent sexual advancements. She was given two chances to keep her actions professional, and she failed miserably. That's why she was relieved of her duties. I don't know where you got your information, but there's no truth to it."

Kenyatta didn't seem completely convinced, but she turned her attention toward Jan, who was nodding her support of Jade's enlightenment. "And aren't you the same woman that almost got arrested for fighting your own cousin over your man?"

Jan leaned forward in her seat and seemed overly delighted to plead guilty as charged. "I sure did, sister girl, but that was totally different. Pete isn't just my man, he's my husband. And I had just found out that my quote/unquote best friend and cousin had done some vile and vicious things to try and break us up. So, yes, I sure did beat her tail, and I'd do it again if I had to.

"I believe in bud nipping and butt whipping. If I had caught Rachel's antics early, I could have nipped it in the bud. But since I found out after she sent bogus letters and made up lies to try and tear up my marriage, I whipped her butt. But the fact of the matter is, Jerome ain't neither one of y'all's husband, and he got y'all acting like straight-up fools."

"It's her fault," Kenyatta said, looking at Jan, but pointing an accusing finger toward Ingrid. "I was here first, and me and Jerome were talking way before she moved to Atlanta. Any woman with any class wouldn't step up in another woman's relationship."

"Jerome is the one who approached me," Ingrid defended. "I didn't step up in anything."

"Both of you are to blame," Jade butted in. "I fault Jerome for dating both of you for months without a commitment to either, but an even bigger responsibility falls on the two of you for allowing him to do it. It's not like either of you didn't know that he was seeing the other. You both were fully aware that Jerome would take one of you out one night and the next one out two nights later, but you let him do it. And I didn't know this until he confessed it to me yesterday, but he had y'all on a schedule, for crying out loud."

"A schedule?" Jan huffed.

"Yes," Jade said. "One of them would call him and talk for an hour, and then when her time was up, she'd hang up because she knew the next hour was scheduled for the other." She turned her eyes to Ingrid. "I can't believe either one of you put up with that, and Jerome echoed my sentiment. It was disrespectful and degrading, but instead of drawing the line with him, you turned your frustrations toward each other.

My brother is saved, yes. But he hasn't always been. He was lost a lot more years than he's been saved, and he's still learning. What the streets taught Jerome is still a part of him, and he's yet growing in Christ. Underneath it all, he's still a man. A man that had two women vying for his attention. I'm not excusing Jerome for what he did, but Lord have mercy— what did you expect?"

Jan was still bobbing her head up and down in agreement. "Ten years behind bars with no women dangling on his arm and all of a sudden he has two smart, beautiful Christian women wanting to date him and willing to be put on a schedule? Of course, he was gonna go for it."

It was Jade's turn again, and she directed
her words at Kenyatta. "I know Jerome apolo-
gized to you, because he told me he did. But I
am a woman too, and I know that his apology
probably isn't enough. But the fact of the matter is that he finally did what he should have
done some time ago. In his defense, though,
I'd have to say that I don't think he had a clue
of which of you he had true feelings for until
Ingrid walked away and gave him a reality
check. You have to give her a little credit for
walking away, Kenyatta."

At Jade's words, Kenyatta turned her face
away from all of them in protest, but Jade
continued speaking. She knew that, although
she was being forced to talk to the back of Kenyatta's head, the woman could still hear her.

"Ingrid backed away and she basically conceded. She stopped taking his calls and stopped
calling him. She didn't go out on any dates or
anything. For more than two weeks there was
no contact between Jerome and her outside of
church, and you had him all to yourself. Now,
you may not like the outcome of the story, but
the truth of the matter is that when he no longer had the option of taking Ingrid for granted,
my brother realized how much she meant to
him. Nobody forced his hand, Kenyatta."

One quick motion brought Kenyatta's face back toward Jade, and her voice was reproachful when she said, "His hand might not have been forced, but I'll bet you put in a good word for your *best friend*."

Jade raised her right hand as though she was about to be sworn in, in a court of law. "As God is my witness, I didn't. As a matter of fact, Jerome didn't even tell me that they'd stopped talking. I didn't know until Ingrid told me two days before Jerome made his decision. The communication between the two of them had stopped for two weeks before I was made aware. I had absolutely no bearing on his final decision. I found out about it when Ingrid called me the same night Jerome called her."

"And I'll bet she couldn't wait to share the news that he'd picked her over me." Kenyatta's bitterness was obvious.

"Kenyatta, she wasn't—"

"I can answer that for myself, Jade," Ingrid said.

Jade held her breath when Ingrid turned her eyes toward Kenyatta, and Jade prayed that whatever her friend said didn't result in an all-out brawl.

"Yes, I was excited to tell her," Ingrid admitted. "But my excitement wasn't because he chose me over you, Kenyatta. It was because he chose me period. I'm sorry that this has hurt you, I really am, whether you believe that or not. I know how devastated I was when I thought Jerome had decided to move on without me. I can't tell you how many days I second-guessed my decision to walk away and leave it in God's hands. When Jerome didn't initiate any contact during that sixteen-day period, I assumed that God had spoken and it just wasn't meant to be. Just thinking about Jerome with anybody else other than me was hard for me to handle. I love him, and I wanted him to feel the same about me."

Kenyatta's eyes shot in Ingrid's direction, and she coughed out a short laugh. "You *love* him? Girl, please, you don't love Jerome. You haven't known him long enough to love him. You might love the way he looks or love the way he treats you or love the fact that he's the son of a big-time preacher, but there's no way you actually *love* Jerome."

"Yes, I do." Ingrid sounded insulted by Kenyatta's critique of her feelings. "I'm not sixteen. I know what love is, and I know what I feel."

"You tell Jerome that, and this whole li'l dream of yours is gonna turn into a nightmare. That man will think you're half-crazy."

Jade looked at Kenyatta. "You mean you don't love my brother?"

Now it was Jade's turn to get the have-you-lost-your-mind look that Kenyatta delivered so well.

"I talked to Jerome for the first time back when Jan's crazy mama was quoting scriptures to me and trying to shoo me off her property during the time that we all thought Pete was about to get killed in Iraq," Kenyatta said.

"Don't be talking 'bout my mama," Jan warned.

"Oh, please," Kenyatta said. "Stop me when I start lying."

Jade couldn't help but laugh. Kenyatta wasn't the only one who thought the Bible-toting, scripture-spewing, overdramatic woman was a bit unbalanced.

"This isn't about my mother, this is about Jerome," Jan said.

"And as I was saying," Kenyatta broke in, "that day in Ms. Leona's yard was only about a year ago, and me and Jerome didn't go out together until probably three or four months after that. I haven't known Jerome long enough to be in love with him, and neither has Ingrid. I don't care what she says."

"I do love him," Ingrid pressed.

Kenyatta answered with a smack of her lips.

"It's possible, Kenyatta. I fell in love with Hunter inside of a few weeks," Jade said.

Jan raised her hand in the air as though they were in a classroom setting. "And I fell in love with Pete inside of a few hours."

Kenyatta sneered at both of them. "And I fell in love with Joe at first sight, but you see what that got me, right? A half-crazy maniac who threatened me every other day and is now a prime suspect in the stalking of my brother, 'cause he wants me back. What that kind of crazy love taught me is that real love takes time. You have to be careful nowadays. That instant stuff that we call love is most often just something that's gonna lead to a lot of hurt and heartache. That's why Stuart is around here nursing a broken heart right now. He went out with that girl one time, and now that it's over, he acts like he lost the best thing that ever happened to him. That's just stupid. That ain't love."

Jan leaned forward on her elbows. "Pete and I have been married for over fourteen years, Kenyatta. True love doesn't have to take forever."

"You're in the minority, Jan," Kenyatta mumbled. "Your testimony isn't shared by the masses, believe me. I've been in enough relationships to know that it doesn't generally work like that."

"And what about Hunter and me?" Jade asked.

"Well, y'all are happy now, but you're still newlyweds.

Me and Joe were happy too, when our marriage was that young. Besides, look at Hunter. Shoot. What woman in her right mind wouldn't take her chances for a slice of that steak?"

Jade wanted to reprimand Kenyatta for her analogy, but all she could do was blush and laugh. Ingrid and Jan found themselves laughing too.

"But life has never turned out like that for me," Kenyatta continued. "So, this time around, I decided to play it smart and be selective. And just when I find a man that's halfway safe, Miss Thing here comes along and messes everything up."

"Is that what this is really all about?" Jade asked. "You think Jerome is safe and that's why you're drawn to him?"

"I didn't say that," Kenyatta said, just as their food arrived.

It only took Jade a moment to say grace, and as soon as the prayer ended, she resumed right where she left off. "Yes, you did, Kenyatta. You just sat here and said you found a safe one, meaning a safe relationship, in Jerome, and Ingrid messed it up."

"Well, he *was* safe," she said. "I'm not saying that's the only reason I was attracted to him, but it played a big part."

"Safe, how?" Jade challenged while Jan and Ingrid began eating. "Tell me how Jerome is safe. What makes you think that a relationship with him is any less of a risk than a relationship with anyone else?"

"Duh!" Kenyatta said. "He's Reverend Tides's son, for starters."

"Reverend Tides's son who used to be a drug dealer," Jade reminded her. "Reverend Tides's son who used to skip school and pick fights. Reverend Tides's son who used to run through women like a baby runs through diapers. Reverend Tides' son who spent ten years behind bars because of his rebellion and disobedience."

"I can't hold that against him," Kenyatta said. "That was then, and this is now. Jerome is a changed man. He's making different choices now, and the choices he makes now are the ones that I respect."

"So why can't you respect this one?" Jade pointed across the table at Ingrid. "Jerome has made a choice in his life concerning who he wants to pursue a relationship with. Why can't you respect that one?"

Kenyatta's eyes became glued to the table, and for the first time, Jade felt a breakthrough. Not wanting to leave any room for Kenyatta to backtrack, Jade kept talking.

"Nobody is saying that you have to agree with the choice Jerome made, but at least, respect it. As much as I would like for you and Ingrid to get along, I'm not even saying that you have to like her. But what I am saying is that you need to respect the fact that she's the woman my brother chose. If you care anything at all about Jerome, you'll respect her because she's the woman in his life. And if you care anything about me, you'll respect her because she's my closest friend. And the call for respect goes both ways."

Jade looked at Ingrid and then back at Kenyatta. "I'm not asking either one of you to value some tramp off the street that's living like common gutter trash. I'm asking you to respect each other, and both of you are decent human beings. It's time for you to call a truce with one another and be the women that God wants you to be. Kenyatta, you can't keep missing church to avoid Ingrid and, Ingrid, you can't keep trying to dip out of the church through the choir exit so you don't have to run into Kenyatta in the foyer."

Ingrid and Kenyatta glanced at each other and then looked away.

"You'll never reach your full potential in Christ if you don't stop fighting one another," Jade said. "There's a scripture somewhere in the Bible where God asks us how we can say we love Him who we have not seen but can't love our brother or sister that we see every day. I'm not sure exactly where that scripture is found, but—"

"We can always ask Jan's mama," Kenyatta mumbled.

"Shut up." Jan's own laughter stole the rigor from her words.

Jade's voice brought order to the table once more. "Whatever differences the two of you have, what you have in common is so much greater. You both share a friendship with me and with Jan, you both belong to the same spiritual sisterhood in the Women of Hope ministry, and you both love the Lord. Isn't that enough to find some common ground? No man is worth this kind of bitterness between sisters in Christ."

Turning to Kenyatta, Jade said, "Whether you think it's a crazy move or not, Ingrid loves Jerome. You never did, you said so yourself. So, the biggest hurt you are experiencing as a result of what has happened is a bruised ego. If you didn't love him, you can't be suffering from a broken heart. And if your ego is the only thing that took a blow, count yourself blessed and keep moving."

Chapter Twenty-two

The house was quiet. Too quiet, actually. With Kenyatta gone out to dinner with her friends, there were no sounds of pots clanking in the kitchen as dinner was being prepared. Just as well. Stuart hadn't had an appetite to eat all day.

Tyler had been granted permission to go to Greene Pastures after school to ride horses and spend the afternoon with Malik and Kyla. It was a reward for getting an A on Monday's exam. At least, that was the reason Stuart had given his son. But it was only partially true (if it were true at all). The bigger reason Tyler had been instructed to climb into Hunter's SUV along with Malik was for his own safety. The notebook that was still being held as evidence at the precinct had placed a level of fear in Stuart that none of the other threats had even come close to achieving. The stalker knew where Tyler lived, and he knew where he went to school. The boy couldn't stay on Hunter's ranch forever, but right now, Stuart needed time to think. And while he thought, he needed Tyler to be in a place where he could be watched closely.

Sitting in his favorite room, Stuart stared at his computer screen, praying that Candice would log on to the site where their relationship began nearly five months ago. She hadn't answered any of his emails, and she wasn't currently online for him to send an instant message. He desperately needed to talk to her. He needed answers that only she could provide.

Stuart looked at Candice's photograph and studied her biographical information as though some secret code, cracking the mystery of all that had transpired over the past few days, was buried between the lines. He found nothing. But Hunter's phone call this morning made no sense to Stuart. As much as he wanted to believe it was all a case of mistaken identity, the logical side of him knew that it wasn't.

What was Candice doing in Atlanta this past weekend? Was she still there? Who was the guy she was with? Why were they discussing issues surrounding his stalker? Just how much inside information did she know about what's going on?

All of the questions swarming in Stuart's head had him desperately hoping that once Blake was interrogated, the already unstable man would completely crack under the pressure, and both he and his son would be arrested based on details of a full confession. Stuart needed for Blake to admit guilt to the ongoing harassments, so that there would be no doubt that the worst case scenario could be laid to rest.

At this point in the game, he'd even willingly accept Allen's theory about everything being related to the Shelton Heights curse. When Stuart really thought about it, the legend was looking more and more intriguing.

"All my friends are riding high," he spoke aloud as his lips struggled to keep up with his racing mind. "Kwame is getting ready to buy his first home, Jerome is starting a new relationship, Hunter's got a kid on the way, Pete's about to be honored in a few days." Stuart stopped and took a breath.

"These are the same guys I hang out with on a weekly basis. We all attend the same church, we serve the same God, we enjoy the same extracurricular activities," he counted. "The only major difference between me and them is that I live in Shelton Heights and they don't."

Was it possible? He felt foolish for even considering it, but if Blake's name cleared, the only alternative would be Candice, and Stuart would take "the curse" any day over having to face the reality of the other.

The waiting game was nerve-racking, and Stuart could feel himself reaching a breaking point. He needed to talk to someone and soon. Staring at the cordless phone that stood upright on his computer desk, only one person's name settled in his spirit. Stuart picked up the phone, dialed a very familiar number, and waited.

"Hello?" Mildred Tides sounded cheerful, regardless of the time of day she answered the phone.

"Good evening, Mother Tides. This is Stuart Lyons. I'm sorry to be calling you at this hour. How are you?"

"Oh, I can't complain, praise the Lord. How are you?" The sudden sound of concern that shrouded her last three words made Stuart wonder if she'd been informed about his recent challenges.

"I'm good. I'm good," Stuart said. He hoped he could label his answer as a reply spoken in faith and not one that was an outright lie. "Is Reverend Tides available to talk for a moment? I mean, I know it's kinda late. I don't want to disturb him if he's busy with other matters or if he's already turned in for the evening."

Mildred released a quiet titter. "We're getting up in age, Stuart, but we haven't gotten so old yet that we go to bed before nine."

Stuart laughed with her. He'd lost track of time hours ago.

"Pastor is in his study," she reported. "You hold on just a minute, and I'll get him to the phone."

"Thanks, Mother Tides."

A few seconds later, Reverend Tides's mellow voice could be heard from the other end.

"Stuart. How are you, son?" If there was such a thing as sounding like a preacher, Reverend Tides could be the model.

"I'm okay, Pastor. You?"

"Ate a little too much," he said with an energetic chuckle, "but other than that, I'm doing just fine." Reverend Tides sobered. "But I know you didn't call me just to see how I was doing."

Stuart rested his back against the support of his chair. "It's about this whole stalking case. I know the Bible teaches us not to fret because of evildoers, but I'm really wrestling with this one, Pastor."

"That's understandable, Stuart. You're human. Who wouldn't be disturbed by this? I mean, every family has its problems, but when there is a possibility that your own brother-in-law, past or present, is wreaking such havoc on your life—"

"I don't think Joe is doing this." It wasn't until that moment that Stuart realized that Reverend Tides hadn't been brought up to speed. "Joe hasn't been totally cleared yet, but Friday afternoon, some of Tyler's school supplies were taken from his classroom."

Stuart went on to tell his pastor the full story and then explained that the police knew of Joe's whereabouts at the time the property was taken and at the time it was placed on Stuart's doorstep. "He was our most promising suspect," Stuart concluded in a defeated tone.

"I see. So, does this mean you have no other leads?"

"Not entirely." Stuart took a breath. "As we speak, they're checking out Blake, the guy at the prison."

"The young disturbed fella at Phillips State?" Reverend Tides sounded surprised.

"Yes, sir."

"But he's in prison. How could he be doing it? Do they think he's hired someone to do the dirty work for him?"

"Not exactly," Stuart replied.

"I wouldn't think so. He didn't strike me as savvy enough to put together a scheme like the one that's being pulled on you."

Reverend Tides's comment made Stuart stop and think. He was right. Blake couldn't possibly have the mental capacity to contrive this kind of a plan—a plan so brilliant that it had stumped police and civilians alike. But if Blake didn't do it, that would leave Candice and her mystery man.

"Perhaps Blake doesn't have the smarts," Stuart said, determined to rid himself of that last thought, "but his son might. Blake said his son hated his stepfather, and I've been blamed for the reason he even has a stepfather. So, while Blake probably doesn't have the brains for something like this, he could be a link in the chain of events that his son has orchestrated."

"Ah," Reverend Tides said. "That makes good sense. I guess you'd have to have the mind of a lawman to string together a scenario like that."

Stuart's laugh was lifeless. "Not really. The only reason you didn't think of it was because you didn't have all the facts like I do."

"So, your reason for calling is because you want me to continue praying that the mystery be solved quickly so that you can get your peace of mind back? Am I right?"

Another labored breath from Stuart placed a pause in their conversation. He wished it were that simple. "Actually, there's more," he said.

"Oh?"

Telling Reverend Tides about Blake and his son was a much easier task than revealing the story of Candice. Stuart had never mentioned his relationship with Candice to his pastor, so he started at the beginning. But the minister's occasional, unruffled responses of "Uh-huh" and "I see" prompted Stuart to believe that this wasn't the first time Reverend Tides had heard the story. However, the pastor was clearly taken aback by the news of Candice being spotted at the restaurant with the unidentified gentleman companion.

"I would have to agree," Reverend Tides said at the end of Stuart's revelation. "That's very odd for her to be in town and not inform you."

"I've been thinking about that," Stuart said. "Since we'd had the spat over the phone just a couple of days earlier, maybe she didn't think I'd be interested to know."

"Do you really believe that's the reason, Stuart?"

Stuart's eyes shot to the clock on his desk. It was after nine now. Malik would be home soon, and no doubt, so would Kenyatta. He didn't have time to be playing word games with Reverend Tides. No time to try to pretend. "No, sir, I don't," Stuart admitted.

"So, am I reading you correctly? You think Candice might have something to do with the threats and pranks?"

Just the thought of it brought sickness to Stuart's stomach. "I just don't know what she was doing here and who the guy was that she was with." He felt better not giving the pastor a straightforward answer. "But I don't know a reason why she would be doing this to me either."

"You said the two of you had an argument."

"Not really an argument," Stuart defended. "It was more of a difference of opinion that I allowed to get out of hand. Even so, this crazy stuff started happening way before that."

Saying those words brought a sense of relief to Stuart. It was true. All of the letters began coming long before his argument with Candice—long before he'd met her, even. She couldn't be the perpetrator.

"Was this going on before your online association with her began?"

Just like that, all of Stuart's newfound hopes were dashed. It was now official. In taking the Christian dating site route, his losing streak continued. Counting Candice, Stuart was batting zero for four, and from the looks of things, he would have been better off to consider himself "out" at strike three. Strike four was costing him more than just the game.

Stuart massaged his left temple. Admitting the truth to Reverend Tides was physically painful. "Actually, the letters started shortly after we connected online."

"I want to pray for and with you, Stuart," his pastor said, cutting into the quiet, "but not over the phone. Hunter will be here shortly. Mother Tides asked him to bring the children over for some of her homemade ice cream and cake when they were finished in the pasture. As dark as it is now, I'm sure they are on their way or soon will be. Why don't you come over here so that we can pray together? We're going to touch and agree for a breakthrough to this problem. The devil has used you for his playing field for far too long. It's time to put him back in his place."

Stuart inhaled slowly. "You think it's Candice, don't you?" He held his breath as he waited for Reverend Tides's answer.

"I think it's the devil," he replied. "Whomever it is that's doing this is being used as a tool of Satan."

Stuart exhaled. The around-the-way answer didn't help.

"But let me say this," Reverend Tides added. "The police should have *all* of the information that they need in order to work on this case, Stuart. The only way that any one of the suspects can fairly be found guilty or innocent is if they have all of the information they need to do a thorough investigation."

Reverend Tides's instructions made the queasiness in Stuart's stomach increase. "Yes, sir. You're right." Those were the words he said, but in his heart, Stuart was praying more fervently than ever that Blake and his son would be charged.

"So, I can expect your arrival?" Reverend Tides asked.

"Yes, sir. I'll be there in a few."

Stuart's heart was heavier than ever as he placed the cordless phone back on his desk and rolled his chair away from the desk and stood. His hand felt weighty when he reached for his mouse to prepare to shut down his computer system. Pausing before clicking the icon, Stuart stared again at Candice's headshot.

"Can a woman as lovely as you really be capable of being so evil?"

As though serving as an answer to his question, the cell phone on Stuart's right hip vibrated. Lifting it, he saw the number to the station displayed on the screen.

"Please, God," he whispered just before pressing the button and saying, "Lieutenant Lyons speaking."

"Stu." It was Allen, and his voice was barely audible.

Stuart knew right away that Allen must have been around people who he didn't want to hear his conversation. "Allen. What's going on? What's up?"

"I just wanted to give you the heads-up," he whispered. "I know Chief is gonna call you soon, but Marion Blake is being questioned right now."

"Marion Blake?"

"Yeah. Blake is the last name of the guy at the prison, not his first."

"So, his name is Marion?"

"No," Allen said. "The prisoner's name is Larry Blake. Marion is his son. He's the one being questioned."

They had picked the boy up for questioning, and that in itself was a good sign. Something that the senior Blake said must have given them reason to suspect his son. "How's it going?" Stuart asked, hopeful.

"Not so good."

Stuart closed his eyes and sank back into his seat, feeling that he was about to lose all sanity. "What do you mean?"

"I don't think either one of them had anything to do with it. Me and Chief Overstreet watched the interrogation for a while, and he agrees with me. Reinhart and a couple of other detectives are still questioning the boy. You got yourself a lot of enemies, man. I guess all us cops do. But this kid and his daddy admitted to hating you and blaming you for their family falling apart, but ain't neither one of them smart enough to outsmart us. If they were guilty, we would have found out by now."

Stuart listened in silence, all the while feeling himself moving closer and closer to the edge of the cliff.

"We got a search warrant and checked out Marion Blake's house and his mother's house and found nothing, and his alibis have already supported his story. When you saw him at the prison on Friday, he was just being released from Crawford Long Hospital. He'd been in a car accident on Tuesday, and you probably didn't notice it, but his left leg was in a cast during the time he was visiting Larry. Marion lives in Macon, nearly a hundred miles from here, and he was at home, still recuperating when we picked him up for questioning. So, he was in the hospital at the time Tyler's notebook was stolen and at home in Macon at the time the evidence was placed outside your door. It's not looking good, Stuart. I heard Overstreet say that we weren't going to have enough to keep him."

Stuart's eyes remained closed. He heard his security system chime, indicating that Kenyatta had arrived. He couldn't let her see his anguish. Enough chastisement had been endured from her for his having so quickly attached his heart to Candice. If Kenyatta detected his latest suspicions, the result would be unbearable.

"Listen, Allen." Stuart balled his free hand into a fist so tight that he could feel his short fingernails beginning to dig into his palm. "I need you to tell Chief Overstreet to call me at this same number as soon as he can, okay?"

"Sure thing. Can I tell him what it's about?"

"Give him this name, and when he calls, I'll fill him in on all the details."

"Okay." Stuart could hear Allen scrambling for a pad and paper. "Go ahead," he said.

Stuart's mouth felt like it was secreting Elmer's Glue, as he fought to form the words. "Candice Powell."

Chapter Twenty-three

Until this week, eighth grade had been a fun experience for Tyler. It was his last year in middle school, and with the last day of school just weeks away, this was the semester he was supposed to enjoy the most. Eighth grade prom was just around the corner, and although he still hadn't decided which girl he'd ask to accompany him, Tyler knew he wouldn't have any problems getting a date. He'd been blessed with his mother's smooth caramel skin and his father's good looks. At his young age, he already had the bulk of a future football player, and that alone gave him a few brownie points with the girls at Redan Middle School.

Tyler's best friend, Malik, was celebrating the fact that Kyla Jericho had agreed to be his date. Secretly, Tyler had his own crush on the pretty, athletic high school freshman, but he wouldn't dare let Malik know. Besides, there were at least three middle school girls who would be glad to walk into the gymnasium on Tyler's arm. He might not be escorting the popular daughter of hometown hero, Peter Kyle Jericho, but Tyler would be sure to choose a girl who would turn her share of heads.

All of his fun had now been tainted. From the desk where Tyler sat, preparing to be released to the cafeteria where he would share Wednesday's lunch menu with hundreds of his schoolmates, he could see Sergeant Allen Bowden's car nestled in plain view at the edge of the campus parking lot. His father hadn't told him, but Tyler knew that the increased presence of law enforcement was largely due to the fact that Stuart feared for his safety.

The adults in Tyler's life had been doing a lot of whispering around him lately. Now, he knew firsthand what Kyla felt like last year when she was being treated differently due to her father's capture in Iraq and what Malik must have felt like the year before when the city of Atlanta, and Stone Mountain, in particular, had blackballed his dad because of information that was being printed in the *Atlanta Weekly Chronicles*.

"Tyler, make sure you take all of your belongings and place them in your locker before you go into the lunchroom, okay?"

Mrs. Rutherford, his science teacher, had stood by his desk and whispered the words, but those closest to Tyler could easily hear her, and he could feel their eyes fixated on him. He knew the notebook that went missing last week was the reason she wanted him to take extra precautions, but he thought having to lock away his belongings was taking it a bit too far. After all, his couldn't have been the first notebook to be taken by another student.

"Yes, ma'am," he replied.

When directions were filtered into their classroom by way of the intercom system, Tyler and his classmates lined up and dispersed. Admittedly, lunch was one of Tyler's favorite times of the day, but today, what he wanted more than anything else was to have his normal life back.

"Hey, Tyler. I thought I'd wait for you," Malik said as he stood next to Tyler's locker.

"You can get in trouble for loitering in the halls when you're supposed to be at lunch," Tyler replied.

"You mad at me or something?" Malik asked, leaning against the closed locker door beside Tyler's.

Slamming the metal door shut, Tyler said, "Naw, Malik. I ain't mad at you, I'm just sick of school, that's all. I'll be glad when the year is over."

As if Malik knew Tyler wasn't really in the mood for talking, the walk to the school cafeteria was a quiet one. Once the boys had their meals in hand, they found two empty chairs at a table that was being occupied by schoolmates that they had little or nothing to do with on a regular basis. Most of them were seventh graders—pretty much outcasts to eighth graders, considered the upperclassmen of middle school. The kids' faces brightened when Malik and Tyler sat, like they felt special to have the elite share their humble space.

"Is this about Uncle Jerome?" Malik asked, biting into a fish stick. "Are you mad at me 'cause he decided to date Ms. Ingrid instead of your auntie?"

Tyler looked at Malik and curled one corner of his top lip. "What? Man, I don't care nothin' 'bout that mess, and my aunt don't neither. She said she didn't want him anyway, and as far as she was concerned, Mr. Jerome and Ms. Ingrid deserved each other. And for your information, my aunt dumped your uncle, he didn't dump her."

Malik laughed. "Oh, that's what she told you? That's funny right there. But, okay. Whatever makes her happy." He swallowed gulps of milk to wash down the fish stick. "So, if you ain't mad about that, why you ain't talking today?"

Tyler looked around at the other students that sat closest to them, and although they had their own conversations going, he wondered if any of them were listening in on his. For added insurance, he lowered his voice. "I just been thinking about all this stuff that's been going on with my dad."

"The letters and stuff?"

"Yeah. Something big must have happened 'cause, all this week, the police have been sitting out on school property."

Malik wiped his mouth with his napkin. "I heard my parents talking last night about your notebook that got stolen, but I couldn't make out what they were saying. But you *do* know that the real reason you been riding with me and Daddy every afternoon after school is because Mr. Stuart don't want you to catch the bus and be home by yourself anymore, don't you? He just wants you to stay with us until he or your aunt gets home from work."

"Yeah. I know." Tyler pushed his glasses up on his nose and crammed a few fries in his mouth. Stuart hadn't come out and told him the reason for the after-school change, but he'd been smart enough to figure it out on his own. That was the one thing about the whole mess that Tyler didn't mind. He enjoyed going to the *Atlanta Weekly Chronicles* building or to Greene Pastures after school. At either location, there were fun and interesting things to do, once he was finished with his homework.

If Hunter had duties to fulfill at the paper in order to ensure that they met their print deadline, Tyler was able to make a few dollars serving as a go-fer, along with Malik and sometimes, Kyla, assisting Hunter, Kwame, Jerome, or Hunter's secretary, Lorna. And at Greene Pastures the fun was unlimited. But for Tyler, there was nothing exciting about having armed security spend the day at the school, as though they were the secret service and he was the son of the President of the United States.

"I wanna go live with my mom," Tyler mumbled.

"For real?" Malik eyes protruded. "Then you won't be able to come to school with us."

"I don't care. At least I wouldn't have to deal with this stupid stuff. I used to want to be a cop like Daddy, but not no more."

"Did you tell your mom that you wanted to live with her?"

Tyler nodded. "Told her when we talked on the phone the other night. She said we'll talk about it when she gets home next week."

"I thought you said Mr. Stuart told you not to mention this to her."

"He did," Tyler mumbled. He knew his dad wouldn't be happy, but neither was he. So, as far as Tyler was concerned, the score would be even.

Malik grunted. "I can't believe you'd punk out on us like that, man."

"Ain't nobody punking out on nobody." Tyler lowered his voice when he saw inquisitive eyes looking at him from their other table-mates.

"Mama said nobody else might not know who's doing it yet," Malik whispered, "but God has all-seeing eyes and He will lead the authorities to the guilty person soon."

Tyler shook his head in doubt, but didn't verbally reply. He sipped milk through a straw and wondered just how long God planned to wait before He decided to do whatever He was going to do.

"You scared?"

Tyler looked at Malik. "Who? Me?"

"Yeah." Malik's eyes were serious. "You scared of this dude who's doing this to y'all? Is that why you want to go move with your mama?"

"Naw, man, I ain't scared," Tyler said. His eyes dropped to his plate. He knew that if Malik could see his eyes, he would know that he was lying.

Chapter Twenty-four

This was the first time that Jerome would visit Rocky on a Wednesday, and it wasn't by choice. Rocky's phone call request, asking Jerome to stop by and see him, couldn't have been more ill-timed. Jerome had planned the evening down to the minute. The night would be a one-stop shop, filled with dinner, good music, and if Ingrid wanted—dancing, too. Jerome had heard a lot about Sambuca restaurant and for some time had wanted to give the Buckhead hotspot a try. With low lighting and live smooth jazz, Sambuca's ambiance was perfect for romantic couples, and Jerome was looking forward to taking Ingrid.

He had just laid out his professionally cleaned and pressed silk-blend black pants, grey buttondown dress shirt, and the grey, black and white tie to match when Rocky called. Jerome had tried his best to get out of the meeting with Rocky tonight, promising him that he'd be at the prison early on Friday, but Rocky insisted. After a while, Jerome began recalling his last visit with the troubled inmate. He remembered Rocky's words and how depressed and despondent he was. Jerome and Stuart had prayed with the man before they parted ways last week, and Rocky vowed to pray daily and read the New Testament Bible that he'd been given through the prison ministry, as a means to keep himself encouraged. But maybe it wasn't working. Maybe he was having a bad day. Rocky was Jerome's God-given personal mission, and the ministry that was growing inside of Jerome wouldn't allow him to turn down the inopportune request.

Jerome looked at his watch. He was supposed to be pulling up in Ingrid's apartment complex right now, picking her up for their night on the town. Instead, he was navigating his car onto prison property. Thankfully, when he called Ingrid to tell her about what had transpired, she understood.

"It's okay, Jerome," she'd said. "We waited for each other this long; what's another couple of hours? If you feel that this is what God wants you to do, then you need to do it. I'll see you whenever you're done."

The smile that crossed Jerome's lips when Ingrid said it returned as he recalled the moment. His calling into the ministry was inevitable. He remembered the deal he made with God in the men's room at church. Jerome had asked God to send help, and He'd already done it. Ingrid had just the right attitude that any woman standing beside him would need. He couldn't have imagined Kenyatta being so forbearing. More than ever, Jerome was convinced that he'd obeyed God when he made his choice.

Jerome shoved his CD collection, his cell phone and any other valuables that he had inside his vehicle into his trunk, then abandoned his car and set his mind on the task ahead. The wait to see Rocky wasn't as long as Jerome thought it would be. When he came on Fridays, his wait was sometimes twice as long as today's. Once he cleared the metal detector, he was on his way, following the lead of the designated staff person, but knowing the route all too well. They passed many employees along the way who remembered Jerome from his years of confinement there. As always, when he visited, Jerome returned their nods and even shook a few of their hands. All the while, Jerome was thanking God that, of his own free will, he could turn around and walk out the same way he walked in.

As usual, Rocky was shackled when he walked into the visitation area where Jerome sat, waiting. When the guard loosed him, Rocky pulled out a chair and sat. For a moment he showed no emotions, but just as Jerome was about to speak, a smile stretching across Rocky's face muted him.

"I know you got places to be, man, so I ain't gonna hold you," Rocky promised, leaning in close like he had a secret to tell. "My lawyer says I might be walking soon."

Jerome's body jolted as if someone had just poured cold ice down the back of his shirt. "What? Why? When? How?"

"That's what I said." Rocky released a laugh that sounded a lot more genuine than any he'd released before.

"Thank you, Jesus," Jerome whispered. The unexpected news overwhelmed him. "Oh, man," he breathed. "Are you serious, Rocky? What happened?"

"One of them cats that lied on me twenty-some-odd years ago came back and told the truth about everything," Rocky said.

It was too much information for Jerome to absorb. "Why after all these years?"

"'Cause they still doing the same dirt after all these years," Rocky said. A frown made a drive-by appearance on his face. "Smoke—that's the dude who was really behind setting up the whole takedown—scared them other wusses into making me the fall guy." Rocky shrugged. "All us was really scared of Smoke, so I guess I can't blame them too much. But a ni . . . a brotha don't appreciate going to jail for what somebody else did. You know what I mean?"

"Yeah." Jerome's mind was still stuck on Rocky's previous statement. This was the first time he'd ever heard the man admit to being afraid of anyone other than his father. And that was a childhood fear that had fermented into hatred a long time ago.

Rocky continued. "So, basically them other cats got away with a slap on the wrist, Smoke got away scot-free, and the only people to ever serve any real time for what happened is me and Nose-Face."

"Nose-Face?" Jerome came close to laughing.

"Yeah. He's the one who actually shot and killed the dude that night. We called him that 'cause he got in a fight one time and somebody broke his nose. He never went to the doctor, so it didn't never heal right. Smoke always said you could see his nose way before you saw his face. That's how we came up with Nose-Face."

"So, now Smoke is in trouble again for something?" Jerome wanted to hear more, and Rocky seemed anxious to fill him in.

"The guy working on my case says they had moved the operation to Florida and had built a big-time drug empire there in Miami. Smoke was the big man there too, and all but one of the guys who ran the streets with us back in the day was still hanging in strong with him. Solo—that's one of the guys who fingered me way back when—was one of the ones who got arrested this time around, and the lawyer says he's offering a plea bargain to save his own behind."

"What happened? A drug bust?"

"Naw, church boy. That's amateur stuff. I can't even tell you how many drug busts Smoke 'n' 'em done dodged over the years. This was another murder, but this time he didn't get so lucky. Solo is a whole lot braver than I was back in the day."

Jerome had to ask. "Solo?"

"Yeah. We called him that 'cause, when we went partying, he was the only one who didn't go home with a girl. Good looks ain't his strong point. You know?"

"Got it," Jerome said.

"Anyway, some po' dude owed a debt he couldn't pay with his wallet, so Smoke cashed in on his life. A bullet through the heart, I hear. He was gonna try to make Solo take the fall this time, just like he did with me. But Solo's name's got a new meaning now," Rocky said with a laugh. "I hear he's singing like Luther, telling everything he's ever known about Smoke in the deal he's cutting with the Feds. Smoke has put a lot of drugs in the hands of school kids and stuff, and he's responsible for more than a few *accidents*, if you know what I mean."

Jerome leaned forward in his seat. "So, he's telling how they set you up to look like the muscles behind the other deal?"

Rocky nodded. "Like I said, he's telling everything he knows. The lawyer said Solo told the cops that he knew he'd probably get killed for telling it all, but said he'd rather be dead than to be in prison." Rocky looked around the room and then back at Jerome. "I don't blame him," he concluded.

"Wow, Rocky." For a moment, it was all that Jerome could think to say. He rubbed his chin with his hand and then said, "So, how soon will you know?"

"Maybe as soon as a week or two. With the real role that I played in the crime, the most I would have gotten was twenty, and I've already served more than that."

"I'm happy for you, man. I believe it's gonna all work out. Me and the brothers from church will definitely be praying for you. I know you have your doubts, Rocky, but prayer really does work."

"I believe you."

Jerome raised his eyebrows, wondering what had changed his mind. He remembered the time when Rocky thought prayer was for the weak-minded who needed to feel like they had some higher power on their side in order to even put one foot in front of the other. Rocky must have read the questions embedded in Jerome's expression.

"You remember, a couple of months ago, when your old man, I mean, Reverend Tides, had asked us to write down on a piece of paper, what we wanted God to do for us?"

"Yeah."

"That's what I wrote," Rocky revealed. "I wrote on that paper that I wanted to be released from prison. I didn't care how. I just wanted to get out of this place. I ain't lived none of my adult life as a free man. I wanna know what it's like to go to bed and get up when I wanna. I wanna be like the brothas who go to honest jobs and get a paycheck every week. I wanna be like you, church boy. Look at you," Rocky said, pointing at Jerome. "You all dressed up, getting ready to spend time with a lady." He grinned. "I want to do that too."

Jerome fiddled with his tie. "It all took time, Rocky. I got all that stuff now, but it didn't come easy, and I had to do it one step at a time. The first thing I did when I got out of here was got back in the church and started getting my life right with God. That's the most important thing. You do that, and all the other stuff will come."

"Including the girl?" That seemed to rank highest on Rocky's list.

"Hey," Jerome said, spreading his arms out, "you see me, don't you?"

Rocky laughed. "Yeah, man, I see ya. What's her name?"

"Ingrid."

"She pretty?"

"Very," Jerome answered. "We've been out before, but just as friends. Tonight is our first date as a couple. Ingrid's a sweet lady that goes to my dad's church. She's originally from New York. I met her through my sister."

Rocky nodded his approval. "That's good for you, church boy, but *sweet* might not be quite what I need in my life. I'll need a woman that's gonna put me in my place when I get outta line. She need to be pretty and nice and all, but just to be able to put up with me, she gon' have to be a little rough around the edges. Your sister got any friends like that?"

Jerome burst into a jovial laugh. "Actually, yes, she does. Her name is Kenyatta, and the two of you just might be a match made in heaven. I'll be glad to introduce you to her once you get out of here, but only after we get you on the right path. God first, remember?"

"Yeah, I hear ya," Rocky said. "But you can go ahead and put in a good word for a brotha, right?"

The hour was growing late by the time Jerome parked his car in the lot of Ingrid's apartment complex. He couldn't believe it was already eight thirty. The appointment at Phillips had thrown a major wrench in Jerome's well-thought-out plans. Now, they'd never make it to Sambuca in time to see Five Men on a Stool's live performance. He'd especially wanted Ingrid to experience the unique magic of the

Atlanta-based popular jazz/spoken word ensemble. As Jerome made his way up the steps to Ingrid's second-floor dwelling, he prayed that she wouldn't be too disappointed.

"You finally made it." She opened the door before he even knocked. "Come on in."

Delicious smells lured him inside and immediately held his stomach hostage. "I'm so sorry," he said, stepping close to Ingrid and embracing her warmly. "That went a little longer than I expected."

"It's okay," she said as he released her. "Is your friend all right?"

"He's doing great. I'll fill you in on the details later." Jerome's eyes were drawn to the way the little black dress flattered her curves. "You look beautiful."

Ingrid did a complete turn so that he could see the fullness of her beauty. "Thank you. You look quite handsome yourself."

"All dressed up and no place to go," Jerome said in a sympathetic voice. "I'm sorry."

"You're here, Jerome," she said. "I'm not disappointed, so you have nothing to be sorry for."

Jerome couldn't help but be optimistic. He foresaw this being a wonderful relationship.

Looking toward the kitchen, he said, "You cooked?"

Ingrid motioned for him to sit on the couch, and when he did, she sat beside him, crossing her legs with perfection. Soft music played from her stereo.

"Your mom called me when she heard that you were going to see your friend, and she advised me to go ahead and start dinner. She said her years as a pastor's wife have taught her a lot of things, and one of them is that, when Reverend Tides is involved in ministry, always devise a plan B." Ingrid laughed, and Jerome focused on her lips as they parted. "She said I should go ahead and cook something just in case."

"And you did," Jerome observed, making a mental note to thank his mom.

"I did," Ingrid verified. "Peppered steak, rice, green beans and dinner rolls."

"Mmm." Jerome's rumbling stomach approved.

Ingrid smiled. "Whatever happened, the food wouldn't go to waste. If you got here in time for us to go out, I could put the food away and eat it tomorrow. If you were late and didn't really feel like getting back in traffic or waiting in long lines at the restaurant, then we could dine in."

Jerome sat quietly for a long while, just looking into Ingrid's eyes and admiring the soul he could see on the other side of them.

"What?" she asked. "Did I say something wrong?"

"No," he replied, standing and pulling her up with him. He slipped his arms around her waist and began swaying to the music. It wasn't Five Men on a Stool, but for now, it would do. She instantly fell in sync. "Thanks, Ingrid," Jerome said with his lips resting at her ear. "I promise to make it up to you. We'll go out this weekend. Okay?"

"Okay," she whispered. "But we don't have to go out for you to make it up to me. You're making it up to me right now."

Chapter Twenty-five

Stuart sat on his couch trying to catch his breath while several of his colleagues from the precinct combed through his home, looking for fingerprints, blood samples, anything to help them find out who had entered Stuart's house uninvited and ransacked the one room that he cherished most.

The moment Stuart walked into his home after driving around the city for hours trying to clear his head, he knew that something was wrong. There was no doubt in his mind that he'd set the house alarm before he left for work, and since Kenyatta had gone to the spa after work today and Tyler was with Malik, no one had been in the house since they all left this morning. Yet, when he entered shortly after eight, his alarm didn't trigger.

Stuart had immediately drawn his revolver and began tipping through his home, dipping around corners and turning on lights as he went. When he entered his kitchen, he found the place where the prowler had entered. The window to the door that led to his deck had been smashed, but somehow, the intruder had managed to disarm his security system before it had sounded long enough to alert the police or the company who monitored it.

Glass was spattered all over the tile on the kitchen floor, and at first, Stuart counted his blessings. It looked like the worst of the damage was the glass door, and he couldn't see where anything of value had been taken. His flat-screen television, his stereo, his TiVo system all were in place and appeared untouched. Still, he picked up the phone and called Dekalb County's finest to come out to write up the report.

Just as Stuart was about to end the call, he unlocked his den, flipped on the light switch and nearly collapsed at the sight before him.

His computer had not only been raked off of his desk, but it looked as though someone had taken a baseball bat and hammered into the frame, disfiguring the metal casing of the screen as well as the hard drive. A mangled mess that used to be his reading glasses was on the floor beside it. The covering of his sofa and couch had been slashed with some type of sharp object, and the pink fibers from the inside of it had been pulled out, littering the floor like mounds of cotton candy. The bathroom mirror had been shattered, and rolls of tissue had been stuffed into the commode. Glass from the broken television screen was embedded into the fiber of the area rug, and spray painted on the wall in black letters that looked like the work of a fifth grader were the words: DR. A.H. SATAN.

"Lieutenant," Deputy Chief Overstreet said as he sat beside Stuart on the living room sofa. "I know this is probably not the best time to talk about this, but a week from now won't be any better."

Stuart looked at the chief, but said nothing.

"We're bringing in Candice Powell for questioning and I think we'll have enough to make an arrest."

"No," Stuart said, vehemently shaking his head from side to side. "She didn't do this. This was done today. I'm sure she's back in New York by now."

"She doesn't live in New York, Lieutenant," Chief Overstreet revealed.

"What?" If Stuart wasn't already sitting, he would have needed a chair at that moment.

"We've been investigating her since I got off the phone with you yesterday. The investigation is ongoing, but with new evidence from this home invasion, making an arrest stick won't be hard to do."

Stuart was still having difficulty digesting Chief Overstreet's initial claim. "What do you mean, she doesn't live in New York?" He looked up to see Reverend Tides, Hunter and Peter entering his home. Stuart had tried calling Jerome several times, but got no answer. He fixed his eyes back on Chief Overstreet. "What do you mean, she doesn't live in New York?" he repeated.

Assuming it was okay to discuss the issue in the presence of Stuart's friends since he'd posed the question in front of them, the chief pulled out a small pad and flipped open the pages. "Candice Powell lives here in metropolitan Atlanta, Roswell, to be exact," he said. "She's an English teacher at Roswell High School."

"Oh, God." Stuart felt a hand on his shoulder and assumed it was Reverend Tides's. He didn't look around to see.

"There's more," Chief Overstreet told him. "This is not the first time she's stalked a love interest. Seems that some years ago, she reportedly repeatedly harassed an ex-boyfriend and his wife after the gentleman broke up with her and married someone else. We were able to contact the ex late yesterday, and he verified his ordeal with her. Said it wasn't until he threatened to put a restraining order out on her that she backed away and stopped the harassing phone calls and uninvited visits to his home, banging on his door at all hours of the day and night. Apparently, the break-up hit her hard. Although her former doctor won't release any information to us, she did substantiate that Candice underwent long-term therapy at her clinic."

Stuart felt like he was in the twilight zone, or maybe just caught in the middle of the worst nightmare of his life. He wanted the chief to shut up and go away, but the words from his lips just kept right on spilling out.

"Evidence indicates that the footprints that were detected—the ones that lead up to your deck—probably belong to that of a woman. If it is a man, he has unusually small feet. We're still trying to figure out how she or he was able to get into your den without it being forced entry, as was the case with the back door."

The grip on Stuart's shoulder tightened, and he knew it was a silent cue for him to tell the whole truth.

"I gave her a key," he whispered.

Chief Overstreet's posture straightened. "You gave Ms. Powell a key?"

"Yes." Stuart was fighting tears. "I gave her a key last weekend when she supposedly flew in from New York to visit me."

Before the chief could respond, his name could be heard coming through the speakers of the two-way radio clipped to his belt. "Chief Overstreet here. Over."

"The suspect has been brought in for questioning."

Stuart looked directly at the chief for the first time in a while.

"Ten-four," the chief said. "I'm on my way."

"I'm coming too." Stuart stood with him.

"No, Lieutenant." The stern tone of Chief Overstreet's voice indicated that Stuart didn't have a choice in the matter.

"This is about me, Chief."

"Exactly. You're too close and too involved."

Stuart established a firm grip on Chief Overstreet's arm. "I *need* to do this. I need to go to the station with you."

Chief Overstreet looked around the house as detectives still walked in and out, doing their jobs. "What about them? Who's going to be here, just in case they have questions?"

Stuart looked at the men standing around him in support.

"Go ahead, bruh. I'll stay until you get back," Hunter promised.

"So will I," Peter said.

"Thanks," Stuart mumbled, still trying to grasp the reality. As he turned to follow Chief Overstreet, Reverend Tides called his name.

"Son, I know you're carrying a heavy cross right now," he said, "but remember our prayer time last night. We asked God to work it out and bring it to a swift end. We can't tell God how to do what He does, but we have to trust Him and know that even when it doesn't feel like it, the Lord is working it out for our good."

Stuart's body felt too paralyzed to even respond. He willed his legs to follow Chief Overstreet to his car and rode in dead silence to the police station.

If every eye in the building wasn't on Stuart as he trailed the chief through the precinct, it felt like it. Moments after they entered the front door, they were standing at the two-way glass that allowed them to see inside the interrogation room.

Candice's eyes looked swollen, and her face was drenched in tears as two detectives—one male, one female—dished out a major dose of the third degree. The grilling was brutal, but Candice stuck to her story, claiming not to have anything at all to do with the letters, the hang-up phone calls, the vandalism, Tyler's stolen binder, or the break-in. Candice lied like a pro, and her performance was flawless. Ruby Dee, Meryl Streep, Halle Berry . . . there wasn't an actress anywhere who could hold a candle to her. While other box office queens strove to be seen as deserving of an Oscar, it was the Oscar that needed to work to be worthy of Candice. She was phenomenal.

As Stuart watched the showstopper, his anguish turned to anger. "Let me inside," he mumbled to Chief Overstreet.

"No, Lieutenant," Overstreet replied. "Give them time. Eventually, she'll break."

"Let me inside, Chief," Stuart repeated. "No sense in wasting all of this time and energy. You let me inside, and I'll have her confession in no time."

"If you get a confession out of her, Lyons, the courts might see it as unethical. You're the victim. You have a personal relationship with the suspect. We've come too close to blow this now."

"I deserve this, Chief." Stuart's whisper was harsh. "That woman owes me, and she needs to look me in my face and tell me the truth."

Chief Overstreet held up his hands in surrender. "I'm not giving you permission, is that understood? You go in there, and you're doing it on your own. As a matter of fact, I don't even know you're going in. Is that clear, Lieutenant?"

"As a bell," Stuart said.

He watched as the chief shook his head. Then slowly, Chief Overstreet began turning his body. When his back was to Stuart, the lieutenant opened the door to the interrogation room and walked inside, closing himself in with Candice and the two detectives questioning her.

"Stuart!" Candice rose from her chair, only to have the female officer grab her by the shoulders and press her back into a seated position.

"Lyons, what are you doing in here?" the male detective asked.

Stuart offered no response. He simply took his place on the side of the table opposite of where Candice sat, placed his palms flat on the table top, and leaned in close to the woman who, despite it all, still made his heart turn flips.

"Why did you do it? What have I ever done to you to deserve this?" he asked, keeping his voice steady and stern.

Candice gasped, and new tears spilled from her eyes. "You really think I did this? Stuart, please tell me that you don't think I'm capable of doing this."

"Capable? Let's not talk about what you're capable of doing, Candice. How do you even keep the lies straight?"

She had no answer, only more tears.

"So, what did you do?" Stuart continued. "You just packed up some bags and went and stood outside the airport for me to pick you up like you'd flown in from New York?"

"I—I—"

Stuart didn't even give her the chance to fumble out a response. "It all makes so much sense now," he declared with a disgusted laugh. "You wouldn't allow me to book your flight here because there was no flight to book. You never gave me your phone number because you knew that giving it to me would give away the fact that you lived in Atlanta. You didn't want me to walk you through the airport to the security gate because you knew that if I walked inside with you, I'd discover that you didn't even have a flight reservation." Stuart lifted his hands from the table and then slammed them back with such force that Candice and the two detectives who stood nearby all reacted with synchronized flinches. "Stop me when I miss one, Candice!" he yelled.

"I'm so sorry," she wept. "I was going to tell you, I just didn't know how."

"Tell me what? That you were a well-dressed, well-educated, well-poised psychopath who was well versed in how to portray a Christian woman?"

"No," Candice insisted. "That's not what I am, Stuart. Listen—"

"You're not a psychopath?" Stuart was seething. "Oh, really? We have evidence that I'm not the first man you stalked and tormented, Candice. Does the name Ephraim Polk ring a bell?"

Candice's eyes became enlarged, and she looked like he'd just spat in her face. Like the Ephraim situation was Pandora's Box and Stuart had no right to open it.

"That's right, I know all about it," he scoffed. "Honesty. You actually said honesty was the most important quality that you looked for in a man. Do you even know how to spell honesty, Candice?"

"Stuart—"

"What did you do to make Ephraim leave you? Did he leave you because you flipped out on him, too?"

"I'm not crazy, Stuart."

"And when he bailed on you, you followed him around, devastating him and his family, didn't you? You were treated by a psycho-therapist to help you cope with the severed relationship, weren't you?"

She looked even more devastated, but managed to say, "Yes, but—"

"But you're not crazy?"

Candice's weeping became heavier, but Stuart wasn't finished.

"This is why you were so shocked when I told you that a suspect had been caught, isn't it? And it's also why you so easily suggested that he might not be guilty, when I told you that he'd been released. You were so confident it wasn't him because you knew it was you who was doing it all along."

"No. No. That's not true."

As Stuart struggled out his next words, he wanted to cry, too, but swallowed back the rising emotions. "I gave you the key to my den, Candice. The key to my heart . . . and this is how you repay me?"

"Okay, okay," she wailed.

Stuart stood upright. He was hurting inside like he never would have imagined, but he was ready for the ordeal to be over, and he braced himself for the imminent confession.

"Okay," Candice said for the third time, "you're right. I wasn't completely honest with you. When I saw your profile on the site, I noticed that you lived in Atlanta, so before I contacted you, I changed my profile to say that I was from New York so that you wouldn't try to set up some quick meeting between the two of us. I needed to know that you were safe and not somebody who had just registered on the site to try your hand at nabbing naïve church women."

Stuart folded his arms in front of him. He wanted to rush her forward to the part where she confessed to the stalking charges, but he tapped into his patience and remained quiet.

"And, yes, the flight into Atlanta was bogus, but you insisted on picking me up, and it was the only way that I could make it look authentic."

She paused to blow her nose into tissue that the station had provided, and Stuart's patience was tried as he waited for her to continue.

"This whole thing with Ephraim . . . that was a lifetime ago. He didn't break up with me because I was mentally unbalanced. I was *very* good to him, Stuart." Mounting anger seemed to replace her earlier wretchedness. "He and the girl had been having an affair for months, and he left me to marry her because he'd gotten her pregnant. If you ask her, I'm sure she'll verify it. She was my best friend, and I admit that I didn't deal with it well at all. I didn't have the level of maturity that I should have had at the time, and most of all, I didn't have Christ in my life."

Stuart shifted his feet and narrowed his eyes. This wasn't sounding so much like a confession any more.

"Ephraim was my first true love, and I thought he felt the same way about me as I felt about him. I was blindsided by what they did, and I handled it like a foolish woman who didn't know God because I *was* a foolish woman who didn't know God. But my *then* has nothing to do with my *now,* and I resent your quest to make me out to be some mental fruitcake. I didn't do what you're accusing me of, and I can't even believe that you'd think that I did."

She was so convincing that Stuart had to remind himself of why he'd come in the room in the first place. He unfolded his arms and placed his hands on his hips. "And what about last Sunday? You were seen in a Buckhead restaurant with an unidentified gentleman, discussing my case. How do you explain that? And who was the man you were with?" Stuart threw in that last question more so for his own benefit.

"That was one of the ministers at my church. Yes, he wanted to have a relationship with me, but that was the Sunday that I finally laid it on the line and told him that it could never be. Despite everything, he's a great man of God, and as we were clearing the air, I told him about you—the biggest reason that there could be nothing between him and me. The part that was overheard was my confiding in him about the discussion that you and I had, had. The one where you got upset when I suggested that your brother-in-law might not be guilty."

"And he'll corroborate that story?" the male detective injected, taking out a pen and pad.

"Cornell Pratt," Candice barked, offering information they'd not yet asked for. "P-R-A-T-T. He is the associate pastor of Redemption Temple, where I attend church."

Stuart stared at her. The tears had subsided, but her red, puffy eyes remained a constant reminder of her uncompromising denial. Stuart couldn't decide which was worse: the fact that she still declared her innocence or that he was starting to believe her. Candice's voice broke the silence.

"I'm not pretending to be a blameless bystander, Stuart. I'm guilty of pretending to live somewhere that I don't live, but I've never pretended to be someone who I'm not. The woman that you went out with is the woman that I am. I didn't reveal my whole past to you, but that's not so odd, is it? I mean, it *was* our first meeting and our first date. I was going to tell you everything eventually, and it was going to be up to you how to handle it. But I didn't want details of the old Candice Powell to run you away before you got the chance to know the me of today."

Stuart ran his hands over his head then resumed the position he was in when he first entered the room. His palms flat on the table, he leaned toward Candice. "What about my den?"

"What about it?"

"It's ruined, Candice. There was forced entry into my house at some point this afternoon, but no forced entry into my den. The door was locked when I left for work, but when I got home this evening, not only had someone used a key to unlock it, but they completely destroyed my den and then had the unmitigated audacity to lock the door behind them when they finished."

The female officer in the room spoke up. "According to our findings, Ms. Powell, your last class of the day ends at two fifteen P.M. You also have a key to Lieutenant Lyons's den. The incident occurred at some point before seven P.M. You had the time and the means to carry out this deed."

Candice never looked at the woman and responded as though she wasn't even in the room. "I'm sorry for what happened in your home and to your den, Stuart. I don't know what took place or how it took place, but I didn't have anything to do with it."

"I gave you the only spare key that I had, Candice. Unless you allowed someone else access to it—"

Candice reached into her blouse and pulled out the box-linked chain with the key dangling at the end of it. "I've worn this almost constantly ever since you gave it to me."

Seeing the key around her neck, dangling so close to her heart, touched Stuart.

Candice said, "The only time I take this off is when I shower. I even wear it when I sleep. Nobody has touched this key, Stuart. When you gave it to me, I knew that small gesture was a big move for you. You're the first man I've felt this way about in years. I wouldn't have done anything so ludicrous to jeopardize what we were building. You have to believe me. Please say you believe me, Stuart. Please."

Stuart stared down into Candice's eyes, searching for signs of the lies that were being used to cover other lies. Just minutes ago, he was so sure that she was guilty. All arrows pointed to Candice, and there was enough evidence to support every suspicion that Stuart had. She had admitted to misleading him before, so why was he being foolhardy enough to even consider that she was being honest now?

"I believe you," he whispered, drawing murmurs from the two detectives who stood nearby. Stuart could only imagine what Chief Overstreet was thinking while taking it all in from the observation window.

Candice's lips quivered. "Do you?"

Stuart reached out and took both her hands in his. "God help me if I'm being hoodwinked," he said. "But, yes, I believe you."

Candice placed one of her hands on each of his cheeks. Stuart felt mounting tension and ripples of pleasure as she used her hands, still moist with tears, to caress his deep chocolate skin. "I'm telling you the truth, Stuart," she said. "As God is my witness, I'm telling you the truth."

Stuart placed his hands on top of hers and reluctantly pulled them away from his face. He brought Candice's hands to his lips, not kissing them, but allowing them to rest there for a few seconds before releasing them and standing to his full height. His face still tingled from her touch.

"They're gonna have to hold you for now," Stuart informed her in a voice still lowered by a combination of emotions.

"Why?"

"The state has too much evidence not to. I'll do what I can to help clear your name, but other than that—"

Candice seemed to panic. "But I'm not a flight risk. I live here. I work here."

"It doesn't matter. Legal procedures have to be followed. I'm sorry."

"How could you do this to me?" she wailed.

The same tears she shed that made him angry earlier were now breaking Stuart's heart, and he wanted to hold her close until she was completely consoled. Leaving her there seemed callous, but there was no other choice.

Straightening his body to its full height, Stuart shook his head slowly and then turned to walk away. He heard Candice call his name through what he knew was a new burst of tears, but he never stopped to look back. He needed to get out. He needed to breathe. He needed to think. He needed to pray.

Chapter Twenty-six

True to their word, when Stuart walked into his home, the first faces he saw were those of Reverend Tides, Hunter and Peter. They were all sitting in his living room, talking. His entrance drew all of their eyes in his direction, but none of them immediately spoke.

Stuart closed the front door, shutting out the sight of the official yellow tape draped around his yard, overstating the crime scene. Uninformed passers-by probably thought someone had been murdered in the house. Just as well. Stuart felt dead.

Still standing at the door, he heard the noise of an electric drill coming from the kitchen area, and then Tyler rounded the corner, dressed in his pajamas and polishing off the last bit of orange juice from a glass he held in his hand.

"Hey, Daddy," the boy said, walking toward Stuart and offering a much-needed hug.

"Hey, buddy." Stuart held him longer than normal and wondered how much Tyler knew.

"Mr. Kwame and Mr. Jerome are putting in a new door," Tyler reported. "They're almost finished now."

"Oh, okay." Stuart was thankful for resourceful friends. He pumped artificial life into his voice and added, "You should be in bed, shouldn't you, big man?"

"I was," Tyler informed him. "I got thirsty and got up to get something to drink." As if it were a souvenir, the boy handed Stuart his empty glass. "I'm going back now . . . unless you need to talk to me or something."

Stuart knew that his son was really asking for an explanation. Tyler wasn't oblivious to the fact that, in recent weeks, certain aspects of his father's life had gone awry, and by simple association, he had been affected by them as well. Tyler was old enough to understand, and he deserved to be informed of the details, but Stuart was just too tired—both mentally and physically—to get into it tonight.

"We'll talk in the morning, okay?"

"Okay, Daddy. Good night."

Stuart watched his son disappear down the hall. Once Tyler closed the door to his bedroom, Stuart sat on his loveseat and leaned forward with his elbows pressed into his thighs. He stared at his hardwood floors, listening to the sudden silence that took residence after the drilling stopped in the kitchen.

"Are you all right?"

Stuart didn't look up, but he knew it was Jerome. He and Kwame were joining them in the living room. A faint nod of his head was the only response he could immediately muster.

"I'm sorry I missed your calls, man. I was out with Ingrid and had left my phone in the trunk of the car." Jerome sat on the space beside Stuart, leaving only Kwame standing.

"How'd it go?" Stuart asked, still staring at the floor.

"How'd what go?"

"Your date with Ingrid."

Jerome placed his hand on Stuart's shoulder and gave him a firm squeeze. "It went fine, man, but you know we ain't here to talk about that."

Stuart sat up, released a heavy sigh and then looked around. "Where's Kenyatta?"

"At the church with Jade and other Women of Hope members," Hunter answered. "You know my bride believes in calling on the sisters for prayer any time something major goes down that involves a member of the church."

"Has Candice been arrested?" Jerome had apparently gotten tired of waiting for Stuart to willingly offer any information.

"She's being held on suspicion," Stuart said. He put both his hands together and rubbed them over his whole face. "I think I'm losing my mind."

That was all that needed to be said for Reverend Tides to abandon his seat on the sofa and walk in the direction of the couch. Like a silent order had been given, Jerome relinquished his spot and migrated to the place on the sofa that his father left vacant.

Reverend Tides sat beside Stuart and then turned to face him. "Why do you think you're losing your mind, son?"

Stuart paused and then said, "With all the evidence that points to her, Candice is declaring her innocence. And . . . well, I don't know."

"And you believe her?" It was as though Reverend Tides could see straight through to Stuart's heart.

Stuart nodded. He could feel the tears he'd been holding back for hours begin to leak from the corners of his eyes. "I feel like such a fool," he whispered.

"Why?" Reverend Tides asked.

"Because it's so obvious that she did it," Stuart said, wiping away the salty liquid and standing to his feet. "It's as plain as the nose on my face, but she told me she's innocent, and, like a fool, I believe her."

"How is her guilt obvious?" Reverend Tides challenged. "Until it's proven that she did the crimes, nothing is obvious."

"You were here when Chief Overstreet was talking to me, Pastor. You heard how the cards were lining up. Every drop of evidence coincides with the department's beliefs. The timing when the harassments started, Candice's past obsession with a love interest, the small footprints on the deck, the unforced entrance in the den."

"What about the notebook?" Hunter offered.

"What about it?"

"How would she have known what class Tyler was in and which desk inside the class was his?"

Stuart thought for a moment and then said, "I don't know. Me and Candice talked so much on that day we spent together that I probably told her. I was telling her everything about me that day."

432 Kendra Norman-Bellamy

"And you would have told her which desk your son sat in?" Peter's voice was challenging. "That's not just something that you tell somebody, Stu."

"This is Candice, Pete," Jerome reminded. "This is the girl he allowed to enter The Lyons Den."

Peter was undaunted. "Okay, fine. For the sake of argument, let's just say he slipped and told her what class Tyler was in. Realistically, once she found that class, all she'd have to do is fumble through the belongings on each kid's desk until she found his. But the fact of the matter is that she would have had to first find the classroom and then find the desk. C'mon, man. In a school the size of Redan Middle, how likely is that?"

"Unless she'd been watching him," Kwame added. "If she'd been watching Tyler for some time and nobody knew it, there's no telling what she could have found out."

"Thanks a lot, Kwame." Jerome's upper lip was curled into a snarl.

"No, he's right," Stuart said. "I need to hear both sides here, and Kwame's right. If Candice is obsessive, she could easily have been stalking both of us. The team at the station thinks she has trust issues, due to what happened to her in the past, and because of that, when she becomes involved with anyone, she automatically takes obsession to an insane level."

"But you don't believe that, do you?" Reverend Tides said.

Stuart shook his head and then banged the side of his fist against his fireplace mantle. "What is wrong with me!?"

"You're in love," Hunter said. "And ain't nothing wrong with that."

"It is, when the person you love is senile and you walk right into her trap with your eyes wide open."

"Stuart, I don't believe Candice is senile," Reverend Tides said.

Stuart looked at his pastor in bewilderment. "How can you make that kind of assessment? You haven't been adequately informed. You haven't even met Candice."

Reverend Tides rested his back against the cushions of the sofa and looked up at Stuart. "I may not be an informed man, but I'm a praying man. God has a way of feeding things into my spirit, and where Candice is concerned, I just don't feel she's the monster that the evidence is drawing her out to be. Just like the police were wrong about Joseph and the brother at the prison, they could be wrong about Candice."

Peter stood and walked near where Stuart stood. "If your heart tells you she's innocent, you owe it to her to stick by her regardless of what the evidence looks like."

Hunter chimed in. "Remember two years ago, when everybody thought Reverend Tides had been killed and wanted me to stop running those letters of support in my newspaper?"

Stuart knew the story well and nodded his reply.

"There was one woman—only one in the whole city—who wanted those letters to continue, and that was Jade. She needed me to believe in her despite what the church community, the city of Atlanta *and* the police were saying. If I hadn't loved her enough to believe in her, her father would have died. Not in the accident that everybody else thought he'd died in, but at the hands of a madman."

"That's right," Jerome said. "And just like with Candice, all of the evidence said that Dad was dead. All the evidence said he had been killed in that car accident. We had had a funeral and everything."

Hunter came back and took it from there. "Jade's heart told her that there was more to the story, and my heart told me that, as irrational as she sounded, and as much evidence as there was that said otherwise, I had to believe in the woman I loved. I had to believe in the God inside of her."

Stuart looked off into the distance, seeming to talk more to himself than to any of those around him. "When I looked into Candice's eyes, when I looked into her heart . . ." his voice trailed, and all of a sudden, he began walking down the hall that led to his den. He heard the footsteps of his pastor and brothers following him.

"Are you sure you want to look at this again, Stu?" Kwame asked. "We fixed the back door, but we didn't touch the den. Jerome said we shouldn't go in unless you said so."

Stuart already had his hand on the door knob and was turning it. "Might as well," he mumbled as he flipped the switch that turned on the light. It looked even worse now than it did the first time. "Welcome to what *used* to be the Lyons Den." There wasn't an ounce of joy in Stuart's voice.

While the others walked around surveying the extensive damage as though it was the result of a tornado or some other act of God, Stuart spent some time standing beside his desk, staring at the empty space where the computer that introduced him to Candice once stood. Although everything that had been destroyed could be replaced, the sense of loss was unfathomable.

"It's late, and I know you need to get some rest," Reverend Tides said after they'd spent many minutes taking in the degree of the destruction. "I guess we should call it a night. Unless you need us to stay here with you longer."

Shaking his head, Stuart said, "No, sir. I'll be fine. I don't know how much rest I'll get, knowing that Candice is still being held. But I do plan to at least lie down for a few hours.

Not much I can do in here." He stretched his hand out toward the center of the damaged room.

Reverend Tides stepped closer. "You can still pray."

Stuart looked at his pastor, then out at the devastation, then back at Reverend Tides, as if to say, *"You're kidding, right?"* Though the words only rolled through Stuart's mind, they may as well have rolled off his tongue.

"In scripture, the lion's den wasn't an immaculate place, Stuart," Reverend Tides said, as if he'd heard Stuart's thoughts. "It wasn't decorated with upscale furniture or wired with the latest technology. As a matter of fact, Daniel didn't go in it to pray. He was *thrown* in it as a punishment for the prayers that he refused to discontinue. His lion's den represented death and danger, but he prayed in it anyway. The man of God beat the enemy at his own game, and ultimately, the enemy died the death that was orchestrated for Daniel. It was in Daniel's den that he found deliverance. In his lion's den, the Lord answered his prayers."

Reverend Tides stretched his hands toward all of the disarray that covered the floor and walls of the vast space. "This room, its current state, represents death and danger for you and your family. Confuse the devil, Stuart. Use his own ammunition to kill every destructive purpose that he has for your life. Don't you dare give him this victory without a fight, and don't dare try to fight him without prayer. Use the Lyons Den to defeat your enemies in the same manner that Daniel used the lion's den to defeat his. The weapons of our warfare are not carnal, and you can't treat them like they are. Pray your way through, Stuart."

Two hours after his pastor and friends had left his home, Stuart lay tossing and turning, trying to find sleep. He'd heard Kenyatta enter the house more than an hour ago, but didn't bother to get up to meet her. He heard her walking through the house, praying, asking God to anoint their walls and cover their floors. At one point, he could tell that she was standing right outside his bedroom door, and her prayers were specific to him. Stuart had never heard his sister beseech God so passionately before, and he could feel the anointing from her prayer engulfing his bedroom. Without a doubt, the special gathering of the Women of Hope ministry had been a meaningful one.

Now, the house was quiet, and all that Stuart could hear was the sound of his own breathing. Each inhale and exhale seemed amplified in the eerie silence that blanketed the darkness.

It was in Daniel's den that he found deliverance. In his lion's den, the Lord answered his prayers.

Reverend Tides's words eased their way back into Stuart's psyche. Upon locking the front door behind the men's exit, Stuart had set the house alarm, showered, and then dragged himself into bed. It had been a long and grueling day. But even with the heavy fatigue that seemed to double his body's mass, Stuart hadn't been able to find sleep. Every time he closed his eyes, still frames showing the anguish on Candice's face flashed through his mind.

During dinner at The Pecan, she'd told him how her parents ridiculed her for following the ways of Christ, that her father had predicted her Christianity would one day land her in trouble. The thought that the woman he loved was in some holding cell all because he turned her name in to the police made Stuart shudder. He sat up in his bed, resting his back against the headboard.

"I've got to get her out of there," he spoke aloud. Agony gripped him when he remembered the tears that painted Candice's cheeks and the terror in her voice as she called for him when he walked out of the room.

"I can't believe I left you there." Stuart brought his knees up to his chest and buried his face between his thighs.

Guilt and regret served as his chastisement, and the punishment was brutal. More than ever, he believed her. However slim the chance was that Candice was telling the truth, Stuart was holding on to it. He kicked off his covers and walked to the window, peeping out into the pitch black that the half-moon barely cut into. There were no signs of life on the outside, and Stuart barely felt signs of it on the inside either.

"Okay, none of the sensible suspects are guilty, so the person who did this has to be somebody who I never would have thought to suspect—somebody who none of the evidence obviously points to." Stuart's mind was playing detective again, and he paced the floor as he thought. For the first time, he was tempted to consider his closest friends. Hunter, Pete, Kwame . . . even Jerome.

"No," Stuart snapped. He'd trust them with his life. "They wouldn't do this."

Immediately, their names were replaced by the image of Allen Bowden. For a second, Stuart froze in place and couldn't move. He didn't want to linger on Allen, but there was some sense to the possibility that he could be involved. Allen was always there when the letters came, but never there when the few phone calls came. Always the first to respond when it came to other instances, like the day his patrol car was vandalized. Allen was always on top of every suspect's interrogation, seeming to know details before anyone else did. He was a

trained law officer. He'd know how to prevent
fingerprints and unlock doors without a key.

"No," Stuart repeated. Only this time, his
mind wouldn't flush away Allen as quickly as
it did the others.

Sergeant Allen Bowden had been the one
who he'd entrusted to watch out for Tyler.
He was the one sitting on school property,
watching the boy's every move. Realistically,
he could have easily gone in Tyler's room and
swiped his binder, and he definitely had the
time to place it at Stuart's front door.

Beads of sweat began forming in the furrows
carved across Stuart's forehead. "This doesn't
make sense. I've never done anything to Allen to make him do something like this. Why
would he do it?" Stuart was pacing again, and
his breaths were coming in shallow pants. He
couldn't help but think of what had happened
with Pete's wife.

When Jan was being tormented a year ago,
it was her own cousin, Rachel, who was found
to be the inflictor. And just like Rachel did with
Jan, Allen had tried harder than anyone else to
make Stuart believe that the spirit of Shelton
Heights was the one at fault. "Oh, God, no,"
Stuart whispered.

442 Kendra Norman-Bellamy

He did a quick review in his mind, thinking all the way back to the time when Allen first began working with him. Other than this whole bit with Shelton Heights, they'd never even had a noteworthy disagreement. To Stuart, every detail about this case made less and less sense, but every thought of it became more and more painful.

He stood in place again, trembling for seemingly no reason. When he heard Kenyatta praying outside his door earlier in the night, Stuart had sensed the presence of God. Now, he felt like every force of hell was trying to overtake him—mind, body, and soul. He heard voices laughing at him, telling him that he was going to lose his son, telling him he was going to lose Candice, and telling him he was going to lose his mind.

Don't you dare give him this victory without a fight, and don't dare try to fight him without prayer.

Stuart had heard Reverend Tides's earlier spoken words loud and clear, but right now the words that followed those rang loudest in his ears.

Use the Lyons' Den to defeat your enemies in the same manner that Daniel used the lion's den to defeat his. Pray your way through.

Wearing only a pair of royal blue pinstriped boxer shorts and bedroom slippers, Stuart walked out of his bedroom on unsteady legs and returned once more to the scene of the crime. He flipped on the light switch and carefully stepped onto the floor, making sure he avoided any dangerous shards of glass that may have splattered from the smashing of his computer. No matter how many times he'd seen the devastation, the pain of the view only increased.

DR. A.H. SATAN. There they were. The big, bold, ugly words that had been haunting Stuart for months. It had been the signature of every letter he'd received, plastered on the side of his vandalized cruiser, scripted on the cover of Tyler's stolen binder, and now, in lettering larger than life, it covered a hefty portion of the wall opposite the sofa. Tell-tale splotches on the floor signified that the intruder had once again used black paint to make his amateurish markings.

Stuart walked to the sofa with the intention of sitting on one of the few spaces that hadn't been hacked, but found himself kneeling instead. At first, he spoke to God in silence, and the heaviness in his heart began to drain through profound moans and a steady stream of tears. There was no one there to hear or see his impassioned reactions, so Stuart allowed the emotions to flow freely, not even bothering to silence them or wipe them away.

"Lord, I need your help," he said as he neared his conclusion. "I know, as Christians, you warned that we'd have trials and tribulations. You said that they come to make us strong, and though this one has shaken my sanity and my faith, I know I've also been strengthened. Through it, I've learned what it means to totally trust in you for daily security. Through it, I've learned what it means to pray without ceasing. Through it, I've even learned what it means to love in spite of."

Stuart choked on his tears. "Forgive me for doubting Candice. Please, God, cover her with your arms of protection and let no harm come to her as she goes through this with me. I believe in her, and I ask that you reveal the fullness of her innocence. Let her not be charged with a crime she didn't commit, regardless of what the evidence shows."

His mind rested on how badly he'd wanted guilt to be charged to Blake and even Joe. Then he thought of Allen. "Forgive my quickness to pass judgment, God, and let *no one* be charged if they aren't guilty. Lord, you are all-seeing and all-knowing. Please reveal the truth and do it expeditiously so that peace can return to my family and to my relationship. I ask all these things in your son Jesus' name. Amen."

When Stuart stood, an automatic whisper of, "God help me," slipped from his lips. He instantly recalled Peter telling him that he'd whispered that same three-word request many times when he was captured in Iraq. When all hope seemed lost and he could think of nothing else to say, Peter said those words had given him courage to go on. In addition, Stuart remembered something else that Peter had said when he came to New Hope with his family that first Sunday after being delivered to Atlanta following his miraculous rescue.

"This ordeal not only taught me how important it is to pray to my Heavenly Father for all that I desire of Him," Peter had said, "but it also taught me how important it is to listen to God and find out what He desires of me. So many times, we, as children of God, talk to Him constantly, but what we fail to do is spend some quiet time just listening to Him. What I've learned is that in those times when we think God hasn't answered our prayers, He really has, or at least, is trying to. We just haven't shut up long enough to hear His response."

On the day that Peter spoke those words,
they didn't register on a personal level with
Stuart. But now they did, and he sank onto
the tattered sofa and closed his eyes in silence,
waiting to hear divine direction. For many
minutes he sat, meditating, hearing nothing,
but holding to the faith that the answer was on
its way.

When Stuart finally opened his eyes, he still
hadn't heard God's audible voice, but for reasons unknown to him, the words on the wall
in front of him, DR. A.H. SATAN, drew him in
and seemed to magnify themselves.

DR. A.H. SATAN
DR. A.H. SATAN
D—R
A—H
S—A—T—A—N

Stuart closed his eyes and rubbed them,
trying to rid his mind of the letters that had
all but seared themselves on his corneas. But
when he reopened his eyes, the same words—
the same letters—stared him in the face, refusing to allow him to look away.

DR. A.H. SATAN
D—R—A—H—S—A—T—A—N
N—A—T—A—S—H—A—R—D
N—A

T—A

S—H—A—R—D

"Oh . . . my . . . God!"

In a single move, Stuart lifted his body from the sofa and sprinted for the den's door, barely remembering to leap over the broken glass of the television and computer. He dashed down the hall and burst into his son's room, propelled by immeasurable adrenalin. "Tyler!"

The sudden call of his name jolted Tyler into an upright position like an air-filled clown balloon that was returning from being punched by a child. "Huh? Huh? What?" Disoriented, his eyes were wide and red.

Stuart flipped the light switch, to get a clear view of his son. Tyler appeared to be alert, but was anything but fully coherent. "Tyler." Stuart sat on the side of the bed and grabbed the boy by both shoulders, shaking him gently until he answered.

"Sir?" Tyler said the word while trying to free himself from his father's grip so that he could lie back down.

"Tyler, wake up!" Stuart said, shaking him more firmly. "Tyler, wake up, son. I need to talk to you."

Rubbing his eyes, Tyler said, "I thought you said we'd talk tomorrow."

"This can't wait, son. Wake up, Tyler. Wake up!"

"I'm awake, Daddy."

"What's going on in here?"

Stuart took a quick look over his shoulder and saw that he'd awakened Kenyatta. But he didn't have time to explain anything to her just yet. He wasn't even sure what to explain.

"What, Daddy?" Tyler asked. Stuart was still shaking him.

"Where is your key to the den?" Stuart released him, finally convinced his son was lucid.

"You lost your key?"

"No, Tyler." Stuart felt Kenyatta closing in on them from behind, but kept his eyes on his son. "I just need you to tell me . . . *show me* where your key is."

"It's in the pocket of my book bag where I always keep it."

"Show it to me," Stuart ordered just before he stood, pulling Tyler out of the bed with him.

"What's wrong, Stu?" Kenyatta asked, holding her robe closed with her hands.

"I'm not sure yet." Stuart watched Tyler search through his bag. With every pocket that came up empty, his heart pounded harder.

"I don't see it," the boy replied after he'd pulled everything out.

"When was the last time you saw it?" Stuart asked.

"I don't know," Tyler admitted, still trying to wipe the sleep from his eyes. "Why?"

"Who knows you had the key? Did you tell any of your friends?"

"No, sir."

"Who all knows, then?"

Tyler repositioned himself on the floor, sitting Indian-style. "Just me, you and Aunt Kenyatta," he said.

"That's it?" Stuart asked, not wanting to put words in the boy's mouth. "Are you absolutely sure that the two of us are the only people besides you who knew you had the key?"

"Yes, sir." Tyler yawned. "Oh, yeah . . . and Mama."

Chapter Twenty-seven

The following afternoon, Candice was cleared of all charges. It was a bitter-sweet victory for Stuart because he knew the next several weeks—months, even—would be difficult ones for Tyler. This morning, Stuart had, had the challenging task of telling his son that the mother he loved was being arrested on mounting counts of charges, including trespassing, harassment, breaking and entering, vandalism, destruction of private property, destruction of government property, and theft.

Tyler didn't cry, and he insisted that he was fine to go to school today, but Stuart knew that at some point, when the shock of it all ran its course, his son would need major support. He had already made arrangements with Hunter to allow Tyler increased access to Greene Pastures. The horse breeding farm seemed to serve as a God-inspired source of consolation for any

452 Kendra Norman-Bellamy

of their children, whenever they were faced with grown-up heartaches. And Stuart could think of very few things that could hurt Tyler more than knowing that his own mother was the face behind the haunting words that had tortured them both for months.

DR. A.H. SATAN

It was his ex-wife's first name, plus the initials of her middle and last names, printed backward. Natasha Renee Dennis—DR. A.H. SATAN. Stuart still couldn't believe they were one and the same. When he called in his suspicions last night, a big part of Stuart hoped it would be another dead end, but it wasn't.

The answer to why Tasha had done it was still speculation, but concrete evidence had sealed her fate. Still the first to get the inside information, Allen had called Stuart shortly after ten this morning, telling him that a search warrant had been granted and that the police had gone into the suspect's home in Ellenwood, Georgia and found gloves, black paint, letters that hadn't yet been mailed, Tyler's spare key . . . and Tasha. Her medical assignment had ended weeks ago when she was released from Nurse Finders after she was accused of a medical mishap that resulted in a lawsuit. The case was still under investigation in Chicago, but with the charges hanging over Tasha's head, no medical service would risk hiring her.

"Since she'd signed Tyler over to you legally, maybe all this was her way to render you unfit, so she could try and get her son back," Allen suggested. "Or maybe she wanted you back too, and thought that if she could break you down mentally, you'd feel that you needed her. Who knows why she did what she did?"

Stuart had shaken his head at the words. There would have been no chance of the latter, and he would have fought her to the death for the former.

Once all of the legal red tape was finished, the Chief of Police opened the door to let Candice out of the room where she'd been brought to hear the news that she was no longer a suspect.

On the big screen that played the scene in Stuart's mind, Candice ran out of the room and into his waiting arms. In real life, that wasn't the case. He was standing not fifteen feet away, but Candice walked right past him without a word. She barely even looked at him. Stuart watched her walk out the exit doors.

"You're just gonna let her go? Just like that? After all you've put her through?"

Although no one had actually spoken the words, Stuart heard them audibly. And when he looked at Chiefs Reinhart and Overstreet, who remained standing at the door of the conference room from where Candice had been released, and across the way at Allen Bowden, who stood near a coffee-maker, holding a fresh cup, Stuart saw the words exuding from all of their eyes.

Exiting the precinct, he stood on the top step, surveying the grounds around him. Candice had just walked out. She couldn't have gotten too far.

"Candice!" He spotted her standing several yards away, at the mouth of the visitor parking lot, a cell phone to her ear.

Taking the steps two at a time, Stuart raced across the street. "Candice," he said again.

She turned her back to him, never once taking her cell phone from her ear. Stuart approached with caution. When he dared to touch her shoulder, Candice whipped around to face him. Tears gleamed in her eyes.

"Get your hands off me, Stuart! Just leave me alone!"

"I'm sorry, sweetheart." It was all that he could say.

She turned her back to him again.

Deciding that touching her again wouldn't be in his best interest, he only spoke this time. "I was wrong, and I'm sorry. There was just so much evidence and—"

"And what?" She pulled the phone from her ear and faced him again. The tears that her eyes once held hostage were streaming down her cheeks. "I don't know who you think you are, Stuart Lyons." Her eyes were aiming darts at him. "Maybe you're used to women falling at your feet every day of the week. Maybe you're used to them obsessing over you and doing whatever they need to do to get your affection. Well, aren't you just full of yourself!"

"I'm not full of my—"

Candice laughed without smiling. "You must be, to think that I'd go to such ridiculous, absolutely preposterous lengths to get next to you. Well, let me bring you down a few notches, *Lieutenant*. Contrary to what you may have been told, you nor your *kingdom-ordered chocolate skin* don't even come close to being all that!"

The way she'd snarled out his title was condescending enough. That last line . . . well, it was just plain brutal. He'd said that to her as a joke, and it had come back to haunt him. It was a low blow and a direct hit to Stuart's ego.

Just to return her below-the-belt serve, he wanted to yell back, "Well, apparently, Tasha thinks I am!" but he knew that doing so would not only be childish, but it would be the death of any chance he had with making things right with her. Putting things in their proper perspective, Stuart stood quietly and took his due punishment like a man.

Candice glared at him. "How *dare* you stand in front of strangers and throw in my face what happened seven years ago with some man that I dated before I ever came to Christ?"

Stuart dropped his head. The interrogation had indeed been brutal. "I'm sor—"

"I'm not finished!"

Stuart flinched behind Candice's uncharacteristic bellow. She was angry . . . no doubt about it, but her tone lowered as she continued.

"If I go back seven years in your life, would I find the same man that I see today?"

Her challenge hit home. Stuart swallowed and brought his eyes back to meet hers.

"Would I find a man who virtually put his life on the line, providing security for the man of God? Would I find a man who honored his body as a temple of the Holy Ghost? Would I find a man who served in a ministry that reached out to incarcerated felons? Would I find a man who prayed daily in The Lyons Den?"

Shaking his head slowly, Stuart's voice was barely above murmuring when he replied, "No. You're right. Seven years ago, you wouldn't have found any of that." He sighed, feeling shoddier than he had in his whole life. "I'm so sorry, sweetheart. I never meant to hurt you."

"Well, you did."

"I know," Stuart quickly responded. He hesitated, but took a chance and reached for her arm anyway. She allowed him to place his hand there. "I know that apologizing is not enough, baby, but I truly am sorry. Please let me make this up to you, Candice."

"I don't think you can, Stuart," she replied.

The box chain around her neck caught the light of the sun and sent a series of flashes to Stuart's eyes that resembled that of an SOS. Only, that didn't make sense because, in this equation, he was the one in distress. He felt that he was one step away from drowning at sea and losing Candice for good.

Stuart loosed his grip on her arm, and she retreated just a bit when his hand reached to-

ward her neck. Stuart used his finger to graze
the surface of the chain, stealing a touch of her
skin in the process. He gently pulled the chain
outward until the key that dangled at the end
was in view. Stuart closed his hands around
the key and exhaled.

"Don't leave me, Candice." His plea came in
the form of a whisper, but it was a plea none-
theless. "My heart . . ." Stuart paused to try
and organize his thoughts, but no matter how
he regrouped or rearranged them, they still
spelled out the same words. "I love you, Candice, and I'll spend the rest of my life trying
to make this up to you, if that's what it takes.
Please . . . please don't leave me."

Whether she wanted them to or not, his
words touched her, and Stuart watched a
single tear escape down a cheek that was still
stained with the evidence of the sob before it.
He desired to wipe it away, but one hand was
paralyzed by his side, and the other was too
busy holding on to the key, as if releasing it
would symbolize letting go of Candice.

"Let me drive you home," he suggested.
What he really wanted was to buy more time
with her. Time that could make the difference
between whether she remained in his life or
walked away.

Candice looked down at the cell phone she still held in her hand. "I was . . . I was calling for a ride."

Easing the phone from her hand, Stuart placed it to his ear. "Hello?"

Without an introduction, he knew that it was the man Candice had identified as Cornell Pratt on the other end. "You treat her right, you hear me? If you don't, as God is my witness, I'll come looking for you."

With that, Pratt hung up.

Stuart closed the phone and looked at Candice. "He said it's okay if I take you home."

Silently, they walked side by side from the visitor's parking area to the lot where the cruisers lined up like soldiers dressed in black and white. When Stuart closed the door behind Candice once she was seated, he breathed a sigh of relief. This one wasn't over by a long shot. He imagined that he'd spend weeks dealing with the aftermath of it all. But she'd agreed to allow him to take her home, and that was a big step. For the rest, he'd pray his way through . . . from The Lyons Den.

Reading Group
Discussion Questions

1. Do you believe legends such as the one surrounding the Shelton Heights community really exist in the twenty-first century?

2. Discuss your early thoughts on the strange things that happened to Lieutenant Stuart Lyons. Before the full story was unveiled, what was your assessment?

3. There was a brief mention in the story of the bantering that Stuart received as a child because of the dark hue of his skin. Is this something you can directly or indirectly relate to?

4. Stuart and Candice connected through an online dating site. Do you believe it

is appropriate for Christians to go this route to find a mate? Why or why not?

5. Candice was less than honest about her background both before and after she met Stuart. Was she justified in misinforming him?

6. What was your take on Jerome Tides? Discuss his casual dating method as well as his miraculous spiritual experience.

7. Were you surprised with the choice Jerome made in the end? Which of the women did you think was the better mate for him?

8. Though one was never seen, it was implied that Kenyatta carried a gun with her at all times. What are your thoughts on Christians and firearms? Should they be advocates of carrying deadly weapons?

9. The men in *The Lyons Den* had a strong bond of spiritual brotherhood. Please discuss your thoughts on each of them and the roles they played (Stuart, Hunter,

Jerome, Peter, Kwame and Reverend Tides).

10. How did you perceive some of the secondary characters such as Rocky, Sergeant Allen Bowden and Minister Cornell Pratt?

11. When the answer to the mystery of Stuart's misfortunes was revealed, were you surprised?

12. Do you have a special place in your home where you go to pray? If so, where is it, and why do you choose to pray there?

13. Who was your favorite character in this story? Why?

14. Who was your least favorite character in this story? Why?

15. If you could rewrite any part of *The Lyons Den*, which scene would it be? Why?

About the Author

Kendra Norman-Bellamy is a multi-award-winning, national bestselling author as well as founder of KNB Publications, LLC. Beginning her literary career in 2002 as a self-published writer, Kendra has risen, by the grace of God, to become one of the most respected names in Christian fiction.

She and her titles have been featured in *Essence*, *Upscale* and *HOPE for Women* magazines. Kendra is a reoccurring contributing writer for *Precious Times* magazine, *Hope for Women* magazine and *Global Woman* magazine. She is a much-soughtafter motivational speaker, and the mastermind behind The Writer's Hut, an online support group for creators of literary works. In addition, Kendra is the founder of The Writer's Cocoon, a nationally acclaimed four-part clinic for aspiring and published writers, and Cruisin' For Christ, a ground-breaking cruise that celebrates Christian writing, gospel music, and other artistries that glorify God. As a famed publication that celebrates African-American achievements, *Who's Who In Black Atlanta* has featured Kendra for four consecutive years.

A native of West Palm Beach, Florida and a graduate of Valdosta Technical College, Kendra resides in Stone Mountain, Georgia, with her husband, Jonathan, and youngest daughter, Crystal. Her firstborn daughter, Brittney Holmes, is an accomplished award-winning author and resides on the campus of the University of Georgia, where she is a full-time journalism student.

Feel free to visit the author's official web home at *www.knbpublications.com* or connect with her on MySpace at:

www. myspace.com/kendranormanbellamy

UC HIS GLORY BOOK CLUB!

www.uchisglorybookclub.net

UC His Glory Book Club is the spirit-inspired brainchild of Joylynn Jossel, Author and Acquisitions Editor of Urban Christian, and Kendra Norman-Bellamy, Author for Urban Christian. This is an online book club that hosts authors of Urban Christian. We welcome as members all men and women who have a passion for reading Christian-based fiction.

UC His Glory Book Club pledges our commitment to provide support, positive feedback, encouragement, and a forum whereby members can openly discuss and review the literary works of Urban Christian authors.

There is no membership fee associated with UC His Glory Book Club; however, we do ask that you support the authors through purchasing, encouraging, providing book reviews, and of course, your prayers. We also ask that you respect our beliefs and follow the guidelines of the book club. We hope to receive your valuable input, opinions, and reviews that build up, rather than tear down our authors.

WHAT WE BELIEVE

—We believe that Jesus is the Christ, Son of the Living God.

—We believe the Bible is the true, living Word of God.

—We believe all Urban Christian authors should use their God-given writing abilities to honor God and share the message of the written word God has given to each of them uniquely.

—We believe in supporting Urban Christian authors in their literary endeavors by reading, purchasing and sharing their titles with our online community.

—We believe that in everything we do in our literary arena should be done in a manner that will lead to God being glorified and honored.

—We look forward to the online fellowship with you. Please visit us often at:

www.uchisglorybookclub.net.

Many Blessing to You!

Shelia E. Lipsey,
President, UC His Glory Book Club

Coming Soon

When Solomon Sings

by Kendra Norman-Bellamy

Prologue

Cloud nine. This had to be what being on it felt like. Officially, Valentine's Day was over, but what a perfect one it had been! In fact, everything about the past three days had been perfect. The time was nearing one o'clock in the morning when Neil walked—rather *floated*—through his front door and into the warmth of his home. The anticipation of it all had only allowed him two hours of sleep last night, but there wasn't a tired bone in his body. And there was a great deal of irony in that because though there was no fatigue, he felt as if he were sound asleep and having the dream of his life.

She said yes! Neil pumped his fist victoriously as the thought filtered through his head.

Shaylynn Ford had obviously not expected his proposal. Shucks . . . he had barely expected it himself. The young single mother of one was visibly shaking from the moment Neil sank to

his knee and took her hand in his. But as un-
suspecting as she had been, Neil had barely gotten the heartfelt words out of his mouth before
Shaylynn tearfully agreed to be his bride. It was
just too easy. Neil had sweated for weeks . . .
months. They had been an exclusive couple for
just over a year, but he had known from day one
that he wanted to make Shaylynn the next (and
last) Mrs. Neil Solomon Taylor. He would have
proposed on day two had he known it would be
so simple. Now he felt ridiculous for holding on
to the ring for three solid months before taking
the plunge.

Neil stood with his back against the door for
a long while, still trying to digest it all. It was
hard to believe he was the same man who had
avowed himself to lifelong bachelorhood after
the painful dissolution of his first marriage fifteen years ago. And it was equally as mindbog-
gling that Shaylynn had been the same woman
who, in the not too distant past, was still wearing the ring of her first husband; a man who
had now been deceased for more than eight
years. When Neil first met Shaylynn, her heart
had been so committed to the man who'd left
her widowed that seven years after burying
him, she was still insisting that people refer to
her as *Mrs*. Ford. As much as Neil prayed to

God that she'd give him a chance, he wasn't at all sure of how his and Shaylynn's story would end. But here they were, and their ending was on the threshold of fairytale.

Thank you, Jesus. The praise had been silently repeating itself in Neil's mind ever since it all became official; from the second that he slipped that impressive stone on Shaylynn's finger. Two hours had passed since then, but Neil's heart was still doing somersaults. He had almost not done it. As much as he wanted to propose, and despite all of the rehearsing, the prayers, and the spiritual counsel, Neil had come frighteningly close to changing his mind. It wouldn't have been the first time he'd chickened out.

The night had gone without a hitch. It was apparent that Neil had made good choices for celebrating the day set aside for lovers. First he treated Shaylynn to a special Valentine's Day old school R&B concert at the Atlanta Civic Center. Using a broker, Neil managed to secure tickets that placed them in first row center seats; right behind the orchestra pit. As a woman of only thirty-two years, he wondered if Shaylynn would be able to appreciate the music, but all doubts dissipated in short order fashion.

The stage featured a wealth of talent and definitely catered to the ladies. Natalie Cole was the only female to perform on the four-artist ticket. The others were Jeffrey Osborne, Peabo Bryson, and James Ingram. Shaylynn seemed to enjoy them all, but when James took the mic, she got so captivated that Neil felt a twinge of jealousy. And he couldn't believe that Negro had the nerve to step down from the stage while singing his hit song, *Baby, Come to Me*, and single out Shaylynn. Neil struggled to hold on to his counterfeit smile when James kissed the petals of a long stem red rose before handing it to Shaylynn. For years, the smooth vocalist had been, and would probably always be, one of Neil's favorite artists, but at that moment, he wanted to knock the shine off of James's Grammy Award winning baldhead. Until then, Neil didn't even know that he was capable of that level of jealousy. Never before had he felt the desire to physically fight another man over a woman. But how could he not be a little insecure? I mean, this was James Ingram, and Neil was living proof that Shaylynn didn't discriminate against well-kept older men. Reminding himself that James was a married man helped out a little, and all residue doubt was erased when, at the close of the concert, Shaylynn turned to Neil, cupped his cheeks, kissed his lips, and thanked him for bringing her to the show. Then she linked her arm through his and held on tight as they left the auditorium together.

During dinner that followed at Canoe, a romantic restaurant at which they hadn't dined since their first official date, she only had eyes for Neil. All the while, a little black box was nestled inside the pocket of his suit, but no time seemed like the right time to present it. There was that one moment—when they were holding hands across the table at dinner and looking into each other's eyes—that he was right on the verge of going for it, but then Shaylynn said something about how Emmett probably would have loved the desert, and that dampened the mood and changed Neil's mind. It had been weeks since she'd brought up her former husband's name. *Was she ever going to just let that man die?* There was no way Neil would ask her to marry him when she had *the great Emmett Ford* on the brain. If she turned him down—no matter how gently she may have done it—it would have been far too humiliating. So Neil surmised that he'd ask for her hand later; maybe on her birthday.

Neil's mother was playing the role of baby-sitter tonight, so Shaylynn's eight-year-old son, Chase, was one of two children Ella was keeping overnight. After leaving the restaurant, Neil drove Shaylynn home and sat with her for a short while before deciding that it was time to leave. But as he and Shaylynn stood at her front door sharing a long kiss good night, something welled in him. It was that same overwhelming love and passion that Neil felt every time he was alone with her . . . and standing that close to her. That feeling that assured him that he couldn't keep waiting. He wanted Shaylynn in more ways than one. Neil hated saying good-bye and good night to her. His soul desired to stay. He wanted to share his love with her; his life with her; his bed with her, and there was only one way that he could make that happen. That's when he decided to do it.

And she said yes!

Neil couldn't recall a time ever in his forty-six years that he'd been so happy. It was too early in the morning to call his best friend or his mother to share the news, but when the clock alarmed five hours from now for him to rise for work, Neil would begin spreading the joy.

Am I too happy? he questioned himself.

That new thought slowed Neil's movements as he peeled off his jacket and draped it on the arm of the sofa nearest him. The black wool Kenneth Cole design was a gift from Shaylynn. She'd presented it to him last Christmas. They were so in sync. Without even consulting each other, she'd bought him a coat, and he'd done the same for her; a black and white wool Worthington skirted pea coat that hugged her waist and draped her hips with perfection. Neil removed his driving cap and carefully placed it on top of his jacket and released a sigh, but he failed in his effort to shoo away the new notion that had forced its way into his head.

Was he, in fact, too happy?

Family history—especially history among the male population in Neil's bloodline—had taught him not to get prematurely keyed up about anything. Twenty-three years ago, Neil's dad was excited about finishing the new roof on his family's home, because he knew it was something that his sweetheart of forty years was looking forward to. His dad lived to make his beloved Ella Mae happy. But days before completion, the man they all called 'Pop' was killed instantly in a freak automobile accident en route back to the house after purchasing the material needed to finish the job. And then there was Dwayne, Neil's best friend and older brother. Next month would be nineteen years since the family had buried him, and Neil still missed him like it was yesterday. Dwayne had been battling a rare lung ailment for some time, but was doing well and was excited about performing the lead solo for a choir function when he suddenly collapsed and died of what was determined to be acute cardiorespiratory arrest. And then there was the time his uncle . . .

Neil chuckled as he sat on the sofa and leaned back against the cushions. What was he doing? He didn't believe in bad omens. Never had; never would. So why was he becoming his own party pooper? The woman he loved had just agreed to spend a lifetime loving him back, and here he was allowing Satan to steal his joy with all of these foolish, unfounded doubts. He wasn't going to die just because he had found a new level of happiness. Die before he had a chance to marry the love of his life? Die before the honeymoon that every fiber of his being was looking forward to? Absolutely not! Neil's closest friend and pastor, Charles Loather Jr., better known as CJ, had preached about that very thing—allowing the enemy to sap the joy that God gives—just two months ago. Neil's soft chuckle turned into an all-out guffaw. It was one of those loud laughs that seemed to fill the room and free his mind of all of its reservations, but it came to a sudden end at the sound of the doorbell.

Who would be coming to his door at this hour? Neil sat in the quiet darkness for a moment, wondering if he were hearing things. A second chime verified the obvious, and Neil stood and flicked the wall switch that brought light to his living room. There was no sense in pretending no one was home. Whoever was at his door had surely heard him laughing just moments earlier. Neil looked at the watch on his wrist. The little hand was grazing the edge of the one, and the big hand was on the ten. It was probably CJ. It had to be. He was the one person who knew Neil's Valentine's Day plans, and he probably couldn't wait to hear the results. Neil couldn't wait to tell him either. No doubt, CJ had told Theresa by now, and more likely than not, she was the one who had shooed her husband to his house to get the juicy details.

A smile twisted his lips, and he reached for the doorknob. But just to be sure, he asked, "Yes? Who is it?"

"Sean Thomas."

An automatic reaction snatched Neil's hand away from the door. *Sean Thomas?* One moment, the name sounded vaguely familiar, and the next, it was very familiar. This was the mystery man who had called his office twice over the past two months, but had never left a detailed message with Neil's assistant. Neil knew the name, but he didn't know the man. Whoever this Sean Thomas character was, Neil wasn't about to let him in his house at ten minutes before one in the morning.

"Who are you looking for?" Maybe the gentleman was confused. Neil Taylor was a pretty common name. Maybe it was a different Neil Taylor that he was searching for. Maybe—

"Neil Taylor, son of Ernest and Eloise Taylor," the voice replied.

Okay . . . maybe not. Only a few people in Atlanta knew his mother by her given name of Eloise, and even fewer knew his father by anything other than Pop, so this person must have known Neil from his youthful days in Mississippi. But he still wasn't ready to identify himself as the person being sought. He wasn't exactly fearful, but he could hear his heart pounding in his own ears. Neil had no idea who Sean Thomas was or what he wanted, but for some reason, his gut feeling told him that his ride on cloud nine was over.

ONE

"Hi, there. Back again, I see."

At the sound of the familiar accented voice, Neil glanced up from the glass counter and into the face of the same handsome, grey haired gentleman who had waited on him the last time he'd stopped by the store. And the time before that . . . and the time before that. "Hi." Neil was already looking down again by the time he returned the greeting.

"Dr. Neil Taylor, correct?" the salesman said.

Neil brought his attention back to the man and accepted the friendly hand that was extended toward him. "Yes. Rabbi Ezra Bernstein, right?" He was glad that he could recall the Jewish community leader's name as readily as the rabbi had done his.

"Right. Very good." Ezra seemed pleasantly surprised, but he shouldn't have been so impressed. It was Neil's fourth visit to his store in the last six weeks. "I see that you keep gravitating back to this same spot," the man observed. He pulled a copper colored key from his pocket and unlocked the door to the glass casing before carefully sliding it open. "You like *this* one, don't you?"

Neil's eyes followed the direction of Ezra's hand as it navigated toward the two-carat emerald cut diamond set in white gold. It also came in yellow gold, but for some reason, the clearness of the flawless white solitaire against the silver of the brilliant white gold looked more breathtaking. It defined *her*. "Yes." Neil's fingers tingled, but his hand was steady as he took the ring from the jeweler's grasp and studied it carefully. It was his first time holding it, and it felt good. It felt right. "This one catches the light perfectly."

"Yes, it does," Ezra agreed. He hesitated for a brief moment, adjusted the white yarmulke that partially covered his graying hair, and then said, "Am I correct in assuming that you're not quite sure about this one yet?"

"No, it's not that," Neil assured him. "The ring is extraordinary. I love it, I just—"

"No no." Ezra's voice stopped him. "I don't mean the ring. I mean the woman. You're not sure about her just yet."

Neil's posture straightened, and he shook his head from side to side. "That's not it at all, Rabbi. She's the one. Shay—that's her name— she's the one; no doubt about it. I'm just . . ." Neil clamped his lips shut. Why on earth was he about to spill his guts to a practical stranger? This man didn't need to know about his insecurities. "I'm just a careful shopper," he concluded. And he was. So it wasn't a total lie.

"So it would seem." Ezra reached forward and reclaimed the jewelry before gently setting it back in its place in the display. "It's always a good practice to shop with care; especially when you're shopping for something as precious as a diamond." He closed the door of the glass casing, locked it, and then looked across the counter at Neil. "But we do have a thirty-day return policy, you know. If for any reason you're not satisfied, you can return it as long as it's still in the same condition as it was when purchased. That means if the bride-to-be doesn't look at this ring and immediately embrace it, you are at liberty to return it and even bring her in with you and let her pick out something else that better suits her taste."

That wasn't it either. Ezra was totally missing the mark, but Neil didn't want to tell the man that it wasn't the jewelry that he feared

Shaylynn might reject. His reluctance to make
the expensive investment had nothing to do
with the ring. "That's good to know," he opted
to say. "I'll definitely keep that in mind. Thank
you, Rabbi. I suppose I should be getting back
to work. My lunch break will be over soon."
Fridays were particularly busy days at Kingdom Builders Academy, the private Christian
school where Neil served as Director.

"Yes." The store owner reached for his hand
once more. "And I suppose I can look forward
to seeing you again in the next week or so?"

Embarrassment heated Neil's face. If he
weren't a black man, he would have turned
candy apple red. Neil accepted the handshake,
but determined in his mind that whenever or *if*
ever he decided to ring shop any further, he'd
go to a different store. In light of the Rabbi's
comment, he would just be too self-conscious
to return to Menorah Jewelers . . . especially
if he still weren't ready to make a purchase.
"Have a good day." Neil figured it was best
not to give the man's question a direct answer
since he had no plans to return.

Technically, it wasn't even winter yet, but
cold temperatures had arrived in metropolitan Atlanta on an early flight. With the wind
chill factor, the temperatures had been in

single digits for three consecutive days, and
even wearing a coat, hat, gloves, and scarf,
Neil felt chilled to the bones as he climbed in
the driver's seat of his SUV. The black Toyota
Highlander had served him exceptionally well
for seven years. After turning the key in the ig-
nition, Neil sat behind the wheel and listened
for the engine to idle down. While he waited,
a photo caught his eye, and he slowly picked
it up. It was a picture of Shaylynn and Chase.
Shaylynn had given it to him just yesterday.
During the Thanksgiving holiday break, she
and her son had taken Christmas photos at
Stonecrest Mall, and she had given Neil one
eight-by-ten that he'd immediately framed
and hung on his bedroom wall and another
that was so small that she'd presented it to him
in a thermoplastic frame that dangled from
a keychain. Neil had placed the frame in the
built-in cup holder beside his driver's seat.

"That ring would be a great Christmas gift."
He whispered the words while brushing his
thumb over Shaylynn's image. "I wish I were
sure of where your head is . . . and *who* your
heart is truly with."

Neil didn't doubt Shaylynn's love for him.
Every time she looked at him, he could see
the love in her eyes. But as strong as her feel-

ings were for him, he knew they were stronger for someone else. Emmett Ford still owned her heart; or at least the better part of it. The flowers that Emmett had presented to her on the day he proposed were as dead as he was, but eight years after his passing, she still had them. Just the thought of it made Neil subconsciously shake his head. He tried to avoid looking at them whenever he visited Shaylynn, but with them sitting on the mantel of her fireplace, those annoying, dried, pressed violets were like the centerpiece of her entire house. They were like some bizarre kind of urn of Emmett's ashes, and to Neil, they served as a painful, constant reminder that he'd never be Shaylynn's one and only.

Would she accept a marriage proposal from him? The inward battle continued as Neil placed the frame back in the cup holder, shifted gears, and began backing from his parking space. Accepting would mean permanently wearing his ring on the same finger from which she'd only recently been able to remove Emmett's. Was Shaylynn ready for that? Being Neil's steady was one thing, but would she be willing to be his *permanent*? Only when the sound of a horn resonated in the air did Neil realize that he was mindlessly holding up traffic at a green light.

The ride back to Kingdom Builders Academy took twenty minutes. Neil walked through the front doors just as lunchtime was ending, and the children were walking in straight lines on their way back to their classrooms. The enthusiastic reception he received made him forget his troubles. Temporarily anyway.

"High five, Dr. Taylor!"

Neil laughed out loud as he went down the line, slapping the hands that were attached to the chorus of voices that had given him his orders. The children, and especially the boys, loved it when he high-fived them, and Neil loved doing it. Twenty years from now, when he retired from this job he held so dear, Neil was sure that it would be the thing for which he'd be most remembered. Not all of the late hours that he'd put in without pay. Not the many times he'd gone beyond the call of duty and visited the homes of the students to check on their well-being. Not even for the incident last year where he used the Heimlich maneuver to save the life of an eight-year-old student who began choking while eating her lunch. He was honored by the school and the church for his quick reaction in the crisis situation, and the *Atlanta Weekly Chronicles*, the city's most popular newspaper, even printed a feature article about it. But it wouldn't be what the teachers or students would remember most. The high fives would be Neil's legacy, and truthfully, it would probably be what he would miss the most.

"Where've you been, Dr. Taylor? What did you have to do . . . go slaughter the cow before making the burger? And why didn't you answer your phone? I tried to call you twice."

Missing his mother-hen-of-a-secretary would probably run a close second. Margaret Dasher was a sixty-year-old who swore that she would die working. The word *retirement* wasn't in her vocabulary. Although she was somewhat hearing impaired, Margaret was an amazing looking woman who easily looked ten years younger than she was. She had been talking loud all day long, and that was a clear sign that she'd chosen not to wear her hearing aid today. She adamantly denied her constant need for it. Neil stopped in front of her desk and removed his sunglasses. "Sorry, Ms. Dasher. I had some business to take care of and got caught in a little bit of traffic coming back." He glanced at his watch, and then back at her. "But I'm not late. I have five minutes to spare."

Margaret was shaking her head as she rose from her chair. "You must have *Mrs.* Ford on the brain. Is that where you were? I'll bet you did have business to take care of. Did you have *lunch* with her?" She made quotation marks with her fingers when she emphasized the word lunch. "That's about the only person who could make you forget that you had an important one-fifteen conference call with Pastor and the KBA Education Ministry Board."

Neil slapped himself on the forehead. He hated it when Margaret insinuated that he and Shaylynn had already consummated their relationship, and he disliked it even more when she referred to Shaylynn as *Mrs.* Ford. But he was too disappointed with himself for not remembering the important business call to scold her for either offense. "CJ is gonna kill me. How in the world did I forget?" The question was more to himself than her, but Margaret was ready with a reply.

"Dr. Taylor, when you're with that young thing, you forget your own name. It's a wonder you remembered to come back to work at all. I done told you to watch yourself. You can't spend too much time with a person that you're in love with and attracted to. The devil will sneak in the mix and have you doing all kinds of ungodliness. Do you understand what I'm trying to say?" She looked at him over her reading glasses like some crazy mix of school teacher and overbearing mother. Then with an accusing tone, she added, "Of course you do."

Neil released a sigh. He knew he didn't owe Margaret an explanation, but it was the only way he would be able to shut her up. "First of all, Ms. Dasher, I was not with Shay; I was taking care of business just like I said. Okay? Secondly, as I've told you a million and one times already, *Ms.* Ford and I have not broken any rules. We've not gone there, and have no plans to go there, so you can stop worrying." In the back of his mind, Neil wondered if the thought of going *there* with him had ever even entered Shaylynn's mind. He'd be lying if he said it had never entered his, but he couldn't help but wonder if her desires to *go there* with anyone had died right along with her beloved Emmett. Neil swallowed the bitter bile that rose in his throat.

"Never underestimate the power of the enemy," Margaret warned. "The Bible tells us that that filthy, lowdown, stankin' devil is out to kill, steal, and destroy. All you have to do is let your guard down just a little bit, and he'll slither his way in and trip you up. Not a single one of us is so saved that we don't get tempted once in awhile."

Without replying, Neil walked the fifty feet that would deliver him to his own office space, removed his jacket, and hung it on the coat rack behind his desk. He placed his hat, scarf, sunglasses, and gloves on the nearby credenza before pulling out his chair and sitting. He didn't need Margaret to fill him in on the woes of temptation. He and temptation weren't only on a first name basis; they sometimes ate dinner and watched movies together. He looked that little imp in the eyes every time he touched Shaylynn's hair or smelled her perfume. Neil knew all too well that he wasn't beyond being tempted, and he knew he wasn't beyond yielding to temptation either. He'd denied his flesh for more years than he cared to calculate, but that hadn't always been his testimony. Even so, Shaylynn was different. She was worth waiting for. He just wondered how long he'd have to wait.

"Are you hearing me, Dr. Taylor?"

Neil looked at Margaret who was now standing in his doorway, but he avoided her examination. It was time to change the subject.

"What did Pastor Loather say when I wasn't here for the conference call?" He was one of the few church members who knew the pastor intimately enough to refer to him as CJ, but he rarely did so around others.

"He didn't seem upset, if that's what you're worried about." Margaret rested her ample hips against the frame of Neil's open door. "I'm surprised he didn't just call you on your cell."

Neil slapped his forehead again, and then swiveled his chair around so that he could reach for the coat he'd just hung. Just before entering the jewelry store, he had set the volume of his ringer on silent and dropped the phone in his pocket. After leaving the store, he never thought to change the setting. As Neil slipped the Blackberry from its case, the first thing he noticed was the message on the screen that notified him that he'd missed three calls. "Aw, man!" he whispered.

"What's going on with you, Dr. Taylor?" As loveable as she was, Margaret's prying was rarely subtle. She stepped farther into the office space. "For the past few weeks I've noticed that you've had a lot on your mind. You sure that you and that li'l girl are okay? No matter how mature she might be, she's still her age and you're yours. Although the age gap might not seem like a problem going in to a new relationship, it could develop into one the more you get to know a person."

While Margaret's nosiness was obvious, her feelings about Shaylynn weren't. Whenever Shaylynn dropped by the office to see Neil, she and Margaret always exchanged pleasantries and got along well. But sometimes Neil wondered how genuine it was on the part of his executive assistant. When she spoke of Shaylynn in Shaylynn's absence, Margaret's tone sometimes carried an edge. Neil could detect that edge right now, and it caused him to clinch and unclench his jaws. He and Margaret had worked together now for nearly seven years, and because they attended the same church, he'd known her even longer than that. By all accounts, Neil considered Margaret Dasher his friend more than his employee despite the fact that they never referenced each other by their first names. Margaret was fifteen years his senior, and for a while, Neil had carried a secret school boy-like torch in his heart for the attractive, divorced mother of two. But all of that notwithstanding; if Margaret ever crossed the line and said anything disrespectful about the woman he loved, Neil would introduce her to a side of him that she'd never met.

"You mind closing the door on your way out?" He made the abrupt request while quickly typing in the password that would allow him access to his own cell phone. Neil was growing weary of the small talk and the needless insinuations. It was time to get back to business.

"Does that mean everything *isn't* okay?" Margaret could be relentless.

Neil wished he could say something that would convince Margaret that there was absolutely no need for concern, but first he had to convince himself. There was no real evidence of trouble in paradise, but his instinct detected something on the horizon. His hesitations about buying the ring . . . the increase of Emmett's name creeping into his and Shaylynn's conversations . . . the knot that gradually tightened in the pit of his stomach . . .

"Well, does it?" Margaret's voice snatched him from his thoughts.

An exaggerated inhale and exhale nonverbally accused his secretary of being a hopeless case. Neil pressed the code to listen to his messages, and then placed the phone to his ear. He shooed her away with his hand and forced his voice to be confident and unwavering when he replied with, "What it means, Ms. Dasher, is close the door on your way out."

ORDER FORM
URBAN BOOKS, LLC
78 E. Industry Ct
Deer Park, NY 11729

Name: (please print):_____

Address:_____

City/State:_____

Zip:_____

QTY	TITLES	PRICE
	3:57 A.M Timing Is Everything	$14.95
	A Man's Worth	$14.95
	A Woman's Worth	$14.95
	Abundant Rain	$14.95
	After The Feeling	$14.95
	Amaryllis	$14.95
	An Inconvenient Friend	$14.95

Shipping and handling-add $3.50 for 1st book, then $1.75 for each additional book.

Please send a check payable to:

Urban Books, LLC

Please allow 4-6 weeks for delivery

ORDER FORM
URBAN BOOKS, LLC
78 E. Industry Ct
Deer Park, NY 11729

Name: (please print):_____

Address:_____

City/State:___ _____

Zip:_____

QTY	TITLES	PRICE
	Confessions Of A preachers Wife	$14.95
	Dance Into Destiny	$14.95
	Deliver Me From My Enemies	$14.95
	Desperate Decisions	$14.95
	Divorcing the Devil	$14.95

Shipping and handling-add $3.50 for 1st book, then $1.75 for each additional book.

Please send a check payable to:

Urban Books, LLC

Please allow 4-6 weeks for delivery